UNBALANCED LUCK

TWISTED LUCK
BOOK SEVEN

MEL TODD

BAD ASH PUBLISHING

Bad Ash Publishing

86 Desmond Court

Powder Springs, GA 30127

www.badashpublishing.com

Cover by Ampersand Books

Unbalanced Luck/ Mel Todd -- 1st ed.

Paper 5x8 ISBN 978-1-950287-26-0

Hardback 6x9 ISBN 978-1-950287-29-1

Audio ISBN 978-1-950287-34-5

 Created with Vellum

DEDICATION

To John Mersh - thank you for coming into my life and I'm sorry I didn't get to meet you in person. You made my books better and my life richer because of you. I will miss your input.

Mel

CONTENTS

CHAPTER

ONE

There are new rumblings out of congress about changing the Draft scheme. Various branches of the military are requesting to be allowed to extend Draft service for mages with highly specialized degrees. This was countered by a suggestion to extend all Draft terms to a decade as they are for merlins. At this time, it is just rumors, but the OMO has remained silent on this issue.

~ CNN Mage Focus

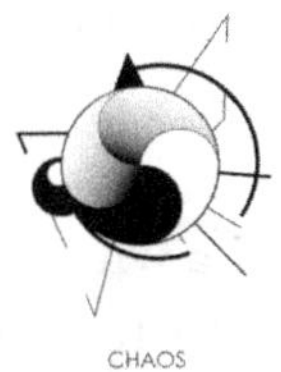

CHAOS

"And it is finalized. The houses, the entire street in fact, are yours. As well as James' remaining assets." Lucille Blanding signed the last piece of paper with a flourish and handed it to me. "Let me get you all the deeds, the final accounts, and your keys."

It all felt surreal, even if I'd known this was coming. My draft had officially finished a week ago, even with the extra six weeks of maternity leave added onto it. It had been a busy few years and now the culmination of what I'd been waiting for was here. Freedom.

"Here you go." Lucille slid a folder and a shoebox over to me. I took it a bit numbly. Curious, I opened the folder. Lucille had included a brief summary document with everything I owned and the current value. I choked.

"Really?"

Lucille laughed. "Two decades of interest and decent stock markets can make anything look good. You have enough to live on and never have to work again if you don't want to. I'm just glad that all this is no longer my responsibility. I hope you enjoy everything he left you, Cori. And I'm glad you're approaching it a different way." She smiled with the first truly warm smile I'd ever seen from her.

"Thank you. But I do want to change one thing. I want to sign over this house to Jo and Sable." I pulled the Tudor house deed out and pushed it to her.

Lucille smiled at me. "That doesn't surprise me. Give me a minute. I need a lawyer and a witness." She made a phone call and a few minutes later a real estate lawyer who had an office in the building showed up as a witness. It took a total of fifteen minutes to get it witnessed and signed.

"Thank you again."

"It has been my pleasure. I hope to see you change the world."

I laughed as I rose and headed out of the office. The last thing I had any desire to do was change the world. Carelian stretched, then moved to walk with me from where he'd been waiting in the outer lobby of the small brownstone office complex.

~It is done?~

I reached out to scritch across the top of his head. He leaned into it with a low rumble. "It is. I'm officially rich, I guess." It still felt odd not to worry about money. I juggled the folder and the shoebox in my arm. I needed to see what was in it, but now really wasn't the right time.

~Jo will be overjoyed. She has lusted greatly over the blocky house.~

I fought a snicker. The Tudor house was much bigger than our Victorian. And Jo lusted after it more for the huge garage and workshop it had than anything else. All the tenants of the four houses I owned had completed their leases in the last year and now the houses were empty. They couldn't sit empty for too long, but I didn't know who to put in them. My brother Kris had stayed with us until he emerged, then went off to school. He had about two more years before he came home, and would he even want to live here? Or live alone? So many questions to be answered.

I shook it off. "Want to walk for a bit before we head home?"

~Yes. That sounds enjoyable. We need to get outside more.~

I pulled the leash out of my bag that held his leash, harness, and a collapsible bowl. I slipped the leash and harness on and we set off for a walk. I wasn't shopping for anything really. I just wanted to give myself some time before everything settled in.

"Is there anything you want to do? I mean, there are still parts of the world we haven't seen." I ignored people's glances as we walked. Lucille's office was in a mixed business section of Albany and we didn't come here often enough for anyone to get used to us. The people in the stores near home didn't even blink an eye at Carelian anymore.

Granted, he'd gotten to be in the Christmas parade last year, but I had no idea how many people thought he was real versus a mechanical cat.

~I enjoy doing the Search and Rescue. My nose is much better than any canine's.~ The arrogance just made me snicker.

"Better than Dahli's?"

He huffed and pulled me over to look at a display in a bar window that had a TV pointing at the street. It was advertising a deep-sea fishing trip and on screen they were pulling up a swordfish.

~That looks like something excellent to do.~

"I've never been on a boat. It could be fun. I think we get to keep all the fish we catch." It did look fun, if a bit wet.

~I wish to do that. I am sure fish tastes much better when you have to fight it.~

I opened my mouth to say they weren't fighting the fish, but from the back-and-forth struggle on the screen, it was as good a description as any. "I can look into that. Anything else? We would need to go renew certifications and my credentials to do S&R."

~I am willing to prove, again, that I have more intelligence than most humans.~

He was arrogant, but he wasn't wrong. The people running the tests for S&R animals didn't seem to understand or remember he had human level intelligence and were constantly looking at me to give him commands. He found the entire process tedious and rather insulting.

A spike of pain splashed through my mind, hard and sharp. "Did someone just open a rip?" I said it out loud as I turned, trying to figure out what that had been. While I was used to tiny spikes of pain, this one was huge. It had been years since I'd felt anything this strong.

~Toward the sun about two stories off the ground. It is an opening to Chaos,~ Carelian whispered in my mind, pulling me in that direction.

I let him pull me as I looked both visually and mentally for the rip. When I finally found it, a shocked gasp escaped me. "That is not good."

~No. This is not right.~ Carelian agreed, his fur rising up with a low growl.

Hanging over a one-story shopping strip, a rip gleamed as a widening gray ripple against a sunny October sky. While the rip was concerning enough, what had me running toward it was the black ribbon-like tentacles that were wiggling out of it as it grew. I could hear the murmurs and gasps as it became large enough that everyone noticed.

"Is that Bob?" I asked as we ran. Bob was one of the Lords of Chaos and resembled nothing more than a blob of tar that could move and create tentacles whenever it desired.

~I do not believe Bob would ever be this unwise or arrogant.~ Carelian sounded hesitant as he loped lazily next to me. Even my sprinting full out couldn't make him actually need to run. Show off Cath.

I didn't reply, mainly because I needed my breath to run, and kept moving. It was a big rip. I skidded to a halt at the edge of a block and looked straight up at it. The tentacles were thin and ribbony, whereas usually Bob had thick octopus-like things.

~It is not Bob. In fact...~ Carelian trailed off and I glanced down at him only to have my stress ratchet up higher as I saw his hackles raised and ears laid back. ~It is an incursion.~

"It's a whatist?" I asked, having never heard that term from anyone.

He snarled but spoke quickly in my mind, as if saying the words were distasteful. ~An area of Chaos accumulated too much magic and is exploding outward, seeking more room to grow. It needs to be lanced and drained for lack of a better word.~

So many questions popped into my mind. Can this happen with other realms? Where does the excess magic go? Is this why there were emergence spikes? I pushed all of them back as I heard more sirens and the sounds of people freaking out around me. "What do I need to do?"

~Seal the rip. Lancing and draining is part of what the council is for.~

I really needed to ask more questions, but every time I did that, I ended up with more things people expected me to fix. Occasionally ignorance was bliss.

"That, I can do." After opening and sealing a rip into a pocket realm to crash an airplane into, I'd gotten very good at managing them.

The rip stood out to my magic like a searing burn on my skin. All I had to do was zip it closed. Which was so much easier said than done. Magic fought me. It wasn't like when I was pregnant, when it was sluggish and unresponsive. No, this time it bucked and wiggled, trying to squirm away. It reminded me of playing catch the kitty with Carelian when he was younger. I used the same technique, corralling the magic, forcing it back in, step by step. It didn't want to go, but I used the elements of Air and Water to block it. They thought it was great fun. If the rip had been closer to the ground, I would have grabbed Fire and Earth, but as it was, I didn't figure setting the sky on fire would help at all.

Sweat poured down my face, and I kept fighting it. There was so much magic.

"Carelian, can you contact your mother, get her here to lance or drain it?"

~Would not Tirsane be better?~ he asked as I leaned on him more and more, now using him to keep myself standing upright.

"You said it was Chaos and I'm not burning a favor for this unless I have no choice." I gritted the words out. There were still two oily ribbons peeking through the gap. I had no idea what would happen if I just cut them off. But that brought an idea.

I called lightning and slammed it into the ribbon. There was a shriek that almost brought me to my knees, though if it was a shriek of pain or outrage, I couldn't have said. The tentacle jerked back in and I slammed the opening shut. The sudden release of the pressure I'd been fighting against sent me reeling backwards and I hit the pavement with a soft whack. Luckily, I landed on my butt.

~See? We didn't need her,~ Carelian purred in my mind.

I glared at him. "What's going on? Normally, you are more than happy to ask your mother to come by."

He avoided my gaze, looking behind me. ~We have company,~ he whispered.

"We will be talking about this," I hissed as I twisted around to see who was approaching. Two cops and someone in a suit that just screamed official—though what type I didn't know—were approaching us. The police had their hands on their weapons and the official just looked arrogant.

They stopped a few feet away from me. I knew I should stand up to face them, but right then I wasn't sure my legs could support me. Fighting with the rip and that aspect of Chaos had exhausted me past anything I'd ever dealt with.

"Are you responsible for that?" demanded the officious one.

"Depends on what that you are talking about," I said mildly. "And you are?" Carelian moved behind me and laid down, creating a backrest. I sagged back against him. At this point, I just wanted to go home.

"Special Agent Jake Arnold, FBI," he said that in a snooty officious voice. "You know that using magic like that and opening rips to other realms can be treated as a criminal offense."

The two cops next to him tensed, and I didn't blame them. Arresting mages was always a risky proposition. Good thing for them I wasn't a criminal and wasn't about to run or make their lives more difficult.

"Excellent. By the way, I'm Cori Munroe." I lifted the hair away from my face so they could see my double marks, then reached into my bag to pull out my phone. I hit the speed dial for Stephen Alixant. He had been promoted to senior director of the FBI Magical task force and reported directly to the head of the FBI. The director of the FBI was a federally appointed position, but about three years ago they'd created Stephen's position to oversee all magical crime investigations.

"Hey Cori, what's up?" His voice came out tinny through my phone.

"Stephen, I'm putting you on speaker. Will you please tell the nice officers and Special Agent Jake Arnold that I'm not the bad guy?" I flipped it to speaker and held it out to them.

The tone and timber of his voice changed and for a minute, I wished I could see him. "This is FBI Magical Crimes Senior Director Stephen Alixant. What is going on there?" It wasn't so much a question as a barked-out demand for information.

"Um, sir, can I um, ask for verification of your identity?" the agent stuttered while the two cops relaxed a bit, but their eyes kept jumping between Carelian and me, unsure as to who was the bigger threat.

"Check your phone," Stephen snapped out.

The agent jumped as his phone went off and he pulled it out, paling at what he saw there.

"Is that enough validation for you?" asked Stephen, though I knew he was a tiny bit impressed the agent had requested verification.

"Sir, yes sir," he snapped out.

"Good. Munroe, tell me what in blazes is going on there."

There were people gathering around us and I winced. "It might be a better idea for us to go somewhere not quite as public as this currently is," I said, giving Jake a hard look.

He shook himself, looked around. I saw red creeping up his neck. "That might be wise. Umm," he looked at the police officers helplessly and I swear I saw them roll their eyes. Fifteen minutes later we were in one of the satellite station's interrogation rooms, with a video conference connected to Stephen. I at least had been able to stop and get a very large iced coffee for me, and water and a tray of sashimi for Carelian. I poured the water into his bowl. I kept one collapsed in his harness storage. Then I unwrapped the sashimi for him—the cellophane gave him nothing but trouble—then focused on my icy goodness of a treat.

"Now what is going on?" Stephen was back in his officious "I am the boss mode" and I glared at him from the corner of my eyes. He quirked a corner of his mouth up at me, but didn't change anything else.

Jake and the cop that had stayed both turned their eyes to me. "We'll let the merlin explain."

"In other words, you have no idea what happened?" Stephen asked. No one responded, and he turned to look at me.

I took a long sip of my iced coffee, trying to organize my thoughts. "I was walking down the street when I felt a rip form—"

Jake interrupted me. "What do you mean, 'felt a rip form'?"

It looked like I'd get to do mage education, too. Jake wasn't a mage, neither was the cop that had stayed here to listen. I fought back a sigh. Teaching would never be something I enjoyed. It was probably a character flaw, but there it was.

"I'm a double merlin. One of the aspects of how I sense magic is that when rips form near me, I feel them appear like a spike of pain through my skull. They are not common in public areas, so when I felt it I looked around." That was at least a white lie. They tended to be common in my life, but not out in public like that.

"Okay, then what?"

I described racing toward it then, highlighting the fact that Indira Humbert had trained me, I explained trying to close it. I talked about the thing trying to come out and using Water, Air, and a bit of lightning to discourage that action.

"Do you know what was coming through the rip? And know that we have already alerted the OMO." Jake said this as if it was supposed to scare or intimidate me. The OMO was the Office of Magical Oversight and they acted as the monitor and regulator for most magic, but mostly they were toothless outside of testing and registration. It wasn't like they could affect the fact that my draft was over or how powerful I was.

"Know? Nope. I think it might have been a Chaos denizen or even just magic manifesting, but I have no way of knowing for sure. And okay? I don't know what the OMO can do besides record that it happened." I went back to my iced coffee, wishing I'd grabbed two.

"What happened when you chased it back in, assuming that is what you did." His voice held more than a hint of accusation, but I ignored it.

I shrugged. "I closed the rift, and it wasn't as easy as it should have been." I ran my hand down my hair. "Most rifts I can close with a few strands. This one cost me almost an eighth of an inch of hair. That rift was very determined to remain open."

Jake opened his mouth to say something, something stupid probably, but Stephen spoke first with a shocked tone. "It cost you that much to get it closed?"

"That and convince those tentacles to go back inside." I shrugged. "They were reaching hard for something."

"You?"

I laughed at Jake. "No. They were nowhere near me. If I had to guess toward freedom. But I'm not exactly an expert at this."

"What about him?" Jake stabbed a finger at Carelian. Carelian wasn't happy with the small room and decided the best way to protect me was to lie across the base of the door. I wasn't sure anyone could force it open if he decided to not let it move.

"Feel free to ask him," I said, leaning back and watching Jake pale.

Carelian yawned, laying his ears back and looking like the vicious predator he could be.

Alixant sighed. "Carelian, do you know anything about what that was?"

~I know many things. But other than Chaos, it was a thing but not in the way you understand beings.~ He licked his paw as his mind spoke in mine and the others'.

Jake went even paler, and I wondered if he was going to pass out, but he managed to speak anyhow. "What does that mean? It was a thing?"

The answer to this question was one I wanted also, so I just waited to see what Carelian would say.

It took him a bit as he licked one claw, then another, and I wondered if he was thinking or stalling for time.

~The best explanation I can give you is that was the Chaos

equivalent of a tornado. Not really alive, but with properties and actions that seem as if it had a purpose or agenda.~

That made an odd sort of sense to me, and I nodded. Didn't make it any easier to deal with, but it not being a direct act did make it feel a bit less directed at me.

The room was quiet for a full three heart beats as we all digested this. "Very well," Stephen said from the video screen. "Is there anything else that happened?"

The cop shrugged, and Jake looked a bit flummoxed.

"Not really. I'd like to go home and think about it," I mentioned, figuring Stephen would understand that I needed to check with a few nonhumans about it. "But I didn't see any damage caused by it, just from people freaking out."

There were a few stammered protests from Jake, but even he had to admit nothing had happened. I managed to get out in another twenty minutes after giving my statement and Stephen promising to get in touch with me soon.

I collected my belongings. Nothing looked like it had been touched. I walked outside, Carelian leaning against me. I knew my actions would be scrutinized, so I called for a rideshare and took the long way home. That was okay. It gave me time to think.

By the time we got back to Hamiada, I'd decided that I really needed to talk to Esmere or Tirsane and figure out what that was about. Plus, what was up with Carelian and Esmere? The thought was taken away from me as I walked into the house and, sitting in the middle of the floor in the entry, was Esmere.

~Cori, the Council requires your attendance immediately.~

CHAPTER

TWO

The rip that occurred in downtown Albany today wasn't the first as many people want to believe. We have evidence that this has been happening worldwide and the government is hiding it from us. Don't believe what they are telling you. The mages aren't saving us when they close these rips—who do you think created them? Mages, of course. Join the cause and force the government to make magic use unconstitutional. ~ Freedom from Magic

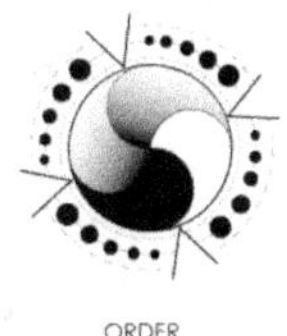

ORDER

I blinked at her. "Good afternoon to you also." I moved past her to hang up my small bag, still holding everything else. Jo and Sable would pick the kids up from school in thirty minutes. I was supposed to start dinner. It might be a sandwich night.

~Cori, this is important.~

"Unless it is about the incursion this morning, it isn't as important as you think. Either way I'm going to go pee, change my clothes, put this away, and then I'll go see the council." As I talked I headed to the stairs.

~Incursion? What incursion?~ Her worried mental voice bounced around in my head as I reached my study. I placed the papers and the box on the desk and resisted the desire to go through it. It looked like that would have to wait.

~There was an incursion in the town earlier. Cori stopped it.~ The amount of pride in Carelian's voice almost made me blush. The ice coffee demanded to be let out and I agreed. After that was taken care of I stripped off the slacks and blouse I was wearing, pulling on jeans and a comfortable Henley in dark green, and slipping on hiking boots. Every time I wore sandals or heels into the realms I regretted it.

I took a minute to pull out my phone and text Jo and Sable.

Esmere here, dragging me to council. Panini's okay?

While I waited for a response, I put my hair back up into something neater and wiped my face. Dried sweat felt icky.

Got it. Don't torture them too much. Jo sent back with a laughing emoji.

I headed back downstairs feeling a bit more comfortable, though not particularly happy. They had decided to cut me out of the conversation, so when I got back to the entry there were two Cath glaring at each other, tails lashing.

"Do I need to give you two some alone time?" I asked archly, even as a niggling doubt burrowed into my soul. In all the time I'd known them both I'd never seen them fight like this. And I couldn't help but feel it was regarding me.

~No. We need to leave. Carelian and I will solve it at a later point.~ Esmere looked at me her eyes almost glowing. I didn't know if that was her emotions or magic.

"He is coming with me." It wasn't a question.

~Of course he is,~ she replied glancing back at me with ears laid back. ~Oh Cori, I... later. We will explain it later.~

I knew it had been about me. "Fine, but we will deal with it later."

She nodded, flicking her tail at me, which I knew meant she would avoid it as long as possible. Cath did not like to be forced into anything. She stepped through the rip she created to the other realm and I followed her.

Every other time I'd gone to the council it had been like walking into a social hour, then everyone settled down. This time it felt like walking into a bar brawl. Magic snapped at the end of being's limbs, fire spurted in the air while some parts of the council chamber were snowing, and a mini twister spun around a Valkyrie.

I blinked, the noise almost overwhelming.

~ENOUGH!~ Brix's voice blew through my mind and cut through the noise, leaving me fighting the desire to throw up. It had hurt that much. ~The Herald of Magic is here as we requested, though much delayed.~ There was a note of censure in Brix's voice that let my irritation push down my nausea.

I wandered over to Shay and Amadahy. They stood almost shoulder to shoulder glaring at everyone. I didn't see Hishatio.

"Hey," I said with a nod of my head. "Any idea what's going on?"

The two of them exchanged a quick glance while Carelian wrapped around my feet.

"They'll tell you in a second. Just remember this wasn't our choice or thought. They have a hard on for you," Shay said with an irreverent grin.

Amadahy slammed her staff down, just missing his foot. "That is crude and unhelpful. We will talk afterward, Merlin Munroe." Her voice was very formal when she addressed me. I preferred Shay's insouciance.

Everyone was settling down, though I noticed there were a lot more spectators than the last time I'd been here.

~Merlin Munroe. Your suggested Lord has missed this session. We have waited for him, but he has not appeared. How are you going to fix this?~

I looked at the rainbow phoenix, then at the two humans. "Really? This is the awful emergency?"

They both nodded, looking exasperated. "Apparently no one ever misses a meeting. They are up in arms as he is two hours late."

The desire to imitate my familiar and hiss and stalk off in a huff very nearly became a reality.

"A few things. One - I am not responsible for him. He is an adult and is capable of managing his own life. Two - did it occur to you he might be sick, or there is something that he has to deal with right now? Three - for Merlin's sake, has anyone called him?"

All of the beings just looked at me. After what seemed like an eternity, Brix spoke.

~You mean injured in a fight?~

"No, I mean sick. Cold, flu, measles, mumps, I don't know. Maybe just allergies. He also could have been in an accident, or maybe there was something he was in the middle of that he couldn't drop. Humans have jobs and responsibilities. We don't just get to do what we want. Others can tell us what to do. For all I know he's in jail for drunk and disorderly. Has anyone checked in on him?"

Again, that silence and I wanted to beat my head on the stone floor. It might help. I turned to Shay and Amadahy. "Seriously? Do either of you have his phone number?"

They both looked at me and shrugged. I sighed. I could ask Tiantang, the Empress Cixi's dragon familiar. But there was an easier way. "Jeorgaz," I called out. Jeorgaz had been James Well's familiar. The man who had left all the houses and the money to me. He also knew Hishatio and didn't particularly like him. But he knew him.

A minute later there was a poof of flame in front of me and Jeorgaz flapped his wings, sending wafts of flame around him.

~Cori?~ He sounded confused as he looked around. ~What is going on?~

~Land. The Herald has a request of you,~ Brix ordered. The feathers on Jeorgaz bristled and I got the distinct impression those two did not get along, but he settled on the perch that flowed up from the council floor.

While he settled himself, I looked around. The usual suspects were here and no one had ever replaced the wall Brix blew out for Zmaug to talk to everyone, leaving it open to a grassy area that held some larger spectators. Some of the lords seemed to have changed or at least the hypnohawk was gone, instead there was a fox with too many tails sitting in the Spirit area. Tirsane was there as usual. I flashed her a smile and she nodded, her snakes hissing and bouncing up and down. She was a regular dinner guest and the twins loved her.

Jeorgaz had settled down, his back to Brix in an obvious move. I did my best not to laugh. The more alien they were, the more they were just like humans. ~Yes? I dislike dealing with the Council.~

There was a snort. ~You're just mad I ascended to this position, not you.~ Brix sounded horribly snooty and I shot the bird a look.

"Do you want this dealt with or do you want to snipe at each other? If you want to snipe, please feel free and I'll go home and do what I need to while you act like my kids." That wasn't inaccurate. They were in the "Mom, she's touching me" phase and all three of us were tired of it.

Esmere choked back a chuff of laughter as I glared at the two birds. They were both at least in their second century and I didn't feel like dealing with them.

~Cori, did you need something?~ Jeorgaz addressed me, as if the rest of the council didn't exist. I understood that sentiment.

"Jeorgaz, Hishatio hasn't shown up for this meeting and we both know that is not like him. Would you find him and inquire as to why he has not attended?"

Jeorgaz, fluffed his feathers, cocking his head to look at me. ~You know I do not care for him.~

I smiled. "I know. But I think you enjoy chewing on him. And if you do, I'll make your berry lemon treat this weekend." Jeorgaz had a major sweet tooth and loved various berries mixed with lemon juice and honey. He'd eat it until he burst if he could.

~That sounds like a reasonable exchange. Hold.~ He launched himself off the post and disappeared in a fiery poof

~Show off.~ Brix's voice was unmistakable but I turned to the other two humans, ignoring the council leader.

"What is going on? Why in the world am I getting dragged here because someone is late?"

Shay had settled down into a chair, while Amadahy had a stool she perched on.

"There was agitation present when we arrived. We have never met outside of here, so we never thought to exchange contact information," Amadahy said with her formal phrasing.

"What she said. No clue what has their feathers in a twist. But the magic feels strange today." Shay waved his left hand around his reddish-orange hair in a circle. "We were told the meeting was about incursions today, but no one wants to explain what that means."

My body went still and I pivoted to find Esmere thoroughly cleaning a hind paw as if her life depended on it.

"I believe there is something that needs to be explained," I said in slow hard tones.

She flinched at each word and Carelian curled into a ball, trying to look inconspicuous.

~Malkin, tell them.~ Carelian's voice was soft, but urging, and I started to think this was what had caused the rift between the two of them. I didn't know if that made me feel better or not.

"Peace, Carelian and Esmere. I will accept responsibility." Tirsane spoke before either of them could say anymore and I could almost see the stress bleed off of Esmere. That alone worried me. I don't think I'd ever seen a Cath that had any amount of stress. Excitement, eagerness, fear, even worry or trepidation, but never stress.

"Tirsane, what is going on?" I turned toward the gorgon, smiling at the snakes, and managed to control the shudder as the tattooed one on my arm wiggled the littlest bit in greeting. It had been years, but it still felt wrong in the worst way.

She inhaled and I laughed as Shay's eyes drifted to her chest. "The council ordered the other lords to not say anything to anyone that isn't on the council." She smirked. "They are welcome to remove my mantle if they wish, but due to the favor I provided you, I have more magic than most." Her smile faltered for a second there, but then she forced her smile wider. "And as it affects all of us, I don't have an issue telling you."

I crossed my arms and waited. I saw Brix pivot our way with wings raised, the ring of office on his leg glinting, and I just knew the feather head was going to butt in.

An exploding wave of flames appeared above the perch and I glanced to see Jeorgaz settling himself down. I had rather expected a smug full of himself phoenix happy to have caught Hishatio in something. Instead, he sat with his feathers slicked down and his wings held tight to his body.

"Jeorgaz, what is wrong?" I asked, my voice loud enough to cut through the chatter in the room. It went silent and every being there, even those without eyes, focused on us.

He lifted his head, even the colors seeming somehow muted, to look at me. ~He is in a hospital. The woman with him said he had a massive heart attack and that they did surgery to fix his heart. He will be unable to talk for another day or more as they have a tube down his throat breathing for him.~

Silence hung in the air as all of us digested that. I took a breath.

"There you have it. He's ill. I am sure he'll be back when he can. Until then, you have two very capable merlin's here to help you." I waved at Shay and Amadahy who didn't look all that capable at the moment. They looked shocked and overwhelmed.

"Enjoy the council you two. I'm headed home. I have family stuff to do."

There was an outburst of chatter and Brix's voice overrode all of them. "The Herald must stay and fill out the council."

I turned and looked at them. "The Herald needs to go home. You'll live one meeting with only two Earth merlins. This is called life. Adapt." I shot a look at Tirsane and Esmere. They both gave me the smallest of nods.

"Carelian, let's go home."

~Gladly.~ Before anyone else could protest or stop us, I stepped through the rip Carelian made and went home.

CHAPTER
THREE

Seeking information exchange for research into the rips. I am a Chaos Merlin, seeking a Spirit Merlin to investigate the rips. I have information and have a contact with the OMO that is providing data about these extra-planar incursions. Terms to be discussed. ~ House of Emrys Board

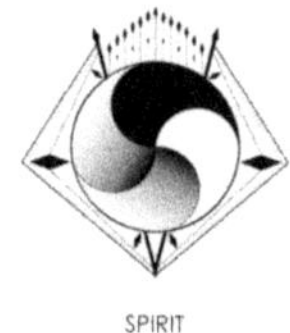

We walked into the kitchen from the rip so I could start making dinner. "Do you want to explain exactly what is going on between you and Esmere?" I kept my voice neutral, but it still worried me.

He threw himself on the floor in a picture-perfect version of teenage moping. ~She knows something is going on that could affect both Earth and you personally, but she won't tell you because of the rules. And I am not happy with anything that puts my queans at risk.~ There was a long pause, then he continued. ~And frustrated my Malkin is putting stupid council rules over family.~

That explained a lot, and I resisted the urge to go pet him. I'd just washed my hands. "Ah. And that is what Tirsane was going to tell me?" I glanced at the clock, three-thirty, and got my butt in gear. I pulled out chicken and set about making a simple chicken casserole. Chicken, rice, cream of cheese soup, frozen veggies, and cheese. The kids loved it, the adults tolerated it, and I had a hard time screwing it up.

~I assume so. I do not like secrets.~

I snorted. "You love secrets. You just don't like them being kept from you."

~There might be some truth in that statement,~ he admitted.

I finished getting dinner ready, then settled down in the study to go over the paperwork. Carelian decided to go lay outside in the yard, enjoying the fall day. It still seemed unreal, even if I'd been working toward this for years. The Tudor house and the Craftsman were mine. A pang shot through me as I realized this meant Jo and Sable would be leaving. That idea caused too many conflicting emotions, and I pushed it away. The Craftsman was the first house on the street and right now I didn't know what I would do with it. Renting it out didn't sound like the right thing to do, but what?

Giving up on the paperwork and decisions I couldn't make right now, I pulled the box over to me and broke the seal. Inside were a few jewelry cases containing two men's rings, a necklace with what looked like a ruby, and one with a pink gold gem in a Trilliant cut, two Patek watches, and a small notebook. I sighed and added it to my "to be read" pile.

I heard the door opening downstairs and laid everything aside to go greet my family. I'd made it to the bottom of the stairs before I got hit with twin missiles that reached my waist. "Good afternoon. How was school?"

Magne looked up at me and grinned. His tight curly black hair, in a low braid, sparkled in the light. Dark eyes and white teeth gleamed up at me. "It was fun. But can I get a dog? I want a dog. Please?"

Carelian didn't react, so I assumed he hadn't heard Magne's comment from outside.

I heard Jo groan, but didn't look away from the kids. "And you Jaz?" She was wrapped around me tighter, not looking up, her fluffy hair hiding her face. "School is stupid. I don't wanna go." That did concern me and I glanced at Jo even while I had my arms around the two five-year-old's.

She sighed and just waved her hand, signifying we'd talk about it later.

I hugged Jaz. "Hmm. Sounds like you've had a busy day." Proof that everyone had made it through an exhausting day solidified as Sable came home about then and looked absolutely wiped. "But if you go change and play for a bit, then we can eat dinner and I can tell everyone the big news.

Jaz jerked her head up to peer at me, her fluffy hair moving with her. All of us were waiting for it to grow out a bit more. Then we could get it braided. "Good news?"

It sounded oddly hopeful and I took my finger and pushed the end of her nose. "Beep. I guess you'll have to decide, won't you?"

She giggled, and they raced upstairs to change. They were still sharing the one room, something else that would change if or when they moved to the Tudor house. I knew we had about seven minutes for the twins to climb the stairs, change, and get back down here.

"What's up?" I asked, looking at Jo while I moved over to give Sable a hug. She leaned into it, sighing.

"No friends at school. There are only two girls in her grade and they are besties. So, she's feeling a bit isolated. While Magne is excited that Bobby is with him and a new kid that seems to share their love of mud, bikes, and collecting Super Familiars."

I laughed at that. It was a game where you went around finding "Super Familiars" and capturing them on your mobile device. Carelian was miffed that anyone believed that a familiar would deign to allow themselves to be captured.

They were both in pre-K, but Bobby Freeman lived not too far from us and they had met on a park outing and become best friends. Magne was stocky, spoke clearly if quickly, with skin the color of dark chocolate. We kept his curly hair in tight braids out of self-preservation, any looser and it just wasn't practical, he was way too active. Bobby, on the other hand, was lanky, with blond hair and blue eyes. He wore glasses with lenses an inch thick, and spoke with a lisp.

Jaz didn't like Bobby, mostly because he was willing to roll in the mud and run around with Magne, where she liked doing art, reading their books, or playing with her dolls. Until this last year, she and her twin had been joined at the hip. But after starting pre-K, Magne had started hanging out with more kids while she still hadn't found any real friends. Partially because she preferred her own company to anyone else's. But the lack of other kids she liked in the class didn't help.

The twins came racing down the steps, and I winced at the sound they made, but Hamiada hadn't complained yet. I think she loved the life they brought with them.

"Can we go out and play?" Magne asked. He had one of his toy trucks in his hand. It had been the last present from Henri he'd received. Just seeing it made a wave of sadness hit me. When the twins were four, Henri had a massive heart attack in his garage. He'd died before anyone had found him. Marisol had been on him to retire and he'd grudgingly agreed to hand over the day-to-day business to Marco and Sanchez as co-managers with the idea of it being their inheritance. Instead, he'd died at sixty-six, leaving it all to them. It still hurt and Marisol still seemed slightly broken, and we didn't know how to help.

"It is may we, and you have an hour, then dinner," Jo told them. They scampered out the back door before she finished speaking. The back yard was safe as Hamiada always kept an eye on them. Where I'd blasted the earth and created a spring, we'd put in a fountain. They had a slide and swing set back there as well.

"You two look exhausted." I scanned both of them. Sable was missing at least an inch of hair since this morning, and Jo had rings under her eyes.

"It was a day. We had issues with the prototype processing, and I had to keep two of them from shattering and create three new ones on the fly." Sable looked ready to drop. She worked for a small company that created water filtration systems for specific needs and right now they'd been working on something for deep ocean drilling and had to get something that could extract the salt from the water, handle the pressure, and do it without requiring electricity. It was a fascinating project.

Jo pulled us both into a hug. "Ditto. Everything at the

machine shop went wonky today and I still have two custom bikes that won't run right, and I have no idea why."

I hugged them both back. "Go. Dinner is in the oven. I'll start a salad and we can talk then." They headed to their room, and I settled down in the sunroom to watch the kids and think. I'd only been there a few minutes when Carelian showed up.

"As we aren't talking about the council drama yet, any thoughts about what you'd like to do? We still have decades in front of us. We don't have to only do things we've done before. We talked about S&R." It wasn't just an idle question, there were lots of options, but my life was richer when Carelian was a part of it.

~I am still in favor of resuming the Search and Rescue, though perhaps not full time. But is there a reason you can't take a vacation for a while? I think you push too hard. Deep sea fishing sounds like an excellent vacation.~ He sprawled out at my feet, tail twitching.

I laughed. "Hmmm. Maybe." My phone rang before I could follow up on anything, though I did like the sound of doing the S&R again. It would help keep me in shape and I still had contacts. "Hey, Stephen. How's Indira?" After all these years his name didn't hurt anymore. It also helped that I never called him Stevie.

"She's good. Wants to come see you, but is caught up in a rush order right now." Indira did custom circuitry chips using her Chaos abilities to manipulate atoms for nanotechnology. It paid very well, but it was exhausting and used up lots of resources. She made about five chips a month and they went for mid six-figures every time.

"Ah. Well, you know where we are. What's up?" I knew darn well he was calling about the incident this afternoon, but no need to volunteer when I didn't know what he was looking for.

"You said you had to struggle a bit to close the rip. Is that unusual?"

I thought about it. "Yes and no. Most rips aren't that big. When I run into random ones, they are like six to ten inches. And the one big rip I closed, I also created. Given that information, I'm not sure I have much experience to base my answer on. Indira would know more." Indira had been the one to teach me to close rips, so I figured she'd know more.

"We've talked about it. She said the largest she's closed that she didn't create was about thirteen feet. It was a bit more difficult, but not enough to worry about. The mages guarding Area 51 have never tried to close them, so you probably have more experience than most." Area 51 held three static rips, one to each realm. All the information about it was restricted, so that was as much as most people knew.

"Why are you asking?"

He was silent for a long moment. "I'll explain later. Thanks, Cori." And with that he hung up, leaving me staring at my phone.

The timer for the casserole went off. I called the kids in, roused Jo and Sable, who had fallen asleep, and got everyone seated and served. Carelian opted out of eating and lay on the window seat in the dining room.

This not working thing might not be too bad. Maybe I could take cooking lessons and actually learn to cook. Italian or Cajun could be fun.

"So, what's the big news?" Jo's question pulled me back to the table from my mental wanderings.

"I signed everything today. The houses are ours." Everyone looked at me for a long moment, then Jo did a slow smile.

"The Tudor house is yours?"

I shook my head. "Nope." I waited, enjoying the confusion

on their faces. "It's been signed over to you and Sable. It's your house."

The look of shock on Jo and Sable's face made me laugh. "Cori, you didn't have to—" Jo started, and I waved my hand.

"I don't need the money from renting it, I have no desire to sell it, you have lusted after it from day one, and you and the kids get everything anyhow. Why not?" And I meant all of that. It was just a house, and I rather loved this one.

"I don't know what to say," Sable stammered. I saw their eyes shining at the idea of their own place, even as my heart cringed at the idea of them leaving.

"Does this mean we're moving? Can we get a dog?" Magne asked.

Carelian's ears laid back, and he hissed, but didn't lift up his head. ~Why would you want one of those ugly stupid things in the house?~ His ears perked up. ~Unless you want to buy one as a treat for me? I don't suppose they would be much work to hunt, but they might taste good. I could use a snack that is interesting.~

" Ewwww." Magne's look of disgust had the three of us turning to hide our smiles and fight the gales of laughter threatening. "No! As a pet."

The huff of disgust from Carelian didn't help my attempt to not burst out laughing. ~Why would you want a pet? They can not talk to you or help you, and they make you clean up their mess. It was bad enough you went through that stage. To have a creature that never gets past it, no.~

"But everyone else has pets." He whined as he said it, but dropped the tone as Jo gave him a hard look. Whining was not permitted.

~And?~ Carelian replied. ~Having a familiar is an honor. Having a pet is simply being a farmer of a creature who makes nothing of value. Besides, you have the dragons waiting for you.~

I kept my face buried in one hand. Carelian had a way of putting things that was both logical and completely wrong.

"But they are never gonna hatch." This time he was borderline whining.

"Excuse me?" Jo said, her tone arch. By this point I had to cup both hands over my face, looking down at my plate. Starting to giggle would have ruined everything and everyone would have probably joined in.

Magne sat up a bit straighter. "Sorry Momma. I just..." He trailed off and stared mournfully at his plate.

"I think there is something more than just wanting a pet here, isn't there?" Sable said. She kept her eyes on him and waited.

"Maybe." He didn't look up.

"He's being a poopy-pants," Jaz said. She then cowered under the glares of three adults.

"What are the rules?" Jo said, her voice flat.

"No calling names," she whispered, starting to pout.

"And what is the punishment for that?" Jo just watched her.

"I have to do all his chores tonight." Her pout grew larger.

"Wonderful. Now that Magne doesn't have any chores tonight, maybe he will feel like telling us what brought all this on." Jo shifted her attention to Magne, while Sable gave him a one-armed hug.

"Everyone brings their pets to school next week. Hamsters, dogs, cats. It's school pet day. And I don't have anything to bring. But Bobby is going to bring his new puppy."

That shed a lot more light on it.

Jaz opened her mouth to say something, but snapped it shut when she saw me watching her.

"Who says it has to be your pet? I'm pretty sure most

animals are the family pets. It would be awfully hard for a kid to take the pet to the vet, buy food, take it for walks," I said mildly, ignoring the alarmed looks from Jo and Sable.

Magne's head jerked up, eyes wide, then he frowned. "But Carelian isn't a pet, neither is Esmere. They are peoples."

I could have hugged him right then, instead I let him see my smile of pride. "Absolutely. But Carelian is an animal according to most humans. I'm sure he could be persuaded to parade around a classroom for a day."

~You are, are you? I do not know about that,~ he said, his voice dry, but he jumped off the window seat to rub against Magne's leg. ~But I dislike seeing you sad.~

"You're the bestest, Carey." He rubbed Carelian's head, who ignored the nickname. "But," he sucked in a breath. "You is people. People aren't pets. So I'm not ever going to say you are. I'll wait. But if the dragons ever hatch, I'm bringing them. Maybe they'll breathe fire on Lindsay."

Chatter had just started up when Tirsane pinged me. ~Cori, I have need to talk to you. May I come over?~

Security Status: SENSITIVE

RE: Rips - Data is being collected and most countries are participating. Under no circumstances should any information slip out that this has been occurring for years and it is just now happening in publicly visible areas and in a volume that makes it obvious to the populace. Research is ongoing as to why and there is a supposition that the sudden decline in sub-par mages that would be phased out under most countries' laws is linked. However, while the data seems to have a correlation this does not guarantee causation and all avenues of research should be continued. ~ Internal OMO memo

---

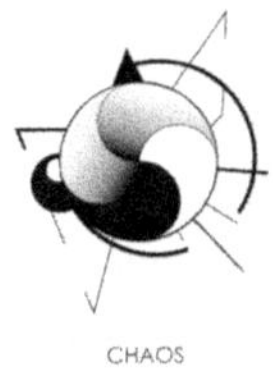

CHAOS

T sighed and looked at everyone. "Tirsane is coming over." I paused so the kids could squeal in excitement.

"Is there a reason?" Jo asked as she finished her dinner.

"Council stuff. I suspect I'm going to find out what Esmere was ordered not to tell me."

"Someone ordered Esmere to do something, and she listened?" Sable's eyes were wide as she stared at me.

"I guess so? Carelian is mad at her and she has avoided talking to me about it. Maybe Tirsane will shed some light on it."

~Can you give us fifteen? We need to clean up and put the kids to bed. Would you like anything to eat or drink?~ I asked Tirsane as I rose, starting to bus the dishes.

~Of course. And not tonight. I shall go home and feast when this is done. The council session was ... exhausting.~ The odd pause before exhausting worried me, but I didn't react.

~We'll see you shortly.~ I turned back to the important stuff. Getting the kids settled in or bribed to chill out, the kitchen cleaned, and mentally prepared for Tirsane. Plus, whatever news she might bring.

Tirsane appeared in the backyard. Most of the time, visitors didn't step directly into the house unless it was important or overly awkward to get to me. Baneyarl didn't navigate house stairs easily with wings, so he would step straight to my study. I opened up the back door as she slithered in, the green hoodie she'd absconded with years ago gracing her upper body.

"That hoodie is looking a bit worn. We've given you new ones. Why don't you wear those?" I said, as we went into the living room. Jo and Sable were there, while the kids had been bribed with watching a cartoon series upstairs with the promise they could come down to see Tirsane and her snakes before she left. They adored her.

She petted the arms of her hoodie possessively. "I like this one. It is fuzzy."

"I can find another polar fleece one. I can get them in different colors so you can wear them on different days. Surely not all areas of the realms remain a balmy temperature?" There was a big bean bag in the corner and she headed for that. I sank into my recliner while Jo and Sable broke off their conversation where they were curled up on the couch.

"Not all of them, no," Tirsane admitted. She kept petting the arms of the hoodie as we arranged ourselves. "That might be interesting? I have had multiple beings mention they liked it," she said slowly, her voice thoughtful.

"Oh, I'm so getting you real clothes for Christmas," Jo said, her eyes glittering. She was still the clotheshorse of all of us.

"Better watch it Tirsane or she's going to addict you to clothes too," Sable teased. Jaz took after Jo in that arena. The more clothes the better.

Carelian sauntered in a minute later and sat next to me, chin on the armrest, demanding pets.

"Tirsane, what is going on?" I asked, my left hand rubbing Carelian's ears to his pleasure.

Her snakes that had previously been bouncing around and hissing softly, drooped and then curled up into tight coils on her head. Her face went to the stony beauty that prevented any emotion from slipping through.

"Brix does not feel you should be told if you are not a councilor and tried to impart what you would call an NDA clause on us. I refused, but Bob said none of his lords would mention it."

"Ah," I said. I couldn't see Esmere listening to Brix, but Bob, yes. He was probably the only being, besides the two upstairs, that could get her to do something she didn't want to do. "And you feel I should know?"

Jo and Sable were listening, their eyes focused on Tirsane, holding hands tightly. A pang of worry slashed through my heart. What if this was more trouble my very existence was bringing their way?

"Yes. I am older than ... well, the other seniors, Bob and Salistra are older than me, and I believe Brix is very old, but most of the others aren't. And unless Brix wants to challenge me, censuring me will just free up my time." Tirsane shrugged, the elegance of it slightly foiled by the fuzzy hoodie. "They will have to live with my decision and I with my actions."

I sensed a strange connotation to the word challenge. "You're making me nervous," I said, suddenly wishing for tea or a hard drink. Whatever this was, it didn't sound good.

"Ah. Yes. Here is the crux of it. Magic is bursting at the seams. Our birth rates are down, meaning fewer beings to breathe in the magic. The magic that is coming to me from your ineligible mages I've been pumping into the realms because I can't hold it all. Even Salistra has quit whining because I'm dumping as much into her as I am Bob, and through them, they dump it into their realms. I didn't think we could overfill them, but we have."

I knew Tirsane had still been getting magic from all the mages that would be killed here on Earth because they couldn't manage their powers. The fact that she was getting that much magic surprised me.

"I see. So, what didn't Brix want me to know?" Nothing that she had said sounded like anything I could change.

"All that magic is why there are more and more rips into your world. At first, they were small ones. But now they are getting bigger. They also aren't getting closed fast enough to prevent things from creeping in. Beings that normally would never have the power or ability to come through on their own, plants, insects, even animals. Brix says you are a key to it one way or the other, but keeps stating that you are not ready for this level of responsibility. And what made me refuse to agree is that this was stated prior to your council members showing up, so they know nothing of this or your role in it."

My mouth moved with no sound coming out. Jo and Sable just stared; their eyes wide. "Do you realize how insane that sounds?"

Tirsane's snakes wiggled. "Which part? Too much magic or you being key to this issue?"

"The absorbing it part. Not only does it sound insane, it isn't even a thing. And even if it was, you're a demigod, I'm human. If you can't handle it, how in the world am I supposed to?"

Tirsane went very quiet, looking down at the ground, but her face remained that mask.

"Tirsane?" I asked. I could almost feel the huge anvil of fate hanging over my head.

"Do you remember Baneyarl teaching you that most of our magic users are full users? As how I can use all the branches of Spirit at full strength? And how odd we find the fracturing of magic users only being able to use some parts of it?"

I glanced at Jo and Sable, trying to remember. That was over a decade ago.

Sable answered first. "Yes. Baneyarl talked about it, and it is why they found Cori so interesting. As a double Merlin, she is closer to being a true user like what your denizens are."

Tirsane nodded. "Cori, have you ever been tested after Frej told you the truth about your twin, about his death?"

Just her saying the words shoved a sharp spurt of grief through my heart, but it faded quickly. His death was part of me and nothing I could change.

"No. Why would I have been?"

Her face didn't change, but her snakes hiding their heads and trying to pull the hoodie up over them said loads.

"You emerged again when you had your... explosion of grief and anger upon finding out about your twin." She spoke in a soft, almost comforting tone.

I blinked, thinking back to that day. It was almost six years ago, as it had been before the twins were born. The realization that I had killed Stevie when I pulled all the magic into me had caused something to snap in me and I exploded. Literally and figuratively. It was why we had a fountain in the back yard now.

"I'm not sure what that means," I said slowly, even as my gut tightened.

Tirsane sighed and the serene mask she wore slipped. "It means you have full access to all branches and all classes. You are, for all intents and purposes, the Herald of Magic, or as your people knew the previous one, Merlin."

The knowledge that I'd maybe realized, though not acknowledged, hit me like a gut punch and air oofed out of me. My hands shook as I tried to reconcile the nauseous idea of being the most powerful mage on Earth. I was fervently glad my draft service was over. Me being a double merlin had been seen as an oddity and yes, I was a bit more powerful, but I'd never really shared with my supervisors exactly what I could do, shifting a lot of my ability onto Carelian.

Over the years, one or two people had come up with the great idea of using him to do things. He'd usually ignored them or just stepped away. One idiot had tried punishment on him in the form of an electric prod. He'd needed thirty-three stitches and Carelian had disappeared from a locked room. No one had ever tried that again.

But this. This explained why things were even easier after the twins were born. I'd just assumed it was the rebound from fighting to use my magic for six months and my perceptions were out of sync.

"You're telling us that Cori is Merlin reincarnated?" Sable said incredulously.

Tirsane laughed at this, the first relaxed sound I'd heard from her today, and it helped me center. "No. If there is reincarnation, I've never had it proven to me. She is simply on the same power levels. There have been a few before, but she is the most recent."

"Recent? Can you name some others?" Jo leaned forward eyes intent.

"Oh, let's see, Solomon." Tirsane frowned as if trying to remember and recite the state capitals. "Aquiliane. Enoch. Gilgamesh. Zenobia was the last one before the Undoing. There were a few, but we are talking over thousands of your years, and none of them after Merlin and he was an oddity. He only managed as he was born in the realms. His mother was brought there by a Lord. Since the Undoing, you are the first human born on Earth to have become a Herald."

I could see Jo wanted to ask more questions, but I needed to know something else. "So, what does this mean? What does that have to do with the magic in the realms and the rips? What does it matter that I'm the Herald? You've called me that for years." The lump lodged in my throat sat there and I was unsure if it would be swallowed or choked up.

"It means you are the only one who has a chance of repairing the realms and Earth. And that Brix will lean on you pretty hard to try to control you." She sounded almost apologetic, but I didn't care.

"I have zero idea how to do that. Do you have an instruction manual? Maybe a how-to guide? None of the magic I've learned has anything to do with dealing with too much magic. I know how to research, how to do specific spells. How in the world am I supposed to be the Herald and solve all this?" My voice rose a bit at the end, my heart raced as I fought not to panic. I had just gotten free. I had the chance to be and do something for Carelian and me. It was so close.

Tirsane just shrugged. "That is why you are the Herald. It is something that only you will know how to do or figure out."

I put my head in my hands and fought to regain control of my emotions. When I thought I had some control and pulled myself back from the edge, I raised my head. "Tirsane, thank you so much. I needed to know this. The twins are desperate to say hi. Do you mind before you go?"

"Of course not. Jasmine is my godchild, after all." She lifted herself from the beanbag at the same time Jo and Sable stood. "I must say, you are taking this without the level of questions I expected."

"I'm sure I'll have questions. I'm just going to process it later." I smiled at Jo and Sable. "I'm headed to bed. I've reached my limit today."

They both gave me a quick hug and Tirsane patted me on the shoulder. I climbed the stairs, slipped into night clothes and threw myself on the bed.

Moments later, Carelian crawled up on the bed, laying down next to me. ~I'm sorry, my quean. I did not know.~

I wrapped my arms around him and snuggled in, trying not to cry. How in the world was I going to save four realms when I couldn't even manage my own life?

CHAPTER
FIVE

Cori Munroe was rumored to have been involved with the rip that occurred in Albany a few days ago. The question that remains on our minds is, did she cause it or close it? As the only double merlin the OMO has admitted to, either is very possible. But over the years she has proved more boring than most to watch. Is all her power a red herring or is she a sign of the things to come? ~ Magical Daily News

---

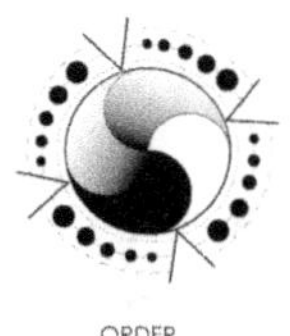

ORDER

My sleep was full of dreams I couldn't remember in the morning, but I did feel better. I pulled away from the roaring furnace that was Carelian and headed to the bathroom. A shower later, I was downstairs. It was early Tuesday morning and I could have slept in, but too much was chewing in my mind. I had my coffee made and in my hands before Jo got down stairs.

"Morning. You okay?" she asked, coming over to drop a kiss on top of my head.

"Define okay," I replied, sipping my coffee. I'd made Sanchez's Mexican chocolate. The extra caffeine sounded good this morning as I tried to chase the last remnants of dreams from my mind.

"Hmmm," she said as she pulled out pre-made egg and chicken burritos for the kids, throwing them in the air fryer. "I'll take that as a no. What are you going to do?"

I snorted. "If I knew that, I'd be the Herald they want. First, I'm going to check on Hishatio." She cast me a curious look, and I thought back. "Ah, I didn't tell you about that or the rip and Stephen, did I?"

Jo paused and gave me a look. If I'd been one of the twins, I might have been worried. As it was, I just smirked, then my smile faded. "Hishatio had a heart attack and is in the hospital. I'd like to check on him the normal way." I looked at my watch. "I think they are thirteen hours ahead of us. That should make it about seven pm. I'll call shortly."

"You have the number of the hospital?" Jo asked, curious.

I laughed and shook my head. "I don't even know what hospital he's in. But he gave me his email and cell phone number. I'm going to hope that works. If not, I'll cheat." I smirked. "A phoenix can go get the number for me. If he's still talking to me." I laughed and relayed what had happened with the council meeting.

The story finished as two sleepy kids tumbled into the kitchen and climbed up on the stools at the kitchen counter.

"Morning, my monsters," I said, hugging them both. "Enjoy school today. And remember, nothing lasts forever." I pulled up Jaz's chin to look at me. "You'll find your own friends." My smile as I nodded at Jo made her smile.

"Yes, Momma Cori."

I let them be. And headed up the stairs. I settled down in my chair in the study and took a minute to just exist. It felt like more of a home than I had ever known and I didn't want to give it up or put it at risk.

The only way through was forward, so I picked up the phone and dialed the international number. It rang five times before it was picked up.

"Good evening, Merlin Munroe. Or I suppose for you it is morning." Hishatio's voice came clearly through the phone and while he sounded exhausted, he still sounded like himself. We'd met occasionally through the years and while we weren't quite friends, we had managed to become decent coworkers. It was the best example I could come up with.

"Hishatio. Jeorgaz brought back word of your condition. How are you doing?" I asked, watching the sky getting lighter out the window.

"What prompted him coming to check on me? The bird can barely stand me."

I snorted. "Your absence at the council meeting disturbed them. Apparently, no one has ever missed one before. I pointed out the frailty of humans and basically told them to deal."

He chuckled softly. "I am sure that put Brix's feathers in a major twist."

"That it did. And even worse, I told them to deal with two councilors and left."

He laughed then broke off in a pained gasp. "I can see how they would have been less than amused."

"So, how are you?" I pressed, trying to figure out just how bad it was.

"I'm alive, which is more than anyone expected about thirty-six hours ago." His voice had a pensive tone and I got the feeling this had really thrown him.

"What happened, if you feel like sharing?"

"Aortic rupture. I dropped walking down the street. A few mages that were nearby stabilized me until they could get me into the operating room. From what they said, it was very touch and go." He coughed again, sounding a bit wet.

"You are lucky. Even with mages, often those just mean immediate death." The memory of Henri flashed through my mind. "I will say the council as a whole isn't happy, but they can't really say anything. Though exchanging numbers with Shay or Amadahy might be wise." I couldn't resist the gentle poke.

"Granted, that would have helped. Honestly, we usually talked for a few hours after the meeting and then met up in a place Amadahy set up monthly. I'd get notified when it was created. Short sighted of us. But they still wouldn't have been notified prior to the meeting. I've only been awake for about twelve hours. You were on my list of people to call, but I've been dealing with doctors most of the day." He paused, and I knew what was coming. "Merlin Munroe, I'm going to need to step down. Even if I respond excellently to the treatment, it is going to take months of rehab and physical therapy to get me back to where I was. The doctors have told me I need to reduce my stress. Even though I stepped down as Majyutsu-Shi, I was still advising and involved. Then the council. My body has said no more, regardless of what my spirit wants."

"I figured as much when Jeorgaz came back. If something minor had been wrong, you would have been at the council meeting."

"And if that isn't proof that I need to reassess my priorities, I don't know what is." His dry humor matched my own.

"Yes, it does. So, do you have any thoughts about whom to recommend to replace you?" He went quiet and my eyes narrowed even though he couldn't see me. "Don't you dare say me."

"Who else could I choose?"

"Not me. This is your responsibility. Figure it out. They need someone with more global views and that isn't me." I could feel my hands clenching and worked to release them.

"As you wish. On that note, may I request the information for Amadahy and Shay?"

"Here, I'll send you Shay's." I matched action to words and shared my contact with him. "I, however, don't know any way to contact Amadahy or if she even has a phone. Wait, I have an idea." I hit mute on the phone and looked at Carelian, who had migrated to the window seat of the study at some point in the conversation. "Can you contact Amadahy's familiar and ask for a contact number for her?"

He flicked an ear at me. ~ Kalihchiia is awfully arrogant, but for my quean yes.~ He closed his eyes.

I unmuted the phone. "I've asked Carelian. I'll let you know if I get an answer."

"Thank you, Merlin Munroe. I do understand this should have been dealt with previously, just..." He trailed off and I couldn't help a sad laugh.

"Just you thought you'd have more time or it would never happen to you?"

"That might be accurate," he said slowly. His voice was getting weaker, and I knew it was time to go.

"I understand. I'll let you know if I get her info and then I'll check in later this week?"

"That is kind of you, Merlin Monroe."

I sighed. "Hishatio, call me Cori. It has been too many years. Just call me Cori." The title always kind of made my skin crawl and now it was worse with what Tirsane had told me.

"Very well. Until later, Cori." We hung up and I looked at Carelian. "I can't decide if you really dislike birds or are just annoyed you can't chase them. Or worse, if you did, they might take their irritation out of your hide."

~Does it have to be either or? I provided Kalihchiia your email address. He said he would pass it on when she woke.~ The entire time, he hadn't bothered to do more than move his tail. ~Can we go hiking today? I long to feel fresh scents and be out in nature.~

There was the slightest bit of a plaintive note in his voice and I felt a stab of guilt that slashed through me. "Absolutely. Let me get changed, get supplies ready, and we'll go. Any place in particular?" I rose, putting action to my words.

He lifted his head, looking at me. ~Really?~

I moved over and dropped a kiss on the top of his head. "Yes. I've neglected you for far too long. It's time to make up for that."

He flicked a tail at me and stepped off the bench. ~I would like Yosemite. The sun should be rising shortly there. We can see it come up from the top of El Capitan?~

"That sounds wonderful, but only if you promise to set us back down at the bottom. I am not up to climbing that mountain." He loved visiting Yosemite. Plus, he found the freestyle climbers fascinating. I was not picking up that hobby, ever.

~Deal.~

I turned to head out of the study when my phone rang. "Good morning, Stephen. What has you up so early?"

"It's almost eight. I've been here for an hour," he said, his voice slightly snippy. "I need to talk to you."

I leaned against the desk, calculating time in my head. We had a little time. "Go for it."

He sighed. "There have been more portal rips appearing. And people are struggling to close them. There is a task force being formed, and I need you to be on it."

"Doing what? I just got done with the draft. I don't need money. I was going to enjoy being unfettered for a while," I protested as my life started to slip out of my grasp in yet another arena.

"You'll hear all of that when we meet. I need you here in an hour," he ordered.

"No." My word was quiet but firm.

"What?" I was annoyed enough that I didn't even enjoy his sputtering. "I need you here to talk to the team so we can come up with a plan on how to deal with these rips."

If I didn't know better, I would have thought I was twenty again with him bellowing at me. Too bad for him I'd met beings that made his anger look as threatening as banana pudding. He couldn't even roast me. "Stephen," I said, my voice icy, "in case you forgot, I am out of my draft. I do not work for you. And I have other plans for today. If you would like to ask me to come discuss something with you next week, nicely, I might consider it. Until then, I'm busy. Good bye." I hung up on him and turned to see Carelian sitting there staring at me.

"What?"

~You really are going to turn him down to spend time with me?~

Just the words felt like a sword shoved into my chest. I knelt next to him and wrapped my arms around him. "Carelian, you are the other half of my soul. Jo is my best friend. Sable is my dearest friend and my best friend's soulmate. You are part of me in a way I didn't realize was possible. I will turn down the world for you."

He laid his head against mine and purred, the rumble vibrating my bones, but I didn't let go. After too short of an eternity, he pulled back. ~You need to get ready if we are going to see the sun rise and hike today.~

I nodded, wiping unshed tears away from my eyes. "Ten minutes." I changed, grabbed his harness, bowl, emergency water, and food, let Jo and Sable know where we were going and that I was leaving my phone here, then Carelian opened a rip to the way point, then another to the top of El Capitan.

We sat down, my arm wrapped around him. Together we watched the sun creep up over the mountains and grace the world with color as I held the one being I never wanted to live without.

CHAPTER
SIX

Japan and China entered new talks today. After the dust-up that saw Empress Cixi take control, relations between the two countries have been warmer than they've been in decades. While there haven't been any drastic changes on the international stage in regards to China, there are many little signs that imply China might be changing policies that have been in force for over a century regarding other countries. ~ CNN News

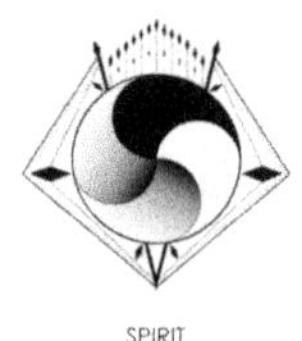

SPIRIT

We stepped back to the house after a long day of hiking through parts of Yosemite few people ever got to see. Carelian had chased animals, ate a few gophers, and basically worn himself out. I'd need to get him a universal hunting license again, something that predator familiars could get as long as they only took older or lamed game.

The smell of pizza caught me off guard and I headed into the kitchen, both of us sweaty and mentally refreshed if exhausted. Three take-out pizza boxes sat on the counter, unusual for us.

"Jo?" I called out.

"In here," she said from the living room. When I stuck my head in, I saw Jaz sitting in a corner pouting, Magne sitting in another corner, and Jo slumped in the recliner looking exhausted.

"Good grief. What happened? I was only gone for what, ten hours?" Carelian sat next to me. While wearing his harness flormping to the floor wasn't very comfortable.

"You know your phone has been ringing nonstop? I finally shut it off, then Alixant started calling me. I answered, and he wanted to know why you weren't picking up your phone. I told him you'd left it here and went hiking. His frustration was greatly amusing." Jo glared at me through heavy-lidded eyes.

"Meh. He's forgetting he's a friend, not my boss, and that I don't report to him. He might also be under a bit of stress. I'll call him in a bit. But what is all this about?" I waved my hand at the twins, who kept glancing back at us, but didn't move from their stools.

"Miss Jaz here decided to cut off Laurel's hair because she made a derogatory comment about Jaz's curly hair."

"She called it a wire brush mess and said that I should shave it all off," Jaz blurted out. I looked at her bushy afro and flinched internally. Jaz's hair was a mixture of Jo and Sable's hair, thick and curly. And when it got longer, it would fall into ringlets. Right now, it was a bit on the frizzy side as she had decided to cut it herself and we'd had to even it out a few weeks ago. Super curly hair tended to look a bit chaotic this short.

Magne's hair was still in close braids. Someday I was sure he'd have long braids, but right now he needed to be convinced it wasn't okay to leave mud and twigs in it. Jaz's just required time, oil, and nurturing.

Jo heaved a sigh. "Be that as it may, you still shouldn't have cut off her hair." She shifted her attention back to me. "I got an emergency call from the school. I spent two hours helping Laurel's hair to grow back using Transform and Pattern, at twice the cost of what I replaced. It was that, or they were going to press charges."

"Over hair?"

"Yes. Sigh." Jo just slumped down a bit more. "I'm exhausted."

"I figured with the pizza. Why is Magne in the corner?" He still hadn't spoken, a pout on his face.

"He decided it was a good idea to laugh at Jaz calling her stupid and said this is why she didn't have friends."

"Oh," I said. "Obviously, no dessert for either of them. They both have time out, and...?"

"Well, Jaz already has his chores to do, but he made fun of her. I'm not quite sure what to do." Jo sounded like she needed an hour in the tub.

"I'd say since he doesn't know how to be a nice person, we don't want to inflict him on Bobby. Hence no play date this weekend."

"What? But that isn't fair," Magne cried out, spinning to give me wide eyes and a pouty lip.

"I don't know. If you can't be nice to your sister, I'm going to assume you don't know how to be a good friend. When you figure out how to be a better person, then maybe you can go back over to Bobby's," I said with no sympathy. Missing one weekend of getting to see Bobby wouldn't hurt him and might make it sink into his horribly stubborn head.

He sagged in his chair and stared at the wall. A timer went off and Jo touched it. "Okay, you two. Upstairs, pick up your room, and then outside to wear off your annoyance."

They both got up and raced upstairs before either of the adults could stop them. I snickered. "They are never going to survive childhood."

"Them? I'm not going to survive it. I owe my mother cases of chocolate and tequila." She rubbed her temples, flinching as her phone rang. Jo picked it up, sighed, and handed it to me. "You talk to him, I'm done."

Low level annoyance sparked along my nerves. I answered. "I'll call you back in ten minutes." Then I hung up the phone. "Jo, go rest. Carelian, after I get all your stuff off of you, will you go watch the kids?"

~As long as I can do it half asleep. I'm exhausted.~

We both snorted. Half asleep, a Cath was more aware than most humans fully wired on coffee. Ten minutes later I had his stuff all sorted. I'd taken a quick shower, changed into comfortable clothes, and was powering my phone back on. It had barely come back on before it was ringing.

"Really? You couldn't wait?" I said, sitting down in my chair, putting my feet on the ottoman.

"Where have you been!" he almost shouted into the phone.

At that point, my patience and vague humor vaporized. "Please attempt to remember, Mr. Alixant, that I do NOT work for you. I am not your child, nor your wife. One more round of shouting at me, and I will block your number and ignore all your attempts of contact." My voice registered in the arctic range. Alixant had always been temperamental, but I would not ever put up with this.

I heard his teeth snap shut. There was heavy breathing on the other end, then a sigh. "I needed you today, Merlin Munroe."

"Too bad. I am not in the draft."

"I will pay you," he gritted out.

"Yes, you will. But that isn't the point. It is my first week out of the draft. Do I need to remind you what you did?" He'd told me one night when all of us got drunk, way before the twins. He'd run away to Australia for a month, dropping completely off the grid. He'd drank too much, surfed badly, and had too much fun with a lot of women.

Another sigh. "It's bad, Cori."

"And you think yelling at me it is going to make it any better?"

"No. Just...no. I never learn, do I?" Frustration seeped down the line and I had to fight not to give in. Even though this might be more my problem than I thought.

"You fall back on bad habits way too often. Indira has mellowed you, but you need to stop before you burn bridges you really can't afford to burn."

"Noted. Are you willing to come to a meeting tomorrow? I am creating a task force, and I need your help."

The rest of what Tirsane had said snapped back to the forefront of my thoughts.

"What is happening?"

"The rips are becoming more common. There are reports of them from all over the world. And things are slipping in. Not a lot, but even one a year is unusual. We need to hunt them down, and preferably return them. Kill them if they're dangerous and close the Merlin-cursed rips."

I wrinkled my nose at that. I still couldn't really accept that I was the equivalent of Merlin.

"Okay, and?" I still didn't understand why they needed me. There were lots of mages and merlins. He had the ability to grab anyone in the draft.

"You shut the rip by yourself," he said with a flat tone that didn't make sense.

"And?"

"On average, it is taking two to three mages of archmage chaos rank to get them to close. You did it alone." The frustration and anger had faded, leaving only exhaustion. "I had one mage lose half their easily available offering. At the rate they are opening, I'm going to run out of mages in a few months. And worse, no one has any idea why this is happening. Is it a new change in magic? Is magic going to go away? What?"

"I see." All my knowledge about why this was happening stayed firmly behind my lips.

"So, yes, I need you. Desperately." He didn't plead. I wasn't sure he could.

"Is it going to explode in the next week? And I mean, literally, is the world going to end?" I pushed him.

He took a deep breath. "No. They are coming one every couple of days, but only every third one is really large. Those are the ones requiring archmages."

"Excellent. I'm off this week. Set the meeting up for next Monday. Have all the numbers there for us. And pull in Charles. I'd like to work with someone I know and trust on the data side. I'm sure you can get him for a short-term contract."

"Do you know how much he costs?" I heard the wince in his voice.

"Yes. Because he is that good. Send me the info and I'll see you Monday. It's better for us to hit this with cool minds, and not panic because it is relatively unheard of. But remember, I've seen smaller rips appear for years. I usually just close them." Mentally, I knew I had a lot more questions for Tirsane, but I was determined to enjoy pizza with Jo, Sable, and the children first. She'd gotten the good kind. "Also, I have a few things personally I need to do and I'd like to enjoy not working for a while before diving back in."

"Okay. Thanks Cori. I don't take obstacles well. I tend to bulldoze them over." It was as close to an apology as I'd get from him.

"I know. But remember, you can't bulldoze me, not anymore." My smugness might have filtered down the line. It wasn't completely true—as a merlin I could be recalled. But this wasn't a natural disaster or something devastating, at least not yet.

"It does seem that way. I'll get you the email by Friday." With that, he hung up. I grabbed a note pad and made some notes. Writing things out always helped organize my mind.

-How could I stop or drain the magic?

-How long until it became a serious issue?

-Why had Esmere listened to anyone?

In all honesty, the last one worried me the most. I set down my pen and headed downstairs.

"What can I help with?" I asked Sable who was walking out of their bedroom, dressed in her standard house clothes, a tank top with built-in bra and loose pants. These happened to be in bright yellow for the tank top and dark gray for the pants.

She smiled at me. "If you'll get the kids in and washed up? Jo has collapsed in the tub and I'm leaving her there."

"Excellent. Will do." I pivoted and headed out back. It didn't take more than five minutes to get them in and convince them they needed their hands and face washed for pizza. We sat down enjoying the treat. Carelian just wanted some kibble and water. He still acted like the energy had been drained out of him.

"Are we moving?" Magne asked after he'd finished off two slices of pizza and was working on a third.

I flinched.

"We will be, yes." Sable's voice was calm. "Why?"

"Do we get our own rooms?" he responded, watching both of us.

"Yes," Sable said. "Is that something you'd like?"

"Oh yes, please?" Jaz all but gushed. "Can mine be green?"

"Slow down both of you," Sable said. "We are moving, but it will be weeks if not months until it happens. There is a lot to work out."

I fought to keep my smile in place. Even though they would only be half a mile away, it seemed like a huge chasm at that moment.

"About that," Hamiada said, emerging out of the woodwork. "I wanted to beg a favor."

Apparently, me quitting the Draft meant my life went back to being Murphy's toy. I checked all of us for Murphy's Cloak, but we were clean.

I braced for the next complication in my life.

"You never have to beg," I said with a smile. Hamiada had green brown skin today and lots of flowers on small branches draping like hair from her head and down her back. I didn't think I'd ever seen her with so many flowers on her head. "How can we help?"

CHAPTER
SEVEN

There have been multiple reports coming out of Europe of monsters slipping out of the rips. So far there has been proof of at least one being killed, but the others still exist only as rumors. France and Spain have created a bounty for any monster that isn't a registered familiar. ~ CNN Mage Focus

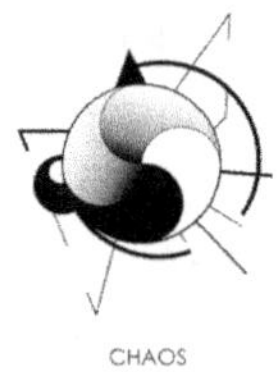

CHAOS

I waited with a slightly forced smile as Hamiada hovered on her toes.

"The children are moving to the big house down the road?" she asked hesitantly.

"We are going too, though not like tomorrow or anything," Sable said giving the kids a glare. "We have lots of work to do to get it ready for us, not to mention cleaning and painting." The kids sagged a bit, but the idea was sparking in their minds even more.

"Ah, yes. That was related to what I wanted to ask?"

I'd never seen Hamiada this hesitant. "Go ahead. You know us. We'll listen," I encouraged.

"It has come time for me to have a sister-daughter. After all these years, I have decided you are worthy of being a friend of dryads. I would like to plant my sister-daughter in your new house. That way she will grow with your children. I would like to request this of you."

We all stared at her. I knew that James had basically trapped Hamiada here against her will and when I got the house, there was no way to free her because she was literally part of the house. For her to offer this?

Sable cleared her throat. "I don't know what to say, Hamiada. We would be honored. What would we need to do?"

Hamiada looked at the floor, bouncing a bit. "Normally sister-daughters are in the same grove as their sister-parent. We create groves of our family. But that isn't possible in this world and Earth is richer in many things than the realms. But with her so far away, I would need a way to reach her." She broke off and the flowers running down her arms closed up tight. "If you are amenable, I would create a realm tunnel between I and she. I would always see and hear her. Making sure she never had to grow alone." The *like I did* was heard clearly between the words.

"Of course." Sable rose and walked over to her. "We would never ask you to be away from your child. Are you sure we can fulfill her needs?"

"Oh yes. This earth is rich and I know you would set up a watering system like I have here. " The surety in her voice made me feel a bit better. "I would create a tunnel. It would literally be a door between here and there."

My head jerked up at that. "Wait, does that mean I could use the door to visit them? Like walking into another room?"

Hamiada tilted her head. "I can make it like that."

"Please? It would make it like we are in one house, but still have our own spaces." It hadn't occurred to me that was possible, but even if it had, I would have never stolen a dryad, much less a child to create it.

"Then yes, that is easily done. I can not let her be on her own until she is mostly grown. Or at least one should not."

The wave of emotion hit me, and I sagged in my chair, accepting the fact that they could go but not go. I didn't know whether to cry in relief or scream with joy. I was fighting through the emotions so hard I almost missed the rest of it.

"Obviously, we will do this. What do we need to do and how long until she is mostly grown?" Sable's eyes were sparkling at the idea.

"Oh, two or three of your decades." Hamiada said. "Willows grow fast."

Sable grinned. "I think we'll be fine. Once we start working on it, do you want to help so it can be the best place for all of us?"

"Oh?" Her entire demeanor lit up, the flowers along her arms opened and her eyes brightened. "Please? I can leave my tree for an hour or two. I would love to make sure my sister-daughter has a home as nice as you have made mine."

Both Sable and I had tears in our eyes. I got up and wrapped my arms around Hamiada. "I am so glad you are part of our lives." That started everything. A minute later there were two almost six-year-olds wrapped around her and two mages that couldn't squeeze her tight enough. Hamiada's flowers burst open, filling the house with the sweetest floral scent I'd ever smelled.

Her arms wrapped back around us. And today we held that hug until the kids started to squirm. We pulled away and Hamaida, who now had flowers across her cheek bones, beamed at us. "We will talk later?"

"Yes!" Sable said with a grin.

A thought popped into my mind. "Hamiada, do you know anything about draining magic out of the realms?"

She looked at me with the long twigs in her head twisting around. "What do you mean?" The odd wariness was back in her voice.

"Didn't you listen to Tirsane?"

"Oh yes. I had never heard of that before. The realms must be very full. It almost makes me glad I pour magic out here."

I leapt on that. "How do you do that? How would I drain the realms?"

She blinked three times. "I am not sure. I pull magic from there and use it here, the closets, the rooms, the garage. There is always plenty to pull. How do you pull magic now?" She tilted her head looking first at me, then the others.

"As far as I'm aware, I don't," I said with a frown. I'd never thought about that. Where does magic come from? I had assumed it just was part of me and what I could do, not that it might have ebbs and flows like water.

"Then I don't know. Magic is used, but I don't know how

humans would take magic from there and use it here. I will go start on my daughter. She will be ready to transplant in three months? Is that okay?"

"That is perfect, though it means we need to get going. A new home for all of us and we get to keep the old home. How awesome is that?" Sable was bouncing on her toes in excitement, looking eerily like Hamiada.

Hamiada faded away and Sable and I looked at each other. "SQUEEE!" The shriek of excitement slipped out of both of our throats at the same time. We hugged each other tightly as the kids went back to their pizza.

A slight stab of pain had me twisting my head, looking for it. A moment later Esmere walked in.

~You seem elated? Are you pregnant again?~

"No. Not happening. Once was enough, thank you very much." The words were out of my mouth before I could consider how they might come across. To my relief, Sable just laughed.

"I think two are enough for us also. What brings you here, Esmere?"

Carelian hissed at her. ~I am most upset with you. How dare you put my quean at risk?~ I flinched. I had wondered if he was still mad at his Malkin. That answered that question.

Esmere sat staring at him, her golden eyes unblinking. ~Do you really want to discuss this in public?~

~Yes. You hurt all of us. Why should it not be publicly revealed?~

"Ah," Sable said, raising a hand at the fascinated look on Magne's and Jaz's face. "You two are just picking at your food. Clear your plates. Jaz, you have chores to do. Magne, go pick up your room. It is an hour until story time and bed. Go," she said with a shooing motion.

Dragging their feet a little, the kids did as told. Though I had no doubt they would try to listen in, Esmere and Carelian would not broadcast to them.

"Now, does Jo need to be part of this discussion?" Sable asked.

"I'm here. I could feel the tension from the tub," Jo said, walking in with a robe wrapped around her. "Besides, the pizza was calling to me." She grabbed three pieces, kissed Sable, and took a seat. "What are we talking about?"

~That my Malkin could not be bothered to provide important information to my quean. Information she needed,~ Carelian said, a sour tone to his words.

Esmere hissed. It was a sight that made me flinch. Having a cat in your house the size of a Shetland pony was fine as long as you ignored her claws and teeth. When she hissed, it was hard to ignore.

~I had no choice. I wanted to prepare her. I was not allowed. I told...Bob I would not.~ Her tail lashed back and forth. ~He required it of me.~

Sable looked at the two annoyed Cath. "I don't understand. I'm not saying that you should break your word, but what is the big deal?"

I agreed with Sable. A little warning would have been nice, but I didn't think it would actually change anything.

Carelian was aggressively grooming his inside hind leg, exposing everything. I could never decide if he knew how rude and shocking that would be as a human or not.

~Cori, would you void your Joining, throw away your ring, because you disagreed with Jo and Sable about what information to give the kids about sex?~ Esmere asked suddenly.

"What? No." The words were said almost reflexively.

~That is the level of what I would be breaking as my Lord required it of me.~ Esmere's tail was still lashing and her tongue licked in and around sharp claws. ~There was nothing that put your life in danger, so I acquiesced.~

"Ah," I said slowly. "It is part of your... commitment?"

~You could say that. It is not a human thing. It is a magical agreement that I accepted when I became a Lord. That Bob may demand certain actions from me. This was one of only two asked in over a hundred years.~ Her tail whacked Carelian on the thigh and he glared at her but dropped his leg

"Okay," I said. "Tirsane didn't break a promise by telling me, did she?"

~No. Brix tried to elicit a vow from her, but she declined. Brix won't be happy, but as nothing was broken, there isn't much he can do.~

I nodded, a bit relieved. "Now that I know, can you talk about it?"

~Yes,~ she replied settling down.

"What does all this mean? How in the world am I supposed to fix it?" I tried to keep the panicked whine out of my voice. Or maybe it was exasperation. Mostly, I think it was a mix of everything plus frustration.

~I don't know.~ Her words fell on me like punches to the heart. ~But while the issue is increasing, it is not about to explode in the next month. This means you have time to figure it out. I think.~

Her adding those last words didn't help. "Where would I do that? Has this ever been done before? I mean, has anyone ever dealt with the realms having excess magic? Or rips forming like this?"

~Not in my memory, but I am not that old. Tirsane did not give you any clues?~

"Not really. Just that I was a magic user like Merlin, Solomon, and a few others." I looked at Jo and Sable, but they just nodded. A thought caused me to frown. "Esmere, what was the Undoing?"

Esmere, whose tail had stopped acting like a whip, canted her ears forward, amber eyes gleaming. ~Why do you ask?~

"Tirsane said I was the first one since the Undoing, other than Merlin. I didn't know what that was. Granted, most of the people she named I only know from the history books, if that."

Sable got up and brought a pot of tea for all of us. "Esmere, do you want something to drink or eat?" All of us fully embraced the idea of if we had people over, we provided food and/or drink.

~Thank you, but no.~ She took her Egyptian cat pose, eyes closed, head tilted. ~It is mentioned occasionally, but only in that it is why magic left your world. I know little else about it. But I am not that old and am the first Cath to ever be part of the Council. Most of my kind find the rules and trappings of magic not worth the benefits.~

I nodded. We'd talked about this before, so that made sense. "Could it have anything to do with the magic surging now?"

~I do not know. You would have to ask ones older than I. They are mostly council members.~ There was something apologetic about her tone that raised the hairs on the back of my neck.

"Great. Then I can go and talk to them?"

Carelian chuffed at that and stretched out, looking impossibly long. ~Could you just go walk up and talk to your president or governor?~ he asked.

"No, of course not," I said, surprised.

~Then do not think you can talk to them any easier.~ His contempt for them came through clearly.

~Carelian is right. Unless you are a councilor, they will not discuss this with you,~ Esmere confirmed.

It was a good thing I held a mug of tea in my hands, because the desire to be over dramatic was high. "Really? This is what Brix wants me to do."

~And Brix isn't as important as Brix believes,~ Esmere snapped.

I groaned and took another sip of tea. Maybe I should add some whiskey.

Please double check the numbers on the emerging mages. While the increase in archmages and merlins is interesting, the ages are concerning. Historically the average age has been 23-25, with over 85% of all mages emerging in that window. However, the newest report is showing the age has skewed to 21-24. As the historical average has held for over 70 years, the change seems a bit drastic. Review and report ~ OMO Internal Memo

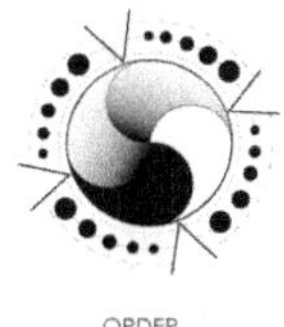

ORDER

On that note, I headed to bed. The next morning Carelian seemed less snappish, literally, and I assumed he and Esmere had made up. The morning chaos of kids, school, and work went through the house like a tornado, until by eight a.m. I was mostly alone as I cleaned up the kitchen.

When the normal chores were done, I headed back to the study, my to-do list firm in my mind. I would call Shay first. Bluetooth headset in, I clicked on his contact.

"Who is calling me at this hour? Don't you know some of us like to sleep?" Shay grumbled into the phone.

"Yes, I know. I'm one of them, but since everything seemed to get dropped in my lap, you get to wake up." I had zero sympathy, but I also had a large cup of Mexican coffee. It was guaranteed to get me through almost anything.

"I can hang up," he responded, but I could hear him moving in the background.

"You could, and then I'd ignore the council. Have you talked to Hishatio?"

"Yeah. He's due to move to rehab by the end of this week. But it is making it a bit difficult for him to find a replacement. Any thoughts?"

"Not my problem," I replied automatically. "But I'm willing to help if you'll help me."

"Sorry, my baby making days are over. You'll have to find another donor."

The mental image threw me off my game and I couldn't even come up with a response for a full thirty seconds. "Shay, I can assure you that would never be an option. Also remember I have a familiar that would be more than delighted to visit you in the middle of the night and urinate all over you while you sleep."

Carelian flicked ears forward at that, tail thumping with amusement. Though it wasn't worth moving from the window seat.

"Ooh, harsh. You play dirty, Munroe. I like that." There was the sound of gurgling and hissing in the background so I figured he was getting some coffee or something like that. "What can I do to you?"

I rolled my eyes. "I need to talk to some of the other councilors. Can you introduce me or get some information for me?"

He snorted. "Good luck with that. They talk just fine in council sessions. Argue, swear, make threats. It's great fun." He fell silent as he drank his coffee. If I closed my eyes I could even remember what I used to make for him back when I worked in the coffeeshop in Rockway.

"Double espresso with an almond milk chaser?" I asked.

"Triple. You got me up too early. I'm retired, remember?"

"Uh huh. Can you finish what you were saying?"

He groaned. "But after the council session, you'd think we were either servants or children. Seen, but not heard. I've never gotten them to talk to me. Amadahy got at least a nod from a few of them. It has been what, five years since we started and I know their races and species and not much else. The only ones even remotely social are Tirsane and Esmere." His voice ended on an odd note.

"What? I can hear you thinking from here." I got up and moved to my desk, setting the coffee down as I opened up my laptop. By the time this was done, I figured I'd need to have taken notes.

"This probably won't make sense, but they are too nice?"

I sat up a bit straighter. "You're right. Explain?"

"Did you have cliques in high school? You know the jocks, losers, nerds, and so on?"

"Sure. Though Jo and I were our own little group of two."

"That surprises me not at all, but as I was saying. These two are the head cheerleader and the homecoming queen who wander over and have lunch with the losers and nerds and when anyone is snide about it, they just smile. I'm not sure if they are planning to stab us in the back or setting up for a coup."

"Oh." I ran my fingers on the keyboard without clicking hard enough to type anything. "I can ask?"

"Mmmm. They are playing a game but... look do you trust them?" He sounded like he actually wanted to know.

"Yes. Tirsane is the godmother of Jaz and Esmere is the godmother of Magne. They are family." I said that without an ounce of doubt. "But there is one thing you have to remember." I paused, thinking how to explain.

"Oh? Though knowing you trust them helps."

"I do, without reservation. But I trust them to keep my children safe and alive, not be socially acceptable. The denizens are NOT human, Shay, and you have to remember that. They are people, but they aren't human. Carelian to this day would eat anyone I killed and be pleased as all get out about it."

~I still say you should have more bodies at your feet. The feasting would be great.~

I ignored him and continued. "You can't expect their motives or actions to relate to anything from human social mores."

"Huh. Point. But yeah, I'll try to introduce you." He left it at that.

"Have you talked to Amadahy? Does she have any ideas?"

"I haven't talked to her yet, but she did deign to give me a number to reach her at. I was going to see if she wanted to meet up this weekend."

"Okay. Let me know if you need something. I'll check in on

Hishatio on Friday. But then I'm going to be pretty busy I think, so don't get worried if I'm not responding quickly."

"Anything I need to worry about?"

"You've got the ability to close portals, yes?" I asked, remembering he had some Spirit.

"Barely. I close them, but it isn't easy."

"Balls," I whispered under my breath.

"Why?" His voice was sharp, not the nonchalant attitude he'd had the entire call so far.

"Did you know the council is hiding stuff from you? Well, humans, to be precise, not you specifically," I countered.

"Did I know? Nope. Does it surprise me? Not even a little bit. But can you shine a bit of light on that statement?"

Part of me wanted to be in the same room as Shay so I could watch his facial expressions and body language. "Do you know about the magic Tirsane has been getting from humans? Shit, do the others?"

There was a long pause and then, "What the fuck are you talking about, Munroe?"

I groaned. "We need to meet. The three of us. Can you arrange that?"

"How am I supposed to do that? Do I look like a travel agency to you?" he snapped back.

"Figure it out. You're a merlin. You have each other's contact information but we need to meet this weekend." I took a deep breath. "Let me ask a favor."

"You'd better have an idea 'cause I don't know how to get all of us here, and Sloan's place isn't that big." He sounded grouchy and I didn't care. This was ridiculous. I thought for sure someone would have mentioned it.

"Hold." I hit the mute button on my phone. "Hamidia?"

Her head emerged out of the book cases a minute later. "Yes?"

"Morning." I smiled at her. "You doing okay?"

"I am busy seeding. My sister-daughter is rooting well." She seemed a brighter green than normal, so I took that as a good sign.

"Excellent. I can't wait to meet her. I have a favor to ask. Would you mind hosting a meeting for a few of us in your glade? We need to talk and trying to travel to all the places is a bit difficult."

"I do not mind. You always have the most interesting things happen around you. Let me know." She faded as the last words were said and I shook my head.

"Why is it that this strikes me as normal in my life?" Still laughing a bit to myself, I unmuted the phone. "I've got a realm glade for us to meet in. I'll ask Jeorgaz to bring Hishatio, Carelian can get you, and I'm assuming the thunderbird can bring Amadahy."

"Uhhhh." He cleared his throat. "Okay. Yeah, sure. I'll get a time set up and let you know."

I smirked. For once, I had Shay off balance. That was always nice. "Sounds good, thanks Shay. I'll catch everyone up at the meeting."

We hung up, and I stared at the walls, not really seeing them. Rips appearing, magic bursting through, councilors hiding things, and for some reason I was in the middle of it.

~Am I a driver now to go and get people?~ Carelian asked archly, though he hadn't moved.

"No, you're my partner and the one I spend way too much on salmon for."

~We should go deep sea fishing or go out on an Alaskan fishing ship.~

I shuddered at the idea of an Alaskan fishing ship, I'd seen those documentaries. "How about just a fishing trip to Alaska and I'll get you a fishing license and you can compete with the bears for salmon?"

~That sounds delightful. I insist.~

I laughed and stood looking at all the journals left from James and that sparked an idea. ~Jeorgaz are you available?~ I pinged. There was still the glade with all his actual research and experiments, but the majority of them were referenced in these journals. I would probably spend another decade getting some of the information out there. The man hoarded information worse than Carelian craved fresh shrimp.

A soft pouf and a wave of heat grabbed my attention, and I saw Jeorgaz hovering in the air. Before I could say anything, a tendril of vine emerged from the wall and transformed into a sturdy perch for him.

~Thank you Hamiada. You are as kind as ever,~ he said, though I heard it too. He turned to look at me. ~Yes?~ There was an odd note of excitement that made me wonder. Or maybe it was expectation.

Denizens weren't much for the social pleasantries, so I didn't try. "Are you willing to get Hishatio this weekend for a human meeting? Hamiada is hosting us in her glade."

His head twisted, and feathers lost some of their puff. ~I will do that...for you.~

I laughed. "Yes, I am still making you the lemon honey berries. It has just been busy. But I also wanted to ask you about too much magic and something called the Undoing?"

Jeorgaz became very busy preening a feather, but I just waited. ~You know, then?~

"Yes, Tirsane told me. Why is this being hidden from Earth's councilors?"

~I do not know Brix's reasoning, but there are always multiple motives when it comes to Brix's actions.~

"That didn't tell me anything. What is going on?" I sighed in exasperation. This is what helped create my relentlessness. I didn't have a choice.

Jeorgaz preened for another moment, a soft hum of laughter filling the air. ~I am unsure. I was never on the council and pay little attention to their machinations. But Brix has strong feelings for you, though I am not sure why or what sort of feelings.~

"Huh? I think I've met Brix what? Three times? Maybe four? Why would there be any feelings toward me at all?" This really did throw me, even after what Tirsane had said.

~Just because we are both avians does not mean I know or like Brix,~ Jeorgaz chided.

"That is not what I meant," I defended myself, though honestly, I had kind of thought that. But then, most of the denizens I had met knew each other. "I just don't know how widely talked about your politics are. For all I know, there is a realm paper sharing the juicy bits."

~True. That might make some of this easier, but most of us don't care. We live in our realms, some in our glades as you call them, and we tend to ignore most of those in the other realms.~ He still waited for something.

"Okay, I give. What do you want me to ask you?" Smug denizens were annoying. Living with one was more than enough.

His excitement seemed to dim a bit. ~I had thought you were going to ask about the phoenix heart.~ The look in his eyes was odd, but I shook my head.

"I'm not sure I know what that is."

~You didn't receive it with the rest of James' possessions along with the manual?~ He sounded worried and flames flickered around his tail.

I opened my mouth to answer, but the phone started ringing before I could say anything. With a frown, not taking my eyes off of Jeorgaz, I answered. The ring told me it was Alixant.

"Yes Stephen?"

"Cori we need you right now," he said, his voice tight with tension and stress.

CHAPTER
NINE

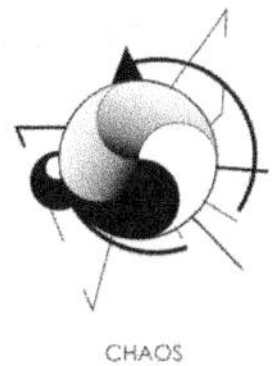

CHAOS

"What's wrong?"

"We've had a spate of rips. I don't have the team put together yet to have response units. You are closer than most. Everyone knows you can teleport, even if they think it has the same huge costs as for most other mages. There is a huge rip in D.C. It's letting things out. Can you get there and seal it?" He was almost begging.

I was already up and moving. "Yes. Where?"

He fumbled for a minute. "I'll text you the address, but it's about a mile from the State department. If you step to your old job, you should be able to get there with a few minutes' run, or you might not need to be that close. It is growing."

"Got it." I shot Jeorgaz a look. "We will talk about it later. Maybe after I meet with Shay, Hishatio, and Amadahy? Thank you again. You have been a good friend, but I have to go."

He nodded, mollified. With a fluff of his feathers, he was gone.

"Come on, Carelian. I'm headed to where I would have gone for the State Department job." I ran into my room, changed into something I could run in, with shoes, texted the group chat with what was going on, grabbed Carelian's harness and kit, then stepped.

As always, or at least since the twins were born, the offering was barely noticeable. I took a minute to orient myself. The text Stephen had sent told me which direction to go. Carelian appeared at my side and I took a minute to strap him in, then we both set off at a jog. I didn't bother with the leash. If they could catch us, they could ask.

Stephen had been right that I would figure it out. I turned a corner into a park and the gash in the middle of the trees was obvious. People were staring, but a few were running away. It wasn't the biggest I'd seen, but unlike the last one, it was only about fifteen feet off the ground. Still moving at a brisk pace, we got there in time to see something with fur and six legs fall out of the tear in reality. It lay there stunned, then shook and stood up, opening a mouth full of sharp teeth.

Crap.

"Carelian, go."

He was already moving, but I felt his laughter in my mind. ~Food or capture?~

~Your call. Just don't tell me what it tasted like,~ I responded as I kept moving so I could get into a clear area. The rip was only about eight feet across, still bigger than what had been normal up until now. I grabbed my Spirit magic and started to close it. Magic fought me.

Something else started to wiggle out, and it was much bigger. I'd managed to get the rip down to about three feet, but the creature coming out didn't notice as it squeezed out, much like Carelian crawling under the bed. It was about six feet long, had scales, four legs, and a long tail. If I had to compare it to something, it looked like a really stretchy Komodo dragon, the Earth type.

~Carelian are you done? I've got something else coming through and you'd better not get hurt.~ I took a second from fighting with the portal to throw a ring of fire around the lizard thing. It hissed and circled, looking for a way out.

A young black woman ran up to me, Spirit tattooed on the side of her head. "How can I help?"

I didn't have time to stare to figure out her skills. "What offensive skills do you have?"

"Well, umm," she stuttered. She sounded new, probably still in college. "I'm strong in Psychic, pale in Soul and Relativity."

"Can you do electricity?" It was one of the few spells in Relativity that could act as an offensive attack.

"Yes!" She almost shouted the answer, obviously glad to be able to say yes to my question. Had I ever been that young?

"Excellent. I'm focusing on sealing this tear. I want you to zap anything that sticks its nose out. Or tentacle."

"Tentacle?" Her voice quavered.

"Just if it moves, zap it," I answered, and I went back to my work. It was like zipping up pants that were just too tight. Everything was there to seal it, but it didn't want to give.

~Coming. That was delicious.~

I groaned. ~I have a lizardy thing that isn't going to pay attention to the fire much longer. Can you trick it back or something?~

~Hmmm,~ I heard in my head. ~These seem to be Order creatures. They are not sentient, as you call it. I can try, but killing it would be much easier.~

I gritted my teeth as I pulled the tear closed. Another two feet to go. Things were still sticking noses, legs, and tentacles out. It reminded me of the internet videos of animals testing something new. Wanting to see what it was and if they fit. I had to get the tear closed. I spent offerings constantly, not that it was all that much in the scheme of things. Rips had never fought me, not wanting to open, and the pants analogy was what stuck in my brain. Was magic forcing it to open or holding it? I pushed harder and with a snap, the last bit slammed closed. I almost fell over with the release of it closing.

Taking a deep breath, I turned to look at the girl. She was about twenty-five and there were chunks missing from her hair.

What had, I assumed, been a nice, even afro puff hair style, now resembled a golf ball with divots taken out of it where she had grabbed offerings.

"You haven't had cosmetic offering as a course yet, have you?" I asked the girl. She had sweat dripping down her face, a bit of a wild look.

"No. That's next semester. Is it done? Are the monsters not coming?"

"You stopped them. Good job," I said trying not to laugh. This no longer even rated as a major event in my life, but for hers, it was probably the most exciting thing she'd ever done.

"Uh huh. Now what?" She still had a panicked aura about her.

I looked around. People had stopped screaming, but everyone looked on edge. Carelian had the lizard thing thrashing under his paw, so while it was contained, it wasn't dead.

"Can you tell if anything else got out?" I called out, though honestly, he probably could have heard me even if I didn't.

~At least two more of the tasty furred things. And one other thing I don't recognize, but it smells delicious.~ The creature under him thrashed a bit more.

~How are you holding that and what it is it?~

~Lizard fast thing?~ he offered. ~If it has a name, I never knew it. And my claws are at the base of its spine. If it thrashes too much, my claws will sever it. It knows this.~

"Does that mean it's sentient?" I had walked closer to them, though I didn't get close by any means. It really did look like the longer relative of a Komodo with better scales.

~Rudimentary. It knows I will kill it.~

"Umm, who are you talking to?" the young woman said. She had trailed me.

"Just my familiar," I replied, waving at Carelian. Movement

from the side caught my eyes. "And here come the authorities." A man, older and obviously out of shape from the huffing and red face he had as he rushed toward us, badge out and suit proclaiming government.

"Agent Stims. You Cori Munroe?" he huffed, eyes glancing at me, then the girl, then locking on Carelian.

"Yes. Did Director Alixant send you?"

"Yes. He says thank you. And see you Monday?" His eyes didn't leave the thrashing lizard. "You are taking that thing with you. Right?"

I snorted. "Yeah, I'll deal with it. But tell the Director I'm charging him."

"Yes, ma'am. And um, who is this?" He nodded at the girl.

"Someone who actually helped. Get her info and turn her in for a reward or something. At the very least, see if you can get her time with a cosmetic expert on evening her hair." I looked at the girl, who seemed somewhere between hyperventilating and running away. "You did good. And thank you."

I waved to both of them and firmly extracted myself from the situation by walking over to Carelian. "What do we do with it?

The creature hissed at me, tail thrashing, but I noted it didn't try to pull away from Carelian's claws.

~I can open a portal to Order. But convincing it to go in will be difficult.~

"I'll create a chute of earth to funnel him through and a spark of lightning to encourage him."

~That would work.~ A spark of pain and a portal sheared open. I created the wall around both of them, though not so high Carelian couldn't easily jump out.

"Go for it," I said, watching carefully. I'd made it a rectangle, so the portal was surrounded by my wall, leaving the creature nowhere else to go. I hoped.

In a blindingly fast move, Carelian retracted his claws, sprang up, and landed to balance on the wall. The creature was almost as fast, whirling and hissing. It looked like it was going to try to climb the wall to chase after Carelian.

"I don't think so," I murmured and slammed a jolt of electricity at its nose. That caused it to yank back and hiss more, showing very sharp teeth. "Go," I ordered and zapped it again. It twisted and writhed in ways that told me it was structured more like a snake than a lizard. But finally, after much hissing and multiple electric zaps, it went through the portal and I sealed it almost before the tail had slipped through.

"That was much more work than I expected," I said. I went to work, putting the earth back where it belonged.

~Earth is fun. Many more creatures to hunt that won't fight back. Besides, humans are easy prey.~ He tilted his head. ~There are still more tasty things that escaped. Should we hunt them, I could do with extra food. Fear makes the flesh taste sweeter.~

I rolled my eyes and turned, only to discover we'd gained a crowd. The amount of wonder and hero worship on those faces, including Agent Sims, made my skin crawl.

"I don't think so. At least not now. Maybe we can come back later?" I smiled at the crowd and gave them a shaky wave. More uncomfortable than I'd been when trying to close the rift, I turned and headed away at a jog. Carelian ran by my side, laughing in my mind.

~You don't like all your worshipers?~

"Shush, you. You may enjoy being worshipped. I don't." I headed toward the state building, ignoring anyone who might have called. When we got far enough away, I slowed down and looked around. We had a few people staring at us, or Carelian, but nothing else. I found a nice area out of the way and called Stephen.

"You okay?" were the first words out of his mouth, better than normal.

"Oh yeah, I'm fine. The rip is closed, but I know at least three things, think rabbits about the size of a medium dog with way too many fangs, slipped out. Carelian said he's willing to hunt them, but not until that crowd disappears. You probably want to put out a wild animal alert." I kept my voice low as I watched people pass by, their eyes lingering on my familiar.

"Will they attack people?"

"Umm." I looked at Carelian. "Would they?"

He licked residue off his paws. ~I would not know. They don't have humans to hunt in their realms.~

"I would say yes. Especially kids." I was guessing, but worst case I was wrong and no one was attacked. Better than the alternative.

"I'll get a warning out. Anything else?"

I shrugged. "Agent Stims should give you the rundown. I'd be surprised if there aren't videos of it already on the web. There's a young mage, Spirit, who showed up and helped. I'd at least talk to her. Most people run the other way. She ran toward me."

"Name?" I could hear keys clacking as he typed.

"No clue. Your agent should have her info. Just saying. Okay, we'll come back tonight and yes, I'll be there Monday. I have news..." I let it trail off both to pique his interest and drive him crazy. "I'll tell you then. See ya." I hung up, smirking a bit.

"Ready to go home? You want me to come with you tonight to hunt?" I turned the corner as I talked.

~Very, though I must admit the idea of hunting this eve sounds delightful,~ he murmured in my head as I sidestepped.

~But in answer to your question: no, I do not need a babysitter to hunt.~

I swallowed down a laugh. "No worries. I never feel like I

am your babysitter. Your archivist maybe, yelling 'oh shit' all the time."

He laughed as we walked into the house, checking the time as I did so. It was a bit after one in the afternoon and I sagged in relief. "I need food and a shower. You?"

~I am full. And showers are only when I get doused with smelly stuff. I shall nap in the sunroom thinking of the hunt tonight.~

"That does not surprise me." I headed to my room. A nice shower and comfy clothes sounded wonderful.

"Cori?" Hamiada's voice grabbed my attention as I stepped onto the landing.

"Yes?" I pivoted slowly but didn't see her.

"I thought you would wish to know. The eggs are starting to hatch."

CHAPTER

TEN

Wild creatures verified roaming in D.C. All people should stay inside as the authorities round them up. They are believed dangerous. Pets and young children should not be outside at all. These creatures are faster than you. Stay inside until the authorities provide an all clear.
~Warning on radio and TV in the DC Area

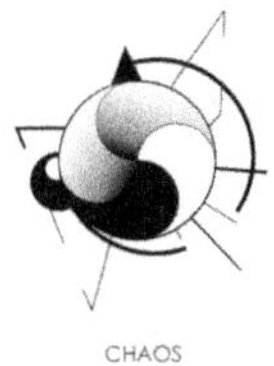

CHAOS

"What?" I swerved to the left instead of heading to my room and stepped into the kids' rooms. What had originally been the green room had been set up with two beds and some ingenious design work by Jo and Hamiada to give them both their own private spaces, yet still share a room. It would probably be good for them to get their own rooms.

I headed to the corner near their bathroom. There, tucked into the corner, was a shell shaped basin filled with sand and two large eggs. In the years that we'd watched over them, they hadn't gotten much larger, but the colors had become more vibrant.

Where originally they had both been a deep metallic brown fading to gold, now one was a bright bronze with gold tracings through it. The other had faded to a rose gold with silver blue crackles across the shell, making it shimmer in the light.

The last few years they had laid there, unmoving, to the point I worried they had died, but Esmere and Tirsane had assured me they were fine. It just took longer on Earth, as the amount of stray magic wasn't as great. But now they were rocking back and forth with cracks starting to run through the shells.

"They can't hatch yet. They need to wait for Jaz and Magne to be here." I said, suddenly panicked. The kids would be devastated if they weren't there.

"So, tell them to wait," Hamiada said as she stepped out of the wall to my left.

"Huh?" I really needed to work on my responses. After a decade, I still sounded like an idiot half the time.

"You are the Herald. Magic will listen to you. Tell them to wait."

It sounded insane, but I had nothing to lose. I placed one

hand on each egg. "Wait, don't hatch yet. A few hours are all we need. Please?" I willed them to hear me, to delay. To my shock, the rocking slowed and the eggs just hummed with magical energy.

I looked at Hamiada, my eyes wide. "What in the world?"

She held out her hands, small green leaves starting to edge into yellow and red at the edges, covering them like gloves. "You are the Herald. It is a small thing you ask."

"They aren't even hatched. How would they know?" Part of me was freaking out. Was there a huge sign on my head that other magical beings could see?

Hamiada spun slowly, flowers tracing down the twigs of her hair. "Your magic has a flavor of power, or Magic. It is like feeling the sun on your skin. You know it versus any other light. The sun warms you in ways you can't articulate, but you know it."

I blinked at her. The analogy actually worked, but it still made me feel like I was a little glowing ball of magic. "Do I leak magic?"

"No. It is simply part of you." She looked at the eggs. "I look forward to their appearance." Then she stepped back into the wall.

It took me a minute, but I chilled out and texted Jo. *Eggs hatching, get kids home right after school.*

Crap. Will we be there in time?

I stared at the eggs and shook my head in bewilderment. *Yes. I'll see you then.*

My list of next steps spooled out in my head. Change clothes, get a dinner going, and welcome two new beings into my crazy family. Family. The word resonated in my head and I smiled. I had an idea. It would still be two hours best case before they got home. After my clothes were changed and a casserole was in the oven to start cooking, I called Marisol.

"Hello, *mi hija*," her voice came through the line.

I sank down into one of the chairs in the sunroom. "Hello, mami. How are you doing?"

"Eh. The house is so empty. I keep expecting to hear the garage door slam. But it never does." Her voice had a distant, empty quality that terrified me.

"What do you have going on this week?"

"Not much. Sanchez will stop by, and I think I'm supposed to see Paolo's kids."

"Sounds like it will be fun." Paolo had moved down to Jacksonville for work. A district manager. It meant she didn't see them often. Sanchez and Marco still lived in town, but they were busy with their own lives and my heart broke a bit.

"It will. I haven't seen them for a while." Her voice still sounded too lifeless. "When do I get to see the twins?"

"That is what I was calling about. The eggs are hatching. Would you like to be here for it?"

"Oh?" Excitement peaked in her voice. "They are? I would like to see them hatch. I've been so curious for ages."

"Good. Do you want me or Carelian to come get you?"

"Oh, Carelian please. Your travel method still leaves much to be desired." The familiar humor bubbled under her words and it did my heart good.

"Get dressed and I'll have him head for you when the kids get here. You will be staying for dinner." That much wasn't a request. But a command given lovingly. We hung up, and I called out. "Did you hear that?"

~Yes. I will go when it is time. You are planning something? What?~

I shook my head, even though he wasn't in the room. "We'll see. It might not work out." Dinner was easily buffed up by adding tortillas, cheese, and salsa. The casserole would taste delicious, wrapped in tortillas with the added ingredients.

I was about to go upstairs to my study, as the kids wouldn't be home for another hour and Carelian wouldn't get her until they were here, which gave me some time to research what Jeorgaz had been talking about. I grabbed the box and pushed my computer back to make space for me to explore the box. I opened the lid and took a look at what lay in there.

The jewelry boxes I set aside. I knew what was in there, but I didn't know what Jeorgaz had been talking about. There were various other little things, but I headed straight for the notebook. It wasn't a large journal like the rest of his stuff, but instead small, as if you'd keep it in your pocket.

The first page had my attention.

"A phoenix heart is a way to focus magic to amplify the effects. But every time I've tried it, the effects have always had a negative effect. Example: use it to focus Earth for Grow. It works, but the plant grows so fast and hard that it saps the soil of all nutrients and dies of age in the space of seconds. Jeorgaz mentioned something about a true and selfless heart, which I do not have. But what I fear is that if anyone got this, they could use it to great harm. As such, these are the only notes I will leave about. In the back is every experiment I tried and the results. I do not see how this could be used for anything positive."

I paused and flipped through the book, and the results were rather horrifying. Every time it went to the extremes of what you could have asked for, though the cost was almost negligible.

The notes called me back. Though there was only a page more.

"Jeorgaz knows this and believes it should be destroyed, but I can't help but feel there is some purpose in me finding it. I will continue to talk to him about how to use this or what to do with it. Otherwise, if this falls into the hands of an idiot, may Merlin shrivel your brain."

A laugh burst out at that comment. That curse was one I hadn't heard before. There on the next page was a drawing of the Trilliant cut gem.

I dug through the box and really looked at it this time. It glowed a dusky pink color with gold reflecting from the facets. The more I looked at it, the more it did remind me of the flames that appeared and disappeared with phoenix transportation.

My eyes were entranced by the play of light along the facets and the more I looked, the more colors I could see in it. With it were all the colors of fire. From white to purple black. It might have been the most beautiful thing I'd ever seen. I would look at it for a while, read some of the experiments, then go back to it. I'd have to get more information from Jeorgaz as to what exactly it was, but it was irresistibly gorgeous.

The slamming of a car door shook me out of the trance and I blinked, my eyes dry. I looked at my watch. I'd been sitting there for almost two hours. Another shake of my head, I put the notebook and jewel away, then I headed down to two bouncing kids, and an excited Jo. "Sable said she'd be home in about twenty minutes."

I nodded, returning hugs from the kids. "Are they hatching? Can we see?"

"Go change. Marisol is coming over to watch and to have dinner with us."

"Yay, Gramma," they cheered and raced up the stairs, making the house shake.

"It's really happening?" Jo sounded wistful, and I hugged her.

"Yep. You always knew they would be powerful mages. This is part of that. At least they are old enough to take care of them hopefully and this should stop the dog requests."

"Oh, that would be nice. I swear no more stories with dogs in them." Jo put her head on my shoulder, groaning. "How did they grow up so fast? I swear it was last week when they were still learning to walk."

"We can throw them in a time bubble?" I offered with a teasing smile.

"Gah, no. Wait... if we did it long enough... no, only works if you are the one casting the spell. Dang it. For a second, I thought I'd found a way to avoid their teenage years." She had a mock pouting face on.

I laughed. "Please. You can't wait. The question is, who is going to gain your mechanical abilities?"

She glanced up the stairs, but they were still up there. Her voice dropped to a secret, sharing whisper. "I was thinking since we own the street, I might build a bicycle with them. Let them customize each part. Then see who really enjoys it as opposed to tolerate."

"And when were you thinking about doing this?"

"Their birthday. They'll be six. That's a great time to learn to ride."

I smiled and grinned. "Do we get to lay bets on how many sparklies Jaz puts on hers?"

"No. Because it will be double the worst-case scenario."

She headed to change, and I walked to the sunroom. It was quiet there and someday it would be quiet throughout the whole house. Would that be a good or a bad thing? Who knew?

"Carelian," I said, stooping down to ruffle his head. "You want to go grab Marisol? I'll take the casserole out, then dragons, and then dinner."

~You really think you can foretell their hatching that exactly?~ His voice was bemused as he stretched out, claws digging into the rug.

"Hamiada thinks I can. She says that the magic that marked me is obvious."

He pulled back and looked at me. First with one eye, then the other, then with both pupils dilated wide so his eyes looked like wells of chaos dragging me in. Then they were back to normal slits. ~I just see my quean, the powerful one I chose.~

I laughed and rubbed his ears. "You are zero help. Go get Marisol please."

~For you.~ His tail stroked across my leg before he stepped into a rip and disappeared.

"They aren't hatching!" The yell came down the stairs, and I sighed. I made sure to pull the casserole out and set the table while I waited for Marisol. The sound of the front door opening signaled Sable being home.

"You ready for drama?" I asked as I stepped into the foyer.

"Why not? Has to be more interesting than fighting with engineers all day. At least the kids are smarter." Her frustrated tone brought a smile to my face.

"I get that." The slight spike of pain had me turning around, and soon enough, Marisol and Carelian walked down the hall.

Her hair had more grey in it, and there were more lines on her face. She'd lost weight the last few years, grieving. It just hurt to see her eroding without Henri. It solidified an idea in my mind: two actually.

I went over and wrapped her in a tight hug, not happy at the bones that met my arms. Sable followed up with her own hug. "I am so glad you came over," she said, ushering Marisol up the stairs. "We've missed you."

"Ah, you're busy with your lives. I get that. I probably should sell my house, but I don't want to live in the city where Marco does. But Paolo and his kids are so busy I only see them about once a week." Her voice didn't sound depressed, it was just life, but her sadness resonated in her words.

"Come on," Magne said from the top of the stairs. "They're rocking."

We stepped up our pace and gathered around the small basin, with the twins peering at the two eggs intently. Then the rose gold one cracked.

CHAPTER

ELEVEN

These monsters that are being registered as "familiars" are a risk to our families and the safety of our real pets. The idea that they are tame or able to be controlled is fantasy. There is a reason why most states outlaw keeping big cats as pets. These are monsters, they aren't even proper Earth animals. They should be sent back to where they came from, anything less is setting a precedent for them to be declared endangered species and start chunking out land for sanctuaries. ~ Freedom from Magic

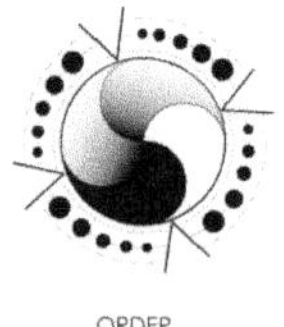

ORDER

It felt like we all held our breath as the egg rocked back and forth; the crack getting larger. The other egg, the one that looked bronze, had started to rock too, but there weren't any cracks. A bit of gold shell flew off as a nose pushed through.

"Look!" Jaz squealed as an icy blue nose poked out, wiggling to break the shell apart. I'd never seen anything so mesmerizing as watching this little creature press and push apart the shell.

Jo put a hand on Jaz to prevent her from helping. "Let it be. It needs to push the shell away by itself."

Jaz all but wiggled in place, her hair bouncing like a cloud of curls.

"Mine is hatching too," Magne whispered and my eyes went to the bronze one. Sure enough, the shell had started to crack, and a nose was bumping out.

"Look," Jaz whispered in a hushed voice as the foot-long dragon moved over to her. The dragon raised itself up on its tail and stared at her, their eyes locked. It was about ten inches long, with forearms and wings. The scales on the little quetzalcoatl dragon, though I called them quetzos, started at pale icy blue and darkened as it went to the tail into a dark blue that was almost black. The tail was covered in tiny feathers in all the colors of the scales. The two feathered wings went from light blue to indigo. Rose gold eyes looked out of the pale face that was half snake and half Zmaug. A longer snout than a snake, but not so defined as Zmaug's. A quick flick of the tongue revealed it to be forked.

"She's mine?" Jaz asked, wonder in her voice.

"Maybe. We don't know if they are pets or people. Carelian?" Jo asked, her voice a bit wary. Just because Tirsane said they were for the kids, they were still an unknown creature.

~They are bonding. Magic will let them talk. It is a baby,

don't expect much until they get older.~ He tried to sound bored, but he was staring down at them too with rapt attention, ears out flat.

~You try to chase either of them until they are older, I will shave you,~ I mentally hissed at him.

~I would never,~ he denied, but his ears flicked up and his body relaxed.

~MINE.~

The phrase echoed in my mind and Jaz gasped, her eyes going wide. "Was that the dragon?"

~Yes. A very loud dragon. Teaching it how to talk to you and not everyone is very high on my agenda.~ Carelian's voice was sharp and the quetzo curled up a bit as if it knew the words were directed toward it.

"Carelian, don't be mean to my dragon," Jaz said with a pout as she reached out and scooped the dragon up. "What's its name?"

~That is between you and the quetzo. But I believe it is a her.~ Carelian flicked his ears toward the other egg. ~But you might want to see this.~

I whipped my attention over to the bronze egg, noting that Magne's eyes hadn't moved, still staring at it with a laser focus. A similar creature wiggled out, but instead of feathers, it had leathery wings, with tiny scales that reflected the light. His head was the bright green of Esmere's fur and it darkened to almost black at the tail. He had a ruff like a walking lizard that flared up and down as dark bronze eyes scanned us. Where the quetzo in Jaz's arms had almost human-like hands, this one had more like claws, but the arms were longer, almost a third of its ten inches, instead of a quarter.

It wobbled as it finished shaking the egg shell off and latched on to Magne. ~MINE.~ The word reverberated and Carelian hissed.

~Yes. Speaking training. That is way too loud.~

I would have chastised him, but he was right. It hurt like crazy. But that didn't slow Magne down, and in a second the green quetzo was curled around him like clinging to a life raft.

"I've never seen anything so amazing," Marisol whispered. She wrapped an arm around my waist as she peered. "Thank you so much for this." I simply kissed her cheek and plotted.

~HUNGRY. FOOD.~

I had no idea which one said that, but the empathic demand was unmistakable. My head rang with the force of their cries. "Carelian, any changes in what we had thought they would eat?"

~No. Small pieces of raw fish, poultry, insects, or eggs.~ He dropped down and moved toward the door. ~I'm going hunting. Don't wait up.~

"Don't get caught," I replied as he stepped away.

"Come on, the food for them is downstairs," Jo ordered. Twenty minutes later, after the fun, if disgusting, process of letting the quetzos gorge themselves, they each lay in their chosen twin's lap with distended bellies.

The rest of us focused on eating, or the adults ate and tried to convince the kids to eat and not stare at their new familiars every moment.

~They are young. They will sleep. In a few months they might become interesting.~ Carelian stepped back into the house with those words.

"How was the hunt?" I asked, making myself another casserole burrito.

~Successful. They are excellent food. I may have to find where they come from and go hunt there.~ He threw himself down and began cleaning his claws.

"Hunt? Is there something we should know?" Jo asked, looking between Carelian and me.

"Ah, right." I proceeded to tell them about the rip this morning in DC and the creatures that escaped. I didn't mention Jeorgaz, but I still wasn't sure what all that meant. I figured he had another dire warning that probably wasn't needed, but then denizens thought in patterns that made no sense to me.

Conversation drifted back to the house and moving. Marisol looked so much more alive with the kids and her daughter talking to her, and it just made my idea seem more right.

"This has been wonderful. Your little dragons are beautiful," Marisol said, smiling at the kids, who at this point looked as exhausted as the quetzos. "Have you decided what you want to name them? Or do they have their own names?"

Jaz stroked the back of her familiar, which had curled up in a ball. "Azul."

The smile that lit up Marisol's face made me ache. I didn't think I'd seen it since Henri died. "Blue. I like that. And you Magne?"

"Vert. It feels right." The quetzo in question preened a bit.

~LIKE.~ The word burst across my mind and I flinched.

~They must learn to not yell,~ Carelian groused.

"You'd better teach them then, because I still yell sometimes if I push too hard," I said with a smirk. "Welcome to parenting 101."

He flicked his tail at me, then went back to grooming, obviously more important than us.

"This was so much fun, but I suppose I should go home." I watched the light leave her eyes and I shuddered at the thought of an empty house with only ghosts of memories there.

"About that, I had an idea. Well, a couple of them actually," I said slowly, all too aware of everyone now looking at me, even Carelian.

"An idea about what?" Jo leaned forward, eyes locked on me and I knew she'd seen the sadness wash over Marisol.

"We have the Craftsman that we don't know what to do with. It is only a single bedroom and a study, with that garden in back. I was thinking, what if Marisol moved in there?" I focused on her, trying to project the right emotions. "It would put you near us, but still give you your own space. It would be easy for us to get you back to see Marco or Paolo or Sanchez. Then you could either sell the house or let Paolo or Sanchez have it. Let one of them turn your house into their home. You would be near the twins, Carelian, Esmere, even Tirsane. She drops in more than you think. We could help you remodel it to look like anything you wanted."

She blinked in surprise, even as everyone else's faces had huge smiles on them.

"Oh, Mami, please? I have missed you. The kids would love to have you close, as would I. You're really their only grand-mother." Jo leaned forward, her face glowing.

Sable nodded. "Really, we would love it."

A thoughtful smile crossed her face. "I wouldn't mind doing something new, being someplace new. Every place I go at home, I expect to see him. The shop, the store, the streets. Being some-place without his ghost in every item might be nice."

I could see she was hesitating, but I had one more idea. "There was one more thing. Hamiada?"

"Yes?" She floated up from the floor, the flowers in her hair so thick you couldn't see the twigs.

In the last few years, she was happier and more relaxed than I'd ever seen her. Now if I didn't ruin it. I'd read what James did, and would gladly go back in time to beat him half to death, but he had talked about the fact that dryads had saplings they raised from seeds and usually they had three to four at any time, because they never knew when they might be chopped down or find the perfect place for a sister-daughter and a sapling was ready to be planted, while if you planted a seed, she would grow up alone with no idea of anything. Large dryad families really only occurred in groves where you had the time to let them grow with protection.

"I was wondering, would you like to have twin sister-daughters and put another child in the Craftsman and have Marisol help take care of her?" I didn't have any issue volunteering Marisol, one because she had a much better record with plants than any of us, and two, it would give her something fascinating to do. And if she was busy doing that, she wouldn't be grieving over Henri.

Hamiada tilted her head so far to the right I winced. "You would help me have two sister-daughters? Give them safe homes that will be protected?"

I smiled. "They will be more protected than you know. All these houses are on the historical register. They can't be torn down. And I promise I will leave them to my children and their children. I can't imagine they would ever allow anything to happen to your children."

Jaz and Magne exchanged confused glances. "We don't hurt people," Jaz said. "Well, I mean I try not to."

Most of the adults laughed, but I saw shiny eyes around the table.

"Are you interested?"

"I would get a grove? A grove?" She sounded like I had given her the best gift ever and I just nodded. She spun and stared at Marisol. "You would do this? Help my sister-daughters? Keep them healthy?"

Marisol took a deep breath and I think we all held ours as we waited. I hadn't meant to push her into the corner, but I also didn't want her to have time to convince herself otherwise.

"Si. I'll help with your sister-daughters. I'll move here."

The joy that exploded around the table had a physical presence as hugs were exchanged. Carelian didn't manage to escape it, though he didn't try too hard, and got plenty of hugs himself. We stayed up way too late making plans, but I saw parts of Marisol starting to heal, and that made it all worth it. We would have everyone here.

Well, almost everyone, but Kris would come back when he could and until he said otherwise, the garage apartment would be his.

CHAPTER

TWELVE

The Queen has stepped down. Britain's Monarchy is in a mess. Per British Law, the monarch must be a merlin. But the last drama with the prince has implied he is not fit to rule. There is no other merlin available. Parliament has declared an emergency meeting to review the laws of succession to see what options there are. They may have to search outside the immediate family. ~ CNN Mage Focus

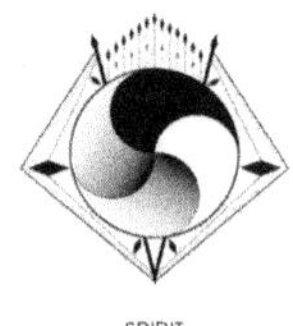

SPIRIT

We all headed to bed with smiles on our faces, but I awoke to remembering that I had a meeting today with the other councilors. Shay had messaged me late last night that we needed to meet late today, as there was another meeting on Saturday. Hamiada worked on the glade while I came up with food, and made Jeorgaz his berries.

My phone rang around one in the afternoon and I took a deep breath when I saw it was Sanchez. This meant Marisol had broken the news to them. I was worried that her sons would resist and try to guilt her to stay.

"Morning, Sanchez."

"I can't thank you enough for this, Cori," were the first words out of his mouth. "This is the best thing you could have done."

I sagged in relief. "Honestly, I was a bit worried you guys would be mad."

"Not at all. Running the garage with Marco isn't nine to five and then we are exhausted. I never realized how much work *Papi* did. We don't have time. Honestly, with the three of you she will feel needed and we know, we all KNOW Cori, that you will never keep her away from us. You are the best thing to happen to our family. What can we do to help?"

My smile hurt my face, it was so wide. "Help her pack. We can get a moving van, but I suspect you'll need a huge garage sale. A lot of stuff she won't want to keep or won't fit here. She has more than enough to buy everything new if she wants. Is she going to sell?"

"No. Paolo is going to move in and pay her rent for a year, then apply to buy it. It is much bigger than where he and his family are living now, so it totally works out."

We continued to chat until we both needed to go. Time flew by and before I knew it, Carelian was stepping away to grab

Shay, while Jeorgaz agreed to get Hishatio, as long as he could stay. He kept giving me funny looks, but I didn't follow up on it. I really wanted to get this meeting done first before worrying about anything else.

"You're sure Amadahy will be here?" I checked with Carelian as he got ready to grab Shay.

~I provided the information to her bird, the rest is on them,~ was his response as he leapt through the rip.

The glade was ready as it would get, and I curled up in a chair of grass. After experiencing it during labor, I'd decided Hamiada's chairs were just as, if not more, comfortable than any fancy chair.

The flash of pain as Carelian stepped through had me looking up and smiling as Shay entered. The dichotomy of how I remembered him and now threw me off for a minute. I still remembered the man in his late thirties with shocking red hair, Japanese features, and a wiry body. Now his hair was blending to white, and the braids no longer had fanciful items in them, they were just braids. He still wore jeans, but the science joke t-shirts were gone.

When did he get old?

"Hey Shay. Coffee, pizza rolls, and fruit." I waved at the table.

"I guess if we need to meet, having food is a good thing." He collapsed into the chair and reached for the coffee.

"Are you okay?"

He shrugged. "This getting old stuff isn't for the old." He sighed and put way too much sugar in his coffee, but I just let him.

I opened my mouth to ask a question, but dual spikes of pain that had my eyes crossing heralded incoming guests. I had to blink to get my eyes to focus as Hishatio and Amadahy stepped through.

"You look like shit," Shay said to Hishatio. I didn't complain because that was my reaction, too. His skin was gray, his hair had been shortened to the middle of his back, and he shook as he walked with a cane.

"It is good to see you too, though I must admit I have felt better." His voice was mild, yet I heard the rebuke in it and managed not to laugh.

"Sit. Would you like some tea?" I waved at the chair.

"Please," he said as he carefully lowered himself into the chair. I made him tea, placing it on the wide arm that formed for him. "Thank you."

"I have to agree with Shay. You look awful," I said, frowning.

Amadahy moved over and peered at him. She didn't seem to have changed much. Granted, last time I saw her I only gave her a cursory glance like I did Shay. But from the woman I'd met more than six years ago to now, she seemed the same—ancient. Long white hair in braids, a wrinkled apple face, and sharp eyes that looked like they were lasers.

"I agree. You look most unwell. Did they replace the heart?" Her voice was huskier than I remembered, but if that was true or just my memory being faulty, who knew?

I turned to look for her familiar, Kachil something. There. He sat on one of the trees, a huge branch supporting what was undoubtedly a significant amount of weight.

"No. But I have two new valves and my leg offered up two veins. But that is what we need to talk about." His voice wasn't ponderous, but I could tell he was exhausted already.

"Amadahy, would you like something to eat or drink?" I figured liquid would be needed for this conversation. I'd even hidden a bottle of whiskey if it got too heavy.

She accepted lemonade, and I set out the bowl of berries for Jeorgaz, then settled back down. Carelian sprawled at my feet.

"Why don't I go first, then we'll see if the information I tell you changes anything." They all gave me sudden wary glances, and I shrugged. "I assume all of you are aware of the rips that are occurring worldwide?"

Shay and Hishatio nodded. Amadahy looked confused.

"There are rips to the planes happening randomly all over the world and creatures and beings are slipping in if they aren't closed fast enough. I've been invited to a task force meeting regarding them next week, but for now that is about all I know." I tilted my head, focused on the AIN member. "You aren't seeing these in your lands?"

She shook her head. "No. Or at least not that I have been informed of. Though in comparison, our lands are very small. Do you have numbers and places?"

"Not yet. Probably Monday." She simply nodded her assent, and I continued. "But what I really wanted to talk about was both what Brix said and what I was told. I'm sure you sensed that Esmere and Tirsane had information to impart."

"Yes. But neither of them would tell us, which frankly I found a bit odd. Of all of them, they treat us with the most equality. Or maybe more accurately, the least amount of disdain," Shay said, his tone sour.

I heaved a sigh. I wasn't sure I still understood all this. "Part of it has to do with me being the Herald of Magic." All three of them stared at me. "I mentioned that, right?"

They shook their heads in unison. It was creepy.

"Fine, though I don't know what difference it makes. The denizens think I am the Herald of Magic, but as far as I can tell other than me being a double merlin, it doesn't change anything," I stumbled over that, and Shay shot me a look. "Okay, fine, a full merlin," I muttered.

"And what does calling yourself a full merlin entail?" Hishatio asked slowly.

I wiggled my shoulders to try to relax a bit. "That I emerged again and now I am strong in everything. And I am NOT telling the OMO."

They just blinked at me. Shay broke the silence with a soft, "Well Merlin's balls."

"Whatever. The important part is the realms are bursting with magic and that magic is ripping portals and spilling onto Earth," I said as fast as I could to get them off of me and the stupid herald business.

This caused them all to sharpen and look at me. But I continued, trying to lay everything out logically.

"Brix has something against me or believes in me or something, and believes that I am the key to dealing with it, but didn't want me told. Brix made the councilors promise to not tell me. Esmere only agreed because Bob required her to." I saw the questions and just waved them off. "Assume fealty-like requirements and leave it at that. But Tirsane said no and came to talk to me. She said I am a full magic user and even all the denizens are only full in their realm. I have them all and that means I'm the only one with a chance of repairing the rips." I took a gulp of my lemonade after that spiel.

The three of them sat back, just watching me.

"Exactly how do you plan on repairing the rips?" Amadahy asked slowly.

"I don't have a clue. No one seems to have any idea, but since I'm the 'herald' they think I'll figure it out. But this is also what they have been purposefully keeping from you. And it makes me worry there are other things they are not telling you."

"Wait, what?" Shay said, sitting up, all signs of relaxation gone. "They are specifically not telling us things?"

~They are treating you like very bright pets.~

We all jumped at Jeorgaz's voice and I snapped my attention to him. I'd pretty much forgotten he was there.

"Explain," Shay snapped out, staring at the phoenix.

Jeorgaz lifted his head and trilled out something that was unmistakably laughter. ~Humans have assumed for centuries that we are dumb creatures. Why is it so surprising that many in the realms think the same of humans?~

Shay sputtered. "Because we aren't! We have tools, use magic, have gone to the moon." His level of outrage amused me, but Jeorgaz's comment didn't really surprise me.

~So? We have towns, arts, councils. We can read and understand your legal systems and yet you still tend to think we are creatures. Most of the councilors haven't dealt with humans in centuries, if ever. They still believe you are talking monkeys, except some of the simians get very insulted with that analogy.~

Amadahy looked thoughtful, while Shay still looked insulted on everyone's behalf.

~I am a perfect example,~ Carelian commented. ~No one expected me to be accepted as a person. Esmere warned me multiple times that humans never treated anyone as equals. They even treated each other as less than them based on magic, skin color, height, gender. She tried very hard to convince me to not become a focus.~ He lifted up his head and licked my hand lightly. ~Cori proved them all wrong, which has brought Esmere and Tirsane here. She and those she calls family have never treated us as anything other than persons. Even her children understand that implicitly. But if I had never taken the risk, neither would have the council.~

His words fell with the impact of small asteroids. All I could think was how could anyone not see they were people? But then I'd received enough abuse in my life to know what he said wasn't wrong.

Shay sighed. "Point. How do we change that?"

"By doing what we are doing. Creating relationships and talking to everyone. We have been too insular." It was

Amadahy, and I glanced at her with a brow arched. A smile cracked the weathered face. "And yes, I am well aware of the irony in a so-called AIN member saying this. So basically, we need to talk to more councilors and not just about what the topic is." The sarcasm on AIN was almost enough to make me smile.

"That sounds like a good idea, but you will need to do it without me," Hishatio put in, his voice weighted with exhaustion. "I'm resigning effective immediately."

Shay sighed. "I figured. Mainly 'cause you still look like shit. Jeorgaz, don't your tears heal or something?"

The phoenix in question flipped his tail at Shay. ~I am not, nor have I ever been, that sort of phoenix.~

"Wait, I heard that before. Tear suckers. The comment was in reference to Brix. What does that mean? Why is there a difference?" I asked, following a random comment.

Jeorgaz huffed. "It had to do with what I wanted to talk to you about. But the short answer is no. My tears can not heal. Brix's don't heal exactly, they just stop and can reverse age-related effects. Not repair active damage done to the body. Think about rewinding cell decay, not preventing fat from clogging arteries. Though I do not believe Brix has shared tears in decades or centuries."

"So, immortality?" Shay asked, though he didn't look excited, more thoughtful.

~From old age, yes. Not from disease or violence.~

"Be that as it may, we still will need a replacement for Hishatio and I myself will be stepping down in the next year. But I at least have been grooming a replacement," Amadahy said. Her sharp eyes turned to Hishatio. "Do you have any suggestions?"

"I'm not sure there is even a question. It has to be Cori."

I snorted the lemonade out of my nose. Then hissed in pain.

Lemon juice in your sinuses burns. While Shay snickered and Amadahy and Hishatio just stared at me, I cleaned up.

"No. I don't want to. Besides," I countered, a bit desperate "at least one person shouldn't be from this continent. I don't know anything about other nations, much less have that sort of view on how magic is treated in other countries."

They just stared at me, and I stared back.

"I'm not doing it," I protested.

THIRTEEN

Big news ladies, Scott Randolph has officially moved to Rockway. If you are looking for a handsome man to spend your affections on, you won't find better. In his sixties, he is still single and with a huge doglike familiar you know you would be safe. Hopefully he will find reasons to stay in Rockway. ~Gossip section of Rockway Newspaper

---

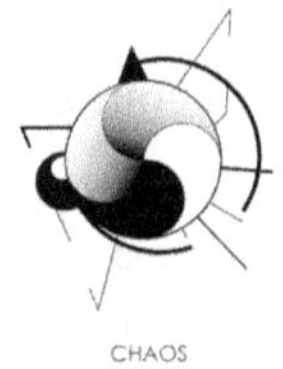

CHAOS

It had been a busy weekend starting the ball rolling on moving two households and creating two new dryads. The kids were reluctantly leaving the quetzos but they had gorged again that morning and would probably sleep for a few hours. Right now, they still enjoyed the warm sand, and Hamiada would keep an eye on them.

Dressed in jeans, a tank top, overshirt, and boots, I stepped to DC. Part of my outfit was a jab at Stephen from the early days, but mostly it was because I was done dressing the way other people wanted. This was comfortable and I could move in it if I needed to. Carelian wore his harness, just in case, though I didn't pull out his leash. I didn't know who to expect here, and freedom of movement was always a good thing.

I'd marked out a place to step to years ago, and Stephen had verified he was running this task force out of the same building. I walked up to the guard. It felt odd to not have a badge. Instead, I provided my ID.

"You check out. What about the animal?" The guard, an older Asian man, glared at Carelian.

"He comes with me," I said mildly, though I really wanted to sigh. There'd been a thread on the House of Emrys board a few years ago about identification cards for our familiars. I might have to revisit that and see if I could help get it passed.

"He isn't on the list."

The man was stubborn, I had to admit. I just stared at him. "Then maybe you should call and verify."

He glared back, but I didn't care. My days of explaining myself or being intimidated had faded to almost nonexistent after surviving a plane crash and giving birth.

With a mutinous frown he picked up the phone, still watching us as if he expected me to pull a weapon and start firing. I wanted to sigh. I was a Merlin. A gun was the last thing I'd depend on.

"Mr. Alixant, there's a lady here, and she's on the list, but she's got a vicious-looking animal with her and she says it goes with her."

Carelian practically preened at the vicious animal part. But I couldn't really argue for all that he was often more of my security blanket than guard dog.

The guard flinched and Carelian smirked. He could easily hear both sides of most phone conversations. I didn't need to ask. I knew Stephen well enough to guess at the lambasting this guard was getting.

"Yes, sir, Mr. Alixant. Right away, sir." He was almost stammering, and I fought to keep my amusement to myself. He hung up the phone abruptly and typed fast. A minute later, he shoved two badges towards me. "Here are passes for both of you. He said to meet him on floor 2."

"Thank you," I said as I took the two visitor badges, clipping one on me and the other on Carelian's harness. He managed to keep his snark in until we reached the elevators.

~You are nicer than I. Though his estimation of a vicious creature was accurate.~

"I figured Stephen would solve the problem. And if not, we could go for a hike."

Carelian flicked an ear at me. ~Now I wish you had gotten mad and left in a huff. The mountains are always more interesting than a man-made building.~

I rubbed his ears. "I agree, but if this has anything to do with what Tirsane talked about, I don't think I can afford to not come."

The elevator doors opened, and he stepped in with a sigh. ~Truth. Will we ever have time to just live?~

My hand sunk into his fur as I didn't have an answer for his question. Moments later the door whispered open to reveal Alixant standing there. As usual he was in a suit, though I noted he'd dropped the tie. Stephen arched a brow at my attire, and I gave him a huge grin as we stepped out.

"Good morning. Exciting so far?"

He snorted. "Idiots. Denying a merlin her familiar because it's scary. You'd think they'd realize a merlin is much scarier than a familiar, even Carelian."

~You just respect my quean and understand death can hide in plain sight,~ Carelian said with pleasure. ~When she finally decides to hunt, it will be glorious.~

"I'm not hunting anything," I said, exasperated. Lately, Alixant and Carelian had a weird pissing contest going on and I couldn't quite figure it out. It was polite and always talked me up. It landed somewhere between embarrassing and exasperating.

"Oh, I hope you are. Rips to be exact. Come on, I have people waiting." He pivoted on one foot, his hair in a long simple braid, but it only went past his shoulders, not further from where it had been two months ago.

He led me into a small auditorium and I gritted my teeth. I'd expected a conference room with a few people, not an auditorium with at least 30, plus a back wall of video connections with faces watching me as we walked in.

"Take a seat there, Cori. I need to get this going." He waved to a row of chairs with two other people in them at the back of the stage. "I couldn't get Charles for this, but I'm pulling him in later. Right now, just roll with it."

I gave him my best "I will get you for this" look, but he ignored me and walked over to the podium. Trying not to growl, I headed to the chairs. Carelian paced beside me, his alert state much higher than it had been about two minutes ago.

One of the chairs held an older black man in a dress uniform with two little stars on his collar. I thought it was Army but it might have been Marines. The green gave me that much information, as I was sure Navy was white and Air Force was blue. He assessed me in a quick seeking glance, eyes lingering on my temple for a moment, then did the same with Carelian. A nod, more to himself than us, and he shifted his focus to Alixant.

"Everyone, take a seat. We have everyone here. I'll start in a moment."

The other person was a tall thin man, with skin so pale I could see every place to stick an IV. His hair was the whitish blonde that suggested no pigments. He had on dark sun glasses, his hand was wrapped around a computer, and next to him hung a collapsed cane.

Neither were mages and I was pretty sure the blonde suffered from albinism, and was probably functionally blind. I nodded to both of them and took a seat, leaving a chair between us. Carelian sat in the gap between us, both a guard and a warning.

I tuned into Stephen as I needed to figure out what I'd been suckered into.

"Thank you everyone for coming. I know this is high importance for many of our agencies. As such, I have a few experts here to talk about what is going on and what we can do to help." He glanced down at his notes and I took a moment to try to peer past the lights into the rows of people.

There were a lot of first responders, a few military, and a bunch of mages. But what was I an expert on?

"The first person I'd like to invite up is Joel Flansky. He is an expert on the amount of magic coming out of the rips and the frequency they are occurring. Joel?" Stephen turned and looked at the man sitting next to us.

With a jerky nod the man rose, leaving his cane at the chair and carefully pacing toward the podium, hand grabbing it as he got close. Stephen had moved directly out of the way. A bit of a fumble with the wires at the podium, but then his computer was connected.

A graph appeared up on the screen behind him and I craned to see it. It was a graph of blue dots spaced out, but slowly climbing up as it went down the X axis. The title said Power Output of Portals. I leaned forward, interest spiking.

"I am Joel Flansky, data analyst for the OMO. Whenever portals are found we check the sensors in the local area. We then, using existing algorithms for power output degradation based on distance, calculate the estimated magic that is leaking from the rips."

I'm not sure what surprised me more: that OMO had the ability to calculate that or that they were publicly sharing this information.

"As you can see, there is a significant growth over the last month." The little mouse circled an area on the screen. "So far there have been sixty-three verified rips." That number was larger than I thought, but much smaller than I had feared. "In the United States alone."

Shit.

"If we include the data from other countries, a larger standard deviation also appears due to lower quality monitoring stations and the data becomes fuzzier." He clicked another button, and the screen changed with a lot more dots, green this time, all ramping upward. "However, as you can see, there is a steady increase. To correlate with that, the number of emergences in these areas have also spiked." Another tap of the keys and a new scatter graph, this one with black dots appeared. "As you can see, the emergences have spiked and when we account for geographic areas, they align almost perfectly with rips."

There was murmuring in the crowd and I reminded myself

to never mention the double emergences that could happen around rips, but there hadn't been death and the rips had been to a single realm, not multiples, which I knew was a factor in re-emerging.

"At the rate the rips are going, assuming they remain consistent, we will have rips appearing at the rate of three an hour per continent, roughly, in the next six months." A gasp went through the room. "A commensurate rate of emergences is expected. This means that if these rips continue unabated, mages will no longer make up only 35% of the population. By the end of two years, they will be over 50%." His blunt voice held no emotions, providing only facts.

He cleared his throat. "All of this is based on interpretation of existing data and may change when new data is added." Not waiting for questions, he snapped the laptop closed, unplugged it and all but made a frantic dash back to his chair, collapsing in it and shaking.

Stephen walked back to the podium, though I knew him enough to realize he'd expected Joel to stay for questions, but the man shook as he sat there, looking damn near pitiful.

"Thank you, Joel, for that data. As you can see, this is growing into a bigger issue. However, if it was just the rips and the increase in emergences, we would not be here. I would like to introduce General Matthew Stone to discuss the next issue." Stephen stepped back and glanced over at us and I tried to kill him with my glare.

It didn't work.

The military officer got up and marched toward the podium. The difference between the two men was like looking at a reversed prism. One stoic and dark, the other light and frazzled. I shook my head and focused on the general.

"As Mr. Alixant said, I'm General Stone. I oversee all groups that respond to magical events, including Rogue Hunters, Mage

SEAL, and all unsanctioned breaches over two feet in width. The reason for that is micro or very small rips occur daily all over the world and 99% of the time people are unaware they exist and they tend to close naturally or a mage will sense them and just close them without much thought."

He nodded toward the screen. "I don't have pretty pictures to convince you of what I'm going to talk about, but I'm sure you've been following the news. Or at least if you haven't, I'm not sure why you're here." There was a low-level chuckle around the room at that. "Many of the rips are large enough to let creatures slip through. While some are unremarkable, a great many of them are deadly, vicious, and capable of treating humans as snacks."

I winced a bit but I couldn't really argue with that.

"We, so far, have had to stop—and by stop I mean kill with great prejudice—what appear to match these creatures: naga, manticore, Venus fly trap, snakes, boar, deer, and rats." He lifted his head from the notes he had been reading from. "I don't want you to think this is an overreaction. The snake was over thirty feet long and moved at the rate of twenty miles an hour. Each of the rats were over fifty pounds and had killed two people before we got to them. The naga and the manticore were intelligent, and it took three rogue Mage teams to bring them down. I would like to state we did ask them to surrender peacefully, and we'd have opened a portal for them back to the appropriate plane. They declined with comments similar to: 'humans are tasty and this is more entertainment than I've had in years.'"

He cleared his throat. "If this phenomenon is not stopped quickly, we may have creatures we can not stop slip through and treat Earth as their hunting grounds. And this is only what my teams have dealt with. I have no idea what might have slipped out in other countries. Any questions?"

There was a general murmur in the room and a few questions about what the creatures were and how had they been stopped; what sort of warning should be sent out. Discussion about whom to contact and how. Meanwhile, I raced trying to figure out what to do next. How biased was my view of the denizens?

"Thank you, General Stone. Next, we have Cori Munroe, to talk about the creatures and what can be done to help prevent them from killing, and get the rips closed sooner. Cori?" Stephen turned and looked at me and I tried to decide if I was going to feed him to Zmaug or Esmere.

CHAPTER
FOURTEEN

Senior government officials have been pulled into a meeting over in Langley and no one will say what is going on. The President and his staff are not saying anything, but certain key individuals are missing today. Those in the know are worried there is more going on than anyone realizes. How dangerous are these rips? ~ House of Emrys politics board

---

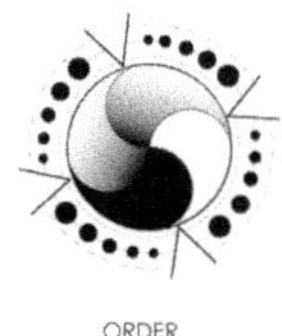

ORDER

I stopped a few feet away from the podium next to Stephen. "I am going to get you back for this. And what exactly am I supposed to say?" I whispered fiercely.

He sighed and dragged his hands over his face looking exhausted. "Yes, you are, and Indira is going to help you. I am sorry, but I'm trapped as badly as you are and really all of this was dropped on me last night. I didn't have much time to warn you. Talk to them about the denizens and how to work with the creatures that come out. And how to close the rips. You might have to pull the power move to get them to listen. Regardless of what you think, most people have no idea what a double merlin is or who you are." He grimaced as the sound of people getting restless was clear. "I swear the president is calling me three times a day asking what the plan is, and no one has one."

If he hadn't looked so exhausted, I might have had less sympathy. "You still could have called."

"And told you what? You would have refused to come and then it would be even worse."

There was something else going on here, but I didn't have time to figure it out. I approached the podium and stared out at the people. I knew there were truth sensors out here, so this would all be a dance to tell the truth.

"I'm Cori Munroe. The last time I was tested, the OMO registered me as a double merlin. This means magic has a very low cost for me. Then when you add in my focus, Carelian, it means the cost is even less." I petted him gently as I spoke. He sat on the side of the podium, looking regal and deadly.

I could see people staring at me, trying to analyze exactly why I was there. If they figured it out, I hoped they would tell me. Time to dance.

"Many people are unaware that I count some of the realm denizens as friends. Not only my focus, but his mother, the gorgon Tirsane, and others. Because of this, I have greater insight into some of the dynamics at play in the realms. First, some of the beings are aware of these rips." I practically heard Stephen jerk upright when I said this. "But at this time, they have not disclosed to me exactly how they can be closed. Also, there is a wide range of beings that make up the realms." On this part, I was on much firmer ground. Though I'd kill for a glass of water right now.

"Some are smarter than humans, others are nothing more than animals. As General Stone relayed, they are capable of talking and making decisions. However, their view on life is different from ours. For the most part, few humans would ever think of hunting and eating another human, both because of the taboo of cannibalism, but also the idea of eating a sentient creature. Many of the realm denizens do not feel this way. They believe in the survival of the fittest and that an intelligent, slow creature tastes just as good as a fast, stupid animal."

The sound of shock that rippled through the room had me shaking my head. We really were the most arrogant creatures. "There are some that do not regard humans as prey, but I couldn't tell you for sure how many that is." I suspected the answer was five or maybe less. I still didn't know if Zmaug or Onyx would eat me.

My phone started buzzing in my pocket. I ignored it. Now wasn't a good time to see what Jo and Sable wanted for dinner.

"Part of the reason the rips to the realms are so strong is they are places where the magic is so high the reality dividing our realms is ripping. As I've been able to figure out, it is the equivalent of a bubble bursting."

My phone was still buzzing, and I gritted my teeth. ~Can you tell Jo and Sable I'll respond in a bit?~

~Of course.~

"Other than that, I know they can be closed. Anyone with

Spirit can close a rip, but because they are large and basically being fueled by magic, they are more difficult to close than most." I cleared my throat, out of things to say. I didn't want to say I'd been tasked with closing them, or it was technically my fault for feeding Tirsane so much magic. With luck, I'd never have to mention that.

"What else would you like to know?" I hoped they'd make it short.

~Jo and Sable said neither of them are trying to contact you and the kids are fine.~

I frowned at this information, but I couldn't focus in on who could be calling or texting me as the room seemed full of hands.

I pointed at someone at random. "You're sure this isn't an invasion? Most of the monsters coming through are overly aggressive." It was part question, part accusation.

"If it is an invasion, I don't know about it, and no one has mentioned it. As to the overly aggressive, their world isn't as nice or stable as ours. They have to be aggressive to survive, even with magic. Remember what I said about everyone being prey? To live, you are stronger, faster, smarter than what is hunting you."

"You," I said, jabbing at someone else. The darkness of the auditorium made it hard to see who people were.

"How intelligent is intelligent?"

I shrugged. "They are absolutely smarter than most of the politicians I've met. You decide."

A snort of laughter rippled through the room. Another finger jab from me.

"Can we stop them? Can they? Do they want to?" A man's voice, but more curious than accusatory.

"The rips? As far as I know, the method to stopping them is unknown. Do they want this?" I shrugged. "I don't think so, but again, what I think and what they actually want may not be the same. You." My finger jabbed, eager to move on.

"Why aren't you stopping it? You're supposed to be like uber powerful?"

I wasn't sure who had asked that question, but I couldn't stop the snort. "If you figure out how I can do that, please tell me and I'd be delighted to stop them."

Another question that just rehashed the answers I'd already given.

"Is there anything else that I haven't answered?"

There were shakes of heads and it felt like it had taken forever, but probably less than ten minutes. I started to step back to let Stephen back up, though I still had no idea what we could do besides rush to close them as soon as they appeared.

He started to walk toward me when I felt a spike of pain and I pivoted, seeking the source. It made no sense. Why would a rip randomly happen here, of all places?

The wavering distortion of reality appeared in the middle of the stage and then Esmere stepped out of it. I sagged in relief, then went tense, even as most everyone around us screamed. My feet were moving before my brain had caught up.

"Esmere, is everything okay? Why are you here?" Her popping into my world like this had never happened before. Usually, she only showed up at home. Already I could see flashes of camera phones going off as she stalked across the stage, her green fur sparkling in the light.

~Herald Munroe. The other councilors have been trying to get a hold of you. You must come.~ Her voice was imperative and Carelian was at my side. His hackles weren't raised.

What she called me clicked in. "Lord Esmere, I apologize. But I have other duties today. May I attend another time?" I kept my tone as formal as I could while cataloging all the things that were wrong about this. Her tail was lashing, her pupils were pinpricks, and the reactions of everyone around us didn't help. She was my friend, Carelian's mom, and sometimes I forgot that she was also terrifying. She was the size of a small horse and took up a significant amount of space on the stage. I could see Joel behind her, laptop grasped across his chest so tight it might crack if he wasn't careful.

~There is an emergency session. The Herald is directed to attend.~ There was a level of formality in her words that made no sense and set off all my alarms. Her voice wasn't projecting to everyone, so the odds were it looked like me facing down a giant green cat. The media was going to have a field day with that.

I turned to look at Stephen, who stood a few feet from me, eyes narrowed as he watched us. "I'm afraid I need to step away. Please make sure to send me the details on how I can help. You know I will assist as needed."

His face was a shuttered mask, and I gave him a hard look. I would be calling him tonight. If I had to, I'd enlist Indira in the fight. This wasn't acceptable. He nodded just the teeniest bit.

"Then I shall leave with you, Lord Esmere. Carelian, will you attend?" The formal phrasing sounded ridiculous.

Rather than responding, he did a sort of bow I don't believe I'd ever seen before. One leg extended, the other pulled back, and he stretched out his head and neck over the extended leg. If it had been any other situation, I might have been pestering him non-stop about what that meant. Right now, I just nodded and moved with Esmere to step through the rip.

"Stop right there, young lady!" The barked order made me stumble as I tried to turn and walk at the same time. I regained my footing and turned to see General Stone storming towards us. "What do you think you are doing? Leaving with this crea-ture? You should hold it captive here until they stop letting their trash into our world." His chest heaved as he shouted into my face.

Carelian snarled and moved forward, but I put my hand on his head. "General, may I introduce you to Lord Esmere?" I waved my hand to her. "Lord Esmere, this is General Stone."

She had sat down, tail wrapping around her feet. ~General,~ her voice whispered across my mind. ~You are delaying us from a required appearance.~ I heard the warning and wondered once again what was driving her.

He jerked back and glared at me. "What is it with this talking in my head nonsense? I know animals can't talk."

My mouth opened, closed, then I took a deep breath. "General. This is Lord Esmere. I can guarantee you that she is at least as intelligent as you, if not more, as she isn't the one insulting someone who has claws that are almost five inches long and can cut through a picnic table like it is Styrofoam." To back up my words, Esmere lifted one paw and extended her lethally sharp claws then dug them into the floor, carving up strips. "Now I would advise you to treat her with the same level of respect you would a merlin from Russia or Germany, because I can guarantee you if she was to kill you where you stand there isn't a force in the world that would be able to put her on trial for removing an idiot from Earth's population."

My words almost echoed in the auditorium, and then Carelian just had to chime in as he licked his claws. ~I have heard that humans taste excellent with the extra flavoring adrenaline adds to the meat. I bet I could convince Lord Esmere to help me chase you for a bit. Make sure the chemicals are fully flushed through all your muscles.~

I wanted to groan, but I managed to keep a straight face as the man paled to an unhealthy color of gray. What caught my eye was Joel, still in the chair, laptop held to his chest, and a hand across his mouth. It wasn't fear I saw, but laughter. I flicked my eyes away before I lost it and fell into howls of laughter to match.

"Mr. Alixant, why don't you explain to the General exactly who he is insulting and I will go to the meeting where I am needed." Just to put the fear of me into everyone, as I still heard rumblings and the occasional squeak of terror, I held up one hand and pulled out one of the showier bits of power Jo, Sable, and I created for the kids.

A column of flame and water twisted and weaved in the palm of my hand. It was hypnotic. Fire and Water thought it was great fun to dance with each other and never touch. I stared right in the general's eyes as the magic danced on my palm.

"Until later," I said with a smile and then threw the two columns on the floor where they twisted and danced their way through the rip. The three of us followed them through, not even casting a backward glance at the freaked-out humans.

FIFTEEN

Rumors abound of a monster appearing at a restricted meeting for selected government personnel. The damage discovered to the floor of the auditorium provides evidence that something happened, but the odds of a "giant green monster" appearing implies that maybe there was less meeting going on and more drug sampling than normal. ~ CNN Mage Focus

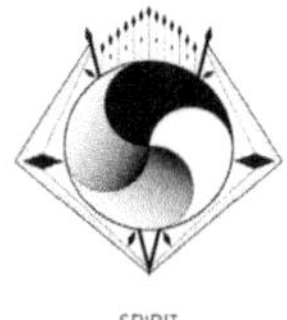

SPIRIT

To my surprise and relief, we didn't step into the council chamber, but instead into a glade that didn't feel familiar. I crossed my arms and stared at Esmere. "Do you want to explain what all that was about?"

She snarled a bit, pacing even as Carelian stood guard in front of me. His stance worried me, and I feared Esmere was under more pressure than I understood.

~This is an ambush that I'm forced into participating with and I detest that. You are about to be backed into a corner, but I am unsure how or why. Brix is up to something and that is normal, but the machinations being done now make no sense. The realms are not stable for the first time in my memory, but I am not that old.~ Her words jabbed into my mind with the force of daggers and I fought to hide my flinches.

"Why does Brix care about me one way or another? Tirsane mentioned that too." I wasn't sure how to deal with this aspect of Esmere. Cath didn't take well to being forced to do things.

~I am unsure. But Brix is old, very old.~ She paused her stalking back and forth, but her tail still cracked back and forth. ~In fact, Brix might be the oldest being I know of. Even Zmaug remembers Brix from when she was only a hatchling.~ If she had human expressions, I would have expected narrowed eyes and pursed lips. As it was, she had just gone completely still, on the hunt for prey.

"Okay? And? I'm not. Heck, I don't even have half a century on me. And really, outside my friends, it isn't like I've had a lot of interactions with the realms."

She flicked an ear at me. ~We are all about manipulation and plans. Your very friendship has created waves. It is amusing, but I prefer to be the one generating waves, not being affected by them.~ She heaved out a sigh and shook her entire body. ~Come. Just be prepared.~

I noted that she didn't say for what, so I brought my best offensive spells to the forefront, cast Lady Luck on Carelian and myself, then I asked Air to stay near, even as I set up a bio-electric shield. That would drain me, but I had time until I figured out what was going on.

~Ready?~ She glanced at me with ears flicking.

"No, but let's go anyhow." I kept my hand on Carelian, glad I'd put the harness on him. It had extra supplies that just might be needed if this blew up.

The rip opened and I stepped through to the council chamber, closing my eyes between one location and the next. I opened my eyes to bedlam. Zmaug was in the yard, smoke slipping out of her nostrils, and flames licking at the corners of her mouth.

Tirsane was talking to what I thought was a naga and Salistra, her snakes agitated and hissing at everyone. Bob all but writhed, and I was glad he wasn't talking. There was a small contingent of Valkyries in full battle armor, their wings out and acting like shields around them.

Then there was Shay, Amadahy, and a short man with dark brown skin and hair that I didn't recognize. They were huddled together near the end of the council chamber, their backs against the wall. Magic was so heavy I could feel it in the air, taste it on my tongue. I stood there for a moment, unnoticed, and watched. This time, paying attention to the dynamics.

Everyone talked to everyone else, barging in, demanding attention, and not being shy about using magic to gain it. If you didn't know the realm a being was from, or what they represented, you would have no idea. Everyone mingled and argued, except the humans.

Shit, culture is screwing us again. Though I wouldn't have thought of Shay as shy.

Watching for a bit longer, I realized the problem. All of the denizens were dangerous. Tirsane had snakes, Esmere claws. Others had fangs, fire, sharp feathers, they could all harm soft squishy humans without magic. We didn't even wear armor anymore.

~Esmere, when was the last time humans were on the council?~ I sent the question to her quietly.

She had moved over to talk to a mix of species from Chaos and Spirit with normal cat invisibility and hadn't garnered much attention.

~Long before I was born. Why?~

~Just a theory. Thanks.~ Right then, I would have bet a lot of money the last time humans were here we wore armor and carried swords. Our current existence made us much too soft, physically.

"Crap," I whispered to myself, and headed over to the other humans. I felt beings take notice of me as I moved through, sounds fluctuating as their attention wavered.

"You finally showed up. There is a reason you are supposed to answer your phone," Shay snapped as I stepped close enough they didn't need to shout.

"Oh, so it was you blowing up my phone. Well since you did it while I was in the middle of speaking to a bunch of people for the FBI, with a General from the Army and a data analyst from the OMO sitting behind me, I didn't think it was a good time to check my messages." I gave him a withering look, and he just shrugged, dismissing my complaint, but he also didn't take his eyes off the beings behind us. Of all of us, I was the only one with my back to them.

I'll have to address that in a bit.

"Now that I'm here, want to tell me what was so all fired important that it couldn't wait until I could read the messages and respond. You know, like another fifteen minutes?" My voice held a note of sharpness because I still didn't understand why I had to be here.

"Oh, yeah." All his indignation and irritation drained out of him. He took a deep breath. "Hishatio is dead."

It felt like I'd been gut punched. We weren't friends, but we'd finally moved into respected colleague territory and I had wanted there to be more. More time, more discussion, more... something. I closed my eyes and processed it.

"How?"

"Massive heart attack early this morning, for him at least. I was contacted about it and they let me know. Funeral is next week and we are all invited."

I'd never been a big fan of weddings and baby showers, even my own, but they were infinitely preferable to the number of funerals I was going to. Granted, even one was one too many.

"I see. I am sorry to hear that." The grief stuck in my throat, a lump of might-have-beens that I struggled to swallow. "But I'm not sure why I had to be here." Dealing with Hishatio's death would come later. Right now, there was a more important item.

"Was this a scheduled council meeting? Why am I here? For that matter, why did Esmere come and grab me and probably set back human and denizen relations about a hundred years?" That one annoyed me and I knew I probably could have handled it better, but still.

"No clue. I got pinged about an hour ago that there was an emergency meeting and that you had to attend with us. I have no idea if they knew Hishatio had died or what caused it."

"Huh." I turned and looked at everyone, aware once again how only the humans were isolated. "Okay, I'll deal with this in a moment. Amadahy?" I said, facing her and the man next to her. He wasn't as old as she was, but he had to be at least as old as Shay. Which, as always, made me the baby of the group.

Then why am I the one in charge?

I pushed the thought away and waited for Amadahy.

"This is Ngarra. He is who the AIN has chosen as my replacement."

"G'day," he said in a soft accent that sounded more Australian than anything else. "Tis an honor to be here." He glanced back at the vibrant room. "If it be a bit overwhelming."

"Australian?" I asked with a bit of confusion.

Amadahy shrugged. "We never said all the AIN members were from North America. We have been collecting indigenous people for a century. You'd be amazed at how much a Mongol or what your cultures call an Aborigine enjoys living a life with no white man telling them what to do. We tend to refer to ourselves as First Nations Peoples."

The jab wasn't subtle, but I just shrugged. "Sounds good to me. Hopefully, Ngarra, you have some experience with dealing with fractious other beings?"

"Ay. Some." He just shrugged and looked around, more curious than wary.

I started to ask more questions, but a trill that cut through my brain and soul stopped me. Everyone pivoted toward the source of the trill. Brix sat there in colorful, feathery glory. It was probably my imagination, but I could have sworn Brix was staring at our small cluster.

~As the last councilor has arrived, please get situated. Visitors, please retreat to the gallery.~ The words cut through the chatter with a crystal sharp edge. Beings nodded to each other and went back to their places.

"Showtime," Shay said, his smile trembling a bit at the edges. He and Amadahy went to the chairs in the Earth area. The other beings had filtered into their spots, with Brix at the head on his perch.

It still felt like he was watching me, but it was difficult to tell. I shrugged it off and went to stand behind Shay, while Ngarra stood behind Amadahy. What disturbed me the most was the glances I kept getting from beings. Not Tirsane or Esmere, but the rest. Lightning-fast glimpses my direction. Then they'd look away. At this point, it was only Bob and Salistra that weren't doing that. And I didn't know if Bob even had eyes.

It took another minute for the watchers to disappear. For the first time, I realized that above us was actually a gallery, but the shadows were such that you couldn't easily see anyone up there. The light in the chamber was bright enough that it kept the shadows all but impenetrable. However, I could hear the rustling and sounds telling me there were many beings up there watching.

Brix's wings waved up and down, the ring clacked against the wooden perch, drawing all eyes to the phoenix. ~We have gathered for an emergency meeting.~ His head rotated through each section, then fastened on us. ~Earth, where is your third councilor?~ The empty chair screamed a banshee cry of emptiness in this place.

Shay stood, moving up a bit. "Our third councilor died this morning and we have not had time to find another representative."

Brix hesitated, then head dipped in our direction. ~Your loss is noted. However, three is required.~

Shay shrugged. "Amadahy and I can handle it until we have a third. Ngarra here is apprenticing to take over for Amadahy when she steps down."

~That is not acceptable. There must be three,~ Brix snapped out, the words cutting literally.

"Then Ngarra can step up," Shay suggested, his voice still calm.

~No. We do not need more than one representative from the Beasts realm. There must be three.~

For some reason the realm denizens tended to refer to the AIN as the Beast realm, which made zero sense to me. I just rolled with it. Though I didn't understand the emphatic statement. Why was it such a big deal?

~Herald Cori Munroe can serve as the third councilor.~ The amount of smugness in Brix's voice made me grit my teeth. I didn't want anything to do with this.

"Not happening. I'm not a good person to be a councilor. Let Ngarra stand in for a while." I spoke clearly, even though everyone in the room was focused on me, except Tirsane. She watched Brix, her snakes coiled in tight. Esmere had her eyes shut, but her ears were flicked back toward me, tracking everything.

~No accepti-~

"Why?" I demanded, cutting Brix off. Half the beings in there froze at my rudeness, or whatever. Maybe you didn't do that.

Brix flared up, flames licking across the multi-colored body. ~Because it is required for councilors of the realms to have three each to support the different aspects of magic. We required merlins from Earth as your mages are corrupted and do not understand or use magic to its fullest. Your delegation must be complete.~

"Then wait," I snapped out. "Someone died and you can bloody well wait." I almost felt the shock at my words ripple around the room. "Most of you are well over a hundred years old and some of you live for thousands of years. We don't. Living to a hundred is rare and we die from the stupidest things. You have time. Give us the few weeks we need to get this straightened out."

Shay and Amadahy were staring at me like I'd grown

another head, but my patience level had gone. Between my family moving out of the house, the rips, everyone wanting me to solve things, and information being kept from me, I didn't care. And if they wanted to get nasty, go for it.

Carelian pressed against my leg and purred. It was all I needed to know. I had to put my foot down now.

Flames were shooting up around Brix and I reached for Water, more than willing to make this into a fight.

~Corisande Munroe, I am calling in one of the debts you owe me and mine.~ Salistra demanded across the chamber.

Brix had nothing on Salistra for a cutting voice. It sliced through my anger and my left arm burned. I glanced down at it to see the unicorn horn glowing on it. Snapping my mouth shut, I pivoted a bit to face her. She had walked out into the ring facing me. Her horn glowed in the light and silver hooves glimmered with malevolence as she focused on me.

Fuck.

CHAPTER
SIXTEEN

Is anyone else having weird conversations with your familiar? We know they talk to each other, just not to other mages, but are they dropping weird comments? Mine mentioned "the Council is having issues" or this random comment, "The Earth Lords aren't effective." Yet when I ask what they are talking about they just give me this look. And I swear it is a pitying look. If anyone is having the same, could you contact me? I'm starting to wonder if I'm going crazy or my familiar is. ~House of Emrys Message Board

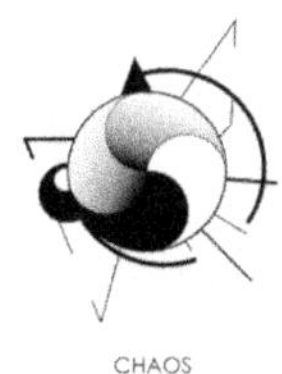

With a force of will, I pushed down my annoyance at this entire situation and nodded to her, one hand still on Carelian's head. He'd stopped purring, and that worried me a touch.

"Yes, Salistra, I owe you a favor, one of three. What is it that you ask of me?"

I couldn't even think as I waited. She had the right to ask almost anything of me.

~I require of you to take the position of Earth Lord and represent your realm in the council.~ Her voice was like a crystal-clear bell slicing through my mind, and I fought off the pain.

"Why?" The word slipped out, and I knew it shouldn't have. I had no right to ask why. They were debts I owed her. Technically, she could ask for me to cut off my left hand and I wouldn't have much wiggle room.

She turned her head so one eye peered directly at me. ~Because that is the debt I collect.~ Her tone didn't change, though the feel of the bell got colder.

I had zero choice.

"Very well, Salistra." I glared at Brix, knowing the bird had something to do with this, but why? "I accept the position as councilor."

~Earth Lord,~ Brix replied with smugness in his voice that really had me itching to ice his tail feathers.

If I spoke, I might say something that would create even more problems. My head jerked down in what could be called a nod and I stepped backward toward the chair. When had I walked so far out?

~You must swear the oath, first.~ Brix's voice stopped me mid-step.

"Excuse me?"

~The oath. It is required for Realm Lords.~

It was certain. I was icing his tail when I got a chance. I glanced back at Shay and Amadahy. "Did you two swear an oath?"

Neither of them looked worried. "Sure," Shay said shrugging. "It was the 'I promise to do my job to the best of my ability' boilerplate. Nothing that I worried about."

Amadahy nodded. "Very similar to the swearing in people do in your court systems."

In the justice system, witnesses swore on a copy of the Bill of Rights to tell the truth and uphold it as they knew it.

I nodded, my teeth clenched. ~I might just kill everyone,~ I sent to Carelian.

Rather than chiding me, he rubbed his face along my hand. ~A blood bath would be glorious. We would feast for days.~

I dropped my head and tried not to laugh.

Blood-thirsty Cath.

"What is the oath?" I asked, facing Brix once again.

The bird fluffed up and multi-colored eyes twinkled at me. ~Repeat after me.~

I nodded, waiting.

~I, Corisande Munroe, swear to tell nothing but the truth to the council.~ Brix paused, and I shook my head.

"The whole oath first."

If that bird could turn glares into lasers, Brix's eyes would have burned me.

~I, Name of Lord, swear to tell nothing but the truth to the council. I swear to share all information pertinent to council inquiries. I will respect and defer to my senior Lord's requests. I swear to protect and serve Magic to the best of my ability and the safety of the realms.~ Brix's feathers were puffed up as the tension stretched out.

"I won't be swearing that," I said, my gaze never drifting off of Brix. A chatter broke out among everyone but my eyes stayed on Brix.

~That is unacceptable. You must take this oath.~

"Not that one." I held up my hand as the noise erupted again. "There are a few things that will need to change. First, I usually tell the truth, but I can not swear to tell nothing but the truth. I may tell you a lie, believing it is the truth and I won't be forsworn on my oath." Brix's feathers unruffled a tiny bit at that, but I kept going. "Second, I can not swear to share all information. Some knowledge I have is not mine to share and I will not tell you. I can tell you what I can share, but I won't spill secrets that aren't mine." I heard a bit of hissing at that, but I could have sworn some of the noises were approving. "Third, I'm not deferring to anyone based on age. You are all older than me. By centuries in many cases, and I'm not ever going to outlive you. So, no. I won't automatically cave to what you want me to do. I can swear to give the fellow councilors the same level of respect they give me." I smiled, showing my teeth with that comment. Carelian laughed quietly in the back of my mind.

I paused, letting the murmurs and other sounds surround me while I thought it out. Writing this out on a piece of paper would have been much easier.

"Here is what I will swear," I said once I had it in my mind cleanly. "I, Corisande Munroe, swear to deal fairly with the council. I will seek advice from other members, and I will protect and honor Magic to the best of my ability." I had planned to see if Brix accepted that, but as the last words fell from my mouth, magic washed through me and on my right arm a band of glowing symbols appeared. It was similar to what had happened during the joining, but instead of fading on my inner arm the symbols of Chaos, Order, and Spirit appeared in a row, each lined with precision and all the sections filled with an iridescent color that changed in the light as I moved.

"And Magic has accepted her oath," Tirsane's voice rang out loud and clear.

~So mote it be,~ rang out in my head and my ears through the chamber.

I managed to drag my focus away from the new marks on my skin and look at Brix. The rage in Brix's eyes should have been enough to turn me into a crisp little pile of ash. Instead, every feather was clamped tight to the phoenix's body, though flames licked at the bottom of the multicolored tail.

~Welcome to the council, Lord Munroe.~ Every word sounding like it had been forced out between two ice cubes.

"Thank you," I said with a smile as false as the welcome. With a pivot that would have made Stephen proud, I spun on my heel and stepped back into the Earth Realm ring. They all stood there staring at me, eyes wide and mouths agape.

"What?" I asked when I got nearer.

"You back-talked them. You defied them. You defied Brix," Shay whispered, seeming more cowed than I thought he knew how to be.

"Whispering is a waste of time. Most of them have much better hearing than we do. And yes. Don't you?"

He and Amadahy traded lightning-fast glances. "Not really. We are usually polite and keep everything civil."

"Have they threatened you?" I asked, all the pieces falling in place.

Shay shook his head. "No, but we saw Brix flame someone that argued with him. It was made very clear to keep our place."

"No. I keep Kalihchiia here on his perch. They just are unfailingly polite even while they brandish claws and fangs." Amadahy narrowed her eyes, inspecting me. "You aren't surprised."

"Kalihchiia, why didn't you tell her?"

The thunderbird stared at me for a long moment, and I started to think he wouldn't answer. ~Tell her what?~

"That polite and deferential isn't the way to go?" I was staring at him, ignoring the shock behind me, though I knew I didn't have much time.

~They are higher rank. They have precedence.~

Birds. Pecking order. Shit.

I sighed. "I'll explain later. For right now, let's see what exactly the issue is." I slumped in the chair, already exhausted from all the posturing.

~Now that Earth has decided to grace us with three councilors, settle down so we can discuss the matter at hand.~

This time, I paid attention to everyone as they settled down. No one looked at me directly, though Tirsane's snakes bobbled hello every time they caught me glancing at them.

~The matter at hand is the magic over spillage and it being wasted on the Earth realm.~

Energy sizzled through me. What was this? Tirsane had talked about the magic bursting over, but not wasted or calling it spillage. I glanced over at her, but other than the snakes bouncing in glee, her face remained an alabaster statue, beautiful but emotionless.

~Here are the ideas that have been suggested to utilize the excess magic and keep it here.~ Brix paused and fluffed wings.

"Did you know about this?" I said quickly. Amadahy and Shay shook their heads, while Ngarra just looked terrified and out of his depth. I felt for him.

~First is the best one, but has the longest lead time. We need more offspring that want to follow our footsteps. Too many of our children are looking at the study and sacrifice involved in becoming an active part of the magical world and they are choosing the life of the beasts.~ Brix didn't so much as send a feather in Kalihchiia's direction, but the thunderbird bristled. ~We need to encourage them to follow in the path of magic. How can we do that?~ Brix cast the question out.

~I do not see that we should, bird,~ Esmere drawled, sitting demurely straight up, tail wrapped around her. ~The realms are full of lands created long ago. Their magic keeps those lands healthy and who are we to dictate the choices of the young?~

~Their parent,~ Brix retorted in a sneering tone. ~Who else should guide them, if not you?~

~What would you know of it? Avians lay eggs. You know nothing of the feel of children in you, squirming, dying. It is not up to you to say how we should raise or guide those we birth.~ Her posture didn't change, but Esmere's scathing tone scalded my mind.

~Feckless cat. You let your litter die rather than protect them.~

I heard the shock at that remark and I glanced over at Shay and Amadahy. They just seemed bored. "You can hear them, right?"

Shay nodded. "Yeah, but they do this all the time. It's just banter."

"No. That was the equivalent of calling someone a fucking bitch," I countered as I went back to watching Esmere's ears.

She didn't move them, but the tip of her tail had gone still. ~At least I had them. I encouraged them to live the lives they chose. Carelian is here. His brother Alin is happy with his pride, roaming the planes and managing the rodent population. Biain is enjoying the Beast realm and has great fun working with their herds. The others were born mindless and followed their nature. My litters are my business, not something to discuss in public. Next time you do so, I'll have new feather toys.~ Her whiskers flipped forward and her body trembled with the need to pounce.

Brix turned on the perch, tail flipping. ~As so illustrated, even lords have a difficult time getting our offspring to submit to magic. Salistra has her quarterly dedications, but where there used to be dozens striving for each spot, now there is barely any competition. Does anyone have any ideas?~

I kept my mouth firmly clamped shut. I had no idea how to address population growth in the realms. I still didn't understand what parts were static and which were fluid. They were both and neither at the same time.

~That being said, creating another four to five pocket glades would use a great deal of magic, especially if they are filled with growing things so magic could seep into it and flood the area. Chaos has been working on that.~ He nodded toward Chaos. Bob seemed to swell, though it was hard to tell with an amorphous blob. Esmere didn't move, but her whiskers were flat against her face.

~We need others to do this. It is a commitment of a few decades, but it will help give magic something to flood and fill, which will prevent it from spilling over into Earth.~

Tirsane seemed to shrug. The ones with her barely seemed to be paying attention, but you could never tell.

At the lack of reaction, Brix huffed and continued. ~The last option is to build more great works. Those disturb the design of the realm or pocket area and magic has to flow into the work to resolve the changes. These are like the Arena of Order. If each realm built a new one, it would absorb large quantities of magic.~

This had a few heads perking up, but even though Zmaug seemed bored with the proceedings, she still had smoke trickling out of her nose.

Brix's wings flapped once. ~We must do something and none of you have anything useful to suggest.~

"I could always ask Tirsane to quit collecting magic from humans on Earth that would otherwise be killed." The words slipped out and hit the room like a shotgun blast.

SEVENTEEN

The death of Hishatio Yamato has created a wave of sorrow across large parts of Japan. Hishatio was well known as the Maiyutsu-shi for the Emperor for years. A large funeral is being planned to honor him. The Emperor was quoted as saying-"He [Hishatio] was the one who found the way to seal our borders and while it didn't work due to the cost in Japanese lives, the effort changed our country. He will be missed. We fully expect his funeral to be attended by representatives from all over the world as is due his legacy." ~ CNN Mage Focus

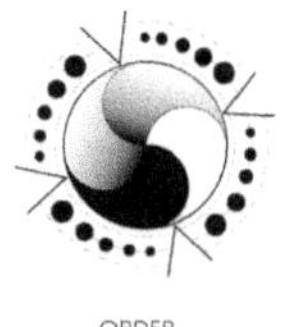

ORDER

I hadn't moved from the chair, though I was beating my head against a wall mentally. Apparently, keeping my mouth shut wasn't one of my skills.

Every head in the room had snapped in my direction. The only one I cared about was Tirsane—from this distance her face was still a perfect mask, but her snakes were waving gently. I took that as a positive.

~What are you talking about?~ Every word from Brix felt like a knife jab in my brain.

"Oh, you weren't aware? I'm sorry. I thought you knew everything that was going on." I kept my tone normal and almost apologetic. Behind me, I heard Shay choking.

~Obviously not. Explain.~ It took everything I had to not wince at that. But I didn't follow up on the words. I just smiled.

"A few years ago, I made a request of Tirsane to take the magic of someone that was about to be killed because she couldn't use her magic the way the government believes it should be used. Tirsane asked if I wanted her to do that for anyone that either due to mental or health reasons was at risk of dying by our laws. I was desperate and said yes." I lifted up one shoulder, still slouched in the chair, though next time I was bringing a more comfortable club chair.

Or I could transform this.

The idea flickered through my mind and I focused on the chair. Here magic was even easier to do, as I could touch all of it. The image of the club chair in my study held firm in my mind, I offered to Magic. With barely any cost, the chair changed and I settled down in my rich leather chair. "Ah, much better."

"We can do that?" I heard Shay mutter.

~Tirsane, why did you not tell us? Do the other lords know? ~ Brix demanded, though I noted his words weren't stabs of pain this time.

"You never asked, and when I tried to tell you, you told me it wasn't my turn to speak. You just went on about how Magic was so rich here and overflowing because we weren't using it properly. I didn't see any reason to fight to disabuse you of that notion." She shrugged in an elegant manner that I could never copy. Her snakes were braided back and none of them were looking at the phoenix. "And of course, they know. I have been dumping magic into them and their realms. It is just more than we realized, hence why it is bursting from all the realms."

I'd never seen a bird splutter before and I had to fight not to laugh. That wouldn't gain me anything.

~Why did you not say something when I brought this up?~

"Because it didn't change the problem. I can't keep all the magic I've been absorbing, and now it is too much for the realms, so the problem is still the same."

Brix whirled to face me. ~Make her stop. We can't deal with this influx of magic.~ These words sounded like they were pulled from him. I just didn't know if it was asking me or admitting they couldn't handle the magic amounts.

"It won't do any good," Tirsane said before I could reply. "I've tried to stop. I set it into motion, assuming it was going to be a small power boost. The number of people this affected made me drunk for weeks. But the magic has fused into a pipe I can't shut off. Magic won't let go for reasons I do not understand."

Zmaug had lifted her head, looking interested for the first time.

Brix hopped up and down on the perch, wings flailing and fire licking around. ~Council is dismissed.~ The words were still ringing in my mind when he vanished in a flash of angry flames. It was like a wire had been cut and various beings laughed or disappeared.

"Come on. This is part of the problem," I said to Shay and

Amadahy as I headed over to Tirsane. They followed behind me like lost chicks.

"Tirsane, what was that all about?" I asked, standing in front of her.

"Brix thinks Brix knows best. I tried twice to explain. Even Salistra mentioned something, but Brix blew past all our explanations. It was easier to let it be run like this. Like I said, we still need to deal with the magic that is flooding us."

"Argh. And me?"

"Games. Salistra surprised me, but you can ask her." Tirsane bent to peer at my new marks on my arms. They didn't really qualify as tattoos, as there was no ink involved, but still. The unicorn horn had one section filled with a pearly dark pink. On my right arm, the symbols of the realms created a line of power. I stared for a minute and my joining band around my wrist popped into existence, then faded.

"You know she won't tell me anything. I'll wait. Somehow, I think she'll be calling in her other debts soon."

~I would talk to you,~ Zmaug said in my head, but I saw Tirsane turn to look at her as well.

I met Tirsane's eyes and nodded. "Come on, let's go talk to Zmaug."

"Wait, we're going to talk to the dragon?" Shay asked, and even Amadahy seemed apprehensive. "I've seen that dragon get pissed and had to throw up a shield when it flamed everyone."

Amadahy nodded. "We have Cath, Aralez, the birds, but the dragons were never involved. The few times we sent representatives, they were eaten."

"Yeah, that sounds like them. She tries to eat me and she'll get the worst case of indigestion she's ever had. Come on." I started that way. Tirsane had already slithered over and rested in a coil talking to Zmaug.

"Zmaug, this is Shay and Amadahy and her apprentice

Ngarra. Please include them in this discussion." I didn't bother to stand, I just dropped down on the ground. Carelian lay behind me acting like a pillow. "What's up?"

Zmaug blew smoke out at both humans, but then turned her gaze to me. ~You gifted Tirsane this power?~ There was an odd note of hurt in her voice.

I sighed. "That is not exactly the right way to look at it. I asked for one girl to be rescued. She asked if I wanted to rescue more than just her and I said yes. The rest is completely on Tirsane. Besides, this was before I met you or Tiantang."

This wasn't me throwing Tirsane under the bus. Simply the truth. I had no idea how she had done it or why she didn't immediately stop.

"By the time I realized how much magic this involved, the channels were fused, so I've been dumping magic everywhere. Why?" she asked, her snakes stretching toward me. I gave in and petted them. They were almost as bad as Carelian. Maybe worse, as so many beings feared her and her snakes.

Zmaug tilted her head. ~Cori, do you remember my explanation about why the quetzo's took so long to hatch?~

"Sure, the magic on Earth is so much lower it took them longer to develop."

~Many of the regions or pockets that we dragons prefer are still magic poor from being created. It is taking longer and longer of late. To the point some eggs are being abandoned.~

Tirsane tilted her head, her brows drawn together. "But they were created eons ago. Surely magic would have filled them back up. I remember when your hatchlings were fast and strong."

Zmaug looked away, smoke wreathing her head. ~Dragons take more magic to live than most. We have absorbed most of the excess to fly and exist. For the first time in a long time our numbers are going down.~ She paused, but I didn't dare speak, waiting. ~It would be appreciated if you have any excess to dump in our realms.~

Tirsane looked at her for a long moment. "Of course. One favor?"

Zmaugs' response was full of teeth and I shuddered. Dragon smiles weren't friendly. ~Two favors that the dragons owe.~

I blinked at that. Not just a personal favor, but a species one. That was rare. Esmere had been teaching me the currency of most denizens and favors or barter were really the only type. This was a huge price.

"I would be honored. I will see you soon. When the magic builds up again." She glanced at me. "If Zmaug's realms are as dry as she says, it should stop the rips from opening, for a while at least. But there is still an issue. The magic influx isn't stopping, and I don't know if it ever will."

"At least it gives us some time." I rubbed my temple. "Any idea when the next meeting is?"

"That is up to Brix. They are called when Brix feels there is enough going on to warrant one." Tirsane looked at me. "We are still friends?"

I stared at her in surprise. "Of course, we are. This is all Brix, and I'm not sure what is going on. I'll have to go talk to Salistra, but later." I stood and nodded at Shay, Amadahy, and Ngarra. "You want to stop at my place and talk or are you done?"

"Talk," came out of all of their mouths before I barely finished speaking.

"Carelian? Home please?" He stood up, stretching, then a sharp pain and a rip sat there. We walked through and were home. "The weather is nice. I need something to drink." I glanced at my watch and sighed. It was barely after noon. It had been a crazy busy day. "But I guess I'm having coffee. You want something?"

They requested their chosen drinks, and I waved to the sun

room as I headed to the kitchen. Ten minutes later, we were all sitting there, drinks in hand and at least some of them looking a bit shell shocked.

"So," Shay said finally. "This means you're on the council."

"Unfortunately, but I owe Salistra too much to be able to deny it. This is going to suck." I sighed and made a mental note to pull something out of the freezer for dinner. If Stephen and Indira were coming over, we'd need more.

Amadahy shook her head. "We were taught to be respectful to the denizens, as you call them. To honor their wisdom. I have spent my time trying to play diplomat, as did Hishatio."

"And I tried to be a wise ass, but they don't react to sarcasm correctly, nor do they get my jokes. It's been exhausting," Shay admitted. His hands were wrapped around a Mexican coffee, as were mine. I felt exhausted, and the day wasn't even near done.

"I told you I wanted merlins for a reason. They respect power, not words. You have to ignore all their posturing." I shrugged. It seemed obvious to me, but then I'd been dealing with them for a while.

"The dragon wouldn't have really incinerated you?" Shay asked slowly.

"Oh, she absolutely would. Her son would be pissed about it, but she'd shrug and point out I had the means to protect myself. It wasn't her fault I was too dumb or slow."

"Oh," he said. Then "Oh shit. Really? I should have called them on everything and shoved it down their throat?"

"Yep." I gave him a wan smile. "They respect blunt power. Lying is a waste of time for almost anyone, as you never can tell who can detect lies, but playing with the truth is a pastime they all enjoy. Never quite lying, but never leaving you with the right idea. The other problem is you play the human card a bit too much."

"Huh?" came from Shay while Amadahy just looked concerned.

"You stay and talk only to yourselves. They wander, butt in, force everyone to treat them as equals or there is a slap, snarl, spell, something to prove they are too dangerous to be ignored. And you don't. You, well, we now, have to go talk to them, bug them, ask them out for drinks afterwards for Merlin's sake."

"They drink?" Shay asked in surprise.

"They are people. They drink or do catnip or whatever. Sometimes it is alcoholic or druggy or it is tea. Many of them like our teas or ciders. The Valkyries prefer craft beers or mead." I'd had the occasion to talk to Frej once or twice over the years. We weren't friends, but friendly.

"Oh."

"We talk about wanting to treat everyone equal, but yet we didn't. I fear the AIN has hidden away from the world for too long." Amadahy's voice was quiet and heavy. "It is time for me to step down. We need new fresh outlooks. I still remember when the sky was free from contrails. That might not be a good thing in this situation."

I revised how old I had thought she was and added another twenty years.

"Now you know. Anything else?"

They asked questions about the rips, a few more about the way to interact with denizens.

"You know, Cori," Shay said as they both rose to go home. I looked at him, waiting. "I'm beginning to understand why the moniker Cori Catastrophe was so accurate. You don't cause problems, you simply attract them." He gave me a wan grin. Then they went home.

I looked at my phone and the multiple missed messages. I didn't bother to respond to any of the messages from Stephen. Instead, I texted Indira.

Dinner? My house? 7? Carelian can come get you.

Excellent. See you then. The text flashed across my screen and I smiled. Indira was so much easier to deal with than Stephen.

CHAPTER

EIGHTEEN

The government has finally decided to deal with these attacks on our country. A task force has been created to address these issues. The military, FBI, and the OMO are working together to address these issues. With luck, they will stop this egregious assault against our hardworking citizens. ~ Pro-magic radio talk show host

SPIRIT

Chaos abounded in the house while Carelian went to get our dinner guests. Vert and Azul were nestled in the kids' hair after spending twenty minutes running around, then gorging themselves again. They'd luckily slept most of the day, and their one feeding Hamiada had taken care of. The two quetzos hadn't figured out how to fly yet, but they thought riding in the hair and flapping their wings was excellent. So far their words were: food, hungry, and mine—all at headache causing levels.

Carelian was working on that.

I turned at the stab of pain to see Stephen and Indira walking in from the sunroom. He was still wearing the same suit as this morning, minus the tie, though he looked as exhausted as I felt. Indira looked gorgeous as always. Silver had crept up at her temples, making it look like she had silver wings. At over sixty, she still looked twenty years younger.

"Cori, how are you?" She swept forward and pulled me into a hug. I returned it warmly. Over the years, she had become a big sister that I enjoyed very much.

"Ask me again after dinner. That is, if he doesn't strangle me." I tilted my head toward Stephen.

He sighed and gave me a hug. "I'm not planning on strangling you, though I wouldn't blame you if you did that to me. I am sorry."

I waved my hand. "It's been a weird day. Explain when everyone can hear you."

By mutual decision, we kept the chatter to life, school, the twins, and their familiars until the steaks, salad, and potatoes were inhaled, and the kids were upstairs with their quetzos. They had decided to read to them, and had books out that they were "reading" to the dragons. In reality, they were making up words to go with the pictures, but it amused them and the quetzo's seemed very excited, or hungry. They were hard to read at this stage.

We gathered in the sunroom, stoking the fire. All of us had adult beverages, mainly because after today I knew I needed one, and I suspected by the time it was over Jo and Sable would be very glad of a few drinks.

"So, explain what that was about, Stephen." I gave him a hard look. I wasn't mad, exactly, but being blindsided like that was annoying, to say the least.

He sighed and buried his nose in his whiskey. "I know I said I had a response team, and I wanted you on it. And as of Friday, that was what I had. First thing this morning, and I mean first, the head of the FBI was calling me at five am." We all winced at that. It was one of the things I was looking forward to the most, a new schedule where I didn't need to get up until after 9 am.

"That five am call told me they had an auditorium scheduled. The general and a report analyst from OMO would be there and they already had sent out the invitations." He took another sip of whiskey, then obviously relaxed his grip on the glass. "I asked what I was supposed to do, and the director said he'd given me the tools. My pet super merlin would be there. I should figure it out and stop this problem. I probably should have called you, but at this point I figured everyone was going to be pissed at me. I might as well have you pissed too. Besides, I didn't know what else to do." He quirked up a side of his mouth. "It turns out having a portal open, a cat the size of a 'horse on steroids' come out and lambast generals is actually a good way to nip issues in the bud."

We all choked, and even Carelian found that funny. Esmere wasn't that large, but I suspected the adrenaline had exaggerated a lot.

"After that I read the director the riot act and told him if he ever pulls that shit again, I'll quit. Then he can find someone new to deal with it. He apologized and said it had been dumped on him too. It turned out someone above both of us from the president's advisors had set it up, then had their star back out. So, they dumped it on me."

"Ah. That makes much more sense now. Joel was way too prepared, as was everyone else, to be that random. But it doesn't solve the problem that I don't know how to stop the rips, though I suspect they are going to fall off for a bit."

"Oh?" Indira said. She held a glass of wine in her hands, twirling it more than drinking it.

I took a deep breath and explained, everything tumbling out, the magic, Tirsane, the dumping, then the dragons.

By the end of it, Stephen looked shell shocked and drained his whiskey. He got up and refilled it, bringing the bottle of Zinfandel back for Indira. She gave it a long look, and I waited for her to grab the bottle and start chugging, but instead she filled her glass all the way up, which all but emptied the bottle.

"Are you saying your desire to save one girl started this domino? And you're now a Lord of Earth to a council that I didn't even know existed, and the dragons want the extra magic dumped into where they live so their eggs will hatch faster," he said slowly, his eyes bouncing between me, Jo, and Sable. To be honest, Jo and Sable were surprised with everything that had changed in one day too.

"Pretty much," I admitted, sipping my gin and tonic. I liked the bitter edge. It reminded me not to get too complacent.

"Cori Catastrophe indeed," he muttered, taking another sip.

A flicker of annoyance bubbled up, but I couldn't really disagree. And here I'd thought I'd left that moniker behind a decade ago.

"I think I understand everything, but from what you said, it is only going to slow down the ruptures, not stop them," he clarified with a far off look on his face.

"Correct. It will completely screw up the calculations done by Joel, but in the end, there will still be a massive issue." That didn't make me happy, especially as I still wasn't sure what the ultimate answer was. There was so much history going on and there was stuff here I didn't understand and that drove me crazy. Unanswered questions usually did.

"Okay. And I can't really tell anyone this. They wouldn't believe me or worse, they would and they'd demand to be on the council and control the information being provided."

Jo laughed out loud. "Ha! Good luck with that. They can plead their case to Zmaug or Brix. They wouldn't return to complain about anything." We all snickered at that.

"What I don't understand," Indira said finally, the level in her wine glass much lower, "is why this is happening? Most of the resources we have are static or renew at a steady rate." I looked at her with a blank look and the others must have too. "As I understand it, there is only so much gold, iron, or coal in the Earth. Once that is gone, we can't effectively make more. But air, food, wood, all of that is replaceable and we know the rates at which we can make it. Which is magic? Most of the mages I've ever talked to just assumed it was a natural thing like a mineral. What is there is there, and your ability to use it is based off your skills."

We all nodded, and my mind started to race, following her logic.

Indira continued in the same thoughtful voice. "But if you say Tirsane is pulling the magic from people, that means it is a live thing that changes and grows. What determines how it grows and is it something we need to stop? Do we use it up? If there is too much, will Earth rupture into the realms? Why now? Why not two hundred years ago? Is that what started all of this in the first place?"

"Argh," I muttered as I took another sip. "I don't know, but I think you're right and there is something we very much don't understand. But I don't get the feeling the council does, or at least not all the council. I can force the issue and ask, but it will be complicated."

"It always is," Stephen said with a smile. "For now, I still need to set up task forces and work with the army, but can you offer classes on shutting down rips? You can open them, right?"

"I guess. They need to be Soul, but I can start running people through. But I can tell you the rips I open are much easier to close than what that rip was." It looked like my retirement was going to be spent going crazy again.

"What do you mean?" Indira leaned forward, looking at me.

I couldn't think of any way to explain, so I showed her. "Here, close this rip." I created a small rip about a foot across to the crossroad area that Carelian used so much.

"That's new," she said slowly.

I blinked and flushed. I hadn't mentioned the full Merlin thing to them. I floundered, trying to come up with a non-lie to tell them, then shrugged. "Yeah. Tirsane pointed something out to me that I am strong in all branches and classes. It's a thing. But I didn't think bringing it to the attention of the OMO or anyone else was necessarily a good thing."

"How long?" This was from Stephen, and I sighed.

"Before the twins were born."

He opened his mouth, but Jo jumped in. "Let it be. She was still in the draft. I know you tend to see people as problems to solve, but she isn't yours. We have first dibs and you don't get to steal her."

Stephen glared at them, then sighed. "Yes, ma'am. " He

turned to look at Indira with a pout. "See, I must be getting old. My glares don't even phase them anymore."

Indira's brow arched up. "I was unaware they ever had."

"Now I'm feeling picked on. You were going to show us something, Cori?" Stephen redirected a side glare at Indira.

Not bothering to hide my laughter at him, I glanced at Indira. "Can you feel the rip? Close it."

She nodded, then a moment later the rip closed. "Okay."

"How much did that cost?"

"Oh, about an eighth of a nail." She peered at her fingers. "This is why I never bother to get manicures."

"Carelian, can you open a rip about the same size?" I hadn't actually tested this, but I had a suspicion.

A flash of pain and another rip. She reached out and closed it, frowning. "That was much more difficult. Were they different places?"

"No, both to a stable neutral pocket. How much more?"

Her brows drew together. "Say a tenth of an inch from all my hair."

"This is just my theory, but I think when magic itself tears the fabric between the realms, you have to be stronger than it was to rip it open. Whereas when we open the rips they are low energy and effort." I shrugged. "But that is just my guess. When Carelian opens them, he does it by imagining a claw ripping open the curtain. I use a sharp knife and minimal effort. Or I'm completely wrong." I shook my head to the chuckles. "Whatever it is, the rips are much harder so you will need fast reacting teams and at least archmages, if not merlins."

"Hmm, that gives me an idea. Enough of that for now. Cori, you okay with the disaster I sprang on you?" Stephen asked, giving me a quirked-up mouth for a smile, but his shoulders were rigid.

"Merlin, no. You owe me. Per Carelian, he says you owe us a deep-sea fishing trip where we get to keep our prey."

The flicker of shock on all their faces, then laughter made me grin.

Stephen laughed the loudest, the stress bleeding away from him. "Deal. Let's get this dealt with, and we'll all go fishing."

The evening ended with laughter and Carelian rhapsodizing over the idea of fresh swordfish.

CHAPTER
NINETEEN

Do we ask enough of mages? We all know any mage over a hedgie is required to do Draft service, but is it enough? Mages after draft are consistently in the top ten percent of all earners in the US. They get jobs that no one else, regardless of their intelligence, could get. They are paid obscenely well, and other than taxes return nothing to their communities. Is this enough compensation for the largess they receive? I don't think so. I think mages should be taxed at higher rates and all their estates that do not go to blood kin should be seized for distribution to the lowest earners in our country. ~ Editorial Opinion

CHAOS

I woke up the next morning way too early for a Tuesday, but my brain was buzzing with ideas. The logic of the rips and the OMO data wouldn't leave my mind as well as an idea about how to deal with getting them closed fast enough.

The coffee maker beeped, and I grabbed my coffee before I slipped into the sunroom to stare at the slowly brightening day.

"Are you okay, Cori?" Hamiada's voice came from my right and I glanced at her.

"Just thinking. Does anyone know the origin of magic? What makes it?"

"Magic just is. Like the air and light. I would not exist without it." She seemed confused by my question and I couldn't blame her.

"Okay. How are your sister-daughters coming?" Jo and Sable were headed over to the house after they got home to decide what remodeling they wanted to do, and what they needed to do before the dryad was planted in the house.

Hamiada's face glowed, with little green leaves tracing along her cheekbones. "They are growing so fast. I think they know they will be planted someplace wonderful."

I grinned. "When do we need to be ready to plant them?"

"Not any sooner than two months, no longer than two years," she said after spinning in a circle for a while.

"I think we can handle that." I heard the sounds of kids getting up and happy hisses of the quetzos, then a ~FOOD~ that cut through my mind. Hamiada winced too. "Yeah, they are loud. Hopefully soon they'll chill out."

"Sister-daughters are much easier. They do not shriek like that." Her eyes narrowed. "Or at least mine will not. "

I laughed and rose to go in and start breakfast, then I had plans that involved a Cath. One hour later, after food, dressing, arguments about "No, you can't take them to school", the house was finally empty. The two dragons were glutted and curled back up in their sand basin snoozing. Zmaug had verified this was normal for the first month. They would grow very fast, but they would primarily eat and sleep.

Carelian had only bothered to bestir himself when he smelled the bacon. "You ready to talk to your mother?"

He flicked an ear at me from where he lay on the floor. I had the fireplace going in the sunroom with all the windows shut, so the heat with the cool autumn view was relaxing.

~Would it matter if I said no?~

"Of course," I said, slightly hurt. "I'm not looking to make you uncomfortable."

~You are a strange creature, my quean. But that is why I chose you.~ He closed his eyes and went back to enjoying the heat.

I pinged Esmere. ~Interested in talking?~ Before I'd finished the words, a tiny slash of pain and she was there.

For the first time, she looked small and I couldn't understand why until I realized she was contained. Her fur flat, tail tucked in, whiskers back. It felt and looked wrong.

I stared at her, trying to figure out where to start, and she just waited. "Can I still trust you? Will you hurt me or my family?"

If I had attacked her, I don't think she could have been more shocked. ~I will never hurt you or your family. Bob and Salistra can both go to the void if they think that would happen. You are mine as much as Carelian is. Family is odd among Cath. Either very tight or almost strangers. But you are my child's quean. I would never hurt you.~

I stood up and walked over to her, then I wrapped my arms around her neck. "I love you, Esmere. I know I'm human, but you are loved just the same. And I will always trust you."

Her purr rumbled through my body as she relaxed into my arms.

~You are the most powerful quean I have ever seen, Cori Munroe.~ Her words were soft.

~See. I choose my queans well,~ Carelian slipped in, his voice smug.

I rolled my eyes as I released her and sat back down. "So, what is going on? I see the problems with the humans and I'll address that. But why did Salistra call in my favor like that and Brix require three? Surely you've had other councilors miss meetings. "

She curled up in a loaf, the light flickering off her fur. ~Yes. But we've had more meetings in the last five years than we've had in the last twenty. Part of it is the magic influx, but Brix is agitated about something and I think Bob knows.~

"Knows what? What does this have to do with me being a councilor?" I rubbed my face, exhausted already with all the political games.

~Cori, you are very direct and honest. We have been playing these games for centuries. I'm not sure that Bob isn't the same as the primordial essence of Chaos that arose when magic did. But he might also be a creature that is a week old. He doesn't talk much to anyone. ~ She looked like she was about to fall asleep but her tail still twitched, occasionally going out to tap Carelian. A soft touch, more of a caress than anything else.

"That I can buy. But Salistra?"

~The horse and I don't talk as much as we once did. She prefers Tirsane, of course most of us do. She is a ... good person, even if she isn't always nice. Most of us aren't. But Brix is your real problem and I don't know what the issue is. Brix is forcing things and no one is fighting back. I've only been on the council for a few decades, and most of them have been snooze fests. I think the last excitement before you came into our lives was

Zmaug and Onyx eating some animals the Valkyries had been raising. That took a week to come to an agreement.~ She laughed in my mind. ~It was amusing. But since you came to Brix's notice, something has changed. But I do not know what.~

I sighed. "Okay. I'll fumble through as usual. But I'm going to push it next meeting. They might not like it."

~Good. Your other councilors are too placating.~

"Yeah. I'll deal. We good?"

~Always. Are the children here?~ Her ears twitched. ~I do not hear them.~

"No, they went to school. But do you want to meet their dragons?" I rose up as I spoke.

~Yes, let's investigate the small dragons.~ We arrived in the room and two little heads, one green, one blue, popped up over the basin, blinking at us. Two sets of wings flapped, spreading sand everywhere.

"This is Vert, and this is Azul." I picked them up one at a time and introduced them to Esmere.

~PLAY!~ The word burst through my mind and I flinched in pain. Anyone that hasn't experienced it can't understand what it is like to have a voice at the decibel level of an air horn screaming words in your mind.

Esmere hissed. ~No! You do not talk like that.~ It wasn't to me, but it felt like she had whacked my nose with her tail. ~Focus on the word and say it. Shouting is not allowed unless it is an emergency.~

~FOOD?~

Another whack on the nose. I started to figure out how she was doing it, which was probably why she was including me.

~That is not an emergency. You are not in pain. No one is in danger. That is a want. Now try again.~

~foOD?~

She whacked again. ~Quiet and focused all the way through

the word.~ I started to see how she was whacking them. It was the equivalent of making a popping sound with your mouth, but directing it as a mental tap at someone. It was odd, but it worked as it felt like a nose bop in your mind.

~Food?~

~Yes. Better. Cori?~

I reached for the little food storage space Hamiada had set up. She'd tried to explain how she kept the food in a vacuum of cold until we opened it. Then the food would be available not in a vacuum, but it made zero sense and I couldn't replicate it. Either way, it worked and kept the food cold. I pulled out slices of fish and chicken for them with the tongs sitting there for that purpose. They inhaled, but the sounds of pleasure didn't make my brain want to bleed.

After the round of gorging, they curled back up to sleep and we went down stairs. ~I will see if I can corner Brix and find out where the antagonism comes from, but I promise nothing.~

"Either way, it doesn't matter. I'll still be a councilor. I'm more concerned with why or what I'm being manipulated toward."

~I agree. I will investigate.~ Esmere hesitated, then looked at me as we stood in the entrance to the sunroom. Carelian hadn't moved, still laying there like a red rug. ~Cori, you are special and unique. I find myself wishing that Magic doesn't change who you are.~ Before I could respond, she was gone.

"What was that Carelian?" I asked, staring at where she had stepped back to the realms.

He rolled over on his back, stretching out and yawning. Inside my head, he replied. ~She was saying she loved you. We don't love the way you humans do. It is rather addictive.~

I don't know how long I would have stood there like that in a state of shock and surprise if my phone hadn't rung.

"Hey Stephen, what's up?" Making separate ring tones for everyone was one of my best ideas.

"So, the Army denied my request for help from their various bases, which means I still have no way to respond correctly. There hasn't been another rip yet, or at least not that I've heard about, but if they do start spewing out more creatures, most humans can't handle them."

The random idea that had flitted through my brain surfaced. "Contact the societies."

"What?" He sounded lost, and I didn't blame him.

"You have all the societies that mostly have people that are out of the draft in them. Put out a call, see if they'll establish a hotline or something. Rip here. Close it and get X from the government. The House of Emrys at least would have a ball getting to study them, as Area 51 is off limits. Most of them are more than strong enough to deal with creatures and close it. Merlin, if I know those mages, you might have people fighting for the chance if you can tell them when and where it is."

There was a long moment of silence on the other end. "I'm not sure why that didn't occur to me. Any other brilliant ideas I can steal?"

"Depends on if you are asking how to close them or if you are talking about something else?" I had moved to stare out at the fountain, proof of my power when I didn't pay attention.

"You have another idea for closing them?" He sounded curious, and while he could be an ass, he was still a good man.

"Create response units with seniors in college. Focus on those in the Spirit track and arrange for them to get credit through the college for responding. There are enough colleges across the nation that the odds of them being closer to an incident are pretty good."

Stephen started laughing. "You sure you don't want my job? You're thinking circles around me."

"Thanks, but not a chance. You are just too lost in the bureaucratic process. You can't break out of it. I'm ignoring all of it and treating it as a game problem where the only things that are impossible are what you haven't tried. But I'm more than happy to accept my consultant's fee."

"Deal. What other words of wisdom do you feel like dropping?" He laughed as he said it.

"Don't know if this is a word of wisdom, but don't you find it very interesting that when the rips have only been happening for a few weeks, the OMO already had all the algorithms figured out and a forecast created? It's almost as if they know how much magic is getting siphoned away by Tirsane."

"Well, I mean," he trailed off. "Do you think they know about Tirsane?"

"Why not? I got questioned about it, I explained what happened. While I might not talk about it, I can't imagine it wasn't reported up the chain."

"But that would mean they have some idea of how many people should be mages or were mages and aren't now."

"Isn't that the entire point of the OMO?"

"Cori. I don't like talking to you. You upset my world view way too much."

I laughed. "Happy to help." He hung up, and I stood there wondering what else was going to happen.

CHAPTER

TWENTY

Troop movements have been spotted in China, Russia, Poland, and the Ukraine. But contrary to normal troop movements where you would see them massing at certain points or borders, these are the opposite. Everything from tanks to SAMs to infantry personnel is being scattered everywhere. While this has been rumored to be a response to rips from the realms, this level of deployment indicates maybe something else is going on. ~ CNN

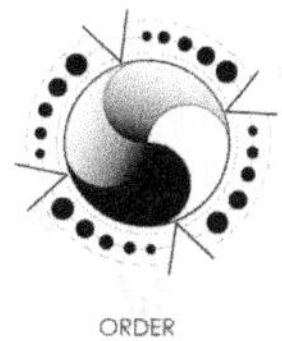

ORDER

E verything stayed quiet for the next few days, though it felt like I was holding my breath the entire time. But nothing ripped, blew up, changed, or fell apart before Saturday morning, which let us start our brand new adventure.

A horn outside the house blew at the agonizingly early seven a.m. However, we had already been up since the even more horridly early six a.m. The group of us tumbled outside, the two quetzos on the kids' shoulders.

Sanchez sat in the driveway behind a huge moving truck, with Marisol waving from the front seat. The smile on her face burned away any lingering concerns we had.

"Sleepy heads, let's get going. We've been driving since three this morning. Someone couldn't sleep 'cause she was too excited." Sanchez grinned and nodded at Marisol.

"Sure, blame it on Mami," Jo said with a laugh, headed toward them. "Back up and go to the Craftsman down the street. It's ready for you." She waved toward the house that was the first one on our street. We'd had a cleaning crew come in and scour it from top to bottom. Then we'd been over in the evenings to get it ready for a dryad.

"Aye, Aye, Capitan!" Sanchez saluted as Marisol laughed and slapped his shoulder. The twins raced after them, the quetzos with their claws anchored in hair or clothing streaming like banners behind them.

The adults moved a bit slower, coffee in hand as we headed there.

"Thank you, Cori," Jo said as we walked.

"For?" I glanced at her, confused.

"You gave the house to Mami. You could have rented it out and made lots of money. Kept it as a retreat. Anything. But you gave it to her."

"Jo." I stopped and pulled on her arm to make her stop with

me. "She has been more of a mother than mine ever was. She is the grandmother of my children. Carelian and Esmere adore her. Why wouldn't I? Money used to be important, but now I can get what I need. So, I'd rather have her here, happy, and get to spend more time with the kids. There is nothing to thank me for. It is literally the very least I could do."

Jo burst out into laughter and pulled me into a tight hug, smacking me on the cheek with a kiss. "Only you would think that, Cori. We are the luckiest people in the world to have you as part of our family." She held me and I sank into it. It felt good in a way only my heart understood.

"Hey, you two coming? Or are you going to let us do all the work?" Sanchez yelled from the driveway.

Jo yelled back. "Let you do it all, of course. That's what brothers are for." But we sped up our walk and got there about the time he had the doors open to the back of the moving truck and Marisol was inside, pointing out where things should go.

The only magic any of us knew to making things lighter was Air, and Marisol threatened to never cook for us again if we did that. Control wasn't something easy with air. We lifted it all the hard way. But three hours later, everything was in the house.

It was a decent sized Craftsman house with simple details, but having seen how Hamiada changed our house, I had no doubt it would become more intricate as time went by. On the main floor was a master bedroom with ensuite, open living room leading to the kitchen, a half bath, and a study. It had a big front porch and a smaller back one that Jo and Sanchez had already decided needed to be a sun room like ours. Downstairs were what had been created as a bathroom and two bedrooms, but the previous owners had made it into storage and a laundry room. Perfect for what we needed.

"Are you ready?"

I turned to see Hamiada at the backdoor peeking in.

"Marisol? Are you ready to plant and take care of a dryad?" I asked rather than answering for her.

Marisol stuck her head around the corner. Dressed in jeans, a t-shirt, and a scarf over her head, she looked about ten years younger than she had two months ago. "If you are ready, Hamiada, then I am." She smiled, but swallowed nervously. "I hope you'll help me take good care of your child."

Hamiada's smile revealed moss green teeth, with joy radiating out of her. "I know you will. It will be good to create a grove here on Earth. Shall we?"

We traipsed down the stairs to where we'd plant Elina. Over the last few weeks, Sanchez, Jo, and Hamiada had created a hidden room in the basement that was a haven for a tree. Water systems, UV lights until she got older, food, and rich soil. Hamiada had worked to alter the framing of the house so that her sister-daughter could grow into it, become it. There was much I didn't understand on how it worked, but she seemed very certain and was glowing. After this, they would start the same process on the Tudor house, but there was much more work to be done there. Hamiada was okay with waiting, as it was such a big house she wanted her child to mature a bit more before separating her.

As far as I could gather, dryads didn't seed, they sent out saplings. Normally they treated these like extra limbs, but they could choose to make the sapling fully independent of their systems. That action created a child. All in all, I had to admit it sounded less stressful than being pregnant for nine months.

The small room was behind a hidden door, which entertained all of them greatly when they created it. It looked just like a wall when you came down the stairs and there was nothing to indicate anything else should be there. Right next to the stairs was a light switch that turned on the lights. But if you pressed gently on the wall right above it, the door unlatched and swung inward. It had me grinning too.

We all moved in. The kids were losing energy after moving things into the bedroom and unpacking boxes. But still, everyone wanted to see the start of Elina's life. Even Carelian followed, though I think it was more boredom than any real level of interest. Besides, maybe there would be a mouse to chase.

On the far wall, a divot in the floor sat waiting. They'd torn up the concrete there to expose the earth underneath. There was a low wall around it holding soil, with bags of fertilizer stored across the room. Water was set to drip in when moisture contents got too low, and alarms were set to Jo's phone if nutrients needed changed. It was an odd mix of high-tech and magic, since magic was about to be planted here.

"Yes. This is an excellent environment for my sister-daughter." She spun, fading away as we watched, then a minute later stepped back in holding a sapling. The stick of green had leaves and small branches, but it was only about as thick as two fingers put together, though half my height. She moved over to the calf high wall and nestled the sapling in. Her hands moved dirt up and around it, like a mother tucking in a child for sleep.

"Water?"

"Here." Jo handed her a small hose that was connected above the water sensor system and turned it on.

Humming softly, she soaked everything down, then added a bit more dirt and dampened it. "There. That should feed her. I don't think she'll wake, but would you like to see her?"

I glanced at everyone, but they looked as confused as I felt. "See her how?"

She laughed, the sound of leaves in the trees. "Come, I will show you." With a wave of her hand, a door appeared, and she opened it to her glade.

"Why do you do doors? Everyone else does tears in reality?" I asked as we followed her through. Her glade glittered in the diffuse light, even the leaves on the trees seemed to be sparkling with extra brightness.

Hamiada rotated as she floated across her glade to her trees. "Carelian hasn't told you?"

~I am not sure I know. I don't believe I have ever created a door,~ he said, ears flicking forward as he stalked over to a shady spot.

"Rips are either open or closed. With a door, the portal is there, but I can control who enters or exits." She had moved over to a set of three trees. One was huge, tall and straight, the other two were younger, both with large boles in their trunks, about three feet off the ground. It almost looked like they had huge balls in the middle of them, but the wood was smooth, almost supple.

~That is both obvious and elegant. I need to remember to tell Malkin.~ Carelian sounded surprised, and I couldn't blame him. It was obvious, and I'd never thought about it. I'd have to see if I could create doors.

"This is me. Or my essence." Hamiada laid a hand on the largest tree. Obviously a deciduous, with bright green leaves just starting to turn orange, it held a position of importance in the glade I was just beginning to see. Everything radiated out from this tree. I suspected if I could fly, I would see a spiral pattern to the glade. Either way, I couldn't ever remember seeing it before.

"This has always been hidden, hasn't it?" Sable asked this as she walked up, arm in arm with Marisol, who looked around at everything with awe. If she'd ever been to a glade or pocket realm before, I didn't know it.

"Yes. I do not share my true self with many. I can be harmed here." She just stated it as a fact and I had to resist going over to hug her and promise her we never would.

~You know my queans would never do that. I choose queans well. Their family is honorable too.~ Carelian's words helped cut the weight of those words.

"I know. That is why I am willing to share. This one here is Elina. She will wake soon." She touched the other tree. Hamiada traced her hand over the bole, and bark and flesh peeled away. Cradled in the tree was a little girl dryad. Her skin was supple green like a new branch, her limbs still undefined, and her face oddly smooth. "Another few months and she'll feel the house around her. Her leaves will be the roof shingles pulling in the sun. Soon she will wake with a sense of who she will be."

I couldn't take my eyes off the child nestled in the tree. I turned and stared at Jo. "Next time you decide you want kids, talk to Hamiada. That looks much more pleasant."

The adults choked, and Jo grinned at me. "Nah. This way, when they are bad, I can tell them to go talk to Momma Cori. Besides, you love them."

Two sets of brown eyes peered up at me with wide eyes, the quetzos on their shoulders mimicking their actions. "You do love us, Momma Cori?"

I moved over and kissed to tops of their heads. "More than Magic. It is mostly teasing your moms."

They both cast me sideways looks, but Hamiada moved and pulled our attention away. "This one will be my other sister-daughter, Zelinka." The tree she stroked had thicker bark, and somehow it just seemed like a different tree. I was no expert on trees, but if I had to guess, I would have said Hamiada and now Elina were poplar trees, with vaguely heart-shaped leaves and silvery smooth bark. This tree looked different. Its bark was grooved with lines, the leaves more fernlike and spread out, and already it looked like it would grow to be huge.

"Hamiada, is Zelinka different from you and Elina?" Marisol asked as we moved to stare at the trees. The bole where Elina lay had closed back up. She didn't open up the bole where I assumed Zelinka was curled.

Hamiada smiled. "Yes. Usually sister-daughters are you, almost clones in your words. But if we try, we can either cross pollinate, our version of sex, or we can graft a child." The kids giggled a bit at sex, but dropped it at glares from the three of us.

"Oh," Marisol said, her face lighting up. "I've been reading up on trees. Like how you might put a pear branch into an apple tree."

"Yes, I believe so. This is a mixture. I took my seeds and traded with a dryad far from here. We merged and exchanged. I'd been hoping you would someday take over your Tudor house." She stumbled a bit over the word Tudor. It was such an odd word. "It was so much bigger. I thought it would need a dryad who was strong and unique." Her hand caressed down the trunk, but this one didn't split open. "She will be a dawn redwood. It should give her strength to guard the house for centuries."

I made a quick mental note to look up what a dawn redwood was.

"You amaze me, Hamiada." Sable said, releasing Marisol's arm and walking over to her. "Thank you for everything." Slowly Sable reached out and offered a hug. Little leaves of green traced down Hamiada's arms, but she reached out just as slowly.

I fought back tears as they hugged and couldn't believe how lucky I was with my life.

CHAPTER
TWENTY-ONE

Calling on merlins with strong Spirit, specifically Relativity. Task forces are being formed in all areas of the United States as emergency response units to close rips. Congress has passed an emergency budget to pay for these units. Everyone that joins will be paid a monthly stipend to reward their on-call status. For all responders that help to close a rift, a bounty will be paid. Contact ripresponse@dmc.gov ~Notice sent out to all the societies.

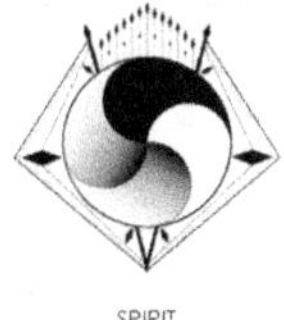

Everything had been going so well the last few weeks that it felt odd. Tirsane had offloaded magic into the dragon pockets. No meetings had been called, no rips had appeared, and all the reports that had been created by the OMO were wrong. Life was good.

Given the quiet, I felt like I could risk taking the time to pry information out of Salistra, but first I had to get her to talk to me. I'd pinged three or four times and got no response. I had the definite feeling she was avoiding me and I needed to figure out what her game was. She wasn't a friend, but she was more than an acquaintance.

~I do not know where Salistra lives. I have never had a reason to visit her. Malkin might,~ Carelian said when I asked. It was early November, and we were already planning a huge Thanksgiving at the Tudor house. Jo, Sable, and the kids were going to move over there next weekend and the dinner would be the first event held there.

They had spent a fortune on the new furnishings and getting it ready, but they both were so excited it radiated from them. The twins went back and forth, especially since Hamiada couldn't or wouldn't plant Zelinka until winter solstice. Why that day I didn't know, but she just shook her head. And until Zelinka was planted, there was no door between the houses.

Granted, a half-mile walk wasn't that far, but when it was five degrees outside, that seemed like forever. It was Saturday, and everyone else was over at the Tudor house tossing ideas out for the final week. Or the kids were and Jo and Sable were trying to keep their wants somewhere in the realm of possibility.

Carelian and I were lying in bed. I was reading a medical journal, leaning against him while he provided more heat than I needed.

"I can do that." I focused, then pinged Esmere. ~Evening. Would you have an address or location for Salistra? I need to talk to her.~

It could take a while for her to respond, so I picked up the magazine.

~No,~ she replied almost immediately. ~While I know her and we are...friendly, I have never been to her glade, as you call it.~ There was something else lingering in her tone, but I couldn't figure out what.

~What else would I call it? And who would know?~ I asked.

~Tirsane probably. Most of the senior lords interact. Or I suppose you could ask Bob, but I wouldn't suggest that.~

I flinched and gagged at the same time, just thinking of how much it would hurt to speak with Bob.

~Tirsane I think. You are coming over for Thanksgiving, right?~

~Do you really think I would miss such a food extravaganza as that? Of course. Besides, I wish to see the new abode and it has been too long since I have seen the children. Have they grown much?~

~Too long? You saw them last week. Remember, human children grow slowly. Look how long it has been since they were born. In two years Carelian was almost this size, and they are almost seven.~

It amused me how fascinated the realm denizens were with the kids. They treated them both as miracles and the most amazing toy ever.

~Yes, but they still change,~ she responded vaguely, and I narrowed my eyes but she couldn't see me. ~However, ask Tirsane. This information I do not have and it is not mine to share.~

That I understood.

~Very well. All the love.~ I grinned as I said that.

The amused humph just added to my humor.

~You do realize you confuse most of us.~ Carelian stretched a bit, making me tilt to one side.

I sank my fingers in and scratched. "I sure do. That is half the fun."

~And you say Cath are sadistic?~ He was laughing as he said it.

It was only five in the afternoon. I'd ping Tirsane and see if she would share, but the way Esmere had sounded made me think I was about to run into odd complications. I still knew there were cultural issues that I wasn't aware of. Oh well. The only way to find out was to do.

~Tirsane, do you have a moment?~ I leaned my head back, enjoying his rumbling purr.

~Yes, Cori?~ I could almost see her snakes perk up just from her voice.

~Would you have time for Carelian and me to come see you? ~

There was a long pause. ~Come see me?~

~Yes? Unless you don't want us to. I mean you can come here.~ The note of surprise in her voice made me blink. I'd been to Esmere's place, Zmaug's, Hamiada's, but I'd never been to Tirsane's. A flush of sheer embarrassment rushed through me. It had always been my place. How could I have been so oblivious all these years? Some friend I was. ~I would love to come see you. Fifteen minutes?~ There was no way I was going to show up for the first time to Tirsane's place and not bring a hostess gift.

~That would be nice.~ The bemused tone still hung in my mind, even as I was up and changing clothes.

"Come on. We are going visiting and I need a gift." I had two ideas in mind, and would probably grab both.

I grabbed my phone and called Jo. "Jo? I'm headed over to see Tirsane. Will be awhile probably."

"Sounds good. Pizza for dinner later? We're exhausted."

"Works for me, but don't wait if I'm not back by the time you need to eat. You know how it goes."

"Yep. You disappear for a hundred years though, and I'm going to be annoyed. No way am I doing Christmas and dealing with family and the kids, quetzos, and Esmere all by myself."

Laughter slipped out. "Promise, no disappearing for a hundred years."

"See ya," she said, and I heard the kids yelling "pizza, pizza" in the background.

I changed clothes into jeans and a soft t-shirt, braided my hair into a thick ponytail braid, then hit my present closet and grabbed what I'd thought about, then I headed to the memento room. Even after all that time, it stayed like a museum, but I was starting to think I needed to change that.

"What do you think, Carelian, should I start to return these things? I was thinking we could make this into something for us both."

He blinked up at me, still stretching as he walked. He would elongate, then catch back up with his head. It was rather amusing.

~That might be wise. There are many things in there that are precious, but the memory stones are yours. You have time now to learn the secrets they hold. But I would not give gifts as freely as you are.~ His voice was hesitant as he said that.

He was right about the secrets. I'd almost forgotten about them. My mind always locked on the statues of the other heralds that had chosen poorly. I pushed open the door and stared at them. These I'd gladly get rid of, except I still didn't know what to do with them. They were people, or at least had been. I hated the idea of treating them like statues, even if they were. So, they sat here, hidden warnings to me.

I'd been through most of the memory or learning stones, but there were two that I just couldn't sink into. The way of thinking was too different. I doubted James had ever gone through them. He in some ways had been a hoarder. It just reminded me I needed to try to get rid of more stuff.

"Don't be silly, you give gifts when you go over to someone's house the first time. It's kinda rude not to. You think Tirsane would like this one?" I pointed to one that looked almost like sea glass. It had a slippery feel that reminded me of her snakes. The mind had been cold, large, and viewed the world as something to combat. There had been magic there, Spirit magic, but it had seen everything as either food or obstacle and I just couldn't do it. Of course, if it was a dragon, Zmaug would be annoyed, but it didn't feel like a dragon to me.

~Possibly. If nothing else, she might know better whose mind it was or is. There are beings out there that sleep for ages compared to your life spans.~ He wandered through the room, tail twitching along the statues. He didn't seem to trust them anymore than I did.

I grabbed it and dropped it in my pocket. "Ready?"

~Yes.~ We headed to the sunroom to leave. It just seemed easier and not as rude to create doors in the house. I wasn't sure why I felt that way, but I did.

~Tirsane? Location?~ I asked, as we didn't know where she was. An image of a pool by the water with a feeling of her magic came through. Carelian nodded and opened a rip. We stepped through to the scene in my mind. A blue sky with blue water burbling nearby, the ground white sand. Warmth caressed me, hot enough I wanted to change to shorts. The light was the same as it had been in all the realms, the warmth diffusing over everything. I turned to see that we were in a courtyard. Ahead was a building made out of the same white stone as the rest of the area.

The courtyard walls were about seven feet high and covered with vines with heart-shaped leaves with small berries.

"Cori, welcome to my home." I finished turning to see Tirsane curled around an odd chair with another chair near a table. The table had olives, cheese, and a carafe of something clear.

"Your home is gorgeous. It never occurred to me that I'd never visited you," I said as I moved over toward her. Carelian prowled along, nose and whiskers twitching.

"I must admit, I prefer to visit Earth. The warmth of the sun is oddly addictive. But please sit," she waved at the chair. "Would you like to try grappa?"

That derailed my thoughts. "Grappa?"

"It is a human drink that was popular when my family was on Earth. I still enjoy it." She poured a small amount into the glass on the table in front of me, then some for herself.

Derailed and curious, I sipped it. I blinked as the alcohol slammed into me. "Whoa. That is strong."

"Oh?" She sipped and smiled, her obsidian teeth gleaming. "I've always found it refreshing, though I do love your citrus drinks." She set the small crystal glass down. "So, what is going on?"

That got me back on track. "First, I wanted to bring you a hostess gift. I'm sorry that I never did before. I thought maybe you could use it in the council meetings. The snakes seem a bit cold at times." I reached into the daypack I'd grabbed and pulled out the gift, handing it to her.

Surprised, she took it, something flickering across her face. She removed it from the small bag and opened up the six-foot emerald green silk scarf. All the snakes were peering around her head, hissing in excitement and delight.

"This is gorgeous," she said slowly. There was a tone under there I couldn't understand. "How would I wear this?"

"Oh, here. May I?" I stood at her nod and took the scarf from her, then I wrapped it loosely around her head, the snakes tucked underneath, but able to slip out if they so desired. "See?"

She uncoiled from the stool and went to peer at herself in the water and smiled. "That is lovely. I never thought about it. But it would explain why they are much more sluggish and love when I wear one of the hoodies you gave me."

Hoodies had become a standard gift, though personally I still thought the sheer one Sable had found last year was hilarious. Tirsane had laughed and immediately put it on, much to most of the men's consternation.

"Good. Here I also brought you this. I'm not sure what it is, but I thought maybe you would enjoy it more than me." I pulled out the glass stone and handed it to her.

There was the oddest wince, but she took it with a smile. "Oh." Her eyes got wide as they unfocused. Her snakes writhed, but I couldn't tell if it was happy or sad writhing. After what seemed forever—I'd even dared to take another sip of grappa— she focused back on me. "Where did you get this?"

"No clue. It was in the memento room James had. There are all sorts of things in there. Honestly, most of the time we forget about it, even though the door is right there." It was almost like half the time it didn't want to be found.

"Ah. This is impressive and I have no idea how he got it. I'm almost more impressed it exists." Her eyes narrowed, but she didn't follow up on whatever thought that was. "It is the memory stone of a great serpent. There are only a few that I even know of. I wonder what he had to trade to get this."

"I'm not sure. But if I ever find it in his journals, I'll tell you."

Tirsane nodded and picked up her glass, watching me, two

snake heads peeking out of the scarf, flicking their tongues at me.

The silence carried for a minute and for the first time in a long time, I felt off balance. "I wanted to see if I could get Salistra's address from you."

"Ah. And what are you willing to pay for that information?"

"Huh?" I stared at her, completely lost. "Pay? Pay for what?"

CHAPTER

TWENTY-TWO

Do you want to be a mage? Is your window for emerging disappearing? Contact Mage Creators for help. Our specially trained archmages will stimulate your body's neurons to help you to emerge as a mage and raise your potential to the stratosphere. All rights reserved, results are not guaranteed, and this advertisement does not constitute a legally binding agreement. ~ Mage Creators Ad

---

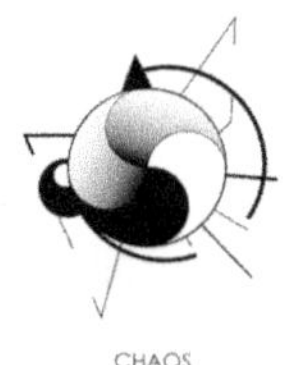

CHAOS

Realization flickered across her face and she took another sip. "Cori, how many things have you ever asked of us denizens?"

I blinked, confused by her question. "Asked how?"

"Help, assistance, favors." Her face was serene as she asked me, but two more snakes snuck out, staring at me.

"Oh, um." I thought. "I don't know that I've tracked the number of things. I know I've asked things of Jeorgaz, I guess. Baneyarl a little. Carelian, of course. Esmere, I guess. I meant I talk to you and the others in councils. Why?"

Tirsane nodded slowly and twisted the crystal glass in her hand, the light sparkling off of it. "You know we don't use money, correct?"

"Sure." I picked up one of the olives and ate it, trying to give myself something to concentrate on.

"We deal in favors, trades, items. Jeorgaz, as he was your master's familiar, is exempt."

"James wasn't my master," I blurted. "In any sense of the word."

Tirsane chuckled a bit. "But he left you his property and his magical items. As far as magic is concerned, he was the master, and you were the apprentice." I frowned at that, but didn't interrupt. "Which means you can ask anything of Jeorgaz without needing to pay for it. Esmere is your familiar's mother. While she could have required payment for any favors, she had the freedom to choose not to."

I stared at her, completely lost. "You mean anything I ask for has to be paid for?"

Tirsane shrugged. "Yes and no. If you ask me to pour you more grappa, no." She waved at the grappa. "If you asked me for a bottle to take home, yes."

I nodded slowly, thinking. "What about Baneyarl?"

"He was your teacher, something he agreed to as a favor to Esmere. Did you ever ask her what that cost?"

"It never occurred to me." I looked at Carelian. "You knew, didn't you, about all of this?"

~Of course. It was why I often did the communication. You asking questions about things you had been tasked with would not generate a cost. You asking for something else would. I avoided you needing to.~

My eyes widened. "What did it cost you?" Images of him being flayed alive slammed into my mind and heart.

A soft chuckle. ~Nothing I had an issue paying. The cost isn't always great.~

I reached out to touch him. The idea of him being hurt for my stupidity made me crave the feel of him.

"Okay, what do you want?"

Her smile had a tinge of sadness to it and the snakes pulled back. "If I had realized how much you still applied human culture to our actions..." She sighed letting the thought fade away. "In the future, as much as I adore your generosity, come and ask, then offer the scarf, the gift. I've been able to participate in your Christmas traditions as they tend to be exchanges. As it is, most don't know what to make of you. You give so freely. I should have told you sooner, but I had thought Esmere would have."

"Why didn't she?"

~She assumed I would or had.~ Carelian laid his head down on his paws. ~I didn't want you to change, to become someone that put a price on everything. Besides, most of it was Magic driven, so you didn't have to pay a price. You are the Herald. There is more leeway for you than most. Future goodwill drives a lot of actions.~ He had his eyes closed and wouldn't look at me.

I sighed, but kept petting him. "What you are saying is that if I had asked the question and then offered the gift, that I wanted to give you regardless, it would have been a fair trade."

"More than. But you gave, without asking. Which I still find amazing, but it is what it is. You don't give things away for free."

I thought back to the price Zmaug agreed to. At the time, I assumed it was politicking. Future favors, trying to keep things on the same level. Not an actual price.

"So Salistra and Bob both paid you for the magic you dumped in their realms?"

"Yes, handsomely." She took another sip of grappa. "Salistra is supplying hair from her mane and tail to a weaver group of Chitterians for a bedspread for me. It will take two years for her to shed that much. Bob will work with me to create some new spaces. Chaos works better than Spirit to pull magic into new and unusual forms that are livable."

"Ah." It felt wrong to pay for something, something that I would have given freely, but I'd learned the hard way that this was their culture and my assumptions didn't work here. The horn on my arm reminded me every time. "Then what would you like for the request?"

Tirsane smiled. It was a bit sad, yet humor lingered at the edges. "I still owe you three favors. They would garner you almost anything from me."

I glanced down at the snake on my arm and shook my head before I finished thinking about it. "No. Those... I...." I looked up at her, biting my lip. "I would prefer to never use them, but if I must, it would be for something I have no other way to pay for."

Tirsane nodded, her snakes hissing in what I thought was delight. "That is a wise choice. Normally you state what you are willing to pay, but for this time..." she trailed off, looking thoughtful. "This courtyard is new and still barren. Do you have any statues you might not want?"

I blinked rapidly and then glared at Carelian. "Do you want-" his tail whapped me hard, and I stuttered to a stop. I'd been about to offer all three, too much for this simple ask. "I happen to have some statues I have no need for. Would you be interested in one of them?"

A slow smile started at the edge of her face. "Why, yes. I believe I would. How about the arrogant male?"

"That can be arranged. Do you need it now, or may I finish my business with Salistra first?" It felt like an elaborate game, but at the same time it almost made sense to me and gave me clues as to the other issues the councilors were having with us and us with them.

"I trust you greatly. Let me know when you are ready to deliver him."

My eyebrows rose at the pronoun, but I didn't say anything about that. "I am honored by your trust."

"It has been well earned." Her smile was broader now. "I will gladly provide her location. Would you like me to let her know you are coming?"

Since I didn't actually know Salistra, for all that she seemed to be more intimately involved in my life than I would have preferred, I'd never dared to ping her.

"Which would be the wiser option?" I was pretty sure that didn't require a trade, as I was asking her opinion, not for something. I hoped.

She tilted her head, the snakes slipping out and hissing. "It depends. If you wish to fight your way through and prove to her you should not be trifled with, then don't. If you think letting her believe she is the one that has something you want, then I would let her know. More grappa?"

I shook my head as she poured herself more. If I drank what was still in my glass, I was pretty sure I'd be drunk. The stuff had to be at least a hundred proof.

~Carelian?~ I whispered to him. There were advantages in both ways.

He hesitated for a minute. ~Tirsane. Does Salistra have contempt for Cori?~

"Cori specifically? No. Cori is an interesting tool, though I do not know how she plans on using her." Tirsane nodded at my left arm and the tattoos there.

There were days when I wondered how long it would be until I had a neck tattoo, which I didn't want at all.

~Don't tell her. Let Cori prove she is not a pawn in their games. I suspect the council will figure that out soon enough.~ Carelian mentally smirked as he said that. If only I had as much faith in myself as he had in me.

~Very well. Here is her address.~ A mental impression, a taste of magic.

~That will work. Cori, I do have an idea about this. But you need to address her from a position of power.~ Carelian was sitting up staring at the featureless sky as he spoke. He could navigate by the impressions, something I'd never heard of a human being able to do.

"And how do I do that?" This was almost worse than China.

"Knowing Salistra, she has defenses. Go through them without damaging but making it clear that she couldn't stop you if she wanted to."

I cast Tirsane a look. "So this sort of advice you can give?"

"Of course. It might be wrong, I might be lying, it could just be speculation. Now, if you had asked me to tell you all the defenses around her place, that would cost you."

A sigh escaped. "It seems awfully variable."

"No better or worse than how relationships work around your world. Carelian won't let you be steered wrong and, thinking about it, you haven't needed to know this until now. Every other interaction has been as a friend trying to help, not someone trying to do something. And you gave Zmaug a gift she will never forget, so she pretends everything is part of what she owes you."

"Oh." That made a lot of things clearer. And I could see that returning her son to her, if I had asked for a boon, would have been enormous. "Is it insulting to say I prefer you better as a friend, not someone dealing with the Herald?"

"No. I take that as a compliment and will do my best to stay as a friend."

I rose, ready to talk to Salistra. "What did Frej cost you?"

Tirsane waved her hand. "It cleared up an old debt that Freya owed me. I had it for decades and never used it. It was nice to get rid of it."

All the questions Esmere and Tirsane had asked for me. The favors and exchanges they had done for me, without ever letting me realize there was a price. All this time I'd thought it was like going to the library or maybe talking to the wisemen in villages. I owed them so very much.

Tirsane had risen too as I stood. I smiled and moved over, hugging her tight. She stiffened, then relaxed in the hug, the snakes giving me soft lick kisses. "Thank you for everything," I whispered, then released her and stepped back. A flush covered her upper body, but a smile graced her face.

"May Magic be with you," she said.

Carelian opened the rip to Salistra's, and we left the warmth and comfort of Tirsane's home.

Given that Salistra was a horse, I'd expected wide plains, grass, gently rolling hills. That wasn't what I walked into. A grove of tightly packed trees with a single path leading toward a mountain. Or at least I assumed it did, as I couldn't see through the trees, but the mountain rose high over them.

The path was the obvious route and I couldn't see any other

means. The trees were so close together, even Carelian couldn't slip through.

"Should have made you wear your harness. Next time we go anywhere in the realms, you are going to be loaded."

~We can go get it.~

I tilted my head and thought. "No. She knows we are here. Let's go."

~Smart quean.~

"Jerk."

~Your jerk.~

"Always," I said with a laugh and stepped onto the path, only to have my foot sink in as if it was quicksand. I barely hesitated, calling Earth and having my footing solidify. Ten more steps in, spiders dropped down around us, casting webs. A little fire took care of that and they scattered, though I was careful to not actually burn them, just their webs.

"Is it going to be like this the whole way?" I peered at Carelian, who paced a step ahead of me.

~This is probably easy stuff. Meant to warn people away.~

"Well, you told me to blow through her defenses. Might as well."

~Try not to kill anything. Often they are fulfilling favors or debts as well.~

"Great. I get to prove I can move past her magic and yet not harm anyone. You'd better hope all my studying has paid off." I stared at the forest that watched me back, though with more curiosity than malice.

~You are a true quean. Powerful and smart. You will be fine.~

The faith of a Cath, what more could I ask for? With that thought, I started down the path.

CHAPTER

TWENTY-THREE

The rips are a sign that man was never meant to use magic. We don't use it correctly and soon all of us will pay the price. Give up magic now, shear your heads, cut off your nails, and turn your back on the addiction magic is. Otherwise, our world shall surely perish due to our own selfishness. ~ Freedom from Magic

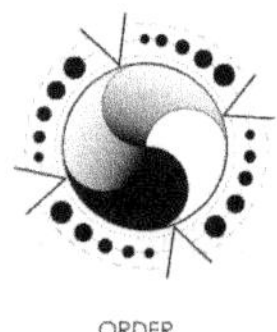

ORDER

The woods around us creaked, and I stopped to listen. I loved the mountains and forests on Earth. Walking through them, listening to the movement of creatures, their sounds, the feel of the air against my face, even the sharp scent of pine.

Here it was different.

There was no breeze to speak of. There were scents, but they seemed to be pale copies, lacking something that most plants on Earth had. And it watched me. At home, occasionally animals would stop and watch us, Carelian usually, but here the woods measured my every step.

I wish I knew how she did that.

Leaves started to drop from the trees and fly toward me. I ducked and one cut into a branch above me. "Ah, getting a bit aggressive, aren't you?" I pulled out Air, who thought this was great fun fighting her sisters, and created a wall of wind whirling around me. Air caught the leaves and flung them back, though not as hard as they could have.

After a few minutes, the leaves faded away and we continued. "This is both too easy and too basic. She is an Order Lord. Why is everything easily countered by elements?" I was talking to myself as much as Carelian.

~She enjoys the long game, and this gives her much information. Be strategic about how you respond. It is meant to deter, but also inform.~

I pondered that a few more steps, then shrieked in surprise as a wall of earth began to form around us. Each brick was three times the size of my hand. They snapped in place quickly until it was fifteen feet high.

After staring at it a minute, there were so many options to take it down, I pulled on Call Mineral and separated out every mineral in the wall into different piles. The bricks crumbled as the various minerals piled up. When there was barely a framework of carbon left, I raked my hands through it and it crumbled into dust.

That had been fun. The offerings weren't much and honestly, I wouldn't mind a bit more as my hair was so freaking long lately. I needed to cut it. With Carelian I could use it even cut and otherwise the headaches were becoming a pain.

Still, the path led on, but a gap in the trees to the right gave me a hint of what was next.

~Ambush coming up,~ Carelian whispered in my mind. I sent back an affirmative response to show I'd heard him but didn't slow down.

A flash of tawny fur and a roar had me diving forward and turning as a manticore pounced. The dark mane filled my vision as Carelian snarled a warning. I had a feeling his advice to not cause harm didn't apply to him. Four pale strips down on the wing grabbed my attention.

"Mi'Kal?" I yelled, half in surprise, half because I really didn't want Carelian to kill him.

The manticore jerked to a halt and peered down at me. ~I know you?~

"Maybe not know me, but Carelian put those scars down your wing." I pointed to his wing and the pale strips where Carelian had healed him.

A twist of that huge leonine head to look at the Cath about to slice his throat. ~Play. I remember.~ He sat back and shook his head and it was almost like a persona fell away or slid on.

~Sorry. What are you doing here? Do you have a pass?~

Carelian snarled, but backed down, licking his claws with a decidedly annoyed air about him.

"Pass, no. I need to see Salistra, and I think she is avoiding me." I looked him up and down. He'd grown a lot in the last few years, definitely not a kid anymore. "What are you doing here?"

~I owed Salistra a favor, so I patrol here. It was my shift.~

His mental voice sounded amused, and I decided not to follow up on what he meant.

"I see. How do we get past you?" I asked as I slowly stood up and brushed the dirt off my clothes.

~Normally, you would have to defeat me, but in this case, I still owe Carelian for healing me. He did not have to.~ I looked at Carelian, but he ignored me. ~So you may continue.~

"You won't get in trouble?"

~No. It is my job to ensure only those worthy to see her get through. I declare you worthy.~

A chuckled escaped. "I see. Can you tell me what I need to do to deal with ahead?"

~I am unaware. This is my area. I patrol until my shift ends, then go home.~

"When does it end?"

~I think another year by your time. I should go. Be well, Herald.~ He rose up to his full height, shook his body and disappeared into the trees.

"This might be harder than it looked."

~You need to impress. Right now, you have just proved you are not easily dissuaded.~ He stretched out, yawning. ~Though I really do need to start hunting bigger prey. My reaction times are too slow.~

There was nothing I could say to that. From my point of view his reactions were lightning fast, but I wasn't him. "Made it this far. Might as well keep going."

The forest faded away as we walked and we found ourselves facing a large chasm, with a river way too far below. There was a bridge stretching over it just wide enough for a single person.

"A balance test?" That didn't make sense, so I moved closer as the color of the bridge changed.

"What?" I moved until I could crouch next to the bridge and

I watched it. It went from granite to lace to concrete to paper to something else. The pattern was the same, strong enough to support—probably strong enough—not strong enough. I timed it, eight seconds for each section. The bridge was about three hundred feet across. Carelian could possibly make it. I didn't have a chance. The river was a very long way down, and while I could probably survive the fall with the assistance of air, I would have failed.

Transformation. That was normally Jo's strongest skill, but I had it strong too.

"Here goes nothing." I reached out with my magic and willed it to turn to steel. For a second it started to change, then flipped back to paper. I offered up more to create steel and held it there, forcing the molecules into the patterns that I wanted. They fought me, trying to twist to other patterns, but I still held.

Until a wave of strength wrested it from me and it changed to glass. Then teased me with steel. We fought trying to change it to the product I wanted, steel, stone, rope, plastic. The longest I could hold any of it was twelve seconds. But that was twelve seconds with me doing nothing but concentrating.

Sweat dripped off my forehead as I sagged back. I could create a volcano in between the chasm, but that might qualify as overkill. How did I breeze past something that was a skill she'd probably practiced for centuries?

The point of this was to show how easily I could beat her at magic, not exhaust myself trying to match her offering for offering. I looked around.

There was no way I could compete with a magic user that had been using Transform for centuries. It also meant she was aware of what I was doing and having great fun blocking me. I stood up and stared at the chasm. It was much too far to leap and the point was to breeze by as if her magic didn't even cause me any effort to bypass. Which was not what I was doing right now.

The shimmer of light way below was hypnotic as I stood there.

Light.

"Got it." I let my shoulders down from where I'd had them scrunched up. "Ready Carelian? I know how to do this, but we still shouldn't dawdle."

He rose up from the ground. ~Yes, but how are we crossing? ~

I pulled on Water. It rushed up from the river far below, at first a trickle, then a solid stream, and I sent it over the arch, then I froze it. Water wasn't happy about having its rushing around slowed down, but it still froze into a hard bridge six inches thick, solidly clamped into each side.

"Ready?" I asked with a grin.

~We fall, I will never let you live it down.~

"I know, and I'd deserve it. But I got this." My assurance didn't stop me from having Air ready to catch me or a sidestep to the house in the back of my mind ready to be called to the front.

He sniffed at me, then sprang forward, moving fast, his claws digging in at each bound.

I held my breath as it shook, but it didn't break. He was across in less than fifteen seconds. Now it was my turn. I didn't run. Slipping would ensure I failed. The surface of the ice bridge was rough as air scoured it and drops of water ran off.

My heart tripled thumped as I realized Salistra was using Air to melt the bridge. I just kept moving. I transformed the top layer into grippy clay, my foot sticking a bit with each step. The air around me heated. I should have created the bridge rather than transformed it but Water was Chaos, not Order. She had to work a bit harder with it than the elements that were in her branch.

But that didn't mean she couldn't.

~I would move a bit faster, it is getting thinner.~

Falling would make this a very bad day. Cracks sounded behind me and I felt it wobble. I moved faster. I'd already been out here for over a minute, way too much time when you were up against a mage of Salistra's caliber and experience.

Ten steps.

I reached, offering up a chunk of hair to turn the entire bridge to rope and wood. I had to stop to do that. The bridge swayed under me as it changed. Then it was solid. The air cooled and I could feel her reassessing. I ran the last few steps, hitting the solid ground on the other side as the ropes started to change into strands of spider web. Still strong, but not strong enough to hold me.

~I didn't know you had that level of risk in you,~ Carelian teased.

"I prefer not to put my life on the line just to talk to someone. Someone that is starting to piss me off. What if Salistra wanted to talk to that person?"

As if in response to my words, a bridge of white marble formed, ancient and steadfast, offering me a way back across. What was it with bridges and the realms?

I rolled my eyes and started walking. The trees had faded into the background as the mountain rose up. The trees that remained were oaks, elms, and poplar trees. The realms didn't seem to care about what grew together. The mountain wasn't as big as I thought, much more the size of the Sutter Buttes instead of the Rockies. At the base was a grove of trees. The weather was perfect as always, and if I hadn't been so annoyed, it might have been a nice walk.

The grove opened to reveal a glade with lush, green grass,

dozens of fluffy rabbit-like creatures, and an opening into the mountain, where I could just glimpse what looked like bedding. Over to one side was a fountain providing crystal clear water that tinkled as it fell into a basin.

All of these were the surrounding details to the unicorn that stood to one side, watching us. A huge mirror hung from a tree next to her. Her pearly silver horn and hooves gleamed, and her coat of white looked like someone had just brushed it. The flexible lips lifted up and sneered at me, revealing long fangs.

~Herald.~ The crystal sharp tones sliced into my mind.

I crossed my arms and glared at her. "Are you really this big of a bitch, or do you just want people to think you are?"

CHAPTER
TWENTY-FOUR

The Merlin wonder-child recently finished her draft. Given her notoriously private attitude, it is a bit of a surprise to find she has been spied at the closing of various rips. Is she working for the government? This would be an odd turn of events, but what is even more odd is finding Stephen Alixant involved. He was rumored to be involved with her emergence as a double merlin. We all know the rips are terrifying, but is something more going on? ~ Magical Daily News

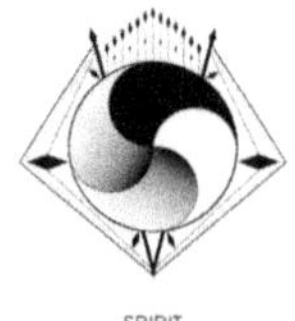
SPIRIT

The wind stopped, everything stopped, then she chuckled in my mind. Her voice always felt too sharp, too orderly. I had the feeling she could moderate it, but chose to speak like that because she knew it caused discomfort.

~You don't fear me, do you?~

"No. Because I still owe you, and you'd never damage me until all my debts are paid," I snapped back. I had forgotten how cranky her voice could make me.

She snorted a very horsey sound. ~Also truth. So why are you here?~ She lowered the volume of her voice or dialed down the intensity, and it didn't hurt as badly. Maybe I'd get my answers before I started to bleed from my ears.

"Why did you call in a debt and require me to accept the position of councilor? What do you gain from it?" My arms were crossed, and I stared at her. Carelian stood next to me. The fact that he hadn't flopped down somewhere told me this wasn't a safe place.

~That was what I chose to do. Should you not be grateful I asked for so little?~ She turned her head to peer at me with one eye, the horn glinting with menace.

"It wasn't little. It puts me in odd situations. Why did you want me there?"

~Are all humans so boring? I have things to do if you are done?~ She turned, flicking her tail at me as she headed inside and stopped at the water basin.

It was obvious she wasn't going to answer my question. "What is Brix's problem?"

~That bird hates humans. The hate has been there for a very long time. Do not expect that hate to fade.~

The fact that she answered me surprised me. "Is Brix my enemy?"

~Enemy? Odd word. That implies you are important to him.~ She walked back out, tail swishing slowly and strode past us. ~Are you?~

"How would I know? I've met Brix what three times? Maybe four? What is the council playing at?" I turned to watch her.

~We are not playing at anything, we are swimming the currents Magic is sending to us, trying to survive. Brix just has more experience than most.~ Salistra moved toward the white fluffs. They moved around nervously but none of them left the glade area.

"What do you mean Brix has more experience?" I pivoted slowly, making sure my back was never to her.

~Brix has been on the council for at least five hundred of your years. I believe magic was still on your Earth when Brix was hatched.~ It was said idly. At the same time, she darted forward, a fast move that made me flinch. Her horn impaled one of the fluffs. It screamed a high sound like nails on a chalkboard. Red blood wound down her horn as it hung impaled.

With another fast movement, Salistra lowered her head then flipped it up fast, the fluff sliding off her horn and into the air. She caught the falling body in her mouth and chewed a few times before swallowing. ~I do love these. Just the perfect snack size, but four or five can easily make a meal.~

I swallowed, more because it was so odd to see something that looked and felt like a horse be a predator.

"So you aren't going to tell me anything?" My exasperation leaked through and I tried to scale it back.

~I have told you many things. If you are wise, you will be a good councilor. If not, well, there are very many humans, I am sure a replacement will be found.~

"Gee thanks," I muttered. "Can you tell me what the rise of magic means? It doesn't make sense—even if Tirsane is siphoning magic from humans, there aren't that many that would qualify."

~I would think the Herald of Magic is the one to answer that question.~ She didn't even deign to look at me as she eyed the fluffs that were scattering back and forth.

"Carelian?" I asked, a bit desperate. I'd hoped she'd tell me something, explain why it had to be me. I knew I'd been railroaded into this, but I still didn't know why.

~What do you believe the Herald of Magic is supposed to do? How does she serve Magic?~ His words were sharper and clearer than I'd ever heard them, almost painful and unable to be ignored. For a minute he sounded like Esmere.

~Watch it Cath. I have no issue killing you,~ Salistra said.

~I welcome you to try. I haven't had horse in a long time,~ he fired back.

"What is it with all of you and your constant threats?" I'd meant the words to stay in my mind, but my mouth opened before my brain caught up, the frustration and exasperation making them shriller than they should have been.

They both looked at me, surprised. ~Does she truly not understand?~

Carelian cocked an ear at me, then they both laid back against his skull as if annoyed and ashamed. ~I thought she had figured it out, but it looks like she has not.~

Salistra cocked an ear at me, then heaved a sigh. ~We are predators and we are crossing into each other's territory all the time. If we were animals, we would hiss and posture and even attack, both mock and real. However, we are not animals. So, we threaten, put down, demean. It is our posturing to remind everyone, including ourselves, that we are not killing the other only because we choose not to.~ She paused to spear, toss, and chew another fluff. ~And it is rather amusing. Esmere is very skilled at her put downs.~

I felt a wave of heat crawl up my face as I flushed. The explanation was obvious once said and highlighted the issues humans were having. We didn't do that.

~When you stood up to me at the beginning of this conversation, you weren't posturing, were you?~ Salistra had turned and peered at me out of a large dark eye.

"Why would I posture? I'm not a predator, and I don't have anything to prove."

They both just looked at me, disbelief clear on their faces.

~Humans are the most efficient and violent of all species,~ Carelian said, still staring at me. ~They kill just to kill.~

"And you don't?" I shot back. I'd seen him play with enough of his "toys" to have zero patience with this line of thinking. "And while humans may be, I'm not. I don't go around killing people and I don't need to prove..." I trailed off. "Let me rephrase that. If I need to prove I'm dangerous, I will, but no, I wasn't trying to posture to you Salistra. I am just trying to figure out what is going on."

I stood there, jaw clenched, arms crossed, feeling vaguely betrayed by Carelian.

~Answer the question, Salistra.~ He walked over to me and rubbed against me. I stumbled a bit as he rumbled against me. ~I thought you understood our interactions, as sometimes you joined in. In all the years I have been blessed by Magic with your presence, I was unaware you still thought those words communicated dislike.~

My arms dropped, and I reached for him. "Have you ever heard me or the others talk like that?"

~Of course.~

I craned my head down to stare at him. "What?"

~Jo will tease you and Sable, well prior to the children, by calling you bitch. Sanchez and his brothers call each other names all the time. You called him Stinky until recently. How is this any different?~ His purrs didn't stop, and I left my hand idly scratching his head while I reassessed everything.

He was right. We did do that. I just hadn't equated that to threatening to kill each other or eat them.

"Someday I will have all the cultural stuff figured out." I wanted to scream. I glanced at Salistra. "Would it have been better if I came in here breathing fire and told you I was going to have unicorn steaks for dinner if you didn't talk?"

~It would have been more amusing and made me respect you more. You humans are so polite. Always asking permission and trying not to offend. You are seen as weak. If you were not the Herald, I would have just killed you a long time ago, though perhaps that might have been a mistake.~

A horrid thought struck me. "None of the councilors or other denizens had anything to do with Hishatio's heart attack, did they?"

~Why would we bother? He was the worst, always so deferential. It will be a relief to have someone else there to talk to. Of all of them, the one you call Shay has the most backbone, but even he is so mild.~ She shook her head, drops of blood flying from her horn and splattering her silver coat.

"I see." It remained to be seen if I was relieved or not. "What about Carelian's question?"

She huffed and walked away from us, lashing her tail back and forth. ~I do not understand why your focus isn't a canine. They hold onto bones like you hold on to questions. We need the Herald to stop what is going on in the realms. The magic leaking out is merely a symptom. We expect the Herald to serve Magic, but what Magic demands, we don't know. She doesn't speak to us like we do to you. She creates opportunities for you to act. For you to solve what is happening.~ She took a drink of water from her basin, it tinting pink as the blood sluiced off her muzzle.

"The realms are fracturing?"

~It seems that way. None of us know what is going on, but per the stories, the last time this happened, Merlin did something and we have been stable until now. Every Herald has always had something Magic needed them to do.~

I grabbed onto that with both hands. "Merlin did something? What did he do?" Here finally was a clue, something that would tell me what I could do or should do. A guidebook.

~Unknown. That was a very long time ago. Brix may know, or if you can find someone else that was alive and involved then. But that is why you are the Herald, so you can take what Magic is presenting to you.~ She turned to look at me, the blood gone, leaving her coated in white and silver. Perfectly pure, virginal, and deadly.

"Why couldn't you just say that?" I wanted to scream. If I'd known this from the beginning, maybe I'd have more information now.

~Because that is not our job. You are the Herald, it is your problem.~

I just stared at her. "I'm not posturing when I say this, but right now, the idea of a unicorn rug is very appealing."

She bared her fangs back at me. ~Try it. I enjoy the taste of mage flesh.~

The comment was so Carelian like that I couldn't help it, I laughed. She just stared at me, blinking.

"Fine. I get it. Magic will show me. The Council just expects me to figure it out."

~Or die. Both are valid options.~

I narrowed my eyes, then shrugged. "We all die. Hopefully I won't until I am old and ready to go. Any last words?"

~Be the Herald and quit being so drearily human.~

There was so much to unwrap in that and I would. Later.

"Carelian?" It would have been polite to walk away. I was done being polite. He opened a rip and we stepped home with the snickering of a homicidal horse bubbling in my mind. I had such a headache.

Anyone else responding to the request for magical response teams? I don't mind closing rips, but they want teams? I get the feeling more is going on that what we're being told. Why isn't this in the news more besides an occasional mention? Does anyone else have any more information? What exactly is happening and how bad is it really? ~ Initial post of a 2000 response string on the House of Emrys forums

CHAOS

Thanksgiving had been delightful, but I hated that I was now viewing all interactions with denizens through a new lens. It didn't change anything, but it did make me think harder about the interactions that I watched.

Christmas was at the end of the month, but Carelian had been being very helpful lately. We'd had a long talk and for him, understanding how to interact with the denizens was like a cat learning how to use a litter box. Absolutely obvious. It never occurred to him I wasn't behaving the way I did out of ignorance. He'd honestly thought I just enjoyed tweaking their tails.

Which in hindsight I had been, I just didn't realize what else they were gathering from it. The next council session was scheduled for after the first of the year. At that point, we would see just how much three humans could do.

But now I had given in, with mock reluctance, and gotten Carelian his deep sea fishing trip. Jo and Sable had both wrinkled their noses. Sable apparently got sea sick and Jo thought managing two six-year-olds on a fishing boat sounded like a fast way to needing to be sedated.

But Stephen, Indira, and Charles said they wanted to go. I'd scheduled it out of Charleston, and Carelian had been pestering me all week about what types of fish we might get. He had mental wish lists and recipes that didn't quit.

"I'm sure you will get something. Just don't count on any specific fish," I'd warned. He'd shrugged and ignored me.

After much discussion, Stephen and Indira decided to do a road trip down, making it a nice break for them. They'd let Carelian know where they were and he'd transport Charles. Then I'd sidestep over to him.

The normal chaos ensued with travel, meeting at the dock,

then getting on board. I'd found a lifejacket for Carelian and he'd agreed to wear it with resistance.

~If I fall in the water, I will just open a rip to the crossroads and step out.~

"And if you're unconscious?" I stared at him.

His ears tilted back, but he'd relented. The captain, Jacob Salls, treated Carelian just like a person and only blinked once when he'd come on board. The first mate was a woman with large blue eyes and blood red hair. Jacob introduced her as Sioban. Jacob got us all situated and soon enough we were sailing out of the Charleston harbor.

"Thank you for inviting us. This is just the change of pace I needed." Indira leaned against the railing with me, her hair wrapped in a tight bun under her cap. Even dressed in jeans, a sweater, and windbreaker, she still looked rather stylish. I'd never figure it out.

"I'm glad you two could come. It makes it more fun and I have a feeling we are going to have a lot of fish." I looked over at the three males all being educated about how the fishing rods worked and anchoring themselves. Charles and Stephen were paying close attention while Carelian listened, but his ears kept twitching toward the ocean. I couldn't remember ever seeing him this excited.

"That, I believe. You did get something to store it in?" Indira asked. "I've been looking up recipes, but still, there is a limit as to how much room there is in the freezer."

I laughed. "Yeah. I cheated. Hamiada says she can create a large null space for us to dump the fish into and basically it is kept perfectly frozen."

Indira slid her eyes to me. "She can create pockets into outer space?" There was hunger for knowledge in her tone and I smirked, as I knew that hunger all too well.

"Not exactly. She said it was more of not space, something

in between our realities, so it has no temperature, it is more of a stasis. It is one of the many things I want to investigate when I can." The wind pulled tendrils of hair out of my braids and shoved them into my mouth.

"Huh. I envy you sometimes. Family, friends, and so much opportunity to research." There was a certain wistfulness to her words, and I peered at her, concerned.

Before I could say anything, Captain Jacob yelled out. "Okay, let's bait these and see what we can catch." Excitement almost poured off the four of them by the stern and by silent agreement Indira and I moved over to watch. There were comfortable chairs back away from the action. We settled into them with bottles of water and got ready for the show.

Charles was fastened into a chair and let the line go. Arachena had declined to come, preferring her food still mostly alive and the idea of that much water when floating had sealed her decision.

I missed her, but at least Indira was here. Carelian wrapped his hands, his claws firmly retracted, around the shaft of the fishing pole and leaned over it, ears forward and tail tight against him. No one wanted that tail to get caught in anything. The poles bent and jumped around as the hooks and floats bobbed up and down in the waves we created as we cut across the choppy ocean.

The silver line flashed in the December sun and Carelian rumbled in purrs as he watched it spin.

"I think you have one. Start reeling it in." Jacob pointed when Carelian's line was jumping up and down.

Carelian started to pull it back, fighting with the line. He was stronger than I was, but the circular motion wasn't one he used often. Even so, soon he was bringing a wriggling fish to the surface while Captain Jacob helped Charles with another fish on his line.

~I have a fish. This is excellent. No waiting or lurking, they come to you and you simply reel them in.~ Carelians' gloating excitement had Indira and me snickering.

The pulling back and forth of the fishing pole as he fought to reel in the first fish almost pulled him out of the boat once or twice. The harness that clipped him in prevented any unexpected swimming lessons. Then the line snapped, throwing him backwards.

"Hey, you okay?" There was a tinge of worry in the Captain's voice as he approached Carelian.

~This is excellent. Again, show me how.~

"Ya ain't upset or nothing?"

~Of course, but prey slips through all the time. That is the joy of the hunt. Now again.~ Carelian handed him the fishing rod. ~I have much prey to capture today.~

The captain shook his head and showed him. Carelian didn't quite have the manual dexterity to tie the hooks on, so the captain did that, though he had no issue threading the bait fish on the hook, then casting it back in. Stephen, meanwhile, had pulled in a fish not much bigger than his arm, and was unhooking it to toss it back. While we were taking a bunch of them home, the smaller ones got tossed back in.

Charles had a wide grin on his face as the water splashed and his rod bent, pulling and bucking with it.

"I might have created monsters," I said in a soft tone to Indira.

"I do believe you are correct. Oh well, there are worse things for them to find exciting, but I see many more of these in my future." She had a fond grin on her face as she watched Stephen live in the moment, something I'd rarely seen.

I chuckled. "I hope everyone else likes fish. We are going to have it as a staple for a while. Though it might make an excellent party offering, as I know many of the denizens regard it a delicacy. I've never gotten them to tell me why they find it such a treat when I know they have oceans and rivers."

We watched them fight with fish and sometimes win, sometimes lose. Carelian purred so loud I could hear him over the rumble of the boat engine and the wind. The entire thing exhilarated him. So far, we had caught a few Mahi Mahi, wahoo, tuna, and a king mackerel. The other two men had given up, with wind burned faces and smiles of delight, but Carelian was wrestling with a marlin. Every time it leapt up in the air, its sharp pointy nose slicing through the air, Carelian screamed.

It was a high sharp sound that was meant to freeze a prey in terror. The first time everyone on the ship jumped and Siobhan stuck her head out of the bridge, eyes wide. Carelian ignored all of us, lost in the thrill of the chase. It was so odd to see him in a harness and life jacket, pulling back on a fishing rod trying to reel it in. The motions were jerky and awkward compared to humans, but he didn't care.

~Look at this, this is prey worthy of the fight.~ He all but crowed in my head. ~Even if I need to use tools to bring it close.~

Captain Jacob just grinned. "He'd make a fine fisherman."

I smothered a snort. "Not if you wanted the catch to make it back to shore. I can guarantee you it will be munched on."

He gave me an appraising look. "Ah. I am thinking perhaps I should start to prep some of the catch prior to returning to port."

I smiled. "That might be wi-" I broke off as pain slashed through my brain. Indira flinched too, and we both looked around. "You felt that?" I asked as I scanned the sky.

"Yes. It was large. Are the rips starting back up again?" Indira scanned the sky like I did looking for anything.

"I don't know. I have no idea how long this peace might

last. I had hoped longer than this." I kept turning slowly, trying to see something, but out here on the ocean everything was so huge and empty it was hard to tell.

"Is something wrong?" Stephen walked over, his brows drawn together as he looked at both of us. Charles followed.

"I felt a rip. Indira did too," I said, still not finding anything.

"Cori?" Charles said slowly, his arm lifting to point off the stern. I followed his finger and about twenty yards to my left, there was a strange ripple in the ocean. It looked like water was pouring down into something.

"Captain," I called, pointing at it. "Is that normal?"

"Fuck. Siobhan, swing her to starboard and step on it."

~No, you are mine, stubborn creature. I have fought you fair and square. I will win this battle.~ Carelian's voice snarled in my mind as he reeled in the marlin, its body leaping up into the air, the nose piercing the sky.

I glanced at him, but yanked my attention back to the ripple of water that had gotten closer.

~What in the void? ~ Carelian said with a note of astonished surprise.

I whirled to see a large tentacle coming up to grab at the marlin coming down. It wasn't a tentacle like Bob or the other chaos creatures, instead, it looked like every movie kraken I'd ever seen.

"What in Merlin's name?" Indira sounded as shocked as I felt.

The captain, on the other hand, went white. "Siobhan, full speed, I don't care if you destroy the engine as long as we get out of here." There was a jerk of the boat that rocked us toward the stern as the boat increased speed.

~No,~ Carelian snarled, sounding like a buzz saw in my brain. I don't think I'd ever heard him quite as enraged. ~Mine!~

The tentacle wrapped around the marlin and dragged it

down. The line snapped recoiling hard and Carelian fell backward as the tension disappeared.

~It took my prey.~ There was lethal anger in his voice and his all too capable hands started to scrabble to unhook the harness. ~No one steals prey from me and survives.~

"Don't you dare. You have zero idea how to fight in water and no matter how strong you are, you still need to breathe. It doesn't." My voice was steely as I moved forward and grabbed his life jacket. "Don't make me lose you."

He turned, snarling at me, and I just stared at him. The hunt lust, I understood, but he could not go after that thing. The tension faded and his ears came back up and he huffed. ~Very well.~ Rage coated his words.

"I think we might have a bigger problem," Charles said softly, and I turned to look at him and the tentacle that was creeping up the hull.

CHAPTER
TWENTY-SIX

The idea of monsters in the sea has woven through human consciousness since we first ventured out on the water. Some of those monsters have been proven to be real. Whales are terrifying if they come up under your boat. Watching an orca grab a seal off an ice floe is guaranteed to make you nervous. However, we have never had any proof of giant kraken that could attack ships. With the number of ships on the oceans, sonar, submarines, and other exploratory devices, I am sure that if there were such creatures, we would have had some proof. Instead, all we have are stories that probably sparked with the first squid ever seen and just kept growing. There is no proof they have ever existed. ~ Mythological Creatures Fact or Fiction?

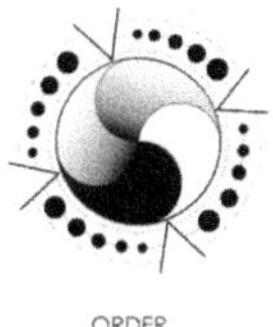

Almost without conscious thought, I grabbed Air and sent a lightning bolt at it. There was a weird screech that sounded oddly muffled, and the tentacle ripped away. Carelian was still snarling and though I let him get out of the harness, we all double checked our life vests.

"You have areas of your realms with water?" Indira asked.

Carelian lowered one ear and shot her a dismissive look. ~Of course. Where do you think the mermaids live?~

I almost responded with "Mermaids? Can I meet some?" but I bit that back before it escaped. One of these days I was sitting down with a mythological creatures book and asking him about every single one.

Instead, I, along with the other three, stood waiting and watching. Jacob had headed to the bridge. He and Siobhan were trying to get the boat going as fast as they could. There was a shudder, and the boat veered to my left. I fell on my ass, but the others managed to grab for support.

"Something grabbed our rudder. We're turning," Jacob shouted out.

Charles snapped his harness to the nearest fishing chair and leaned over the stern.

"It's wrapped around the rudder. Give me a second." Charles was an Order arch-mage. He was strong in patterns, and preferred to work with data, but it didn't mean he didn't have powers. Another muffled scream and he stood back up. "Shattered the tentacle. Break pattern is fun sometimes."

I nodded. I needed to remember that use. Part of me wanted to go hire tutors to teach me all the ways to use the other classes, but for now I'd just have to practice.

"We should probably all secure ourselves. I don't think this is over yet. But make sure you have a knife or a spell to cut yourself free if needed," Stephen said, even as he pulled Indira over and secured the harness under her life jacket, then did the same for himself.

"Carelian?" I asked as I followed Stephen's advice. It also put me in a position to see over the edge of the boat. It had resumed the previous course after Charles had shattered the tentacle.

~I will stay unencumbered. However, I will retain the flotation device. I must be close to fight, like now.~

I spun, trying to follow his movements as he darted behind me. The safety line wouldn't let me turn far enough that way, so I had to rotate the other direction to see what he was doing.

Two more tentacles had reached up on the ship, and were flailing around, looking for something else to grab. Carelian growled, a low sound that was almost subsonic, and attacked. His claws came out and sliced cleanly through the thinner tentacle. The second was a good five inches thick, and he slashed twice at it, fast motions, and the tentacle fell to the ground.

I'd never really seen Carelian fight before. If he hunted, it was by himself, and while he'd protected me once or twice, I'd never seen more than a bite or a claw before whomever it was decided that death by Cath wasn't their preferred way to die. This was another level. Fierce, incredible, deadly. I wanted to just watch him fight and cheer for the blood he spilled.

"Merlin's balls," Charles whispered. I nodded as I stared.

The sudden jolt of the ship shook me out of my fascinated stare. "We've got to close that rip. The creature has to be originating from the underwater rip." My voice might have been a bit more panicked than I would have liked, but I couldn't see how big the rip was or where it was.

"Can you close it if you don't know where it is?" Indira turned to look at me.

"I don't know. I've never done that before," I admitted as another tentacle came up and Indira set it on fire. The muffled screams of pain were getting louder and closer.

"If that thing gets all the way into this world, Jules Verne's stories are going to become reality," Charles pointed out, his eyes searching for a new target. "That would have disastrous consequences for the wildlife and shipping."

"Cori," Indira snapped. "Listen. Close your eyes."

It took a force of will to get my eyes closed as Carelian seemed to anticipate each tentacle that came up. Stephen held his hand up as if he had a knife in it and slashed at each tentacle as it broke the surface of the ocean. I realized he was using Transform Cut to act like an invisible sword. And the offerings it was taking were visible chunks from his hair as he fought.

I needed to stop this before we all ran out of offerings.

My eyes clamped shut.

"Feel for it. You know what rips feel like. Find it. You don't need to see it to close it." Indira's voice pulled me back to my first lessons with her, closing rips.

I pushed away everything and just felt. It was like a huge neon flare, but smothered by water. I'd never seen them anywhere except in the sky. But it was there, obvious to my senses. With nothing visible to guide me, I just had to close it by feel. Usually, I tried to push anything back in, but this time I didn't care. I grabbed that zipper and pulled.

The rip was open wider than any other I'd ever dealt with and I fought to pull it closed. Offerings vaporized, but I kept at it.

"Cori, duck!" Charles screamed out the warning, and I just dropped to my knees. The harness held my torso up as I bent over. Something wet and fleshy whacked right above my back. My eyes stayed shut as I tried to focus on what I needed to do.

A screech shattered my concentration, and I felt water cascade up and soak us, even as the boat lurched down alarmingly. My mental zipper was suddenly easy to pull.

Shit.

I yanked it shut, ignoring the cost, three inches of hair, and sighed in relief as it sealed, but that lasted only seconds. My eyes popped open, and I stood up.

"It's closed, but we have a bigger problem."

The three of them were panting and Carelian was soaked in green tinted fluid. I didn't know if it was blood or ichor and didn't have time to figure it out.

"Whatever owned those tentacles got out of the rip and is now in the water. Probably a bit peeved off at the damage we have done." I glanced around the deck, taking in the bits of sea creature, and the ghost white faces of the two crew members hiding in the bridge. "We need to kill it."

I hated saying that. I had no idea if it was sentient or not, but it couldn't be allowed to stay here. The consequences were too great as whatever it ate normally wouldn't be here. And that meant it would eat what lived here. Prey with no way of knowing how to deal with this predator.

"Any idea how?" Charles looked at me, his face drawn and serious. For a minute, the boy I first met flashed in front of my eyes. Overweight, acne, awkward, not sure how to deal with his familiar. Not the assured man who knew his place and had the strength to stand ready to fight.

The expressions on Indira's and Stephen's face were similar. I had the best family.

"Carelian? Any ideas? I'm starting to understand why

seafood is so rare in the realms." My voice was dry as I watched him.

~You think?~ His sarcasm was drier than my salt drenched skin. ~The beings that inhabit the waters in the realms are mighty. I don't know the exact name of this, but think similar to a kraken of your stories, but with more tentacles.~

"I had kind of guessed that," Charles said dryly. "How do we kill it?"

~Like you would anything else. Cut off its head, stop its heart, cut it into bits. Any of those would work.~

I huffed a sigh. That was so much easier said than done. "You did notice some of these tentacles are bigger than we are, right?"

~You are mages. Do magic,~ was his response.

"One of these days I am so getting you back," I muttered even as I turned to look at the water and the frothing that I just knew was a creature coming after us. "Is it edible? I mean, can other ocean creatures eat it?" I stared at the bits of the creature laying on the deck, some still twitching.

~Yes. Though I find I prefer it fried, like your calamari. It is too tough and bland to eat for enjoyment otherwise.~ He lashed his tail back and forth. ~This is a large one, most do not survive meeting it.~

"I can see why." Stephen looked around. "We are at a severe disadvantage. Any ideas?"

"Either of you strong enough to fly?" Order mages strong in Air could fly, but not like a superhero, well not unless you practiced a lot. Mostly it was a hovering action.

"Technically," Stephen said. "But it isn't a skill set I've used since my college days."

The churning water got closer, and I had the mental image of a colossus rising from the oceans toward us. It was unsettling and probably accurate.

"Indira, how are your water skills?" I asked as I gazed at the endless sea. It would be so easy to disappear here and no one would ever know.

"Rusty. I mean I can ice my drinks easily, but anything else? Besides, this is the ocean. No one can control it. It is too huge and fluid."

She stated a truism. Not even merlins could control the ocean.

"I know, but we don't need to control the ocean. Just the area it is in. If I freeze the water around it, can you dry the creature out?"

"Evaporate? Huh. Sure. But it won't be fast." She said the words slowly, as if trying to figure out how to do it.

I nodded, the precious time to come up with a plan disappearing. "Stephen, can you and Charles distract it? We need it up high enough so Indira can go for the eyes. I'm going to try to freeze the brain."

"Are you sure it has one?" Charles said, with his head tilted as if searching his memory. "Many of our invertebrates don't have their brains structured like mammals."

"No. But I figure if Indira can dehydrate, while I freeze, it should die. Worst case, I'll freeze it completely, then one of you can shatter it." I hoped. If it was as big as I thought, it would take a lot to freeze it.

Stephen and Charles both cast me doubting looks, but unless they had something else to try, we were stuck with my idea. The water roiled as multiple tentacles came up and we were out of time.

CHAPTER

TWENTY-SEVEN

I am researching old maps. There is the possibility that rips are actually static in certain locations. Multiple maps from radically different cultures and time periods all have comments equating to 'Here Be Monsters' at the same spots in the map. It makes no sense for all these sea-faring cultures (Viking, Polynesian, Chinese, Greek) to have the same notations when their cultures rarely interacted at all. ~ House of Emrys Board

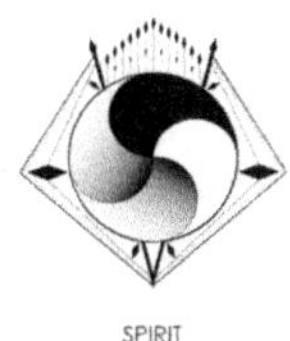

SPIRIT

grabbed the water around the creature, trying to make it colder. There was so much. Water agreed willingly to get colder, sluggish, icy thick, then it was washed away in the next breath. It wasn't that the ocean fought me; it was that I was trying to change something that changed constantly. But I needed to get that thing closer to the surface. There had to be a better way.

Thoughts and ideas rattled around in my head. Salt. Osmosis. Water. Cellular structure. Would that work?

"Indira, flood the cells with Water. Do the reverse of evaporate." I matched my words with actions, shoving water into the cells every time I saw it. While I did that, I tried to convince the water to push it up closer to us, get so I could see it, have an idea of how it was built.

The Water laughed and flowed and was gone before anything else could happen. Now I understood why no one worked with the ocean. It was impossible.

"Here, this should work," Charles called out. His hair had significant length missing. I glanced at him.

"What?"

"Watch." He stared at the water. Trash and seaweed that floated on the top writhed around in the roiling water, twisting and cutting through it. A pattern started to appear, wrapping, weaving over the creature below.

Indira and Stephen had paused also to stare at it. "Oh," Stephen said. "Brilliant." He concentrated, and I watched his hair disappearing into offerings.

"What am I missing?" I couldn't figure out what they were doing.

"Creating a net from the seaweed and the other trash in the ocean. I'm using Reassemble and Replicate to weave everything together and then twist it around the creature. And once I get a section done, I shove air into it, to make it float. Together, we should have it trapped and rising."

I blinked. It was genius. For the first time I was very happy for trash in the ocean.

"And once it is closer to the surface, we can freeze or dehydrate it," I said, elation in my voice.

"Good. Freezing is much easier than evaporation. How can we help?" Indira leaned next to me, already looking exhausted and with her normally elegant hair a bit disheveled, with random bits missing.

"Give us a bit. It really doesn't want to rise to the surface."

~It is a dweller of the depths. But we shall emerge victorious.~ Carelian all but crowed that, and I wondered if he was taunting the thing.

"Is it sentient?" I didn't know if it would change my actions, but I needed to know.

~No more than any of your sharks. It is a creature that hunts, eats, breeds. As far as I'm aware, it has no relationship with Magic other than being a Magical creature.~

Once again, I heard the capital letter. "Good." I turned to focus on the water as Charles and Stephen concentrated. As I watched, strands of plastic and seaweed floated to the surface, then were pulled back down, but more and more appeared, dragging a nightmarish creature with it.

The tentacles had been a green-blue approaching grey. The creature was mottled with green spots on a brown-grey body. It did and didn't resemble the pictures of a giant squid that I had seen before. It had the vaguely arrow shaped head and huge eyes, but there it ended. There were four eyes, one on each quarter of the body. In theory, it would have had a three-hundred-sixty-degree view around itself. There were tentacles with spear points, some with hooks, and the mouth wasn't the beak I'd expected. And I knew exactly what it looked like as it screamed at us, revealing something more like a lamprey.

So many teeth.

My gorge rose, though if it was at the creature, the tossing of the boat, or the scream that seemed to cut through my brain, who knew.

"Now!" Stephen's yell cut through my paralyzed wonderment at the monster. Carelian hissed, but he stayed back. Distance fighting was not his forte.

"Let's go, Indira." I pulled on Water and asked it to freeze. I had no idea where the brain might be located in the giant body. It was enormous. From where the tentacles started to the end, it had to be twenty feet. Some of the tentacles were longer than two school buses. They flailed around trying to hit us, or wrap around the boat. Carelian kept us safe.

He was everywhere, the life jacket barely slowing him down as he rushed from side to side, severing anything that crossed above the sidewalls of the boat. I went for the brute force approach and tried to quarter its body. I asked Water to freeze it in quadrant lines, hoping I'd get lucky and destroy something important.

A scream that had been much more tolerable when muffled by water emitted from the creature, and this time I gagged. I heard the others gagging too. It must have affected our inner ears in some way. We needed to kill it.

"One eye down," Indira announced when there was a break in the screams. "On to the next."

The frantic nature of the thrashing doubled, and I could see the offerings vaporizing from Charles and Stephen. The tentacle with the spear came up and raced toward Charles.

I choked, trying to scream out a warning. A red blur wrapped around the spear and yanked it to the side. And Carelian was there, his claws slicing through the tentacle like a piece of fruit.

~Keep going, it is flailing.~ His voice was hard and commanding. Another flash of red as he darted to the other side.

I doubled down on freezing through the creature.

"Three eyes down," Indira called out. And it was obvious we were affecting the creature. It rolled back and forth, trying to avoid the damage we were doing to it, trying to get away. Many of its tentacles had been severed and its movements were slowing.

I managed to cleave the body in half. A line of crystals shattered along its body, and a long slow screech keened in my ears and brain. It stopped as the body fell apart, broken into two pieces. The tentacles twitched and jerked, but after a few minutes they fell still.

We all stood there, our breaths loud in the sudden silence. At some point in the fight, the engine had stopped. The splash of the waves against the hull and our loud breathing were all I could hear.

"Did you get it? Is it dead?" Captain Jacob whispered as he stuck his head out of the bridge.

I stared at it, watching for any twitch, any chance it wasn't fully dead. "I think so. Creatures are going to eat it, right?"

Carelian was leaning over the side, his tail whipping back and forth. ~I do not think that will be an issue. Already the cycle of life is stepping in.~

We all leaned over to peer into the water. The trash held the creature up at the surface, but I could see small figures darting in and out. When I looked up, I could see fins cutting through the water in a wide swath around us.

"I see. Can we pull that trash in with us?"

"Somehow. Give us a few." Stephen and Charles put their heads together and started talking.

I walked over to the captain. "Are you and Siobhan okay?"

"Yeah. We're okay. Did that just happen?" He stared out at the creature with a dumbfounded look.

"Yeah, it did." I couldn't blame him for his shock as I stared at it.

"My grandfather talked about these creatures and the whaling ships. I always thought they were just tall tales."

"Huh." That idea resonated through my brain. "They might have been real. Creatures that slipped through rips, maybe out, maybe back in." All the old stories of monsters and dragons seemed much less far-fetched.

Jacob shook his head, looking at the broken fishing poles, the flopping tentacles on the deck, and the gouges in the wood. "If you hadn't been here, this thing would have torn my ship up. You're all scary as fuck, but thank you. I'm assuming you don't mind if we cut this short? I'll need to get the engine going again, but I'm ready to head back."

The exhausted chuckles came from all of us. "Not at all," I managed, sagging to the deck of the ship. Carelian padded over to flop down next to me. "You okay?" I ran my hands over him as I asked. There were wet patches and he let out a soft hiss as I touched some areas.

~Yes. Bruises, small cuts, and maybe a cracked rib. But I will heal quickly.~ He laid his head on my lap. ~This was perhaps a bit more excitement than I was looking for.~

Laughter slipped out of me, though low and tired. "You think? Next time you want to fight monsters, can you give me a heads up? I would have prepared better."

"What she said," chimed in Charles. "You do realize Arachena is going to be annoyed she missed this. Though personally, I'm glad she did. Having her here would have had me frantic. She isn't a tank." He had curled up against the bridge, sweat and blood on his face. I narrowed my eyes, but I could only see a small cut on his face, nothing major. "But it definitely was a change from the usual."

"I'm perfectly fine with the usual, thank you very much," Indira muttered. "I'm getting too old for this. And my hair?" She lifted up her hair, that looked like someone had hacked at it. "I'm going to have to spend a week doing magic to get it to even out."

"I'm just putting mine in a tail and ignoring it," Charles muttered.

I snickered and just petted Carelian. The noise of the waves and the boat engine as we headed back to the harbor created an almost meditative sound.

~We still have fish, correct?~ Carelian asked as we were pulling up to the dock.

It pulled me out of the exhausted doze I'd been in. "I believe so. Why?"

~I plan on enjoying every bite. I fought for those fish and I am going to enjoy them.~

We all rose to our feet as Captain Jacob and Siobhan started tying us to the dock. "Carelian?" He twitched an ear at me, though he hadn't moved yet. "Are there any land creatures like that thing?" I could feel the other three all halt in their move-ment and stare at me. "You know, large, hungry, mindless?"

Carelian yawned, exposing his needle-sharp fangs. ~Not that are carnivorous that I know. There are a few of your wooly mammoths in some of the pockets, but the largest carnivores are the dragons. They are all sentient, mostly.~

"Does that mean we don't need to worry about them slip-ping out of the rips?" Stephen had moved closer while Carelian answered and stared at my familiar, his face drawn.

Carelian levered himself up, moving slowly and favoring his

front right paw. ~No? Yes? I am not sure how to answer. I doubt that Onyx or Zmaug would lower themselves to coming here and hunting humans. You are rather boring prey. But some of the others? It is possible. They do not care about the intelligence of their prey. If that happened?~ He flicked ears backward and headed to the edge of the boat. ~Then humans will be snack bags.~ He leapt over the edge, landing neatly on the dock, though I noticed he didn't put weight on his paw.

"Cori?" Stephen said slowly and Charles drew near. "Did you know that?"

"Maybe?" I sighed and scrubbed my hands over my face and into my tangled and seawater-soaked hair. "Zmaug could eat a human and wouldn't feel any remorse about it. I know that there are other dragons that don't have the connection I have with Zmaug or Tiantang. So yes, I guess I always knew that was possible."

If those three could have gotten paler, I think I'd have worried about them passing out.

"But," I said and held up my hand. "As Zmaug proved, the dragons have always had the ability to come here. They don't need rips. I suspect if that was a real issue, it would have happened a long time ago." I didn't bring up the legends of dragons and knights, because part of me wondered if it had been a thing. Stupid teenage games?

"Point," Stephen said, nodding his head. "I wish that made me feel better."

I sighed and got off the boat. "Me too."

CHAPTER

TWENTY-EIGHT

A dragon was reported in Chile yesterday. It apparently stepped out of a rip, looked around, and then stepped back in. The rip then sealed up behind it. Multiple images of it were caught, but unlike many of the rips there was no damage. The dragon seemed annoyed more than anything one witness stated. ~ CNN Mage Focus

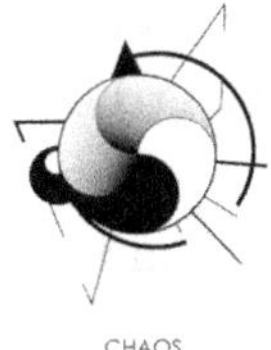

CHAOS

We ended up with about three hundred pounds of fish once it was all processed. We unanimously decided the sea monster was not edible. Indira, Stephen, and Charles took some of the fish, but that still left us with a bit over two hundred pounds. I dragged it home via sidestep. Once there, Jo returned from remodeling at the Tudor house to help me put it in the stasis storage Hamiada had created for us, while I relayed the events of the trip.

"I can't say how glad I am we didn't go. I think I would have been useless freaking out over the kids," she admitted.

"That or all of us would have turned into monsters to protect them? You are much better at the hard, sharp vengeance sort of stuff." I said this as we organized the last of the fish for storage. The remaining was for dinner tonight. Carelian had consented to let me wrap his paw after a quick rinse in the shower. The stuff covering him apparently tasted awful, so he submitted to the shower with only minimal whining. We verified his forearm wasn't broken, just sprained. As best he could tell, a couple of the attacks on tentacles had bent his fingers back a bit too far. Hence the sprain.

"Maybe, but I'd still not like to go that far. Last time I did that, I ended up bald and barren." Jo grinned at me, showing she wasn't upset. "But it means the rips are back."

"I think so. I think we need to change a lot of stuff." The ideas I'd had in the back of my mind started bubbling up. "And I really want to take a nap, but I don't think I can push it off anymore."

Jo glanced at the clock. It was after 4. "Well, we got a lot done at the house today. Sable and the kids will be back here for dinner. Fish is a nice treat. You sure it can't wait until tomorrow?"

I started to say no, then sighed. "No. It can. I'll get the ball rolling and deal tomorrow." The start of the ball rolling was a call to Shay after I had a shower and a strong rum and coke in my hand. I had muscles hurting where I hadn't realized I had muscles. The shower had exposed a lot more bumps, cuts, and bruises than I'd realized I'd collected.

"Cori, I take it the world is ending again?" He answered the phone with this comment and I almost laughed.

"Probably. You free tomorrow? We, the councilors, need to meet." I lay in bed, Carelian by my side. He'd wimped out and took a portal upstairs. It told me he was more tired than he wanted to admit. I suspected if we weren't having fish for dinner, he'd just sleep through it.

"I can make time. Where?" He sounded tired, too. "And I just want to point out this councilor stuff is a lot more than what you sold to me."

I barked out a weak laugh. "Tell me about it. But that is what I want to talk about. Let's just do it here. I have lots of fresh fish."

"Oh? I like fish." His voice had perked up at those words.

"That is part of the story. Noon tomorrow? I'll provide lunch." I had a few quick things I could throw together and Jacob had been nice enough to prep a few slabs that were sushi quality. The nice thing about stasis was it would still be as fresh when I took it out as it was going in, even a few months later.

"Okay. I assume your Cat will come get me?"

"One of these days my Cath will express his displeasure in your denigration of him."

"Probably, but apparently I need to learn to live dangerously when it comes to non-humans." Shay had a wry tone to his voice, and I chuckled in response.

"Not dangerously, just don't put up with them dismissing you. But that is stuff I'll explain. Let me get ahold of Amadahy. I'll let you know if anything changes."

"See ya." He hung up, and I pulled up Amadahy's number.

It rang for a long time and I was about to hang up when it was answered. "Tanisi?"

"Umm, this is Cori Munroe? I needed to talk to Amadahy?"

"One minute," the male voice replied in English this time, to my relief. Though to be fair, it was much closer to three minutes before I heard her come on the line.

"Merlin Munroe. Is there a problem?" She sounded older and tired, but then I'd never talked to her on the phone. Maybe that made a difference.

"Isn't there always? I was hoping you had time tomorrow at lunch to come over so we can discuss things. We need to talk to Ngarra also."

"Ah." She sat silent for a moment and I was about to make sure the line had not been cut. "Yes. We will be there. Explain then."

"I will. I'm serving lunch. Is fish okay?"

"Oh," a note of excitement entered her voice. "That will be delightful. Thank you."

We hung up and from the scent, I knew dinner was done. "Come on fuzz face. Let's go eat the fish we caught. "

~If it had not been such a glorious battle and I hunger for the fruits of my victory, I would pass.~

I frowned. "Is there anything I can do?"

~No. Food and sleep are the best remedy. I shall be down shortly.~

I leaned over and brushed a kiss on the top of his head, ignoring the fur left on my lips. "Love you, Carelian."

~Silly quean. You know I am yours,~ he murmured in my head as he gingerly stretched, preparing to get up.

I headed downstairs to find Sable and two excited kids and quetzos racing around the sun room.

"We have our own rooms!" they chattered at me.

"I know. Did you get to look at them today?" I asked as I leaned into the hugs.

"We pulled up carpet and removed doors. We have our own closets," Jaz said with a grin.

"Oh? Do you think all your clothes will fit?" I teased her as I moved to the table, still stiff and sore.

"I think there will be room for more," she said with wide eyes as she climbed up on her chair. Azul clung in her hair. They were almost ready to fly and were about too big to continue to cling to the kids' heads, but that was something they'd figure out.

Vert, his green scales all but glowing with health, had reached about a foot long and was starting to thicken. His body was about the width of a silver dollar. His leathery wings were building muscle, and I suspected he'd fly first.

Azul was leaner and longer and given that Jaz loved to play with her tail, I figured we needed to see about some scarfs for the quetzo to hide in. I bet that I had a nice infinity scarf in dark grey that might work.

"Carelian!" The cry from the kids pulled me back from my mental rambling as Carelian stepped into the dining room from a rip, his forearm held up, and then climbed carefully into his chair.

"He's hurt!" Jaz glared at me as if I'd done it. "How did he get hurt?"

Magne had moved over to him, brows drawn together in a frown. "Are you hurt? Do you need your ouchies kissed?" It was a very serious question and was so adorable I had to fight back my giggle.

~I was hurt fighting a giant monster. Cori has already kissed my wounds. Now I need sustenance to fuel my healing,~ Carelian replied just as gravely to Magne. ~Sit and hear about the fight for the dinner we have tonight.~ He nodded at the fish that Jo had brought out.

She'd decided to go with the swordfish and Mahi-mahi. The swordfish had been grilled and there were five big steaks, while she'd baked the Mahi with lemon, zucchini, and garlic. She'd also made a mushroom risotto and a quick fruit salad.

"You got that? How? That is fish, it's wet. You don't like to get wet." Jaz kept looking back and forth between him and the fish.

"He'll tell you in a minute. Now here are cooked and raw cubes of both types of fish for your quetzos. Remember how we've been working on table manners?" Jo said as she set down a bowl to the side of both of them.

Knowing that we needed to convince them to eat neatly in public, we'd been working on table manners. We'd added the panel back into the table, making it a bit big for the six of us, but it put an entire setting space next to each kid. It was there Jo put the bowl.

"Yes, Mami," the twins said.

~Food?~ chirped one of the quetzos. I hadn't managed to figure out their tones yet. Hopefully, by the time they were grown they would have recognizable voices, at least to me. Carelian had no issue with it.

"Food," Jaz said sternly. "You need to eat neatly. No tearing into food." Her mama voice was adorable, and I glanced up to see Sable and Jo smothering smiles. Magne was just as focused on Vert, so neither twin saw our amusement.

The two quetzos slithered down to their spots and picked up the small cube. Both of them had flexible necks so they could easily eat from their short hands. They were watched carefully for a minute by the kids, but then the lure of their own food called too loudly.

"You caught this, Carelian?" Magne asked as he stared at the two pieces of fish on his plate. Neither of the kids were picky eaters. The looks of astonishment from Carelian and Esmere the first time they'd tried the "I don't like that" routine and the snarky comments from Esmere had nipped that in the bud. There were days when I suspected we had no idea how much easier our lives were because of the denizens' effects on the twins.

~I did, or at least many of them. I have no idea if I caught this specific fish or if it was Alixant or Charles.~ I could never tell what Carelian was going to call the others. It really depended on his mood. Today, I think he was too tired and hungry to be quite as dismissive of others as he would normally be. That or they had managed to impress him. ~But those fights were nothing compared to the monster that attacked the boat we were on.~

"What?" Sable and the kids had the same reaction and looked at me with surprise and worry on their faces.

"Yep. That is why he is hurt and I'm moving slowly. Let him tell you." I focused on the food. It was delicious. It did taste better knowing we'd wrested this food out of the water, as opposed to getting it from a store shelf. After the day we'd had, that extra sense of victory just added to the flavor.

Better watch it, or you'll be out hunting with Carelian.

I snickered to myself and let Carelian tell the story. He had seen more than I, and was a natural storyteller, even if he was the hero of the story. Though as I listened and put together the flashes of red or the sounds I'd heard as we worked to disable the leviathan, he wasn't far wrong. None of us could have reacted fast enough, nor been able to move on a rocking ship the way he had.

A cold shiver went down my spine as I realized we might have very well died today without him. I took a hasty drink of my soda, letting the carbonation and rum burn through the sudden fear.

"Wow. Carelian's a hero!" Magne gushed, and I nodded.

"He is. More than I realized. I don't think we would have made it without him."

Carelian's ears and whiskers flicked forward as his green eyes caught mine. ~I will always fight for my queans.~ There was a rumble purr behind his words and I nodded.

How in the world would I live up to this trust in me? Did Esmere, Tirsane, Salistra, heck Bob, also believe in me this much? If I had died today, I would have missed all this. The twins, Jo and Sable. A fierce need to see them grow up and us to grow old slammed into me.

Fine. If everyone thought I could fix this, I would. I didn't want anyone to lose their futures because of these rips.

The gloves were coming off.

CHAPTER

TWENTY-NINE

A ship came into the Charleston Harbor the other day, looking like it had been attacked by pirates. Spied leaving the ship was Director of Magical Crimes Stephen Alixant, his longtime girlfriend Indira Humbert, and double merlin Cori Munroe. One has to ask if they were attacked and if so, by what? The captain and crew member would not talk to us when asked for information, so we are left wondering what happened. ~ Magical Daily News

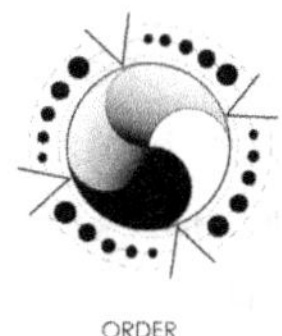

ORDER

I had spent the night sound asleep. I thought for sure I'd toss and turn what with the rips, the council, the herald crap, and realizing we almost died. Instead, I'd crawled into bed, Carelian sprawled out next to me, and the last thing I remembered was his rumbling purr.

By noon I was ready for guests. I had fresh sashimi plated, and threatened to cut off Carelian's tail if he ate it. He had his own personal stash. He didn't need to eat what I had for the council members. I also created a quick pasta salad and grilled a few swordfish I'd started marinating that morning. Fire was so useful in keeping things warm.

~I'm off to play bus driver,~ Carelian said as he stood and walked over to me, rubbing his head on my ribs.

"Sounds good. I figured Amadahy will get here via Kali-hchiia. See you shortly."

I had iced tea, sodas, and some lemonade on ice. And a large coffee just for Shay. It amused me that I still remembered his favorites.

A stab of pain went through me, much stronger and more intrusive than Carelian's rips. I headed out to the backyard where Amadahy and Ngarra were walking forward.

"Merlin," Amadahy said, nodding her head, Ngarra mimicking her.

"Please, Cori. It makes me feel ridiculous, especially when we need to be equals and united." I invited them in and to the dining room. While it wasn't as comfortable a place to talk, I thought the ability to face each other, not try to juggle plates, and the fact that I could take notes trumped anything else.

Everyone else, including Hamiada, were over at the Tudor house working on it. All the low-level remodeling Jo and Sable wanted to do themselves, and had the kids helping create their rooms and the family room. I'd watched them tugging up the carpet. It was amusing how hard they worked, but it made it theirs and had the benefit of exhausting them by the end of the day. Win, win.

Carelian strode in, followed by Shay.

"Hey, Cori." He nodded to Amadahy and Ngarra. "Others. So, what's the what?"

"Afternoon Shay. Help yourself." I pointed to the food and the plates. I took a minute to fill drink orders, giving Shay his coffee with a smirk, then I settled down myself. Carelian was in the window seat. He was walking much better this morning, but you could tell his paw was still tender.

"Let me tell you about our deep-sea fishing adventure." I laid out everything, with Carelian filling in parts, about the creature, the effort, and what it had taken. By the time I was done, all three of them had paled drastically. Amadahy looked the worst with her pallor at a sickly grey brown.

Shay cleared his throat as he twisted his coffee in his hand. "Cori, I get that I'm a merlin, but we can't fight these. And I'm not sure what we are missing in the council sessions."

"I don't know either, but I know there is one after the first of the year, so about three weeks. I'm going to find out what is going on then," I said calmly. There was no choice at this point.

"And if they obfuscate or refuse to tell you?" Amadahy's voice was quiet as she asked that, but both she and Ngarra had enjoyed the fish.

"Then I make them. I'm not playing the malleable person anymore. All they do is go on about how I am the Herald of Magic and that it is my problem. So be it. It is my problem and I'm going to solve it."

Ngarra sighed, a low, deep sound that seemed to come from the depths of his soul. "I gotta say sorry, but I ain't the right bloke for this role. I'm a pacifist and a diplomat. Ya need a true-blue warrior, someone who's up for drawing blood, or taking a life. Usually, I'd say ya gotta work to find fair ground in this situation. But here ya gotta to prove ya are equals and I'm not the one to make that happen."

I nodded to the man, understanding his point. "I don't disagree. I have no choice but to be the Herald and a councilor at this point."

Shay broke in. "That. Would you explain why you caved when the unicorn asked you?"

I sighed and pointed to my arm. The horn, one section of three full, the snake, one section of four full, and the cat nose and whiskers, just sitting there as if smirking, all but gleamed as if they knew we were talking about them. "There was a situation." I blinked, trying to figure out how to explain it. "They wanted me to prove I could be the herald, or that I was worthy of magic. I wasn't interested in their games, so they kidnapped Jo and Sable, telling me their lives were on the line if I didn't compete." The three looked at me, eyes wide. "I didn't have a choice. During that competition, I made an assumption, a bad one, and almost cost beings dearly. Salistra extracted a price from me. I owe her three favors. The tattoo shows them. She called in the first one that day. There was no option, as she could have just as easily demanded my life and Magic would have enforced it."

They blinked at me and once again it occurred to me just how weird my life was.

"And the snake?" Shay asked, looking at me curiously.

I sighed. "Tirsane thought Salistra had a good idea, but she felt that she owed me favors. I called in one of them a while ago." I wasn't getting into Carelian almost dying. That had been terrifying. "So technically, I have three more favors she owes me. But most of the time, I don't think about it."

The blasted snake knew we were talking about it, and it lifted its head and wiggled a bit, like a squirming puppy. The three of them jerked back. "What was that?" Shay didn't quite squeak out the words, but I couldn't follow up on that as I was fighting down the shudders myself.

"That was the snake. It is one of hers under my skin. It moves sometimes." All three of them shuddered in unison and I took a gulp of my iced tea to push down the revulsion. I hated it when it did that.

"Dare we ask about the whiskers?"

"That I don't know what to tell you. Apparently Bob was jealous he didn't have a mark on me, so Esmere pressed her nose into my arm, and cat tattoo. It at least doesn't do anything."

~It marks you as Cath, protected and honored by us, and blessed by Chaos. It is both a warning, a brand, and a blessing,~ Carelian said as he sprawled out.

"Wait, what... you know, never mind. That actually makes perfect sense and sounds like your mother." I rubbed my head. "Where were we?"

"Warriors needed," Ngarra said simply. If I had to guess, he was very glad that he wasn't the right person for this.

"Right. Here is the problem: they are requiring one of the councilors be from what they call the Beast Realm, but it isn't a separate realm, right?" That I'd been a bit fuzzy on.

"No. It is us." Amadahy sighed. "There is a story there. I do not believe we have time to share it today, but I will ensure the tale is shared with you. I believe it is imperative that you understand. There is a book of the Enclave, as we call it, that explains our history, our separation from the world, and the deal we made with what you call denizens. But other than their requirement for one of our people to be on the council, it doesn't matter now. I will take this back to the lodge and we will discuss."

"You know he will refuse," Ngarra said quietly.

"He may not have a choice," Amadahy responded with exhaustion lacing her tone. "What else do we need to know?"

I pushed away curiosity about who they were discussing. Right now, it didn't matter. "We have rips, the magic that Tirsane is still feeding into the realms, Brix being a jerk, and the task forces being set up. The US government at least is starting to freak out and they want to begin to fight back. Which I can't blame them, but I have zero idea what the results of that will be or what other countries might be doing."

Shay tilted his head and stared at me. "You can't ask China?"

I shrank a bit, then forced myself to stand up. "You're right I can. Want to talk to a dragon?"

"Will it try to eat us?" Shay asked this, but I could see the question on the faces of Ngarra and Amadahy.

"Tiantang? Doubt it. He's like a huge puppy. Come on."

We all walked out to the back lawn. The mid December weather had a light dusting of snow, but nothing major. The weather called for more snow tonight, but that was Albany, New York, for you.

~Tiantang, do you have a minute to talk to me and some friends?~ I pinged him, not worried about the time difference. If he was anything like Carelian, the hours he slept and were awake had little to do with the time of day.

~Cori! Always.~ The words had barely finished ringing in my mind before he was stepping through to wiggle around the lawn. He was almost as bad as the quetzos. His red scales shimmered in the light as he zoomed around, almost flying.

"Tiantang, can you fly?" I asked, curious. I knew the Chinese dragons of legend could fly without wings, but all the others I'd seen fly had wings.

~Soon. Zmaug says soon I will be mature enough to manipulate Air and have it let me fly by flaring out my scales. Look.~

He shook himself and all of his scales snapped out just a bit, creating little flairs of air. ~I can't wait.~

I grinned at the image. "I am sure you will be wonderful. Tiantang these are my fellow councilors from the Lords Council. And we had a question." The information I was about to ask for might be considered state secrets, but if no one knew I knew it, then it didn't matter.

~Of course, anything for Cori!~ He settled down in front of us, his tendril whiskers drifting around him.

The lessons I'd been learning the hard way slipped into my mind. "Do I need to pay for this information?" My tone was wary, and I ignored the frowns from the others. That was another thing I needed to explain to them.

~Zmaug would say yes, but you are Cori. You found my family. There is nothing I won't do to help you.~ He squirmed a bit in excitement.

Guilt and amusement warred with each other, but I pushed it away. I couldn't afford to not get this information. "Are the rips from the realms appearing in China also?"

~Oh yes. They are many and are scaring people badly. Cixi is not happy.~

That answered one concern and proved that the OMO wasn't wrong about it happening everywhere. "Can you tell me what Cixi is planning on doing about them?"

~Ah. She is creating mixed groups of mages, tanks, and many soldiers. We have found a few areas where they are more likely to occur. If they do, the orders are to kill anything that comes out of there.~ His shimmering slowed down. ~We fought about this, but she wants any rips that are near tanks to have shells shot into them and is trying to get missiles that can be shot into any rip before the mages close them. They have to close them no matter the cost. Even if it is their life.~ His voice had dropped to a whisper. ~She does not believe me that this could be very bad.~

"Oh shit." I tried to remember how to breathe. "Does she realize she could start a war between the realms and Earth? If she shoots it into the wrong thing? If she took out dragons or Cath or any of the others, they would react very badly.

~She says they have declared war on us and she won't be a placid lotus.~ His head dropped and he looked miserable.

"I see. I'm trying to stop them, Tiantang. It might be a good idea to ask Zmaug to talk to Cixi?" It was all I could think of. I could try to talk to her too, but Cixi was an odd mix of arrogant and low self-esteem. If you approached it the wrong way, she'd dig her heels in and refuse to change just because she felt she'd lose face.

~She said no. She said if the silly human I chose was that stupid, she would remove her and bring me home. I could learn the joy of living with others of my kind.~ In what sounded like a side whisper, but I knew everyone could hear it. ~She thinks I should have chosen you, challenged Carelian for you.~

~You would have lost and I would be sad to lose a friend,~ Carelian said, his voice dry. ~Zmaug forgets things sometimes.~

~That is what I told her.~ He rippled in a whole-body shrug. ~You are my friend. I like having friends. Play later?~

~Maybe in a week. We can go hiking in the Himalayas again,~ Carelian agreed mildly. I cast him a look, as that wasn't a trip I'd been aware of. He ignored me, curled up with his paws tucked under him.

~Yes! Cori can I help more?~ Tiantang turned his luminous eyes to me.

"No thank you. That helped a lot." I said, trying to hide my dismay.

~Very well. Bye council members, bye Cori, bye Carelian.~

He wiggled around and slipped out of the yard via a sidestep. It was nice not to get the portal spike.

I turned to the councilors, who looked as worried as I felt. "I have to figure out how to stop these rips before our worlds destroy each other."

CHAPTER
THIRTY

The rips that have been plaguing our country and others have all but disappeared over the last month. Perhaps the problem has been solved. If so, what do we make of the continued unrest being seen in China, Russia, and Brazil at this time. Are they experiencing things we aren't, or is the United States just lucky? ~ CNN Mage Focus

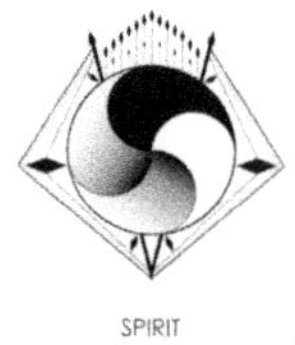

Christmas had been delightful, with Sable's dad, John, and her aunt Larissa, Stephen, Indira, Charles, Marisol, Kris, Tirsane, and Esmere here for a Christmas Eve dinner and gift exchange. Then for Christmas morning, thanks to Carelian, our family, plus Kris, went over to Paolo's house. The rest of the Guzmans were there. Carelian had the kids fawning over him all day while we exchanged gifts, ate too much, and generally had a wonderful relaxing time. Kris filled us in on all the drama at college and his grades, and basically we just leaned into being a family.

None of the denizens mentioned anything, and neither did the mages. We all pretended none of the problems with the rips existed. We did get Kris up to speed, though not the Guzman family. Only Sanchez was given a high-level review, just in case we needed Marisol to take the kids. He'd be able to step in and help. For now, Sanchez was still a favored uncle, but someday we knew we'd explain to the kids where they came from. At the moment he was still single, though I thought he had someone he was getting serious about.

January 3rd, though, we had the council meeting. I had no idea how to run it other than I needed answers. Amadahy said she would be sending her replacement in her stead. It seemed like everyone was getting older. There hadn't been any reports of rips that I knew of since our trip, but I was also aware that many of them could be unreported. Rips would close on their own, but I'd never seen anything that said how long it could take. There were reports of it taking anywhere from minutes to months. And in that time anything could come through, though most people couldn't walk into them. They had tried to explain it to me, but basically the magic that created them made them mostly one way unless you were a plane walker.

That morning I stared at my closet. How did you dress when you were about to declare war? Nothing seemed right so I settled for my comfort mobility clothes. Cargo pants with thick socks and hiking boots, a tank top, a long-sleeved top over it, a travel jacket that had more pockets than even I could fill up, and my backpack. Something told me this might be a very long session. I made sure I had water, food, lip balm, emergency rations for Carelian, and caffeine.

"Carelian, I need you to wear your harness," I called out.

~Why? I have no need to pacify the council members that I am nothing more than a tame animal.~ He walked into the closet as I finished getting dressed. His forearm was all better, and he moved normally again.

"Because I'm not sure that we won't be hitting the ground running, and I'm worried we might need what you have in there." I couldn't swear to it, but something was niggling, and I'd rather be over prepared than under.

He laid his ears back as he stared at me, and I did understand his opinion. I waited.

~How full is your backpack?~ he finally asked.

I lifted it up. I had thrown in a book, and a few other miscellaneous things, but since I wasn't packing extra clothes, my computer, or anything more than a notebook, it wasn't that full. "You're saying see if I can fit it in there?"

~Yes. I am part of you and I do not want them to think you view me as a pet. That would not be good for either of us.~

"Ah. Point." I sat back down and did some repacking. His harness by itself wasn't that big, but when I added the bags that held his leash, bowl, booties, and brush, it took up a bit more room. I compromised by making the tumbler I was carrying with me bigger, and I would grab some coffee concentrate. Making water boil, even pulling water out of the air wasn't that hard. I still had two bottles, just in case, but I'd refill my coffee via magic and concentrate. A jug of concentrate.

~Thank you.~

I paused to look at him. "Carelian, you are and always will be my partner. There are very few things I will ever force you to do."

He followed me down the stairs toward the kitchen. Everyone else was at work or school. The quetzos were snoozing, though Hamiada had agreed to watch them. They were pretty easy to entertain to be honest. She just let them run around her glade and chase insects until tired.

~What things might those be?~ He sounded curious, not mad.

"You roll in stuff that reeks to me. Regardless of how you think it smells, you're getting a bath before you sleep in my bedroom." I stated this with absolute assurance. He'd found a dead something one day and thought it smelled wonderful. I was pretty sure a skunk would have smelled better. He finally agreed to take a bath with soap when all three adults pulled out perfumed body sprays and were covering him in them. He whined the entire time about how awful the chemicals smelled. We didn't care. It was everything we could do not to gag.

He chuckled in a low, rumbling purr. ~Fair enough, I suppose. Do you know what you are going to do?~

"Not a clue besides forcing Brix to answer me. I'm a bit concerned about Amadahy's replacement, but honestly, if I have to, I'll do this by myself." I didn't add that I was pretty sure when all of this was said and done I'd be alone anyhow. No matter what anyone wanted.

~So you will hunt the prey that appears?~

"Exactly. You ready?" I had my pack and everything else I could think of. Jo and Sable knew where I would be and

Stephen had been warned of the council meeting, though I'd given him an out this time. If he called the house, we still had a landline and Hamiada would answer it. She could get a message to me and Carelian almost no matter where we were.

I stood there for a second and let myself realize how truly blessed I was. No matter what else happened, even if I died today, I had been truly and deeply loved.

"If you please?" I waved at the air and he gave me a cat smirk. The rip opened and together we stepped in. The familiar grey stone of the council chambers appeared. It seemed we were early as only Bob and Zmaug were here. Bob raised a tentacle to quiver at me. I waved back, mostly just amused. Of all the denizens here, Bob was the one I didn't know, didn't understand, and had no clue if it even had thoughts the way I did.

I headed over to our area, created a chair for myself, pulled out my thermos, and settled in to watch.

~Would you create a bed for me? I feel like being ostentatious.~ Carelian rubbed his head against my knee from where I sat cross legged in my large chair.

"Any color preference?" I asked as I assembled a large bed mat from the cobblestones next to me.

~Gold I think. It should contrast with my fur.~

I fought back a snicker and colored it gold, or more accurately changed it so it reflected all the wavelengths except for the ones we regarded as gold. I needed to take more science classes.

~Why do I sense you are here to cause trouble?~ Zmaug asked quietly in my mind. Carelian didn't even twitch his tail, so it was a private comment.

~Because I feel the need for some new feathers to put in my hat,~ I responded with a glance in her direction.

~Oh?~ Zmaug lifted her head slightly. ~Is roast bird on the menu?~

~I am not ruling anything out at this point.~ I paused, then went all in. ~Has Tiantang talked to you about what his mage is doing?~

Zmaug tilted her head so one eye had me fully in her view. ~Should he have?~ A hint of wariness slipped into her amused tone.

~Most likely. It will come out during this meeting, but feel free to talk to me about it afterward if you need more information.~ I stressed the word free and her head lifted a bit higher.

~I find myself feeling that I may have preferred the boring meetings prior to you joining us.~

~Most likely.~ I gave her a brilliant smile, showing too many teeth.

~Whose tail are you pulling?~ Carelian asked, still curled up on the bed I'd created.

~Just giving Zmaug a warning.~

~Ah. Yes. This shall not be boring.~

As we watched, more and more drifted in. I saw Frej, the kitsune, the naga, and Tirsane come in. The snakes bobbed at me, flicking tongues as Tirsane glided over to me.

"Good morn, Cori. Are you ready for this?" Her voice was kind, and I smiled. My smile wasn't.

"I think a better question is if you are ready for me."

Her face went immobile for a split second, and then she gave me a slow, brilliant smile. "Oh, this will be fun, will it not?"

I just kept my smile up. "If you sell popcorn, I expect a cut."

Tirsane burst out into a peal of breathtakingly beautiful laughter that stopped everyone else in the room and focused their attention on us. She kept laughing, and I grinned wider.

"Cori, you are just the best thing to happen. I look forward to this," she managed, as she kept chuckling. She slid away, her shoulders still shaking occasionally. It was amusing to watch people drift over to question her, and she just waved them off, saying nothing, but from her snakes, I knew she was still snickering.

~I see you have started the show without me,~ Esmere purred as she walked out from the shadows. She stopped to lick the top of Carelian's head, then rubbed her cheek across mine. ~If I did not express how delicious the fish you sent back with me was, let me tell you again. That was wonderful.~

I snorted a bit. "Now that I've fought what lives in your seas, I'm starting to think I should start a seafood company that sells to denizens. The problem would be figuring out what to charge. I don't need reams of favors owed me, and trying to liquidate gems and gold is a pain."

~True. But if anyone can figure it out, you can. Have you figured out what you are going to do?~

"I believe I need some new feathers for a quill set I'm making," I replied out loud. More than one ear twitched my way, and I ignored them. Esmere froze and looked at me, her tail still.

~I see. This will indeed be an interesting council meeting.~ She licked my hand and headed over to her corner, brushing off people with her tail as anyone that interacted with me was garnering more and more attention.

~My quean is causing them to worry. This is a good thing,~ Carelian murmured, for all that he looked like he was oblivious to the world.

I didn't reply, just reached down to scratch his ear.

"Cori?" Shay called from my right. I glanced over my shoulder to see him approaching. "This is a new look. Making yourself at home?"

"Oh, I plan on being very comfortable." I grinned. "Let's just say I have lots of marshmallows to roast today."

He snorted and stared at the stool. "Would you please? Transform is not my best skill and my ass hurts just looking at that stupid thing."

I tilted my head, looking at him, then focused. A minute later a Roman chaise lounge began to form, complete with pillows the shade of Esmere's fur.

"Ooh, I like." He flopped down and got comfortable. More and more eyes were drifting toward us and I just smiled at anyone who dared meet my eyes.

"Merlin Munroe, Merlin O'Shaugnessy. I have brought your new council member. I am no longer the right fit for this role." I stood and turned at Amadahy's voice. It sounded older and frailer than a few weeks ago.

She was to my left, leaning heavily on her staff, while Kalihchiia stood on the ground next to her, his eyes not leaving her form. Amadahy nodded to the woman who stood next to her. "She will introduce herself. I must go. I apologize for the short notice, but I wish to die in my home with my children."

"Go, honored elder. You have served your people wisely for many years. I will take the burden from here." The woman spoke in a rich tone that made me think she could sing. Between one breath and the next, Amadahy was gone.

Worried, I focused on the woman. She was tall, at least six feet, with a mane of silver hair that was in the Native American braids the history books had told me were traditional. She wore a pair of beige moccasins, skinny leg jeans, a green tank top, and a Harley Davidson leather jacket. Her dark brown eyes turned on us, assessing, weighing us, and I noted she did not dismiss Carelian at all.

Movement caught my eye and a smoke grey fox the size of a

lynx slipped up behind her, almost invisible against the cobble-stone floor.

I lifted an eyebrow but didn't move.

She finished her appraisal and nodded once. "You will do. I am Citlali Taliance and this is Kesis. I believe you know my nephew, John."

CHAPTER

THIRTY-ONE

Foxes appear in multiple cultures as mystical beings. Japan has the kitsune, many Native American tribes held foxes as second only to coyotes in trickster roles. It makes you wonder then about any mage with a fox or foxlike being as a familiar. What sort of mage would have a creature known for its mischievous ways as their companion? ~ Daily Magical News Editorial.

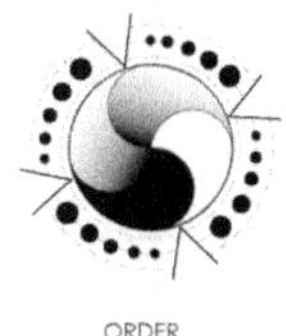

ORDER

I blinked and was about to ask a question when a burst of flame in the middle of the room signaled Brix's arrival.

~Councilors, take your seats.~ Brix's words cut through my brain and I saw Shay wince and Citlali blink.

She glanced at the stool, then our chairs with a flick of an eyebrow toward me. I grinned at her and pulled on Transform to create a seat that I'd seen in a TV series about a land with magic and dragons. A throne made of swords formed, dark, foreboding, and absolutely a declaration of my mood. She raised an eyebrow at me and I just nodded. I'd have to explain later. If I lived through this.

The spectators had moved from the floor to their seats, though I noted Onyx had shown up, something I'd never seen before. He lay next to Zmaug, their bulk taking up the majority of the lawn. They both appeared to have their eyes closed and to be ignoring the discussions. I had no doubt they were paying very close attention.

Another crystal chime, then Brix spoke. ~Council is called. Earth, where is your third?~ The snide tone from the bird set my teeth on edge. I saw Citlali about to rise and I waved at her to remain seated.

"We are all here. The representative from the Beast realm is called Citlali." I didn't stand and barely seemed to pay attention to the phoenix, but I tracked every ruffle of vibrant colored feathers.

~Very well. Is there other business before we deal with the rips?~ he asked, and I practiced my breathing to deal with the slices of pain.

Frej stood, Salistra behind her, acting like a docile animal. "We are reporting that the magic levels in Spirit are at the highest we have seen and there has been a slight increase in births, but many of the beings that live there are long lived and may not be ready for children for another decade or ten. Though more seem interested in Magic than normal. The Valkyries, as always, are all fully dedicated to Magic's needs." She went back to standing behind Salistra and a large Chitterian that sent my hind brain into spasms of fear.

~That does little good when we need the magic to be used now. And your words mean even less when your kind only have children but rarely and then dispose of all the males.~ Brix's words cut, but Frej just shrugged her wings, unmoved by the insult or truth. I had no idea of the social structure of the Valkyries.

~Anyone else?~

No one else moved, and I waited. I had a very good idea of what would happen next. Brix had proven to be a bit predictable.

~Very well then, Herald, when will the rips be halted?~

I rose, moving into the circle that surrounded him. The chamber itself always reminded me of a large castle hold, long and rectangular. But where we stood was all about the circles laid out in the stone by lighter colored stones. There was a huge ring that Brix perched in the middle of and four large circles on the outside, one for each of the realms. As a general rule whomever was speaking would step just inside of the central ring to speak, then step back. It wasn't always followed, but it was obvious it was what passed for conduct rules for them.

I reminded myself that strangling the bird would be counter productive. My steps took me into grasping distance of Brix which only increased the temptation. There was a slight shift in tension as I did so. I kept my back to my fellow humans and everyone else in my peripheral vision. But Brix was who I focused on.

"Yes, about that. I'm still waiting for the information on how I am to close them." My words were calm and even. It was odd. I thought I'd be antsy or worried at this point. I wasn't. If anything, I felt more centered and surer of myself than I'd felt in ages.

~Is that not your job, Herald?~ The sneer was almost a physical assault in the tone. ~But be assured that if you don't, it is Earth that will suffer. The realms will be fine and destruction of your home is no feathers off my back. You were the ones that caused the Undoing, so it would be only fitting for you to suffer for the choices of your ancestors.~

"I see. So if I can't close the rips, oh well? It isn't your problem and you don't need to help?" My voice was mild, curious.

~Exactly. Humans are fragile and too numerous. It would be only fitting if your numbers were cut down a bit.~

I didn't hear disagreement from the others, but a few snickers did slip in from the spectators.

"I can see your point, but you might decide that you need to give me a bit more information. Because the rips are about to become a very real problem for you and every other creature that lives in the realms."

~And how is that? Are you going to leave in a huff? Will you refuse the special favors you grant your friends?~ Brix didn't look at me. Instead, Brix's head attacked feathers that seemed to be in desperate need of being preened.

I wanted to follow up on that. There were so many things that he was hiding behind his words.

"No. But what do you know of our wars?"

The non sequitur seemed to catch the bird off guard. ~Wars? Your wars are human problems. Why would we care or know about them?~ Brix stared at me from under a colorful wing.

"Esmere, do you remember the little pocket realm you

helped me create?" I turned to face her, ignoring the puffed-up bird.

She blinked her amber eyes at me, but nodded. ~Yes.~

"Would you show that universe to everyone? Don't open it all the way up, just show it to them." I'd looked at it a week ago, basically peered through the peephole. It was still awash in fire, radiation, and power. Even looking at it had given me a headache.

~Very well.~ She licked her tail as she showed everyone. It was like having an image presented in front of you. And you almost instinctively leaned closer to see into it.

The room exploded in shrieks and hisses of horror and almost everyone took a step back. The weight of the combined stares felt physical as I turned to focus on Brix. The bird had almost fallen off the perch and he was beating his wings to get back to balance.

~What is that? That makes Chaos look simple and tame.~ The words were hissed into my mind, all but spitting the venom in the voice.

"That was the smallest of our nuclear weapons. We have many that are much bigger. We have what we call bombs that can level cities, dig craters, even leave dents in the moon. Humans are very, very good at destruction. Right now, multiple countries are preparing to launch these weapons into the rips." I knew the US and China were for sure. That counted as multiple, so I was safe from lie sensing. "Imagine if they launch these into an open rip? I know some have opened and let loose creatures. Small, vicious ones. There was one that let in a leviathan. Others may not go anywhere. But can you imagine what would happen if one opened over the dragon's nesting grounds? Or Salistra's grove? What about the plains the Cath hunt on?"

Zmaug and Onyx were both sitting up and staring at me. Dragon faces weren't good at expressing emotion, but the black smoke billowing up from their nostrils and wreathing their heads said worlds about their current state.

There was an explosion of chatter and fear as the other councilors whispered among themselves. I kept staring at Brix.

"So, you're right, Earth might be destroyed. But I'm betting there is a much better chance that if we launch a few nukes into the rips that the resulting death and destruction will take centuries for magic to heal. And that would drain the magic overload. So, I mean, I guess I can do nothing. Let each country deal with it as they choose."

Brix actively squawked, launching himself into the air and hovering right in front of me.

~You dare? You are the Herald. Your job is to protect Magic and repair the damage. This is your fault from the beginning, giving away so much magic.~

"You say I'm the herald." I leaned in, my nose less than five inches from his beak. "Excellent. Then the herald demands your assistance to save the realms."

~You should not need it. This is your job!~ Brix turned brighter with flames flicking around feathers as the phoenix shouted at me.

"Then why should I care? You won't help me; therefore, I don't need to worry about your realms. I can make sure Earth knows exactly where to send their weapons. We will be fine if that happens." I turned and managed two steps toward my chair.

~You will listen to the council.~ The words were shrieked and an involuntary wince pulled my head down just enough to miss the buffet of wings that slapped across where my head had been.

I whipped around, my left hand covered in water, as I swung at the bird. It was a hard backhand that slammed into the fire-covered chest. There was a lot of force in my hit and Brix cartwheeled in the air three times before catching the air.

~You dare?~ The words were hissed ice that stabbed into my brain doing nothing but raising my anger.

"Yes. You are not my master and you hit me first. Come at me," I taunted the puffed-up bird. My right hand was held up with a ball of ice in it. Part of me was aware of the shock rippling around me. Most of me didn't care. The attitude had to go.

A wing was waved at me, feathers of flame darting toward me. I flipped my left hand pushing air in front of me as I flung the ice hard. I didn't dare pull my punches in this fight. The ice headed for the center of Brix's chest. A few flaps of wings and it looked like my ice would miss but I sent a gust of Air under it and it went straight up, catching the tail where it exploded into water that I froze as it soaked the feathers.

Brix fell to the ground like a rock. For a moment, all you could see was colored feathers flapping in an effort to sit up correctly. A flash of flames, a cloud of steam, and the bird was back on the perch. I turned, glaring at him, ready to incinerate the wood he stood on.

~Pax~,"Pax," Tirsane called, her voice cutting through the chatter, the mindspeak cutting off everyone.

"Brix, you have shown enough arrogance for a while. Cori has proven she is not to be dismissed nor used as a pawn. Either run this council with equality or I will call for a vote of no confidence and we will vote in a new Head Lord." Her words caused a ripple of shock and approval as Brix and I faced off.

He ruffled his feathers twice, not looking away from me. ~Humans were what caused the Undoing. It is up to her to fix it. Learn your history human. The answers are there if you are strong enough to find them. If not, then Magic chose poorly. She has before. Council is ended.~

Before anyone could respond, he flared up and disappeared, but this time I felt how he flew away. It was similar to sidestepping, smaller, focused, but I was pretty sure I could stop it if I wanted to. I nodded to myself and turned. Everyone stared at me. The attitudes ranged from shock to reconsidering, with a few smirks in there mostly from those who knew me.

Shay and Citlali just stared at me, Shay more openly than Citlali. I strode back to them. "Come on, next step."

"Are you insane?" Shay muttered as he rose, his face paler than it had been.

"No. I'm a merlin. And I Merlin blasted won't be treated as lesser by a bird."

Citlali gave me a long look. "We should talk later."

"Yes, after. Now come on." I spared a glance at Carelian. He was still curled up, looking like he hadn't moved a hair with all the fuss. Kesis was curled up next to him, as far as I could tell, sound asleep.

With two humans in tow, I headed directly to Order. Tirsane, I was pretty sure would tell me what I wanted. Chaos was next. I didn't bother to hide my smile as I stalked toward the unicorn, Valkyrie, and Chitterian. I needed information.

Never attempt to win by force what can be won by deception. – Niccolo Machiavelli

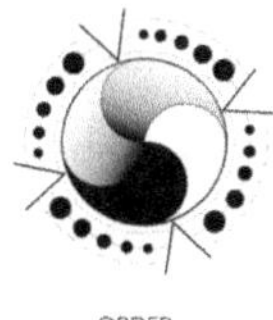

ORDER

"Frej, it is good to see you. At some point you should come over for some more of the mead. I found a new supplier." My voice was light and friendly and I saw all of them blink and try to reorient. What had they expected— me to come over swinging a sword?

"I, well, yes. You are looking much better than the last time I visited. I take it the birth went well?" she managed after a stutter or two. Her hand didn't stray far from her sword and I didn't blame her at all.

"It definitely qualified as a once in a lifetime event and one I have zero desire to repeat," I said with a smile. "Salistra, I see you are looking - horsey." I had no idea what else to say that wouldn't be a lie.

A snicker came from the horse. ~You are finally becoming a Herald. It took you long enough. I had feared it would never happen.~

"I still believe that you shouldn't need one, but you won't see that there are better ways to handle things. Since no one will give me any other options, I'll do it." I pivoted to nod to the huge creature next to me. "And the other Lord?" The Chitterian had at least twelve legs, maybe more depending on if smaller ones were hidden by being tucked up under her.

Frej cleared her throat. "This is Cesttark. I am surprised you did not back away screaming from her. Most find her discomfiting."

I shot Frej a look. "I try very hard to not be a bigot." I turned a bit to face Cesttark. "I am honored to meet you. One of my friends has a focus that is Chitterian, Arachena. She is delightful."

The Chitterian flushed to a bright pink, almost neon. ~Arachena. Friend. Smart. Good hunter. Fast weaver.~

"So is her mage. He helped me defeat a leviathan."

All three of the Order lords stared at me. "Leviathan?" Frej asked slowly.

"Well, that is my name for it. Carelian said they don't really have names. Huge, like more than sixty feet huge, with four eyes and a mouth full of teeth." I shuddered at the memory of that thing.

"You killed one?" Frej asked, just staring at me.

"Me? Yes, well no, not by myself. I had two other merlins

and an archmage with me, plus Carelian. He saved the day more than we realized. But yeah, it was definitely dead." That much I was sure of.

~I must admit I am impressed. They are not easily killed,~ Salistra said, her crystal bell tones softer than normal.

"No shit. That thing almost took out our boat," I said.

"Wait, you were on the water and you killed it?" Frej burst in, her voice hitting a sharp note.

"Well, yeah. We were out fishing." I looked at them. "Don't tell me none of you have ever killed one."

"I am unaware of anyone that has succeeded in doing that. You are either braver than I thought or an idiot." Frej was still looking at me with a weird look.

"Neither, she simply responded to the situation. The fish she caught was delicious, though," Tirsane said, sliding into the conversation. "The retelling of that battle would make for an excellent epic poem."

The three Order Lords nodded to Tirsane as she joined the conversation.

"Hey, Tirsane. So, do you have any idea where to find the information bird-brain is talking about? I'm not even sure what the Undoing was or why he seems to be blaming me. And I'd like to remind you, this is the Herald of Magic asking for help to solve a problem that affects all of us." I so didn't have time to deal with the trading of favors or anything else of that nature.

~I not know. Our lives not long. Undoing ancient, ancient story,~ Cesttark said, waving two front mandibles.

Frej frowned for a minute, her eyes locked on me. "It doesn't mean much to me. I mean, I know what the Undoing was, but the Valkyrie were never locked out the way others were. For a while, the worship gave us access to our lands. It has only been in the last two hundred years or so that the calls to Earth have lessened." She must have seen the confusion on my face and flickered her wings. "Faith and the cry of a battle can open a portal for our realm specifically. But if you don't believe, it doesn't open. Like I said, those have been fainter, and we have few other reasons to go to Earth."

"Do you really collect souls?" Shay asked. I glanced at him and he seemed completely captivated by the conversation.

Frej laughed. "Do you still think that? That we take heroes to Valhalla?"

"It is what the myths say," he countered.

"No. We grab men worthy of living a bit longer and take those who would otherwise die without our interference. And contrary to Brix's insinuations, we don't kill male children. They are placed in homes on Earth where most men eventually go back to." She shrugged. "It works."

The lure to ask more questions was there, but that wasn't my purpose today. I needed information more than I needed legends.

"So, what was the Undoing?"

Tirsane replied, her snakes coiled up tight. "It was when Magic and Earth were separated, but I don't know what caused it or when. I know the Heralds before that, so there are rough Earth timelines, but for many it was unnoticed, and those that cared have long since died. We are not immortal and even for us, three thousand or more years is a very long time."

"So why is he harping on it? I've never heard anyone wishing for the 'good ole days' while I've been here. Is it a thing?"

Tirsane and Salistra stared at each other for a minute, then back at me. "Actually no," Tirsane said. "I don't believe I've heard much bemoaning about that."

~Some of the older ones talked about the gifts their ancestors used to receive,~ Salistra said. ~Like there would be offerings of honey and mead for help with one thing or another. The ability to get things that your people made was higher, but for actually missing it? Not that I have heard of.~

All of them sounded unsure of anything.

I scrubbed my hands across my face. "Fine. I'll go talk to Bob. But this is a serious request, order if you want an order from the Herald. I need some information if you want me to do this. Otherwise, the cost is going to be greater than I think anyone wants to pay. I killed one leviathan, but too many more of them would devastate our oceans. If creatures keep slipping out into populated areas, there will be repercussions. I get that this seems a someday thing. It isn't. It is a now thing that could become a never if we aren't careful."

I started to turn away, seeing the shuttered expression on Citlali and considering expression on Shay. They needed information badly, but it would have to wait until we weren't here.

I paused, giving them one last hard look. "Oh, one last thing to consider. If I die, you lose the primary chance you have of stopping Earth from retaliating. You might want to think about that." I didn't glance back as I headed over to Chaos.

"Cori, are you sure you know what you are doing?" Shay asked in a low whisper.

"I keep telling you, everyone here has better hearing than you do. Whispering is a wasted effort. And nope. But I do know if they don't help, we are all in a world of hurt. I promise I'll explain as soon as we are done here." Bob was the last being I wanted to deal with, but he was the major one left and while Esmere could ask, I suspected I had the ability to force answers.

I reached the ring where the Chaos lords lounged and I walked right in. Esmere flipped her tail at me but didn't say anything. "Esmere, Bob. I don't believe I've met your third lord." I focused on the Naga, who watched me like I was a mongoose getting ready to pounce. The imagery amused me, as it was a bit more accurate than she might think.

~Cori, this is Shiarissa of the Venom Nagas. Shiarissa, Cori Munroe - Herald.~ Esmere's voice was dry enough to make me want my tumbler, but instead I gave the Naga a nod. She was taller than me on her tail, but not as tall as Tirsane. They both had the lower bodies of snakes, but while Tirsane had scales, the naga had banded leather like skin instead. She was a medium brown color, about what a blond roast with a splash of espresso in it would look like. Her hair was lustrous black. And fell to her shoulder blades. The eyes that stared at me were light green with obsidian pupils slit vertically. She was pretty, but there was something about her eyes and the structure of her face that made her look more reptilian than Tirsane did.

"I have seen you. You think you are more important than us because you are the herald," she said. Her voice had a soft level of sibilance to it, making the difference between her and Tirsane more apparent.

"No. You all say I'm the Herald. I just quit arguing. And if you're going to treat me like I'm the Herald and demand impossible things from me, screw it, I'll go with it, but don't lay this on me." I raised my hand as I talked, having zero care if I offended or not.

"You don't want the power, the honor of the role?" Her eyes were locked on me, questioning.

"Honor? Power? I'm sorry, are there benefits someone didn't bother to share with me? So far I've gotten shit dumped on me, told it is my problem, and then everyone bails. If there is some benefit to this other than bragging rights, which I don't need, please tell me." I didn't give an inch.

Her mouth opened then closed and dark brows drew down heavily over her eyes, but she didn't say anything else.

"So, girls and blobs, does anyone have any information or know where I can find it? At this point, do you know someone that was alive and witnessed the Undoing?" I gazed at each of them in turn, arms across my chest and gaze direct.

Esmere flicked her tail at me. ~Cath only live a few hundred years. I don't even know of any whose great-grandparents were around at that time. We don't write books, we tell all of our stories orally. And the only story of the Undoing Carelian should know.~

~I do? What is that?~ Carelian asked, though a quick glance showed him still curled up in the bed peacefully with Kesis.

~It would be Fish Now Gone,~ Esmere said her voice calm.

~Oh. Yes, that one. I can tell that one but I do not think there will be much information.~

"Okay, later at home." Just from the name and all the Cath's fascination with fish, I had a strong suspicion of what the tale would contain, but I'd listen anyhow. I took a deep breath and faced the blob of Chaos. "Bob, do you know anything about this Undoing? Or someone that is old enough to remember being there?"

The blob of black tarriness had shifted somehow facing me. I braced myself. ~You were child on field. You were weak. You strong enough to make me tell?~

Where Salistra was crystal when she spoke to me, Esmere the rumble of a purr, Bob was a mace made of needle-sharp points that slammed into my head. I heard Shay and Citlali groan behind me. A trickle of blood tickled as it slipped down to my lip.

"Maybe, maybe not. It would be easier to let it be known that Chaos is in favor of the rips and doesn't care if other realms are destroyed. Then the other lords can deal with you." I lifted my hand and wiped the blood off with my thumb, not bothering to look at my hand.

~Smart. But no. Am old, but memory of before not real, not detailed. Know it happened. Not remember whys, whos, or whats.~ The attack felt less brutal this time, but I still felt blood ooze from both nostrils now.

"Very well. If you know or remember something, tell me, please. I can't do anything if I don't know what to do."

The blob bobbled, then slumped down, leaving a tarry stain on the cobblestones.

~Well done, Cori.~

I glanced at Esmere. "Maybe. They don't discount me now, but I still don't have anything to go on."

She hissed a bit. ~I know. We will keep looking. Go, take medicine for your head. The others are hurting.~

I turned at that to see a pale Shay with blood running from his nose and ears, while Citlali had one eye red with burst vessels and blood oozed from where she had clenched her hands so hard the nails cut into the skin.

"Come on, my fellow lords. You look like you could use a drink and some painkillers." I headed to Carelian, who had stood stretching.

"Or ten," muttered Shay, as he and Citlali turned to follow me.

THIRTY-THREE

As more rips occur and the government is reaching out to the Houses and colleges for assistance in closing them, the recall of merlins is coming up again and again. Merlins are the most powerful of mages and they are able to close rips like these with a smaller amount of offering as opposed to even an arch mage. And those with familiars are even less. The rules to recall merlins state that there must be a national disaster or emergency. If the President declares the rips either of those, then they will be open to being recalled to active duty. ~ CNN Mage Focus

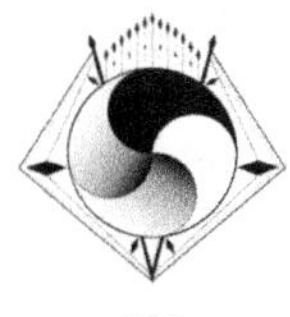
SPIRIT

I left the furniture, curious as to if it would still be there next time, and stepped through the portal to home. I moaned with relief as we entered the house and I stripped off my backpack and jacket. It had definitely been overkill, but made me feel better and I was all for that.

I glanced at the clock, one p.m. Time had gone faster than I thought.

"Lunch? I'm starving? And I'm grabbing ibuprofen. You want some?"

"Painkillers, so much, yes. And yes, please. More fish," Shay said eagerly.

I glanced at Citlali, who had the best poker face I'd ever seen. "I'm going to go wash up. If you two would like, there is a bathroom right around the corner." They both nodded, and I headed upstairs to wash my face. The two trails of blood had dried on my face, my hair was shorter, and the eyes that looked back at me seemed foreign and old. I stared at myself in the mirror, wondering who the mage was that looked back at me.

It didn't matter. I grabbed a bottle of pills and headed back downstairs. I found both of them standing awkwardly in the kitchen. "Take a seat at the bar." I set the bottle down, pulled out glasses, and filled them with water. We all reached for them and swallowed the pills and icy water.

"Citlali, hi. I'm Cori. I'm sorry your introduction was so..." I fumbled for the right word.

"Adventure filled?" she said dryly.

I grinned. "That. I'm sure you both have questions, and Citlali, do you mind sharing why you were picked and what was the dying thing Amadahy mentioned?" That part worried and confused me.

"We know when our time is coming, especially a mage of

her age. She wanted to prepare. I think she has a few weeks at most," Citlali said, her voice calm.

"Oh. Is there something I can do?" Guilt slammed into me with the force of a sledgehammer.

Citlali smiled, a hint of joy in that. "No. There is nothing to grieve about. She has lived a full good life. She is ready to join our ancestors."

It wasn't the words as much as how she said them that reassured me. "Okay. So, what do we need to know about you and what do you need to know about us?"

She took another drink of water as I started pulling food out for all of us. "Oh, and does Kesis like fish?"

~Kesis loves fish, thank you very much,~ a new voice said in my head.

I twisted to see the fox sitting in the fourth bar seat, watching me with bright brownish red eyes.

"So noted. Kesis, I'm Cori, it's nice to meet you." I caught the look of surprise on Citlali's face as I moved back to the fridge.

"She spoke to you." Her voice was flat.

"Yeah, most of them do, and I'm not sure why," I said with a shrug.

~It is because you see beings, not creatures or animals. You accept all of us and your mind welcomes our words. So many, even those that are mages with focuses, can not do that. It makes you comfortable to speak to,~ Kesis said.

"Ah. Okay." I wasn't sure what to do with that.

"Is that why, when you speak to me, it always sounds slightly muffled and distorted?" Shay asked Carelian suddenly.

~Yes,~ Carelian said. ~We have to push harder for you to hear. For my quean, we have to work to not include her in conversations. Though you have been getting better.~

Citlali sat there looking at me with a strange look on her

face. "I am beginning to understand why Amadahy called you Child of Coyote. You definitely leave Chaos in your wake."

I sighed as I threw swordfish in a pan for a quick sear after seasoning it. I'd prepared Sashimi for the cats, and I set out a bottle of hot sauce for Carelian. "You have no idea how often people tell me that."

She just looked at me, then shook her head. "You asked what you needed to know about me. Need is an unusual word. Not want. You let me choose what I share with you, not demanding answers. Why?"

I shrugged. "You have things that I don't need to know. You're obviously not a teenager, so I'm going to trust you have the ability to choose to tell me what I need for this situation. Later, if we become friends, you can share more as you feel like it or not. Right now, I'd just like to see if we can solve the problem that has been dumped in my lap." The aroma of cooking fish filled the air and everyone glanced at the pan with hungry looks.

Shay just laughed. "Cori has been a vehicle for Chaos since I met her and that was what, twenty years ago? At that time, she was a barista at the only coffee shop in town. Back then I was much more self-centered than I am now."

I cast him a disbelieving glance as I put some cheese and crackers out to nibble on. I handed a few pieces of cheese to Carelian and Kesis. Kesis ate it with apparent gusto.

"I am," he protested. "Sloan has a way of not letting you lie to yourself. It's annoying having a friend who's a psychologist. It was his secondary degree." Shay reached for the crackers and cheese after that, stuffing his face. The meds were kicking in for all of us, as I could see the stress lines fading from faces.

"Amadahy and Ngarra came back and explained the situation to our council, saying they were looking for a warrior who was the equivalent of your merlins. I am one of the few. Most of our people are what you would call archmages. I am also one of the few that hunt in the realms."

~Citlali and I are excellent hunters. We know the forests and the plains. The beasts we hunt always fall to our weapons.~ Kesis had finished the cheese while we were talking.

"Carelian, where do you want to eat?" He had made it clear long ago that eating on the floor was not acceptable. He wasn't a pet. He'd been sitting on the floor watching all of us, but hadn't jumped up into the empty stool between Citlali and Shay. I figured he'd tell me why later.

~Set it on the counter, I'll graze. I am not overly hungry at the moment.~

I nodded and put a plate of sashimi on the end of the counter and a plate in front of Kesis. The fox didn't have hands the way Carelian did, but was a neat eater with her pointed nose and teeth.

"They do, but I was trained in the ways to use magic as a weapon. Most mages find that path too arduous, but Kesis and I enjoy the challenges and opportunities to seek prey." Citlali had regained a calm expression, but her dark brown eyes watched and analyzed everything.

"What branch?" I asked. I was everything. Shay was primarily Chaos.

"Order, though we call it Life."

I shot her a look. So little was known about their land or society.

She provided the information. "Our branches in English would be called Life, Entropy, and Essence. The actual words we use aren't so simple, but it is close enough."

I longed to ask about what language or languages they used, but now wasn't the time. "That makes sense. What do you want to know about me or this whole mess?" I plated the swordfish, grabbed leftover pasta salad from the fridge and set it on the counter while providing some utensils. "Eat up. Let me know if you need something else. I assumed there weren't any allergies to worry about." Mages rarely had food allergies, so if they had, I figured they would have spoken up.

Everyone was silent as we ate a few bites and I felt myself relax as the flavors hit my tongue, then my stomach. It was like my body quit tensing for a blow, the food telling my hind brain I was safe.

"Can you give me an overview about the Magic that is being fed in, the rips, and where you got the information about Earth launching weapons into the rips?" Citlali asked after a few minutes of eating.

"Sure." I filled them in with everything I knew, as well as the fact that I had strong access to all classes. I thought Shay might choke when I said that. "Just keep that one a secret. I really don't want the OMO to know and there is that blasted clause about recall for merlins. The last thing I need is the government coming up with a reason to reactivate me because I'm uber powerful. Besides, even with that, closing these rips is expensive." I pointed to my hair, that was just past my shoulder blades. "I've used up about six inches in the last few months between the leviathan and the rips, and that is with a familiar."

They both sat there not talking while we ate. I didn't rush anyone. It was a lot to take in, and if time allowed us to come up with answers, we could sit here all day.

"I don't know what to say. Can you clarify what was going on with the council meeting today? I felt like I'd walked into a battle of cliques."

"Me too!" Shay said, his head jerking up. "I knew you were going to push things, but that was a bit extreme."

"Remember what I said about us being too polite? Well, when I found out about the weapons and rips on Earth, I realized it wasn't that I needed to be less polite. I needed to be in their faces and force them to deal with me."

"And if they killed you?" Citlali asked slowly. "They are powerful beings."

~And my quean is more powerful,~ Carelian said, a note of warning in his voice. ~They will not think of her as lesser.~

I reached over to scratch his head. He'd been standing on his hind legs picking up the hot sauce and covering pieces of fish with it. He'd passed one over to Kesis per a private request I assumed. The fox had not liked it, taking one lick and pushing it back to him. Carelian ate it gladly. Cath had no fear of cooties at all.

"That was a possibility, but I judged it a low one. They are all about posturing and social standing. They dismiss humans because we have no natural weapons and we are taught to be polite. There is a huge swath of people in our society that can sense lies, so we rarely lie, and we expect others to act the same. The denizens don't. They work on power and strength, and if you can't prove you are strong enough to be taken seriously, they won't." I shrugged. "The draft and everything else pounds it into mages to be polite. Don't use your powers for offence. Make sure you don't break the law. It is a hard mindset to break. And it is exactly the wrong mindset to use with them."

They both looked at me, a dawning look of understanding on Shay's face and calculated thought on Citlali's.

"I begin to see the issue. What about this information you need to stop the rips?" Citlali had finished her food and was just moving the bones around on the plate.

"I wish I knew. Most of them don't write. And if the Undoing was three thousand years ago, that is a long time. We don't have anything talking about it that I know of. Though I need to put up a request on the House of Emrys board, maybe see if anyone has seen some really old texts that mention it."

Shay sighed. "By the time this is done, I'm going to need a case of tequila. Too bad they don't have a library where all this information is stored."

It felt like someone had slapped me in the face. "Of course. How the fuck did I forget?" I wanted to scream at my own stupidity. "Hamiada? Are you here?"

"Of course, Cori," she said as she stepped out of the wall into the kitchen. Shay squeaked, but the look of shock on Citlali's face would have caused me to ask questions. But right now, I had something much more important to ask.

"Hamiada, the trials you put me through to be a Herald. Do you remember those?" I asked, my voice almost desperate.

"I did not really put you through them. That was Magic and the Lords. I believe Tirsane, Salistra, and Bob were directly behind them, but yes." She was almost all green today and the flowers tracing her arms and collar bones were pale yellow and pink. Motherhood was making her all but glow with happiness.

"Okay. The challenge I did for Order. The library," I said, my heart lodged in my throat. "Was the library real?" Everything hung on that question.

THIRTY-FOUR

The Library of Alexandria has always been the lost treasure for those who seek knowledge. But there is so much history in our songs, our poems, those stories that travel down via families. Join the Memory project and submit your stories and memories before they are lost, just like the Library was. ~ Memory Project

CHAOS

"Library?" Hamiada frowned at me, then she grinned. "Oh, yes, the library. You had to get a stone or something. I assume it was real. Why?"

"There were so many books there, including I think, ones written a long time ago." I avoided the memory of the book of Death. If I had seen that then, there would have been my name written on it. The thought saddened me, but it was over and done. All I could do was move forward. "Those books might have the answers I'm looking for."

Hamiada wiggled her shoulders. "I really don't know what was magic-generated, what was realms, and what was real. Obviously, you went to Salistra's realm as part of your challenge. And the villages were mostly magical constructs, basically like your moving pictures? They were there to make you think and react that way based on your past. But the library?"

"That was Spirit, right?"

"Yes. Tirsane helped to create that," Hamiada said with a nod.

"Thank you so much. Maybe we have an answer after all." Hamiada waved at Shay and Citlali and stepped back into the walls, and probably headed to one of the houses.

"Cori, what are you talking about?" Shay asked.

I quickly explained about the trials, the places I had to go. "There are two statues upstairs of mages that didn't pass the tests. There used to be three, but I traded one of them to Tirsane to get some information. Speaking of which." I closed my eyes and focused on Tirsane.

~Tirsane, do you have a minute?~

There was a slight delay, then her voice. ~I am still at the council so anything would be a nice distraction.~

Shay and Citlali were looking at me, and I knew they couldn't hear this. "I'm talking to Tirsane. Give me a minute." I switched to mindspeak. ~Tirsane, when I did the challenges or trials for magic, there was a library in the Spirit trial. Was it real?~

There was a long period of silence. ~Library. I had forgotten about that. I...~ she trailed off. ~I don't understand. I should have remembered about the Library. And even now I forget about it. It is real, but... we don't use or think of it often. I believe there are only five races that can easily write. And only seven or eight that have ever bothered encouraging reading as a species.~ She still sounded odd, as if I'd shaken her world view.

~So, we can go to the Library?~ I couldn't keep the eagerness out of my voice. I enjoyed libraries in the first place, but being able to actually look at those books made my desire to know all but scream in joy.

~Maybe? I mean it is the Library, but I'm not positive how to get there. I... where did you need to go?~ Her voice sounded confused again.

My joy drained out of me like I'd been filled full of sadness holes. ~The Library? It is in your realm.~

~Oh, yes, it is. And?~

If I didn't know better, I'd have said she wasn't paying me any attention, but I knew she was. But Magic was wrapped around this. ~Tirsane, may I have open permission as the Herald to Magic to go through your realm to look for the Library?~

~The Library? Of course, that might hold the answers you need. Feel free, but I don't know where it is.~

~That is okay. Thank you Tirsane.~ I ended the conversation and sagged back against the counter. "I swear I find out one thing and then another obstacle jumps in my way." I peered at the two of them. "Do you remember me asking Hamiada about a library?"

Shay gave me a funny look. "Are you feeling okay, Cori?"

"I don't know. Do you remember?" I held on to the counter, completely unsure as to which answer I wanted or which I'd get.

"Yeah. You just asked the dryad not three minutes ago." He stared at me. "Do you need some coffee or a nap?"

I sagged in relief and glanced at the two familiars who had just as funny of a look on their faces. "You two remember as well?"

~Yes. I take it Tirsane had issues?~ Carelian said with a whisker twitch.

"Yes," I muttered. I started putting the dishes away with a bit more force than was strictly healthy for their integrity.

"I don't understand," Citlali said. "The Spirit Lord didn't remember a library that you visited a decade ago?"

"No, not at all. Which means maybe it isn't real. Maybe it is, and Magic doesn't want it found. Or maybe something else." I stood in the kitchen, not knowing where to go or what to do next. A splash of pain pulled my attention to the back of the house.

Esmere walked in, her emerald green fur shining. ~Carelian said you thought Magic was interfering?~

Citlali took in a sharp breath while Kesis dropped off the stool and hid under the table. Shay just paled and darted his eyes around. I sighed.

"I don't know if it is a good thing or a bad thing, that I consistently forget you're a huge Apex predator and when you lay down in council chambers, you appear much smaller. Shay, I know you've met Esmere. Citlali, this is Esmere, Chaos Lord, as I'm sure you figured out, and Carelian's mother. And my friend." I scratched her forehead for a moment. "I have some sashimi left. Would you like it?"

She rumbled a purr in an answer. ~That would be wonderful. It is good to meet you, Citlali. So, what is the question?~

Citlali blinked and her gaze went from Esmere's large pony size to Carelian's large Saint Bernard size. "Will you get that big?"

~Possibly. But that is years away. My *Malkin* is almost two hundred. We get larger with age and good food.~ Carelian sounded unconcerned. I winced, thinking if he got that big, I'd need a larger bed.

I set out some of the sashimi, pulling it from the stasis realm Hamiada had created. With a few quick moves I had it plated for her. She just sat next to the counter like Carelian had done, but she didn't need to rise up on her hind legs. She just reached out and picked up the pieces, tossing them into her mouth.

~What is the issue?~

"Esmere, do you know of a Library in the realms?" I asked, keeping my voice calm.

~Of course, it is the Library of Magic—" She broke off and froze mid reach. ~Void shards!~ She hissed. ~Why did I not remember about the Library? I have always known of that. Yet when you were pregnant and we were searching for answers, none of us thought of it. When you asked about this not an hour ago, it never occurred to me. With all our fretting, it never popped up as this might be something that could be of use. What is going on?~ There was a level of anger in her voice that would have had me stepping back, if I wasn't already pressed against a counter.

"So, you know of it?" I asked, this time cautious.

~Yes, we all do but...~ She trailed off, setting a piece of sashimi back down on the plate. ~Yet at no time have I thought of it.~ She whacked Carelian on the head. ~Do you remember the library?~

He laid his ears back and hissed a bit at her, but still responded. ~No? Should I? I remember her mentioning it when she entered. But I had never been there before. I did not go with her, I stayed to watch my queans. At that time, Hamiada was not to be trusted, but she has become a friend over the years. ~

Esmere's tail twitched as if it wanted to lash at something. ~Ah, I suppose not.~ She stared at the floor for a long time. I glanced over at the others to see pale faces and I almost felt sorry for them. My normal life made everyone else's crazy lives seem boring by comparison.

"This could be me speaking out of turn, but is it possible you only remember when in the presence of the Herald?" Citlali asked slowly. "Which is why Carelian would never forget, because he is always around her."

Esmere lifted her head to stare at Citlali, who met her gaze for gaze, much to my amusement. ~That is an excellent question. Let us test it. I shall go to my plains.~ She turned and padded out of the room and a splash of pain later, I no longer sensed her in the house.

"You want anything else?" I asked the other two as I turned to put dishes away. I'd gotten better at cooking, but still I preferred quick, easy to grill options to anything else. It meant I couldn't leave it, which was when disasters always happened.

"Whiskey and a more comfortable chair?" Shay asked.

I peered at the circles under his eyes and nodded. "In the sunroom." He nodded and rose, then made his way there. "Citlali?"

"Tea is preferable."

I grabbed a kettle, filled it with water, used a trace of magic to set it boiling, then pulled a mug from the cupboard and a tea selection. "Help yourself."

My own desires led to Mexican coffee. I needed the sugar and the caffeine. Minutes later, all of us were in the sun room, the fireplace going, and Carelian and Kesis sprawled out in front, enjoying the heat.

~Esmere?~ I pinged.

~Yes Cori?~ Her voice a distracted purr.

Just the way she asked that told me she'd forgotten, but I pushed ahead anyhow. ~Do you know anything about the Library of Magic?~

~Of course. That is where you should go. Why haven't you gone already? Didn't you go once?~ She trailed off as if distracted by something. ~Cori, why do I have a craving for your sashimi to the point I can taste it in my mouth?~ Her voice was confused and a bit twitchy.

~It's okay. I'll send Carelian over to you with some later. Thank you.~

~Very well. I do love your fish though.~ She ended the conversation, and I looked at the others and shook my head.

"She didn't even remember being here a short while ago."

~I do not like that anything, even Magic, is messing with memories.~ Carelian didn't move from the fireplace, but his ears were back and his tail twitched a bit harder than normal.

"Agreed. But where does that leave us? Is it the Herald or humans? Will we forget? Will you? What are the options?" Shay asked as he stared morosely into his half full whiskey glass.

"I suppose anyone with a strong in Psychic could do that. You can pull on memories. There is no reason why you couldn't destroy them. I just never tried." I wrapped my hands around my mug, heating it back up as I thought. "Let's plan for the worst case." I groaned as I said that and double checked that none of us had Murphy's Cloak up.

"And that would be?" Citlali asked, her own mug steaming in her hands.

I rose and grabbed a notebook from the pile of things we kept in here for the kids. It had scribbles all over it, but there was a crayon and a blank sheet. It would work. "It would be me writing out that I needed to visit the Library of Magic located in

Spirit. And it means that I need to go sooner rather than later." I wrote carefully as I spoke, recording every bit of information as neatly as I could. Crayons were not the neatest of writing instruments.

Citlali nodded. "Just you, or should all of us go?"

"I don't know." And I didn't. "Last time it was a test, but this time it is like something is specifically hiding that Library from us, and I don't think Brix is that powerful. And I'm really scared the moment we leave each other's company we will all forget." I let a bitter laugh slip out. "And even worse, I don't know if it will have the answers I need."

Shay shrugged. "I guess there isn't a reason we can't go now."

My phone rang, and I recognized the ring tone. "You have got to be kidding me." I sighed and picked it up. "Hello?"

"Cori..." Stephen sounded frantic. "I need your help."

CHAPTER

THIRTY-FIVE

Are the rips the precursor to the end of our way of life? Global warming has been the hot topic for the last two decades, but now the tears between this reality and others are proving a much greater threat. Can humanity survive this or is this what killed civilizations before us? ~ Magical Daily News

---

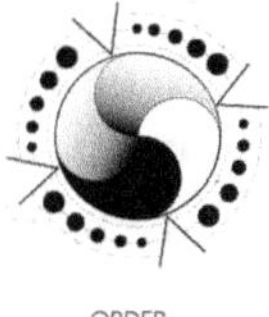

ORDER

"Rip?" I asked, suddenly exhausted.

"Yes. They have two, but the one we have to stop now, actually an hour ago, is the one at Niagara Falls. The ecological impact is going to kill the Northeast if we don't." I could hear sirens and wind blowing.

"What do you mean? What is coming out?" I had risen, standing to look outside at the snowy ground.

"Nothing is coming out. That is the problem. A rip opened before the falls, prior to the hydroelectric dams. The majority of the water is going into it. We're lucky that it is a small rip, so the water is pooling and some is getting past it, but if we keep losing this water and power, commerce is going to be in so much trouble we might never recover."

I frowned, still looking at the water that bubbled up in the fountain outside. It never froze, and it was yet one more question I had about magic. "If it is a small rip, why can't you close it?"

"The water," he said simply. "The volume going in is so fast that you can't close the rips. You're probably the only person strong enough. And I have zero idea how I'm going to explain how you got here."

"Carelian. I'll even travel with him. Give me five minutes." I hung up and turned to them. "I have to go. Write all this down, put it in your phones, copy it on another sheet, but all I can do is hope we remember when we have time. I think I'd like the help. I just don't know if I can use it or if you'll be allowed to give it." Before either of them could say anything, I looked at Carelian. "Go get Sable. I need her help."

He nodded and was gone even as I raced up the stairs. I grabbed my jacket, backpack, and his harness and I raced back down. Then I headed into Sable and Jo's room. She'd left this morning in corporate wear. I needed her in jeans and boots. I grabbed those, a light sweater, tank top, socks, and a heavy jacket. Then I raced back to the sunroom.

"Sorry, either you'll have to make your own way home or wait for us."

They glanced at each other. "We'll wait. Any issue with us using your study?" Shay asked.

"Have at it. Not like I'm worried about it, but stay out of the memento room, if the door would even open for you."

Carelian stepped through that minute with Sable behind him. "Cori? Carelian said it was an emergency?" She was dressed in light gray slacks, a dark blue blouse, low heels, and a jacket.

"Here." I tossed the clothes at her. "Change. I need you in Niagara. We have to close a rip."

I could have kissed Sable. She didn't spend a single second asking questions or arguing, she just stripped down to her underwear with Citlali and Shay right there, pulling on clothes as fast as she could.

"Do you want us to come with? We might be able to help, and given the issue with the Library it might be better for us to maintain our proximities," Citlali said as she watched Sable pull on clothes with lightning speed.

"Can you close rips or deal with water?" I asked. I knew what Shay's strengths were, but not hers.

"Yes to both, though I have rarely had a reason to close rips," she admitted.

"You know I can close. I'm just not very strong," Shay added to the conversation. "But I'll help if I can."

I looked at both of them, thinking. I knew Sable inside and out, but having them there might help. I headed to the hall closet and grabbed two jackets. January in a river was going to be colder than what they were dressed for.

"Here, bundle up. You ready Sable?"

She was twisting her braids up into a large bun on the top of her head. "Yep. Where?"

"Niagara. Carelian, you have the location?" I asked as I put the harness on him.

~Roughly. I can move us closer if I need to once we see the area,~ he replied as I finished buckling him in.

"Go." A moment later Carelian created a rip and we all rushed into the grey crossroad area. It closed behind Shay as he stepped through and another one appeared, a cold breeze bursting in. We walked out onto the walkway of a hydroelectric dam. The water that should be rushing about at the bottom past it was just a trickle in comparison. There was little there but mud, a car, flapping fish, and rocks. I spun and looked on the other side to see a lake of water spinning down into a rip.

"Small my ass," I muttered, but I knew why he'd said that. The last one had been half a mile long, this one was less than thirty yards, but that was still capturing a lot of water. "Let's go. Sable, can you divert the water as much as possible so the volume going into it is less?"

"Yes, but it might be easier to create a dam around the rip to prevent it from going in," she said after looking at it for a minute.

"Ah, that I can do. The riverbed is going to be a mess for years after this," I said.

"That I can help with," Shay said. "You start at the left and I'll start on the right?"

"Go," I replied, and I reached out and pulled. Earth burst up at my request. There was so much of it and its weight pulled on me. I felt an inch vaporize. I'd pulled on earth many times in my life. But prior to this, the largest I'd tried to move was a few hundred pounds. Now I was pulling up literal tons, but I had to create a damn long enough for us to get that rip closed.

The ground shook underneath us. "Merlin's Balls. Citlali,

Sable, can you check the structure of the dam, make sure we aren't creating a bigger problem?"

"I'm on it," Citlali snapped, and I didn't look back. Either I trusted the people I was with or we were all screwed.

Shay to my left groaned, but we had the walls rising. We'd have to be fast or the water would back up and flood areas that weren't used to flooding. I kept pulling, watching dirt, stone, and mud respond. The mixture moved upward as I pulled and shoved, the tectonic forces beneath me complaining at what I asked for. Shay and I worked toward each other. Water poured through the breaks and gaps in the rough earthen works, but I didn't care. It didn't need to be perfect, just slow the flow enough for me to close the rip.

Carelian leaned up against me and I sank one hand into his fur, needing his support. If this disaster kept up much longer, I'd be resorting to blood offerings. Those, while extremely powerful, were also dangerous as you could easily offer too much. I preferred to do exposed blood to internal. Harder to kill yourself that way.

"Got it," Shay gasped as our mud walls met in the middle. I stopped and felt my knees wobble, but I didn't have time to pay attention.

"I'm keeping the water back that is already there, Cori. But you need to get this rip closed. Water does not like to act like this." Sable was leaning on the railing, looking over the edge, eyes focused on the water.

"'Kay," I muttered. Shay was on his knees, his once long braids mostly gone as his hair floated wild and unkempt at shoulder level. Mine wasn't much better riding at my ears. Too much magic lately and I didn't see it stopping.

The rip was obvious at this point, what with Sable keeping the water away. It rippled at the bottom of the river like a wiggling worm of unreality. I took a deep breath and reached for it, the offerings of my toenails and fingernails at the top of my mind. I grabbed and pulled and almost fell over as it just closed. No struggle, nothing, it just let me zip it closed for minimal offering.

Just like that, it vanished. I stood there for probably too long, trying to find the catch or if I hadn't done it correctly, but it had closed.

"That was easy. Shay, you ready to put everything back where it was?"

"I guess." He sounded exhausted. "Let's hope it's easier than putting it up."

Together we released the Earth from the formation we had forced it into. With a soft rumble, the mud flowed, the dirt became mud, and the stone sank down. That part relieved me as I'd been worried about them tumbling forward and slamming into the plant. But the water had been working through our wall, turning everything into thick mud. The water rushed forward, slamming into the walls of the dam, something it could handle. A wave crested up and over and I cringed, bracing myself to get soaked, but it stopped and went around us.

"Ha. I don't like getting wet with clothes on and this stuff is too full of mud to be enjoyable," Sable said with a note of pride in her voice.

~I, for one, thank you. Cori would have made me take yet another bath to get that out of my fur.~ Carelian sighed and sank against me. ~This is not the stress free retirement we were talking about.~

Laughter slipped out as I rubbed his ears. "No, it isn't." I turned to really focus on the others. Shay was grey, circles under his eyes, and his hair was almost as short as mine, for all that he'd created half as much wall as I had. Citlali looked composed, but I noticed a few braids were shorter and Kesis was pressed up against her, just as Carelian was.

Sable seemed composed and gorgeous as always and I just wanted to collapse in my bed in relief and exhaustion.

"Citlali, anything we need to know about the dam?"

"Not that I could see. I looked through it and there was no damage. But it would never be amiss for engineers to go through it. I was not much help here."

I waved my hands tiredly. "You helped. You'd be amazed at how rare that is. Most people run from danger."

"That is because most people aren't crazy like you are," Shay said. He'd managed to stand, but still looked like he needed a week of sleep. "But that is it for me today. I need sleep and lots of vitamins."

I looked at him. He seemed overly exhausted. "Are you going home by yourself?"

"No. I've been staying with Sloan," he said in an odd tone of voice.

"And are you going to let Sloan know you need some TLC?"

He blinked at me. "No?"

I shook my head and dug out my phone. My contact list had Sloan, Scott, and various others from Rockmart. I didn't dare not have access to people there, especially after Henri died.

"Cori, what are you doing? I'm fine," Shay protested.

"Hey Sloan?" I said as the line was answered on the other end.

"Afternoon Ms. Munroe. How may I help?" He sounded confused and wary, and I didn't blame him. I don't think I'd ever called him before.

"We've had an exciting day. I'm sending Shay back, exhausted, and in need of someone to get him to bed and make sure he's eaten. He used up a huge amount of offerings today. Can you do that?"

"Of course. He lives in my house. I'll place some orders for food to be delivered tonight. Get him home and I'll make sure he's taken care of." His voice had firmed up and sounded determined. "Thank you for calling, otherwise he would have snuck in and I'd be trying to figure out why he was sleeping for fifteen hours."

"Ah. He's done this before. That doesn't surprise me. I'll have him home in a minute. Thanks," I said before I hung up.

Shay looked like I'd betrayed him. "I don't need to be coddled."

Citlali responded before I could. "Yes, you do. This is what a leader does, takes care of her people. Go. We will need you later and the only way you will be of use to us is if you are rested."

I smirked. "Carelian, would you, please?"

~Only because I think your sidestep might kill him right now,~ Carelian said, though I could tell he was teasing. ~I will return to take the rest of you home shortly.~

He left with Shay and I watched the churning water below us. How much more would go wrong before I could stop this?

THIRTY-SIX

Workers in Buffalo today were shunted to half shifts as the damage from the lack of power ripples down the state. Brownouts have already started and the impact will take a week or more to recover. Already there are calls for more sustainable energy sources. ~ CNN Mage Focus

---

SPIRIT

An hour later, Citlali and I were deposited in the house. Carelian had taken Sable back to work to pick up her car. Citlali and I sat in the sunroom, the fire stoked back up, and stared at each other.

"Is your life always like this?" she asked after a long minute.

I thought about it. "Yes? No? More often than I would like?"

She shook her head. "I am not sure why Amadahy ever thought Ngarra would be able to handle this."

"This isn't his preference?"

"Ngarra is a full pacificist, he won't even eat meat and he lets mosquitos feed on him." She managed to keep most of the derision out of her voice. I suspected it was for the mosquito part, not the vegetarian part.

"In Amadahy's defense, until I was forced to participate, they all thought it was a diplomatic game," I offered, feeling guilty. In hindsight, there had been so much that I knew that the other councilors had been blindsided by. If I had taken more responsibility would it be this bad? Or maybe it would be worse.

"And it is not?" Citlali wasn't accusatory, just curious.

"No, it is more a game of..." I thought, trying to figure out how to explain it. "Three-way capture the flag. Where the flag is respect and perceived power. It is one of the reasons Esmere is so well known and respected. She doesn't take shit from anyone and while she can use magic, she manages to use her claws and teeth more than her magic. To be honest, I've rarely seen as much magic from them as what I use on a daily basis. But then they are really only with me occasionally. Even Carelian rarely uses magic unless he has no choice."

This stopped her. "Your familiar can use magic?"

I shrugged. "Sure. Yours can't?"

Citlali stared at Kesis, who was curled up on the rug in front of the fire. "Can you use magic?"

~Of course, I am a focus, am I not?~ Kesis replied clearly.

A splash of pain heralded the return of Carelian and a moment later, he walked into the sunroom. ~Why do humans persist in thinking we are just animals?~ he asked, though I didn't know who that was directed to.

Citlali looked at her fox for a long time, and I just sank into the chair.

"On the bright side, I remember about the Library, so maybe it is just denizens that can't remember?" She spoke into the quiet, pulling me out of my zoning out.

"Oh good. I didn't want to ask. If you had forgotten, I would have just dealt with it." I was oddly relieved that humans didn't seem to be as affected.

"What do you want to do?" She turned her brown eyes on me and I shrugged.

"I don't know. But I think I need to talk to people. Shay is going to be out for a day and I'm not sure I'm up to anything else at this moment. What about later this week we have dinner here. You can meet the rest of my partners." I stopped and sighed. "I didn't introduce you to Sable, did I?"

"No." I wasn't sure if that tone was amused or annoyed.

"Sable and Jo, my partners, live here, though we are working on moving them over to the house down the road." She lifted an eyebrow at that and I laughed. "And you haven't seen more than the back of this house. My life is complicated. And I haven't even introduced you to the quetzo's or the kids yet. So yes? Dinner at my place later this week? Now that we know we won't forget the Library. Plus, I'm taping this to my bathroom mirror." I held up the sheet of paper with the crayon scribbles on it.

Citlali laughed. "That sounds good. I will check with my

elders and those of other countries, but I doubt we have much. We are a young country in many ways." She rose from the chair. "Kesis can take me home."

I nodded as she walked toward the fox, exhaustion just pulling at me. "Wait!" I jerked up, pushing the desire to lay down away. "Do you have a phone number? Some way to get ahold of you?"

"Oh," she said, and started laughing. "There are days where I rarely use technology, but right now that would be helpful, wouldn't it?" She rattled off a number, and I entered it into my phone. I then texted her with my name as she hadn't brought her phone with her.

"Thanks. I'll let you know if anything changes, but can you tell your government about the rips and what others are doing? Closing them is becoming problematic, as you can see."

"That might be an understatement. I will need to see if we have noticed any rips." She paused and for a moment I thought she might say more, but she shook her head. "You are not what I expected," Citlali finally said.

"Consider this my shocked face," I said dryly. "Let me guess - rash, rude, a little sweet, but seems to have denizens waiting on her, yet more powerful than she acts?"

Citlali choked and rubbed her nose with her fingers covering up what I thought was a smile. "Add on rough around the edges and a bit dismissive, but yes."

I shook my head, wishing I had coffee. Jo would need to cook dinner. If I made it to my bed I'd be impressed. "And now?"

She tilted her head, looking at me, not past or through, but at me. It was searching and uncomfortable. "A leader not by choice but due to circumstances. You are in way over your head, but determined to do what needs to be done, no matter the cost."

~That is why she is my quean,~ Carelian murmured.

"You chose well," Citlali said, nodding to him. "Kesis, are you ready?"

The fox stretched like a cat, then shook like a dog, her elegant gray fur settling back down. ~Yes.~ She opened a rip and slipped through, Citlali right behind her.

It closed, and I glanced at the clock—only 4. It felt like I'd been up for days already. *Jo, can you get dinner or something or cook?*

I barely moved the phone when there was a ding. *Way ahead of you, Sable called. I've got the kids, we are picking up Thai. And yes, I'm getting Carelian his spicy shrimp.*

"Jo must really love you. She's getting you Thai spicy shrimp," I said after I replied with a *thanks*.

~Of course, I am loveable and she is a smart quean,~ he replied amicably. He'd splayed back out in front of the fireplace and was grooming his paws.

"Thoughts on those two?" I asked, curious as to his viewpoint.

~The woman is deadlier than you might think. They didn't mention what they hunted, but I know what roams in the beast lands. Kesis is swift, smart, and deadly. She may look like a fox and lacks my thumbs, but she has razor claws, and can become bigger than Esmere when needed. Though not big enough for Citlali to ride.~ He paused, tongue extended. ~I like them.~

A soft chuckle escaped me. "Me too. What about the Library?" It was part test, part question.

~I believe we are meant to find it. Shay mentioned it to Sloan when I took him home. So, they have not forgotten.~ His ears laid back. ~Though if that effect ever disappears and everyone remembers it, they will not be happy.~

"Of course. Still, that isn't my doing, no matter what Brix might say. But we need a plan and soon. " I pulled up the calendar on my phone. It was only January 3rd. It felt like a lifetime had passed today. "Next weekend is good for a dinner. But I think I'll leave Stephen and Indira off the list. They both have competing loyalties."

~Agreed. He needs babies to settle him down and teach him to bend more. His thinking is too inflexible.~

I choked, trying to fight back laughter. "Not Indira?"

~She is a smart woman and has no need of humbling, though I suspect he would not want children with anyone else, so she might have to suffer.~

This time, the laughter did come through. When I could breathe again, I looked at him. "You do realize she is in her sixties and mostly well past her child-bearing years, right?"

~So soon? That is a shame. Then perhaps they should keep the twins and the quetzo's for a week. I am sure that would humble him.~

I just chuckled. "You have strange views on children."

~They are important, but they seem to remove most of your stiffness quickly. It is rather nice.~

"That it is. We have to learn to play with them." I brushed the conversation away and started setting up things for a dinner in a week. Halfway through, I paused. "Carelian, do you think there is anything in the memento room that might help?"

His hind leg was up in the air as he licked the fur. ~That room is full of mysteries and other things, so I could not say. But you can look.~

The idea of climbing the stairs made me want to cry. I choked it down. No matter how tired I was, nothing would change or stop the rips if I didn't get my ass in gear. I leveraged myself to my feet and trudged to the stairs. Moving felt easier the more I did and by the time I reached the top stair, my muscles had loosened up and I felt a bit better. Not a lot, but at least I didn't think my knees were about to buckle. I pushed open the door and stood looking at the room. The two statues left seemed to judge me with their immovable expressions. I flipped them off.

There were so many things in here, but I'd touched all the memory stones, and none of them mentioned the Undoing, at least not like that. Everything else were things that James had regarded as precious or rare. But staring at them made me think of something and I went into my study and pulled out the Phoenix Heart and his little note book. Back in the room, I put them on a far shelf. The room wasn't a safe, but most of the time we forgot it was here, and that sounded like an excellent idea.

I was still going through all the notebooks James had left, but the majority of them I had read. But I hadn't asked Jeorgaz.

~Jeorgaz, do you have a minute?~ I looked longingly at the chair, but I feared if I sat down, I'd never manage to get back up.

A burst of sweet-smelling flames heralded his arrival. A perch snuck out of the wall, ready for him as he hovered.

~Cori. I am glad to see you are okay. The stories of what happened in the council chambers are the talk of the realms.~

I laughed. "I'm glad to hear I still entertain people. Do you know anything about the Undoing? Or what Brix is rambling about?"

He lit on the perch and twisted his head to look at me. ~Not really. I know of it, when Earth and Magic separated, but not much else.~

"Merlin," I sighed. "I thought you were immortal?"

~Yes and no. Immortal in that we don't die of old age, we simply egg to be hatched again. But I am only about three hundred of your years. We do reproduce. My parents were killed not long after my first hatching, so if they had been around, then I would not be aware. ~ He flipped his wings at me. ~I know this is not much help.~

"It is more than I had. By the way, I put the Phoenix Heart in the memento room. It seemed like a good place for it."

~That will work. I have hope the Herald will have use of it one day, something that will be for the good of all, not something dark and twisted.~

"I'd just settle that it sits in the corner until it crumbles into dust. Oh well. I've got some freeze-dried strawberries if you'd like to try those? They are downstairs." It gave me a reason to keep moving, otherwise my bed was so close.

~That would be wonderful, Cori,~ he trilled but I couldn't help but feel I wasn't asking the right questions.

THIRTY-SEVEN

"The formulation of the problem is often more essential than its solution, which may be merely a matter of mathematical or experimental skill." ~Albert Einstein

CHAOS

We set a dinner date for two weeks out. I needed to talk to humans about the situation going on, so Tirsane and Esmere were not invited. We compromised on Arachena attending as Carelian and Kesis would be there also. The twins and the quetzos were having dinner with Grandma, giving us some space.

It surprised no one that fish was the star of the dinner. I

looked around the table checking on everyone. Jo was at one end, Sable next to her. I sat at the other end. On my right was Charles, then Shay. On my left was Citlali, Kesis, and Carelian on the chair nearest me. Arachena was in Charles' ever-present hoodie. She'd peeked out to wave at people, then scrambled back in.

The conversation stayed to general chit-chat until most of the eating had slowed down. I faced the inevitable and started the conversation. "We need to talk about the rips." They all quieted down, looking at me. It felt odd to not have Stephen and Indira here, but for now I didn't want to put them in an uncomfortable position. "I asked Charles to look at some data for me. And compare it to what was presented by the OMO at my ambush presentation." That last was a bit sour. I was still annoyed about that.

"Asking before dessert is just mean, you know," he said as he got up to grab his laptop from his bag. Jo grabbed his plate and moved it out of the way. He nodded thanks as he sank back down. "Here is what I have. The energy levels are increasing, though it isn't as obvious a ratio as the OMO wanted you to think. If I had to guess, it is seeking out low magic areas given the reactions."

"Wait, what?" That made no sense to me.

"Basically, the rips seem to be forming more where there are fewer magic users. Big open areas or areas with lots of non-mages," he said as he typed on the laptop.

"What makes you say that?" Citlali asked, her gaze focused.

"Believe it or not, the Amish." Charles turned his laptop so we could see it. It showed a map of the US with small and large circles in various areas, a lot in areas even I recognized as mostly mountains. "They are historically almost never mages or only hedgemages. Those who do emerge end up leaving or never using magic if they are a hedgie. In the last month we've had at least six rips, none really big, appear there. There are also spikes in sensors across the United States for areas in state parks and rural areas. Now we are still getting them in populated areas, but those are bigger and angrier, for lack of a better word."

"I need you to explain," I admitted. "You've been looking at the data and I haven't."

"Basically, the ones in rural or low magic areas are occurring more often, but they are small without much effect and they aren't letting very many creatures out. The huge ones in populated areas cause damage and usually have things trying to cross or come in. These are the ones that are getting the government up in arms."

"Huh," Citlali said slowly. "That matches with what we have seen. All of us have seen little ones on the plains or in the hunting areas, but they close easily and we've ignored them. But two large ones have opened in populated areas and both of those were difficult to seal, all of them with something coming through, but our focuses usually dissuade them."

"My problem is I have access to US data. I also have the information you've given me about China, but I can't tell you what else is going on across the world. We know the US and China are both planning on attacking rips, for all that Stephen is trying to dissuade them, but without active information I can't really tell you more than what I just did." Charles shrugged and closed his laptop. "Get me more data, or convince the OMO to let me get access to their computers, and I might come up with a different answer."

I rubbed my face, pushing my empty plate back. "So again, information. Even if we find the Library, that won't tell us how humans are reacting. The news doesn't have anything else?" This I directed to anyone, but Charles answered.

"Yes and no. I can tell you Russia is mobilizing tanks in

various areas. Japan has pulled all their warships back to their coastline. Australia is doing more drills, but none of them are admitting what it is for or why. I don't think anyone really wants to face what is going on or admit how they are reacting." He sighed too. "Bottom line, if this keeps up, I can't see them not doing what you know we are doing."

I snorted. "Humans." I tapped my fingers on the table. But I'd come into this out of ideas. "Does anyone have any ideas? Because the only thing I've got is seeing if the Library is real, and while I'm going to try, I don't know if it will give me anything useful."

"I have a question," Sable said. We all looked at her. "Carelian, Arachena, Kesis, do you know other familiars or focuses? I mean, we all know Carelian knows Tiantang, but what about others in other countries."

You could almost feel the slap of realization as we all turned to our familiars. Arachena crawled down Charles's arm to participate in the discussion.

~I know a few, many from the awards banquet years ago. The Aralez was from Spain,~ Carelian said slowly. ~I hunted with a not-bear from Russia, but I don't know what or who his mage is.~

~Arachena know Chitterians and gorgons. We weave, trade. Not many focus.~ Her high chittering voice had a note of apology.

~That is a good question,~ Kesis said thinking. ~Most of the ones I know are all part of our lands. You are the first I have interacted with that are not of the Nation.~

Sable shrugged. "Oh well, it was an idea, but for future options, it might be good to encourage the focuses to have friends and connections of their own."

We fell back into silence. Shay twisted his hair, obviously

uncomfortable with its short length. "What about asking Scott?"

"About?" I replied. Scott Randolph was a friend, kind of. He'd been a Rogue Mage hunter once, even had a movie made about him.

"He's retired, but he knows lots of them and they interacted all over the world. Some of the mages they hunted should never have been born, much less emerged. They weren't nice people. He might have contacts that would know what is going on in their own countries." Shay shrugged. "Though I'm not sure what difference knowing how close we are to the Doomsday clock striking twelve really makes. If we can't get the Herald to a point where she can stop this from happening, it's all just a ticking bomb."

I sighed. "I know. I guess I was hoping. So, we need to find the Library or nail Brix to a tree and pull it out of him?" For a minute, the image of Brix nailed to a tree like the poor girl I had found when I had just moved to Atlanta flashed through my mind and I shuddered. "Never mind. Just force him to tell us?"

"If we could," Citlali said. "I talked to my elders, and they knew nothing. We don't even have many stories past a thousand years, and those we do are awfully universal."

"Universal?" Jo asked as she started to collect plates. "And remember, I have Angel food cake and ice cream for dessert."

"Floods, earthquakes, Coyote, Raven, nothing that relates to real people that we can tell. Mostly learning tales, like messing with porcupines ends with new holes in your skin."

We fell silent as I got up to help Jo, and everyone else seemed lost in their thoughts. When I came back, Shay just shrugged forlornly. "I got nothing. This wasn't really what I thought it would be and to a certain extent, I feel like we are trying to fight nature."

I felt like someone had poked me. "Well, aren't we? We do it all the time." Everyone just looked at me with blank faces. "Think about it. We build dams, firebreaks, set up sandbags, alter the flow of rivers. We do this all the time. Why can't we control the flow of magic?"

"Because it's never been done before?" Shay asked slowly.

I just laughed. "Of course not. One of the things I've noticed about the denizens, and Carelian, Kesis, Arachena—I don't mean this as an insult—but they aren't tool users or inventors. The Valkyrie are the most human-like and I'll lay you money everything they have are things humans did first. The naga, gorgons, and a few more are the only ones with actual hands. The Cath only use their thumbs occasionally, they still focus on magic or what we'd regard as naturalistic behaviors. We need to show them how to harness or maybe put a stopper in the magic deluge." I was excited as I said this, visuals of magic flowing like a river.

~Cori?~ Carelian said slowly.

"Don't you think it's a great idea? We'd be able to harness it and use it for other things." I was so excited, and everyone just looked at me like I'd grown another head.

Carelian spoke again. ~Cori, I do not disagree, but Magic is more insubstantial than the wind and it took humans centuries to consistently harness the wind with sails for ships. And aren't your wind turbines something that only developed in the last few decades for anything major?~

"Sure, but we know how to do magic and Sable works with water, the principles have to be the same."

Sable cleared her throat, and I looked at her, feeling my heart fall at her look. "Cori, I think you are right, and it's a brilliant idea. But you are talking years if not decades of work to figure out how to isolate and channel something that we barely understand. Unless you stumble across a manual telling us exactly how to control magic, we'll never figure it out in time to stop the attacks on the rips." Her gentle voice wormed its way through my excitement and I slowly deflated.

"Oh. Now that you say that, it's obvious. So, we're back at the Library."

"Back at the Library," Jo said. She headed into the kitchen and came back with cake and ice cream, dropping a kiss on my head as she came back in. "But maybe you can make that your retirement project. You have two engineers that could help you."

I nodded, still feeling like there was something there, but I let it go as we kept talking. But Brix and the possibility of the Library telling us something were the only things we could come up with. With a note of frustration Citlali and Shay agreed to be ready to go tomorrow and head into Spirit, starting at Tirsane's. Maybe we would find it quickly, but somehow I didn't think it would be that easy.

We were just saying goodbye when a spike of pain had me looking at the back yard. I walked into the sunroom to check. Tiantang writhed there, his whisker drooping. I headed outside with most everyone following.

"Tiantang, what's up?"

~I wanted you to know, it is decided. The next major rip that appears, we will attack. Cixi is starting with missiles, but her advisors are recommending having small nukes available if the rips continue.~ He had curled up in a ball. ~She won't listen but many people have died and they are demanding she do something.~

"What? Why have people died?" I questioned going in to rub his brow.

~One of the rips happened in a large park with many families and kids. A large lizard with teeth and a tail came out. It stared at people and they froze. It killed dozens before a sniper killed it from another building.~

~Basilisk,~ Carelian hissed. ~They are animals and they stun anyone that they look at, then they kill and eat their prey.~

I sighed. "I'm trying, Tiantang. We're going to see if we can find the answer tomorrow."

~Hurry, Cori. I don't want to see what might happen if they get scared enough to launch the nukes.~

CHAPTER

THIRTY-EIGHT

Few countries have active nuclear arsenals after the devastation in Nagasaki and Hiroshima, but that doesn't mean there aren't nuclear weapons. Many have been decommissioned as mages refuse to work them given the known instability around magic use. However, there are still many deadly missiles out there. Which is why the satellite images of China moving its Dongfeng missiles in unprecedented numbers is very stressful. – CNN Mage Focus

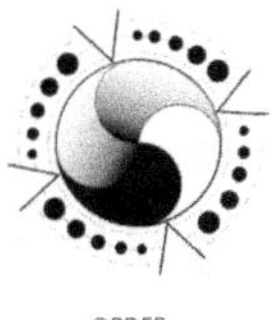

ORDER

Shay and Citlali were ready to go by 8 A.M. Shay didn't even complain, but his mood improved when I handed him Mexican coffee. Sanchez's recipe was still my go to after all these years, so much chocolate and caffeine. It would wake the dead.

Shay wore boots, jeans, a jacket, had a backpack, and interestingly, a walking stick made of metal.

"That isn't what I expected you to bring," I said pointing to it.

"Sloane made me take it. It can unscrew and it has a spear if I need it. I'm so short on offerings, I figured a bit of an advantage wasn't to be ignored."

I couldn't disagree and made a mental note to add one to my bag. Citlali, on the other hand, showed up in leather leggings and a long coat of beige hide, with a powerful recurve bow, and a pack. I noted she had knives strapped to her waist and arms.

"I'm not sure if I'm underdressed or over," I commented as I looked at my clothes mostly from hiking stores recommended by the S&R people. My pack was crammed full this time. I wasn't taking any chances.

"It is my normal hunting gear, minus the coat, but if we end up camping out, the coat will be useful." She moved in it like a ghost and I had to admit it seemed a part of her, but then so had the leather biker jacket.

"Come here, Carelian," I said and pulled out the harness. He flicked his ears back, but let me strap it on him.

"Why that?" Citlali asked as Kesis watched with matching laid-back ears.

"Mostly it is for the people we run into on Earth. It helps convince them he's harmless."

They both looked at me with unbelieving expressions. "Carelian? Harmless?"

I shrugged. "If he has a leash, he's suddenly a pet. I never said people were smart."

Citlali and Shay both laughed a bit at that. "So why now?" Citlali pressed.

"Because it carries food for him, a bowl for water, some booties, and a brush. All stuff he could need and therefore he carries when practical." I finished clipping him in and letting him shake to make sure it was settled correctly.

"Kesis, don't you think that sounds like an excellent idea," Citlali said softly, still watching us.

~No. I do not.~ The fox had her ears back and wasn't impressed by the idea at all. ~Besides, if I change size it would cause issues.~

"True, but I like the idea of letting you carry a few things for your own needs, like the bowl and brush?" Citlali looked like she was sketching out ideas in her head if her twitching hands were any indication.

The fox twitched ears and tail, but just turned away, refusing to respond.

"I find myself suddenly glad I don't have a familiar. Though I have to say neither Dahli nor Elsba are this... ornery." Shay was looking back and forth between the two animals.

~Dahli is a canine. She is all heart and no brains. Elsba is similar to the quetzos. Intelligent but not civilized is the best word.~ Carelian had stalked forward and opened the door to the backyard. ~Are we ready or are you going to continue to avoid what needs to be started?~

His words acted like a prod and we had been delaying. I sighed and followed him out. "Tirsane's please?"

Carelian just twitched a tail at me and opened a rip. This time we went directly there, stepping out into the warm sand in the grotto. A chime echoed as we stepped out and a minute later, a large snake came slithering out, head raised, and a hood expanding. It postured in obvious threat.

"My name is Cori, I'm here to see Tirsane." I pitched my voice to carry, so that we didn't get attacked. I had zero doubt that Carelian could eliminate the snake prior to it getting close enough to cause an issue, but that would be a bad omen to start that trip.

The snake stopped, the hood collapsing and it turned and slithered back into the entrance of what looked like a Greek temple. A minute later Tirsane came out, looking elegant and beautiful. She wore the scarf I'd given her, draped around her neck, various snakes holding it in their teeth and twisting underneath it, like it was a toy.

"Cori, Lords. To what do I owe this visit?" Her voice was wary, and I hated feeling like I was using her, but I didn't know of any way to do this.

"Morning, Tirsane. I wanted to remind you we were going to search the Spirit Realm today for the Library of Magic." I spoke clearly and fastened my eyes on her face, watching for recognition.

She blinked, her eyes lighting up with a Eureka moment. "Of course, why didn't I think of that? The Library will surely have the answers you need. I can't believe we didn't go there or think of it. It is right over," she turned as she spoke, her arm starting to point to a path leading out of her grotto.

Tirsane stopped, her arm hovering in midair. She turned to look at me again, a frown creasing her face. "I...where.. Did you need me to show you something?"

The idea of anyone, anything removing memories like that, made me want to throw up. Yet another dark side of magic. "No. We need to head into the realm, and I wanted to clear it with you first. That is okay?" The words carefully chosen as any lie would spring out at her.

"Of course. Be aware of doors and paths to pockets, but the Spirit realm welcomes you. Just be careful—it is not as welcoming as your world is." She smiled again, and I heard Shay clear his throat as the scarf was pulled up by the snakes to expose her breasts.

"Thank you. I'll let you know if I find anything we need you to explain or perhaps grease the way. I'm hoping as the Herald, Magic might guide our way to what can help."

"Ah, yes. That sounds wonderful." She pointed to a different path. "That will lead you to the heart of it. Please do come back by some time." With a nod she headed back into her home, the snakes bouncing up and down in their approximation of a wave.

"That is..." Shay started, but I shushed him. We headed down the path she had first indicated and I raised my hand every time either of them started to speak until we'd been walking for at least ten minutes. The area was sparse and craggy, but a path led away from the water you could hear on the other side of her walls.

"We safe to speak yet, Carelian?" I asked.

I didn't slow down my pace as his ears twitched back and forth. ~Yes. I can no longer hear the fountain or the waves. I doubt anything will be directly overheard and I sense no sentients near us at this moment.~ His voice was easy and his tail was a normal sway, not an agitated swish.

"You were saying, Shay?" I slowed down to look at the two humans. I'd set a decent pace and Shay was a bit winded, but Citlali looked like we were out for a casual stroll.

"That was uncomfortable to watch. She knew, then it was wiped away. I am very unhappy with the idea of magic doing that to me." He cleared his throat as we continued.

"Agreed, but I don't know what else to do at this point," I said in a frustrated mutter. "She is a friend and has been for years at this point. All I can do is try to work within the stupid game I find myself."

"It is discomforting, but I find it interesting she had full recollection until her eyes turned from you. It makes me wonder if there is more we are missing than just the herald aspect. Especially since Shay didn't forget, and he doesn't have a focus." Citlali didn't pause her stride as she spoke. Kesis scampered ahead, disappearing behind trees and rocks. Her fur blended into this wilderness perfectly. Carelian, with his ruby red coat, stood out just a bit.

"And why would Magic hide this place?" Shay huffed as he spoke, and I slowed down a bit more.

"Well, when I went there it was set up more like a museum, and trust me there were things I wanted to read and stare at. I was so tempted." My voice got softer remembering the Death book and some of the others, not to mention the jewelry. "But I also don't know how much was staged, versus what it is really like, or heck if it is more than just a traveling bookmobile."

Shay snickered at that comment, but Citlali just looked at me, confused.

"Never mind, a social commentary joke." I waved it off, it wasn't important to explain.

We kept wandering up the path, though it had changed from the craggy mountain to a more lush forest. The sounds of life were picking up with birds in the trees and rustles in the leaves and needles.

"Do you have any idea where we're going?" Shay asked after another ten minutes of walking. We were deep in the forest now and the diffuse light was all but blocked out, putting us into dark shadows.

"Not really," I admitted. "I know it is in this realm, but not where." I looked around, but there wasn't anything here to guide me. Carelian had slipped into the trees, and neither he nor Kesis were visible.

"So, we just walk forever?" His voice held all the doubt that rattled around my own head.

"We are trusting Magic wants us to find the Library," Citlali answered.

"Exactly. But be warned, Magic likes challenges. A most of the denizens do." I was getting the feeling we were being watched. ~Carelian, is something out there?~ I sent it privately, not wanting to alarm anyone.

~Yes. We are hunting it.~ Carelian replied in my mind. I shot a look at Citlali, who stiffened for a moment, then continued her smooth pace.

"Which means what?" Shay asked, his breathing finally back to normal now that we weren't climbing up a hill and were moving at a slower pace.

"Ambush," Citlali said as she drew her bow and set an arrow.

I just stopped in the trail, set my feet and waited. Earth was more problematic to use in the realms, but I was done being nice.

~Incoming,~ Carelian called in time with a crashing sound. Out of the woods burst a bear that made even our Kodiaks look like a stuffed animal. I had no idea of how anything that large could have moved through the forest and not have sounded like a herd of elephants. It rose up on its hind legs and roared. The sound hit physically and mentally.

That told me everything. "Don't shoot," I snapped out to Citlali and at the same time I said ~No,~ very firmly and mentally popped it, as if I'd hit it with a newspaper on the nose. I'd figured out how Esmere did it and was doing the same thing, though I popped it much harder than she'd popped the quetzos.

It jerked its head back, the roar cut off mid sound. It blinked tiny eyes at us and dropped back to all fours. Carelian sprang out of the trees and dropped in front of it, hissing, with his fur standing on end. Kesis appeared a moment later looking about the same size as Esmere, her fur tipped with what looked like sparks of electricity, fangs bared.

~No!~ I popped it again, the way I would have popped a misbehaving dog. It whined and sank back. ~Go!~ Another mental swat. It huffed out a sigh and lumbered off to the side and toward the trees.

My shoulders sagged in relief. That had been really lucky.

"What, by the Great Sprits, did you do?" I turned to see Citlali standing there, her bow pointed to the ground and a look of surprise on her face. That was matched with a rolled eye from Shay.

"She was being Cori. Nothing ever works the way you think it should."

~Indeed. I was looking forward to that fight. It would have been a nice challenge and we could have had roast bear for dinner.~ Carelian all but pouted his response, glaring at me.

I threw my hands up in the air and started walking, only for the ground to give out underneath me.

The current death count from the rips is fifty in the US. Which isn't even the number people that die from car accidents a day. However, in Australia it is over seventy, and France saw ninety get killed in the last month. As the rips in reality continue the death toll is going to rise.
~CNN Mage Focus

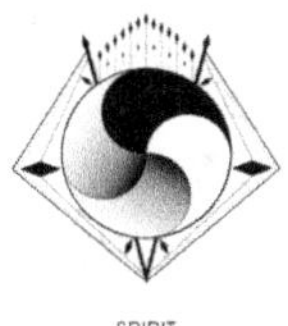

SPIRIT

I didn't have time to react before I slammed into the ground feet first, but the fall threw me onto my back and knocked out all my air. I lay there gasping, staring up at the opening of light much further above me than I was happy with. A second later, a Cath, fox, woman, and man all peered in, looking down at me.

~My quean, are you okay?~ Carelian said, his former annoyance vanished and now just concern.

I didn't respond instantly, still trying to remember how to breathe. "Yeah," I gasped out as I sucked in another lung full of air. "Not hurt. Winded." I levered myself up and sat there, head on my knees as I let the spinning stop.

"How are we going to get you up here?" Shay asked, his voice echoing down the hole.

I lifted my head and asked fire to play out in my hand for a moment, feeding it sawdust. It burst into light and danced on my palm as I looked around. I was in a long, low tunnel that had obviously been carved from stone and wasn't natural at all. It also felt vaguely familiar. It extended into the darkness and disappeared to my left, while to my right was a wall not ten feet away.

"Actually, I think you need to come down here," I managed to say. The words had barely left my mouth when Carelian and Kesis sprang down. That distracted me enough I let the flame die, but there still seemed to be some light.

"I really don't want to use Earth to get down there," Shay said as he looked down at me.

"No worries. This is why I still hunt with a bow," Citlali said. Even from here, I could hear humor in her voice.

"Ack!" Shay yelped. I looked up to see him floating down, with Citlali right behind.

"Air is my domain, in and out." Her voice had a joy that

rippled through the air. "You sure you're, okay?" She directed this question at me.

"Yeah, just knocked the wind out of me and gave me a few new bruises. Nothing new there." I looked around. The tunnel led on. "This is made, not an animal hole, regardless of how large. This was made, and that is a bit too coincidental."

"Ah, I see what you mean." Shay spun slowly. "Only one way to go, and since we have a flyer here, we can always backtrack if we need to."

I nodded. I created little flames that flickered on the walls, and we started down the tunnel. The rock had been chiseled, but it was plain and unornamented. It was about a foot over Citlali's head and the air was cool. I snuffed out the fires as we passed them, just because it took energy to pull food in to keep the flames alive.

We had walked for three minutes when suddenly the cave ended and the library appeared on the other side of a chasm.

"It's the Library, like it was when I visited." I looked at the chasm and smiled. "Except this time there is a bridge that might support my weight."

"This time?" Shay asked, giving the bridge an appropriately dubious look.

I started to respond, stopped, and looked at the bridge again. "Citlali, how good are you at flying people?"

"Very," she said with a smirk.

"You want to fly us over? The bridge is temperamental," I said as I narrowed my eyes at the bridge. As if it heard us, it turned into an ice bridge and began to melt like a blowtorch was held to it.

"So, I see," Citlali said as she leaned over to look at the chasm. "We sure about this?"

I burst out in laughter. "Not at all. But I haven't come up with any other options."

Citlali didn't say anything, instead air just wrapped around us and carried us over to the other side. It seemed strangely anti-climactic, but at this point that didn't strike me as a bad thing. She set us down much more gently than I could have managed, and I stood peering at the steps and the huge doors. It seemed almost the same, but also somehow different.

"Wait," I said as I stared at it, trying to remember. The place had the same imposing architecture as before. With the pillars and pointed roof it still reminded me of a temple as much as a library. But this time there were no gargoyles, and the doors weren't ajar.

"Carelian, are gargoyles real?" I asked, looking at the empty tops of the pillars.

~Gargoyles? Your stone statues?~ He sounded confused.

"Yes, large beasties with wings, claws, fangs, and turn to stone."

~No. We don't know of creatures like that, though we have hunted elephants, but their fur doesn't make them look very rock-like.~ Kesis sat at Citlali's feet, staring at the building.

"Wait, elephants have fur?" Shay looked at the fox with a confused look.

"When you are hunting wooly mammoths, they have fur," Citlali said.

I opened my mouth, then snapped it close. I didn't have time to follow up on that right now. "Noted. Last time, the doors were open." Right now, they were firmly shut. A creak grabbed my attention and over to the side of the building was a door that was closer to a normal human sized, ten feet tall, not the twenty-foot main doors. "I suspect maybe patrons enter there?"

The other two looked at me and shrugged. I glanced back up at the empty gargoyles' posts. What had they looked like? I couldn't remember. They had just been there, figures that I dismissed. Right at that moment I wished that time travel actually worked. But while you could step out of time, freeze it around you, if there was a way to go back in time, I didn't know it.

The collective attitude seemed to be a "why the fuck not?" and we started to climb the stairs. Everything remained quiet as we went up to the main door. The steps were just as intimidating as before, but the door swung open quietly and I stepped in, the heat of Shay and Citlali letting me know they were close.

Last time it had been like wandering into a museum, full of cases, lights, books and objects on display. This time, it felt like a library. We were in a foyer and to the right was a large desk with books stacked on it. Past it were rows and rows of shelves that had to be at least 12 feet high. There were ladders attached to each bookcase. Instinctively, I looked up and breathed a sigh of relief when I verified the imposing cases were anchored into the ceiling which was stone.

"This isn't what it was last time," I murmured. The others stepped around me, standing in the foyer, and I took two steps back to look at the giant doors, then stepped in again. Halfway in between the doors was a wall. "Or maybe it was just a different part of the library?"

Carelian sat looking at all this, his tail twitching. Kesis almost mimicked him, but she was still as if she'd been carved out of resin. The gray of her coat looked almost blue in the diffused light. There was no one behind the desk, but as I walked over, I also didn't see a coating of dust.

"Now what?" Shay asked.

I took a breath trying to come up with a plan. But other than searching for something like the Undoing, I didn't have a clue.

"I guess we-"

~Cori, Hamiada has a message.~ Carelian interrupted.

It threw me off my thought process and I had to think for a minute to get myself on track. "From?"

~Alixant. He said they are having another meeting this afternoon. He wants you there.~ Carelian's tail twitched in annoyance.

"Who is Alixant?" Citlali asked, and I blinked at her.

"Oh, you don't know. Shay, do you know him?"

Shay shrugged. "He was at the wedding and the baby shower. I know he is like FBI or something, but that is the extent of what I know."

"Basically, he's the director of magical crimes, and the government and the OMO have put him in charge of the rips, but the military and political pressure is getting extreme. He's called me in because I'm powerful enough to close most of the rips without issue, plus he's trying to avoid them reactivating my Draft." I paused and looked at her. "You do know about the Draft?"

She nodded. "Are you going to go?"

I huffed out a laugh. "There is no way. I'm not positive magic would even let us back. Carelian, could you find this place again? The way you can find Tirsane's?"

His years twitched back and forth. ~Maybe. Let me try something.~ A spike of pain and he stepped away from us. I felt the loss. It was odd how much I leaned on him.

A minute passed, then two. My panic started to rise. Then a spike and he stepped back. This time his hackles were raised and his tail was puffed.

~The answer to that is no. I could find you. I could not find this place. It is blocked, but I could travel to you.~

"That is interesting and very good to know," Citlali said slowly. "Kesis, would you mind testing that out?"

The fox nodded and disappeared in a flash of pain that was gone before I could even wince. Again, we waited. I buried my hand in Carelian's fur to verify that he was really there. I knew I could sidestep home, but we needed to keep this place accessible.

This time, three minutes passed before Kesis returned. ~He is correct. I can find you, but until I step to you, this place is unable to be seen. I am not sure how to explain it.~

"Kesis, Carelian, if you were stepping to us, could you bring someone else?" I asked, my mind whirling.

They looked at each other, then away. The private conversation was just at the edge of my mental hearing, enough I could tell they were talking, but not that I could hear it.

~Yes,~ Carelian finally answered. ~Hamiada asked if there was a message to pass, apparently Alixant is on the phone.~

"Oh. Yeah. Tell him I have a conflict that cannot be rescheduled. It relates to possibly stopping the rips. I can't guarantee when I'll be available." Nothing in that was a lie, and besides, if Hamiada was relaying it, there wasn't any way to know if the statement was true.

~Done.~ He pressed up against me and I sighed.

"That does give us options," Citlali said. "From your questions, I suspect we are on the same page. And yes, it would make more sense for me to stay here. I am well used to camping in the wilderness, sleeping here would not be an issue, especially if Kesis can find me."

I nodded, relieved she'd seen the same thing.

"I'm glad you two are okay with that. My body isn't," Shay said, looking around. "But it means the time we have is still getting shorter. So where do we start?"

A bang sounded in the depths of the library and I spun, looking for what created the sound. Kesis and Carelian were both on their feet, noses in the air, sniffing. Soft clicks and creaks started moving towards us with a ponderousness that had me readying a KO spell.

"Don't call Fire. We can't risk damaging this knowledge," I hissed.

~Something is coming. I do not know that smell, it is cat yet not. It is... unknown,~ Carelian growled in my mind. His body was tensed as the shadows moved to our left and as one we pivoted to face what was coming.

My heart tried to lodge in my chest, but I pushed it down. Whatever it was, I'd deal. Like everyone said, I was the Herald. I'd face whatever was coming.

Click, click, pad, pad.

The sounds were of Carelian walking through the house, claws clicking the wood, but a warm dusty smell reached my nose. Definitely not Cath.

The shadows parted as globes at the end of each bookshelf sprang into bright luminescence revealing a sphinx stepping out to glare at us.

CHAPTER

FORTY

For the first time in over a hundred years, the AIN has sent representatives to the White House to discuss opening the borders between our countries. Arrangements are still being discussed, but both political insiders and newcomers to this arena are abuzz with the possible opportunities and changes this might make in the political landscape. No one knows the technology level of the AIN and it will be a slow process, but it is possible the walls might fall allowing the US and the AIN to interact once again. ~ CNN Mage Focus

---

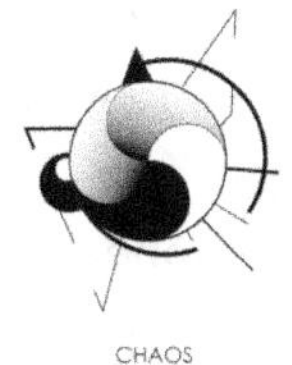

CHAOS

The sphinx's head came to just under the second to the top shelf of the bookcases. I could tell the sphinx was female with a tunic on her top, long hair in dark braids that were pulled back into a tail at the base of her skull. Her face was an odd mixture between human and cat. She took another step out of the shadows to reveal a leonine body with dark burgundy fur and tufted tail that swept from side to side, brushing the tops of books.

Now I know why there's no dust.

The irreverent thought zoomed through my mind as we stared at her. She opened her mouth, and I tensed, waiting for an attack.

"Do you have your library cards?" The voice was rich, echoing through the library, yet it wasn't that loud. Oddly, at least to my ears, she had an English accent. She continued on toward us.

"If not, you can request them here."

We moved back almost in unison as she moved toward us and settled down behind the desk that I had thought absurdly large. Apparently not.

"Well?" She stared at us with amber eyes that told me nothing except that they resembled Esmere's.

I cleared my throat. "Um, yes? I mean, we need to get library cards. We need to research something." My voice might have squeaked a bit at that last part. It was more that even after all the denizens I'd met, there was something about meeting a sphinx that just threw me for a loop.

"That is why the library is here. Please enter your name and magical signature here." A clipboard lifted up from under the counter and settled on top. I moved toward her, still unsure if I was going to be attacked or not. The only expression I could get from her was curiosity, nothing that made me think she would attack—other than being a sphinx.

As I looked at the form, I tried to remember what I knew about sphinx, and the answer was not much. They asked riddles and there was one in Egypt. That covered it.

The form was relatively straightforward, other than it was on papyrus, not paper. The top declared "Library of Magic, library card application." It wanted my name, realm, and a square box.

"Here." A quill and ink appeared on the desk.

I filled out my name, listed Earth as the realm, but stopped at the box. "How do I do a magical signature?"

"Push your senses at the box and think of calling magic."

I followed the instructions, and the box glowed a tiny bit.

"Excellent. Here is your library card." She glanced at the rest of us. "Do any of you wish to receive a library card?"

We all glanced at each other, shrugged, and Shay moved up to get his library card. Carelian was directly behind him.

"Can you read?" Citlali asked, looking at the card Carelian slipped into his harness. He had badges often enough so we created a slot for identity cards and things for him.

~Yes,~ he said flicking his tail at her.

"Kesis?" Citlali looked like someone had slapped her. I was really hard on people's view of reality.

~Yes? No?~ The fox twitched her tail from side to side, the white tip mesmerizing. ~I know words. I can recognize them, but reading from a book, I do not believe so.~

Citlali blinked, then took a deep breath. "I and my focus would like cards please."

The sphinx gave us a blinding smile, revealing even human like teeth except for the very long, sharp canines. "Here is the form." Another form floated up to the top, and it took a bit for all of us to get cards. But soon enough we were all in possession of library cards.

I took a minute to examine mine. Made of a thin metal, it had my name engraved on it, then the symbols of magic, each filled in fully. It was like when I pushed my magic signature into the form, it had weighed and measured my magic.

"Carelian, may I see yours?"

He flipped an ear at me, and I suspected he was laughing, but he pulled it out and handed to me. His name was there also, but instead of each of the symbols of magic, it had a Chaos symbol that was strong in Entropy and Time. Then there was an arrow with my name next to it.

"Interesting." I handed it back to him. Everyone else had received theirs and we stood there aimlessly. I felt like face palming. This was a library, and we had a librarian.

"Excuse me, do you have a name?" I hadn't seen a plaque or anything and she didn't wear a name tag.

"You may call me Cleo," she said after a minute.

"Thank you, Cleo. We are researching the Undoing. Do you have any information on that?" I asked, hope spurting up into me.

"The Undoing?" She tilted her head to one side, suddenly looking very catlike. "Do you know the time period or another name for it?"

"At least three thousand years ago. Carelian, Kesis, do you know of any other names?" That flame of hope that had been so bright and fierce died down when she didn't instantly recognize the name.

Carelian looked at me. ~The Cath called it the Sweet Food Devastation,~ he offered. The sphinx shook her head.

"Then I do not know of what you seek. However, you are welcome to browse the shelves." She waved at the expanse of the library.

"Are there card catalogs?" Shay asked. I wasn't sure what those were. College had every book listed in the computer. You'd do searches to find the books.

"Of course." Cleo rose up and padded around the desk and walked over to what I'd dismissed as a large apothecary system. It was about six feet tall, ten feet long, and about a foot deep. "They are all in here."

Shay narrowed his eyes. "How are they listed?"

"The drawers from one to twenty are alphabetical by author, known name, then family name, and the drawers from twenty-one to forty are alphabetical by title." Her voice sounded like every other librarian's voice, proud and helpful.

Shay however, flinched. "Only by that? You don't use the Dewey Decimal system or a category system?"

Cleo drew back, a bit affronted. "Of course, there is a system. It is listed at the end of each column."

Shay started to sigh in relief when she continued.

"Shelves are arranged by language, then by author. We are the only library in the realms, so we make sure people can find what they are looking for."

"Ummm," Shay said slowly, and I had to agree with his hesitation. "How many are in English?"

Cleo blinked at us. "English? Modern English?" She stood there thoughtfully for a moment. "I believe there was one patron about two hundred years ago that donated a few books in that language. Yes, the two donated were a mythology book called The Bible, and the other was an English copy of the work of Marcus Aurelius, a poor translation, I must say."

I just looked at her. "None of them are in English?"

She laughed, a ripple of sound that in any other situation I might have enjoyed listening to. "Not as such. Magic allows us to all speak English, as I am now, but it is a young language, barely three hundred years old. Most of the books in the library are thousands of years old. I have the first pictographs from the Neanderthals, recopied of course on paper. The stone tablets were too heavy to carry around. Our most prolific period was about four thousand years ago. Interaction with Earth was active and rich. We had great mages on both sides writing treatises about the interactions. But about three thousand years ago the number of patrons to visit us dropped. You are my first in … oh, I'd say a hundred and fifty of your years, if the time is right."

"So, should I cry or scream?" I asked idly as I turned to stare at the shelves.

"I am not sure, but I feel the same way." Shay said. He sounded old and I glanced at him, but he looked fine, just tired.

"What is the primary language for the books presented here after the peak activity?" Citlali asked.

"Oh, that would be Greek, Sumerian, and Hebrew. They had such interesting stories," Cleo said with a smile. "My favorite is still the Iliad, so much death. Those battles must have been glorious."

"How old are you?" I asked.

She sniffed a bit as if affronted. "I am three hundred and fifty, more than old enough to run the library myself."

"That wasn't what I was implying," I rushed to say. "We are trying to find out about what the Undoing was and why it happened. That was when magic and Earth separated."

"Ah. My grandmother mentioned her great-grandmother had talked about that. Apparently, her older brother was upset he would not be able to laze around under the statue of him. She said he'd approved of the likeness. And enjoyed the offerings." Cleo shook her head. "If there is information in here, I would not know what it was under."

I put my hands on my face and rubbed my temples. "Do you mind if we walk around? And where is the display that was here the last time I was?"

"You have never been in my library before, but if you mean the display hall, that is currently closed for rearrangement. It had been set up that way per the order of the council and I am still working on trying to put it back to a proper layout." Cleo snarled that last part, obviously annoyed. "However, the library is yours to peruse. Please do not take books out without checking them out."

She nodded at us and went back to the main desk, humming something under her breath softly.

"Well, this was a waste of time, effort and preparation. We didn't even have to fight anything," Shay muttered.

"Be glad of that," I countered. "But let's wander. If something calls to us, maybe we can find a historian? Maybe there is a way to translate?" I felt like doing a hundred things at once, but instead I settled the backpack more firmly on my back. Then I headed into the stacks with Carelian padding behind me.

I let my intuition just pull me through the stacks. There had to be an answer here, somewhere, but I didn't know what I was looking for. Mostly I just wanted a few minutes without someone looking at me. The smell of dust and paper, wood and fur teased my nose. I just kept moving, my fingers not quite brushing across the volumes. Some were books, but many were scrolls or piles of paper. None of which I could read.

~Are you okay?~ Carelian's voice was soft as he pressed against my leg. I let my hand drop to scratch his forehead.

"Just frustrated. I thought we had found it. But in retrospect, why would there be anything in English here? It is a new language. If I went back 200 years I doubt I could understand anyone, and two thousand? It was stupid. But all the books I saw when I was here last time had English titles. Temptation? Or...." I carefully pulled out one of the books. Why they weren't crumbling when I looked at them, I attributed to magic. There was nothing written on the cover that I could see. I flipped it open.

The third page was covered with marks and swirls and other lines. It meant nothing to me. I stared for a minute, hoping maybe something would change, but it remained unintelligible.

"No, this was all a waste of time and effort. Everyone is going to die and I don't know what to do."

CHAPTER

FORTY-ONE

House of Emrys sues over premier magic books: In the news today, the house of Merlins is suing to allow all mages, regardless of level, access to the expensive books of magic. These books, printed in limited runs and not allowed in e-book form, are controlled by the OMO. Emrys is suing to have these books be treated like any other and available to the public. They are pushing for all magic reference books to be converted to e-books, so they are more widely available to mages. ~ CNN Mage Focus

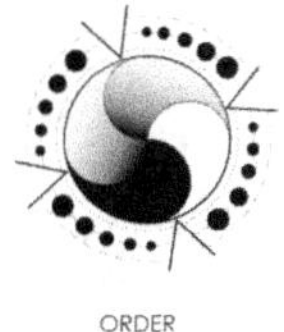

ORDER

I sat at the kitchen counter the next morning staring at my coffee. It felt like too much energy to even lift it.

"Okay, Cori, talk." Jo slipped in next to me and bumped me with her shoulder. "You came in last night, barely said anything, and crawled into bed. So, spill."

"We found the library," I said, still staring at my coffee.

"Well, that is excellent!" Her voice then lost her excited note. "But I take it you didn't find the information you wanted?"

A snort escaped me. "For all I know it could be there. English is a young language, like we aren't even two hundred years old the way we speak and read. The youngest book there is over two thousand." I wanted to cry as I said that. It just seemed impossible.

"Ah," Jo said softly and put her arm around me. "Problems of the world seem a bit insurmountable today?"

I rested my head on her shoulder, too tired and depressed to pretend. "They all think I can fix this. I'm willing to fix this, but I have no clue how to stop any of it."

Jo squeezed me tight for a moment. "How about a perspective reset?" she asked.

The way she said that, I knew I should be wary, but that didn't matter. If I couldn't trust her, there was no one left. "Sure. What should I do?"

Jo laughed, lifted my head to kiss my forehead. "Get on decent clothes. You get to chaperone the kids today." She stepped out of reach as she said that, headed to the refrigerator.

"Wait, what?" I asked. That had derailed my train of thought from the rips to the kids with enough speed to give me a headache.

"I volunteered to be one of the parents for the zoo trip. Now you get to. It will help clear your mind, make sure you get back in touch with your family, and gives me the day to finish getting the house ready. I'm thinking we can move in at the end of January." Her smile was brilliant as she glanced back at me.

"This month?" I doubled checked it was still January.

"Yes, this month. Go enjoy a day with your delightful children and I'll finish up the aspects that are easier done without kids underfoot." She was cooking as she talked and the aroma of her staple breakfast burrito mixings filled the air.

"What about work?" I managed to sip my coffee, the dark richness hitting me and helping to lift my mood.

"I had already taken today off to chaperone, so I'll use it. Otherwise, I was going to try to get Mami to watch them this weekend."

I thought about it. Other than dinner time, I hadn't seen much of them, what with working on all the council stuff and everyone else being at the Tudor house. "Sure, why not? What do I need to know?" If nothing else, the chaos involved in a bunch of pre-k's at the zoo should distract me appropriately.

"Folder is with my purse. If you grab it, all the information should be in there."

Taking another sip of coffee gave me the fortitude to rise and grab the folder. It sounded pretty easy. I was to manage the four to six kids they assigned me and follow the tours through the zoo. The kids would have money for snacks and lunch had already been paid for.

"Sure, this gets me out of the house. I'll go change." I was still in my sleeping shorts and a tank top. Making coffee had been the height of my powers.

"Better get going. The kids will be down in about five, given how hyped they were when they woke up." Jo grinned and I groaned, but got going.

I gave Carelian the offer to come, but he very firmly

declined. He'd much rather sleep all day than deal with that many children.

Three hours later, we were at the Utica Zoo. I had a new appreciation for teachers and their ability to not hex every child in sight, especially when at least two teachers were magician level. It was for two classrooms totaling forty-three kids. Apparently taking sympathy on me, I was only assigned five children, of which Jaz was one of them. She'd been ecstatic I was coming and had babbled the entire drive in. Magne had been happy, but he zoomed right over to Bobby and had stuck with him when groups were divvied up.

Along with Jaz, I had two girls, Sheliah and Adrienne, then two boys, John and Mark. At least everyone was wearing name badges. We would move through as a group and break at 11:45 for lunch. The teacher waved us in and we started with the barnyard animals, the neon yellow name badges making it obvious we were here as a group.

Jaz instantly fell in love with the goats, and I couldn't blame her. "No, we aren't getting any goats."

"But Momma Cori, they are so cute," Jaz whined a bit, looking up at me with luminous brown eyes.

"Yes, they are. Do you really think Carelian won't try to eat it? Or Azul and Vert? All of them would think you'd brought them a live snack, and that is not a habit I want to get into."

Her mouth opened to argue, stopped, stared at the goat, then sighed. "They'd eat it."

"Yep. Now let's catch up."

By lunch time we'd made it all the way to the Scales and Tails reptile house. Jaz loved the zoo but was bored by the reptile house. I guess snakes that just sat there were a bit boring compared to having your own dragon. We had to backtrack back to the Rotary Pavilion, where hotdogs, potato chips, and fruit had been provided.

I talked to the other parents a little, but the questioning looks and probing questions weren't how I wanted to spend the day. That had me wandering over to look at the "World's Largest Watering Can" and check in on Carelian.

~You enjoying yourself?~ I asked as I sipped on a soda—at least that I'd been able to purchase. The kids were stuck with milk, juice, and water.

~Very much so. The sun coming through the windows is just warm enough, the house is quiet, and I have a full stomach.~

I snickered at that. If only my needs could be so easily met. ~Did you talk to your mother about the Library?~

~Not yet, though I did discover something new. I can go to the library now. It is visible and welcomes me almost. Though there is little there I can read it is a comfortable space.~

That caught me and I stared at the watering can without really seeing it. ~You have a library card,~ I finally said as it clicked. ~You must go to the library the first time. After that you have a card and can come and go as you please.~ It all made sense, but it still didn't help me with what I needed.

~Ah.~ He fell silent. ~I think you are right, but in that case I suppose I had better get moving.~ He sounded like he was yawning as he spoke, a weird ripple in the mind speak. It mixed with the sounds of kids becoming more active. I'd have to get back in a minute.

~To do?~ I swallowed the last of my soda and turned to the kids.

~Do you really think my Malkin or Baneyarl would ever forgive me if I found this library and did not take them to it? Besides, they can research while they are there.~ He sounded smug, and I laughed as I reached the picnic tables and started to help the kids clean up.

~Point. You do that. Maybe they can read some of the

languages.~ I let him go and found my little group of kids. Our next stop was the Asian realm as the wallaby enclosure was currently under construction. I found the cranes and the pigs uninteresting, but we were moving toward the lions and that had everyone excited.

A slash of pain slammed into my brain so hard that I cried out, brought to my knees. Jaz was at my side in a split second. "Momma Cori! What's wrong?"

I forced myself to breathe as the pain lessened and I stood slowly. The kids looked at me with horror. With a shaking hand I wiped blood from my nostril, but I paid no attention to it. Instead, I turned, seeking the rip I'd felt form. "Shit," I muttered as I found it. Huge and gaping right over the lion enclosure. What was worse were the tentacles emerging from the gash.

"Chaos," I said with an odd sense of inevitability. "Jaz, hold on to my belt loop and the rest of you hold hands now." I snapped out the commands, taking over as I reached to close the rip. It didn't want to close.

The bulging blackness had everyone's attention and people were starting to scream and rush every which way, but I fought with trying to close it. Even the animals were upset and you could hear shrieks and growls rumbling through the zoo. It didn't matter, I had to get it closed.

"Children, come over here now," a voice screamed. It sounded like one of the teachers, but I couldn't be sure.

"Don't move," I warned Jaz. I wasn't sure of anything else, but I could and would destroy the zoo to protect her. I fought not to turn and look for Magne, but I needed to focus on this. Outside the rip, the only thing I was aware of was Jaz's hand clenched on my belt and the heat of her body.

The black ooze coming out was thick and heavy. Not as bad as water, but it resisted and squirmed, pressing the sides as I tried to seal, ripping back open the tear. The tentacles were lashing out, and wrapping around things, pulling them up. I had to move faster before a person was grabbed.

"You need to let her go!" a woman yelled right in my ear. "We have to get them to safety."

"She's safer here with me. In fact, all of them are. Now quit distracting me," I ground out as I fought. My hair was creeping away fast, and I'd be at nails, blood, and urine soon—or I'd be bald.

"Let me go!" Jaz screamed. It broke my concentration. A woman with her own badge was pulling at Jaz. All the other kids had been pulled away and I could see them racing toward the reptile building.

"That isn't safe in there. I'm keeping her with me. Where is Magne?" I spun, ignoring the rip that was getting larger. "MAGNE!"

"Momma Cori, I'm here!" He wiggled out from the gaggle of kids and raced to me, arms clamping around my waist.

"They have to come!" the woman screamed.

"Get down!" I grabbed her and yanked as a tentacle came swinging toward us. It missed and went into the nearest animal enclosure. To my horror and astonishment, it came back up with an enraged lioness in its grip. The poor cat shredded the tentacle that held it and fell—directly in front of us.

Oh shit.

~CARELIAN!~ I screamed the word in my mind as I vaporized a full inch of hair to slam a huge lightning bolt into the squirming blob trying to escape into our world. A shriek of outrage had it pulling back as I backed up, not wanting to kill the animal in front of me.

~Cori?~ Carelian said even as he appeared in front of me. One look at the lioness and he snarled, all the fur on his body poofed up. The woman behind me was screaming. The sound added an extra level of agitation to my already frazzled nerves.

"Knock it out or get it back in its pen. I have to get this closed," I ordered as I tried to pull enough power to close it. I needed blood. There was no time to try to cut myself, and I knew from experience that biting your own tongue on purpose hard enough to draw blood was more difficult than you might expect. I raked my uterus. Cramps hit hard enough that I wanted to double over crying, but I pushed them aside and used the power. Blood had always been magic's favorite and menstrual blood was even more powerful. I slammed another lightning bolt at it, splitting the electricity so it hit multiple places at once and it screamed pulling back. With a grunt, I sealed the rip, and my knees buckled.

I staggered, the kids holding me up, and focused my eyes on the red blur. Carelian spun around the lioness, confusing her, and as she charged he opened up a portal that she dove through, him following. A second later, another one opened in the enclosure and the lioness rushed out. She had a few light scratches, probably love taps from Carelian, but nothing else.

He stepped back out a second later and rushed to us.

The teacher started screaming. "A monster, he's going to eat the kids!"

I KO'd her. She crumpled to the ground and the zoo went quiet. Or quieter. The animals were still making a ruckus, but even that seemed muted and less dramatic. Everyone in the area just stared at my little group. Jaz and Magne released me and rushed to Carelian, burying their heads in his fur as they wrapped arms around him. Not crying, but very close.

I turned to see the woman I'd knocked out laying there, the other teacher and parents all staring at me, sheer terror in their eyes.

"I should have stayed in bed."

CHAPTER

FORTY-TWO

Panic at the Zoo! The strange invasions are getting more dangerous every day. The recent attack at a zoo in New York has parents screaming. Already emergency meetings are being called and restrictions are being suggested to ensure people are being kept safe. The information that wild animals had gotten loose has been disproved however, as all animals were accounted for in their enclosures. There were no confirmed injuries of children, though several parents needed to be treated for anxiety attacks. Merlin Cori Munroe was present, but no one has been able to validate what her level of involvement was, and the authorities are not providing any information. ~ CNN Mage Focus

The aftermath of the zoo didn't surprise me, but did result in the school declaring I was never allowed as a chaperone again. The zoo gave us a lifetime membership for rescuing and not killing their lion—they apparently had no doubt Carelian could have done that easily. The various government agencies were called, reports taken, witness statements collected, questioning, and on and on and on. The whole time the kids would not leave my side, Carelian snarled and hissed at anyone who came too close, and the cops had no idea how to record the incident.

Eventually Alixant showed up, took over and got me released, though with a "I'll talk to you later" glare that was unmistakable. By that time, Jo showed up, loaded us all up in the van and took us home.

I didn't talk the whole way home. I was numb and didn't know how to feel or what I should express. When we got home the kids urged me out of the car and up the stairs into the sitting room. I curled up there, Carelian at my feet, still trying to figure out everything.

Jo brought me a coffee, and I took a drink, almost choking from the amount of coffee liqueur in it, but it did help to get me to unwind.

"Are you okay?" Jo asked. She was crouched across from me, one hand on Carelian.

"Yeah. Tired. Mostly I'm trying to figure various things out."

"So, tell me," she requested, and sank down. The kids had

shaken off most of their terror and had gone to get their quetzos. The faint sounds of them telling the mini dragons everything that had happened filtered down the stairs.

"Why there? Why now? This world has seven billion people on it and last check, we were getting fifteen to thirty rips a day across the globe. Now these are the ones that are reported, so let's triple that and say it's a hundred a day. For that matter, assume there are still more happening in the water and in places with no humans and multiply that by a hundred. That is ten thousand. Still a drop in the bucket for the number of places and people in this world. Why would a major rip happen above me?"

Jo settled herself, dark eyes on me. "Charles did mention large amounts of magic users and no magic users affect the appearance," she offered.

"He did, but that leads me to a few other possibilities that don't make me happy. It implies that my presence with a few other mages is such a draw that magic can't resist. I have no idea how many mages were at the zoo that day, either guests or employees. All the kids were too young to be emerging. So, if my presence there and some other unknown aspect drew the rip, it means just being in public with me increases the chances of a rip exponentially." I looked up at her, my eyes bleak. "It means I'm a danger to everyone, especially my family."

Jo took a deep breath but didn't look away. "What else?"

With her question, I finally addressed the real problem, the one that had my rage wrapped into a source of incandescent power. Where it took all my concentration to keep from exploding again.

"I have asked for help. I have been told it is my job to resolve it. I have tried, I have looked. I don't know how. And because I cannot get the help I need, the information I need, my children were put at risk. Everyone in that zoo was put at risk, but my children could have been killed." I swallowed and forced myself to relax. The anger didn't fade, I just locked it down hard and tight so that it didn't slip out of my control.

"I'm aware that people have died, and I care. But my children, your children, the two beings I helped create were almost killed." I closed my eyes for a long moment, then looked at Jo. "I'm not sure the world would have survived if they had."

Jo started to laugh. It was a giggle, then a snort, then a full out laugh that had her on the floor holding her stomach. I just stared at her, confused.

When she could breathe again, she pushed herself back up and looked at me with a grin still on her face. "Welcome to parenthood, Cori. That is what every parent feels the first time their children are endangered. Did you ever take the Mage Statistics class?"

I looked at her, unsure where this was going. "I took Research and Statistics, but not that one. You're saying this is a common occurrence?"

"No. I'm saying the number of child molesters that have died, and parents that have used magic to kill their child's attacker, is through the roof. More children are left with relatives because of their parents killing their attackers than through accidental deaths. And the number of parents that flee the country to a place that doesn't have as harsh penalties for those sorts of murders or attacks is sky high. I'm saying Sable and I would do that same thing for them." She stopped and looked me right in the eye. "And for you and Carelian. You do anything to protect family, Cori. We know that, we've always known that."

I broke down. The fear that had been wrapped around me snapped and I started crying. Jo surged up from the floor and wrapped her arms around me. The kids stopped and in seconds were racing down the stairs, the quetzo's clinging to them, tails and wings streaming behind them. Jaz climbed into my lap while Magne curled up on top of Carelian to hold my legs.

"Don't cry, Momma Cori," Jaz ordered. "You saved us. You were awesome. Teachers were dumb."

"Jaz," Jo warned.

Even through my tears, I could see Jaz's bottom lip stick out. "They were dumb. It's not calling names if they are."

Jo had pulled away and I could see her face. Her lips were pressed together, holding back a smile. "Hmm," was all she said. Jaz squeezed me harder.

"You and Carelian were heroes. I wanna be like you when I get bigger."

I just held her tighter and fought to get my tears under control. The idea of not having them here felt like someone threatened to rip out my heart. I wouldn't allow that to happen. Instead, I kissed the top of her head and blew a kiss to Magne, who caught it and slapped it on his cheek.

We stayed cuddled like that for at least five minutes before the kids began to squirm. "You gonna be okay, Momma Cori?" Magne asked hesitantly.

"Yes, Magne. Go. I'll be fine." He wiggled away from my legs and Carelian while Jaz squeezed me extra hard.

"You go, Jaz. I'll be fine. I need to do boring grownup stuff."

She gave me a look that I'd seen in Jo's eyes so often, showing she wasn't sure she believed me, but she finally let got and scampered off to the upstairs with Magne.

"You sound better," Jo said. She still sat next to me on the couch.

"Not sure I feel better, but this is ending now. It has to. The risks are way too great and I can't let my presence endanger you, Sable, the kids, Hamiada, and her daughters. I just can't. I'm done playing nice. If I have to pluck that merlin blasted bird, I will."

~Excellent. I bet phoenix tastes like chicken.~

I blinked, then Jo and I fell into helpless giggles. There wasn't much else we could do to a statement like that. The worst part was I couldn't really disagree with his comment.

I went in and washed my face, flinching away from the hack job on my hair. It looked like I'd let the kids attack it with scissors leaving it mostly above my shoulders with sections shorter and longer. If I was lucky my magic use in the near future wouldn't be under pressure and I could choose where the offerings came from to neaten it up. Or I could chop it off and keep it with me to use. I sighed and moved to my study, pulling Carelian with me. "Are you okay?" In all the drama, I'd forgotten to check on him, but I also knew he was pretty good at telling me when he was hurt.

~I was not hurt. The lion was amusing. Though too slow and stupid for real entertainment. Even the quetzos will be smarter and more of a challenge.~ He jumped up on the window seat to clean his claws. ~Not even the blood tastes good. Too tame.~

I gave him a narrow-eyed look, but let it be. My Cath would never change. "Did you get a chance to take Esmere and Bane-yarl to the Library?"

~No. I was moving slow and figured I still had hours. Then you called.~

I nodded, biting my lip. "Let's see if I can offer them library access in exchange for information."

~Malkin would give you much because of me. She rather enjoys your definition of family.~ He had stopped grooming to look up at me, his green eyes bright.

"I know, but this I think I want to pay for, as I'm going to ruffle a lot of feathers."

~Very well. I will let you do that.~ He settled back down, but I could swear I heard a note of approval in his tone.

Setting up a three-way mindspeak took me a minute. Most of the time, if they were near me, I could just broadcast. This involved calling each of them and joining the calls, so to speak. When they had both "answered" I started right in.

~Baneyarl, Esmere, I would like to trade for some information or assistance.~ I wasn't asking favors this time. I was trading for it.

I could hear the stunned shock in their silence, but I just waited. The memory of Jaz and Magne holding on to me was more than enough to keep me on my course.

~I see, Herald Munroe. What is it you would like to trade for?~ Esmere asked slowly.

~I want the information on how to call a council meeting myself and what the rules are for council proceedings. And for both of you to serve as my advisor for all future council meetings even if you need to quit being a lord.~ At no point had I been told anything, and they didn't tend to provide info if you didn't ask it. I knew this would cut deep, but I'd rather have Esmere quit being a lord than risk us being on opposite sides. This wasn't something I could offer Tirsane, I just knew that somehow, but Esmere wasn't primary, Bob was.

~And what are you trading for this?~ Baneyarl asked warily. I couldn't blame him as this was asking a lot.

~You will be brought to the Library of Magic where you can request permanent access to it,~ I stated and this time I had the feeling they wouldn't forget. After all, I had a library card.

If I had slapped them across the face with a live fish, I think they would have been less shocked.

~You found it,~ Esmere hissed. ~It has books?~

~More books than I can count and most I can't read. But it has wonders that I can't even begin to explain or show you, but I'm sure the librarian can.~

~There's a librarian?~ Baneyarl sounded more excited than I'd heard in a decade. ~There is someone to help find things.~

~Yes.~ I didn't bother to keep the smugness out of my voice. ~Her name is Cleo, and she is a sphinx.~ If a feather had fallen, you would have heard it hit the ground in the resounding silence.

~They still exist?~ Baneyarl's voice was almost a whisper.

~Um, I guess. I mean I talked to her and got a library card. I was unaware they were not supposed to exist.~ That part did surprise me. Carelian hadn't been astonished by her existence. But then he was a Cath. He rarely showed any reactions that weren't aggressive or posturing.

~I will agree. I have no council oaths that I need to worry about. I never dreamed it still existed.~ Baneyarl's voice was all but reverent. I couldn't remember any other denizen ever sounding reverent about something.

~Esmere?~ I asked softly.

~The offer is fair. I am torn. With the storm approaching, I will not be able to remain neutral, but I fought hard for my right to be a lord. Also, while I can read, it is not something I excel at as Baneyarl does. But there is history there and other ways of doing magic. What was common prior to the Undoing. It is information that gives me leverage and favors to trade to anyone.~ Her voice sounded very thoughtful.

~I must warn you, many of the books are written in languages that aren't even spoken on Earth anymore. None are in English.~

~So? The librarian can translate it into any language for you.~

"WHAT?!" The word came out of my mouth and mind at the same time. I could feel the shock of the two denizens. "She can do that?"

~Of course,~ Baneyarl said. ~It is the magic of librarians.

What good would it do to have a library where no one can read what you have.~

~Why didn't she tell us? Why didn't you tell us?~ I glared at Carelian for that.

He licked his paw, but his tail thrashed. ~I was unaware,~ he muttered.

~Did you ask?~ Esmere sounded curious.

~It never occurred to us, we just asked for things in English and there really weren't any.~

I took a deep breath and pushed that away. I needed to share that, but it didn't change what needed to be done now. ~What is your decision, Lord Esmere?~

CHAPTER

FORTY-THREE

Looking for three mages for a research project. Must be passionate about history and the origins of Magic. Experience with the syntax of other languages, especially Babylonian, Greek, and Hebrew. Willing to do all research on site. Must be willing to sign an NDA that will be strongly enforced. Contact Shay for more information. ~ House of Emrys Message board

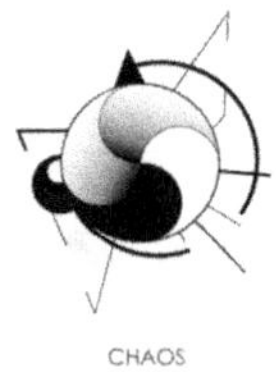

CHAOS

It took me two days. Mainly because I wanted to make sure my family was safe and Shay and Citlali knew what I was going to do. But I didn't discuss it with them, I just let them know. Jo and Sable got the kids moved over to the Tudor house so that I didn't need to worry about them being in the house if there was some sort of retaliation. Marisol and the Guzman's were warned, and I took the time to call Kris and get him up to speed. He wanted to come help, but I wanted him way out of the danger zone.

Then I warned Hamiada.

"What do you mean, you want to know if I can survive if the house is destroyed?" There was a note of panic in her voice.

"I need to know if I need to get out of the house." I stated the words as if I was going to the store, but to be honest I had no idea where to go if I couldn't be here. A hotel would be worse? I supposed I could go camping somewhere, but that didn't sound fun at all. I'd have to buy an RV.

I shook my head to get my thoughts under control. "If a rip happens here and I can't stop it and the house gets hurt, will you be okay?"

Her entire body had shut down, turning a dark brown gray. There were no flowers or green leaves on her body. "Cori, are you saying you are worried that an attack might damage my tree?" For once she wasn't floating on the tips of her toes, but instead both feet were flat on the ground as if she was sinking her toes into the wood to reach the ground.

"Yes, basically, that is what I am asking."

"Hmm," She closed her eyes, swaying a bit back and forth. "If my roots are not destroyed I will be fine. But this house is part of my realm. Short of you calling fire here and feeding it, I do not know how I would easily sustain more than minor damage. I can control who comes in here and expel anyone that does not belong. Your presence has made me stronger than I was at the beginning."

"Even chaos beings from a rip?" I pressed the issue, needing to make sure she understood.

"Even so. My realm is Order. This is my realm as much as the glade is. As long as you do not hurt me, I am difficult to .... mortally wound," she said finally, as if she'd tried to figure out how to say it. But it made sense in an odd way. You could prune trees, burn them, and often they came back stronger and healthier than before.

"Good." I almost sagged with relief. "I'm going up against the council, and I wanted to make sure you wouldn't be hurt."

"Should I remove access for those who visit?"

I shook my head. "No, or at least not yet. I am working on the idea that they are still my friends, just we are having a difference of opinion on how to proceed. But thank you for the offer." I moved over and hugged her tightly. She returned the gesture. By the time I stepped back, green had returned to her bark, and leaves were starting to burst out of her hair.

"Very well. I shall return to my sister-daughters. I am surprised, they are growing very fast and with more... essence than I've ever heard of. I had figured years or decades before they awoke. Now I am thinking it might be closer to months. Your family is very good to mine."

"Hamiada, you are family. Don't ever think you aren't. We love you too."

The flush of flowers that burst over her cheeks made me want to laugh in delight, but I kept it tamped down. She just nodded, rose up on her toes and spun away.

I let out a long breath. Everyone was waiting for me and my next move. I moved to the study and curled up in my favorite chair. I sat in the house I'd come to love and just breathed. For the first time, I sank into myself and felt my magic.

Over the years, I'd come to enjoy it, but I'd always treated it as an unwelcome part of me, something I had to deal with, much like my menstrual cycle. It was part of me, but I'd always had a vague resentment at the problems it had caused. Granted, it had brought me Carelian and made my life rich, much like my cycle let me have two of the best kids in the world. It didn't mean there wasn't a part of me that didn't still resent it and the fact that my magic had cost me Stevie.

It was time to let that go.

I closed my eyes and reached for magic. We tried so hard as humans to quantify everything, put it into boxes for easy explanations. In some ways, it worked. Understanding the science made magic so much easier to do, though the entry gate was harder. But we never figured out why we could manipulate the forces of the universe. So, I looked. It was like sensing the air I breathed, there yet not tangible. Magic was part of me, and I was part of it.

I felt it as a part of who I was and knew it had made me who I was as much as my parents and friends. It was time to stop resenting what was in essence me. I let my resentment go and accepted that I was a mage and the Herald of Magic.

Meditation had never been anything I enjoyed, too much sitting quietly and I got bored. But this time, seeking inside and outside myself, I found a sense of wholeness I'd never had. By the time I opened my eyes, I felt more at peace than I'd felt in my life.

Carelian was sitting across from me. Positioned so when I opened my eyes he would be the first thing I saw. He tilted his head, green eyes slowly blinking at me, then nodded.

"I think I'm ready, at least mentally. Let me change." Once again, I dressed for war. I put cut off offerings in my pocket. Braids, nail clippings, the true power of a merlin with a familiar. It basically gave me an extra source of offerings that most didn't have. I had no idea if denizens could do this and I didn't care, but I was ready to spend them all to get my way.

Cargo pants, this time with a very sharp knife if I needed more, though Carelian had gleefully offered to bite me. A tank top, overshirt, light jacket, and boots. My backpack loaded again to the brim. Better safe than sorry, as far as I was concerned.

I checked my hair. It was barely at chin level with the closures lately. It would make me look weaker than I was. Good.

The harness with his accoutrements was stuffed in my bag as well. I knew he wouldn't want to wear it to the council chambers, but I felt better with it, as I never knew where life would take me.

"You ready?" I asked Carelian.

~Yes. I will take you there, then go get Shay. Kesis will bring Citlali as soon as I tell her you are there.~ He rose with a long stretch. ~The battle will be glorious.~

I leaned down and kissed the top of his head. "I suspect it will." It wasn't something I could argue. The odds of this not being a fight were slim to none. "Let's go."

A splash of pain and we stepped into the council chambers. Carelian disappeared almost immediately. I stayed in the shadows, looking at it. I'd never seen it empty before. The chamber should have been pale and lifeless, being simple gray stone with rings of lighter gray, one wall destroyed to open to a courtyard. But it wasn't.

The place rang of quiet majesty and power. The weight of ages had settled into the bones of the building. I realized I'd never seen it from the outside or even gone past this room. For all I knew this was all that existed. The rest might not, or maybe this was the fabled Camelot brought here by Merlin himself.

My ruminating was cut off by twin spikes of pain as Kesis,

bringing Citlali, appeared, and Carelian with Shay and to my surprise Scott Randolph and Dahli.

"Guests?" I asked, glancing at Scott, not that I wasn't glad to see him. His training and experience as a rogue mage hunter meant he was better with offensive uses of his magic than I ever would be.

Shay shrugged. "He was around and I figured everyone else gets their own cheering section. Why not us?"

"Hello Scott, it's good to see you. I assume Shay brought you up to speed?"

Scott gave me a roguish grin. He was now in his late sixties, but I could tell he must have been a charmer back in his prime. "Yep. Should be fun. With Dahli here, I'm not worried about anyone attacking me from behind."

~I protect!~ Dahli barked with enthusiasm.

I had to fight my chuckles as Carelian and Kesis both managed to sneer at the dog and instantly find something that needed to be groomed. As far as I could tell, it was a mix of a cold shoulder and giving someone the bird. It never failed to make me smirk.

"Yes you do, Dahli," I said as she came over to get pets. I introduced Citlali, who also gave pets much to Dahli's excitement from the number of times my legs got whacked with her tail. But the laughter and joy faded.

"Are we ready for this?"

Citlali shrugged, as did Shay. "Are we sure going back and reading the books isn't the answer?" I wanted to be sure. I'd shared with them what Esmere had said, but we all agreed until we knew what we were looking for it did us no good.

"Troy was only discovered because there were clues that led to it. If all there had been was the tale of the battle, we wouldn't have found it. We need more than just the Undoing," Shay said calmly. He was dressed today in jeans, a t-shirt, and a jacket. It was the most informal thing I'd seen him in for a council meeting. Scott had copied it, though with his jean jacket with BAM on the back, he still exuded an air of danger Shay never would.

I nodded. What he said was correct. Once we had more information, maybe the Library would be useful.

~Baneyarl are you ready?~ I sent that and then sent to Esmere the same.

A minute later, there were two beings walking toward me. Baneyarl was dressed for battle, literally. He had a chest plate on that protected his breast bone, the edges of his wings reflected silver, and there was a metal cap on his beak that gleamed with danger.

Esmere, for her part, seemed excited for the coming actions. Her eyes were wide and dilated and her tail twitched even as she tried to restrain it. Across her chest and back, she wore a modified leather breastplate. It looked like a mix between what horses would wear to battle when there were still knights and the harness Carelian wore.

"Are you sure?" I asked her. Baneyarl had less to lose and for the most part was agreeing to be my councilor. Esmere thought she would lose what she'd fought for.

~I am comfortable with my choices. There is much you are unaware of regarding the machinations in the council. I risk less than you might think.~ She sat and looked at me, so I shrugged.

"Very well. Esmere, in exchange for advising me and backing me up in council, I will take you to the Library of Magic. Assuming I survive. If not, the others have agreed to fulfill my debt."

Esmere flashed amber eyes at the others and they all nodded their assent.

~I agree.~ She turned and paced to the center of the ring. ~Stand here.~ She tapped a claw in the center and I looked down. It hadn't been visible in the gloom of the chamber, but where Brix usually perched was a silvery stone with all the symbols etched on it in a triangle. If you weren't looking for it, it was all but invisible.

I moved to stand where she indicated. ~Call on magic. All Lords have the right to call a meeting. Pull the magic into you, then down into the stone and repeat what I told you.~

I did as she instructed. Magic flooded in at my request and much like with the library form I pushed it out, then said in a loud clear voice. "I, Earth Lord Cori Munroe, call an emergency council meeting by the office and oath I took. It will start in one hour."

Magic grabbed it and like an explosion, I felt the magic race away from the center rippling out everywhere. "That was interesting. Why don't we feel it?"

Esmere flicked a tail. ~You do not live in the realms. All those sworn to the council will feel it, not others.~

I nodded processing that and stared at the gray circle. It was done. Now to deal with Brix.

FORTY-FOUR

A new alert system is being rolled out today. After working with major telecommunication companies, the government has arranged for the number 988 to route to a rip hotline. If you see a rip, regardless of the size or area, call 988. They will ask you to provide your location. The nearest mages will be dispatched to deal with it. Please do not enter the rip, nor interact with any creature or thing that might emerge. Many are deadly to humans and they are not easily subdued. ~ Public Announcement

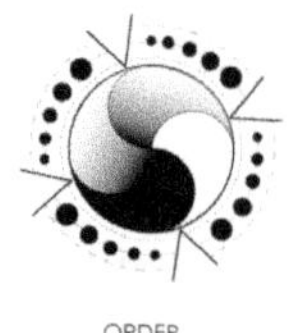

ORDER

With assurance I didn't feel, I moved back to the area for Earth realm lords. The chairs were still there, which vaguely surprised me, but I didn't worry about it. I settled in and reminded myself once more of how lucky they were that my kids had not been hurt. This council might not still be standing if they had been. Shay was sitting in his chair, while Citlali appeared to hold court from her sword chair. She had a poise that said "kneel if you wish to speak to me." It was amusing.

Beings began to appear, all of them glancing at me, but no one dared to walk over until Tirsane appeared. She stood there for a long time, then slithered over to me. She positioned herself so she could see the majority of the Council chamber, but still talk to me.

"A few questions if I may, Cori?" She sounded hesitant. I would have to fix this, I didn't want my friendship with Tirsane to be damaged.

"Of course. Please feel free." I smiled at her, but I doubted it was reflected in my eyes. I was still too angry even though days had passed.

"Did you come by a few days ago? My nest swears you did, but surely you would have spoken with me?" There was worry and a bit of a hurt note in her voice and I silently cursed. Once I had spoken of the Library both Esmere and Baneyarl had remembered. Hopefully Tirsane would once I told her.

"Yes, we were there." I pulled my wallet out of its normal pocket. The library card all but jumped into my hand. "I would be delighted to show you the library so you can get your card, for some future favors?" Not two months ago, I would have just taken her, but now I couldn't afford to give up such a powerful trading option.

She stared at the card, all her snakes coming around to stare in apparent wonder as well. "You found it?" There was a hushed reverence in her voice.

"Yes. And got cards. Assuming I live through this, are you interested in a trade?" The hunger in her eyes was almost physical.

"Yessss," she managed, then cleared her throat. "That would be something worth much, maybe more than I can pay, but we will discuss later." She glanced around and a large portion of the council were showing up with their various entourages." Did you happen to invite anyone else to your council meeting?"

"Uh?" That threw me. At no point had Esmere mentioned inviting anyone. "Like?"

"Zmaug is not a council member, but she wants to say in the loop. Same for a few others. It might behoove you to invite them." Her tone was mild as she rotated. "Basically, anyone you think I might want to eat popcorn with."

"Oh." I felt like slapping my head and instantly sent out a note to Jeorgaz, Zmaug, the Thunderbird, and Tiantang. I doubted two of them would attend, but you never could tell.

"Thank you," I said sincerely.

Tirsane bobbed a bit in acknowledgement. She flicked her eyes over to Baneyarl, who stood there dressed, but completely at ease as he and Citlali chatted, her in low tones. "Support?"

"And then some. I have multiple options in play." The small part of me that wanted to be ten again and eternally a child wailed at how manipulative I'd become. The rest of me just smiled at figuring out how to play their game.

Tirsane gave me one last smile, then turned to head back to her ring. "One thing, Cori," she paused as she talked, not looking back at me, but fixated on the dragon's courtyard. "How bad is it going to be?"

"Somewhere between West Side Story and Rocky." My voice was flat, but I figured that about covered the range.

"Oh, do you plan on singing and dancing as well?" Her voice had an amused tone to it.

"Not currently, but you never know what might happen. Though my singing voice is nothing impressive."

"I see. Then let's hope your opponent is not as prepared as you seem to be."

"We can but hope." My voice was flat as she slid away, but I was glad the Library seemed not to be as big of an issue this time.

Shay leaned forward. "They are showing up and all staring at us. You ready?"

I laughed. "No. But this can't go on any longer and the only way to stop it is to force Brix to answer. If anyone else knows, they aren't talking. And I am reluctant to engage in wholesale slaughter." My voice was dark as I gazed out at the beings moving in and out, more and more arriving as the word spread.

"Reluctant, not opposed?" Citlali asked, her voice quiet.

I didn't look at them. I received enough guilt looking in my mirror. "If you'd asked me at 19, I'd have died before hurting anyone. When the draft started, I would have bent over backward to avoid causing insult. Even now, the last thing I wanted was to be in the halls of power. It isn't my jam." I stopped and looked at them, a cold smile on my face. "I kept trying to ignore all this and see if a solution would pop up, but Brix put my children at risk, children that I never thought I'd love more than I could breathe. I will burn their world down to get the answers I need to protect my family."

Both of them were quiet for a long time, and Carelian had moved over to me, his chin on my leg.

~And how would you live with that afterward?~ Kesis asked from under the sword throne.

"What makes you think I would?" I didn't know how else to answer that other than I'd have zero desire to live as the type of person I would become. Another reason to get this fixed as soon as possible.

"Ah," Citlali said quietly. Shay just looked old and his eyes, when he looked at me, had more understanding than I would have expected, but it was Scott that surprised me. He gave me a bittersweet smile and nodded. It rather surprised me he had never married. From everything I could see, he would have made a good spouse.

The conversation might have continued, but a flash of flame signified Brix's arrival. The phoenix glared at me and at this point, I just felt annoyed. If phoenix's could kill with their eyes, I'd already be dead. Since it didn't seem to be a power they had, the excessive glaring was annoying.

I checked my watch and there were still ten minutes left. "Baneyarl, do you have to wait in the visitor's area, or can you stay here?"

His feathers ruffled as he responded. ~As I am your official advisor, and Shay has declared Scott Randolph to be his, we both may stay in your circle, but we must stay here. We can talk to you or respond for you if you direct us, but we can't argue or leave unless you direct us.~ He tilted his head toward Scott. ~It is a little used clause in the structure of the council as most councilors have little desire to have anyone else provide input into their actions.~

I rolled my eyes. "For a group with little real-world influence, I don't understand why anyone would care."

The gryphon almost choked, and I got alarmed that I might need to figure out how the Heimlich maneuver worked on a bird-lion hybrid body as he struggled to breathe. ~You really don't understand, do you?~

I could see others looking at him with the same expression I had. "I thought I did. They get to help control what happens and have input in what the realms do? Not that I've figured out how that works. Most realm denizens I've met seem pretty independent."

Baneyarl snorted. ~And you think most of us would do anything for that? No. By being a councilor, you get magic dedicated to you and your pocket realms. You don't have to expend your own energy to keep it up. It is part of the oath that being a councilor gives you that bit of power. To the point that other beings can live in your realms knowing that you will keep it steady, safe.~

Everything clicked into place with that. "That is why Esmere talks about our world not changing. They have to work to keep it static."

~Yes, and Esmere is a very strong Councilor. It lets her have the plains that let her children roam. It lets the animals they hunt have places to live, to thrive. She makes it attractive, keeps it stable, keeps the predator prey levels in the right balance, and more. She is the only one I've ever seen to actually try to replicate an ecosystem. We don't have insects and mostly magic pollinates plants. Plus, you get the rights to travel to all the realms. That is usually blocked.~

"You mean the creation of rips to other places?" I pushed, double checking.

~Yes. Why do you think you aren't just overrun? They don't have the right to leave their realms or pockets.~ He stared at us like we were juicy morsels and he couldn't decide which one to eat first.

"What about the Chaos creature that came through with the plane walker?" I was royally confused now.

~That was an existing rip, or one magic created, that let it through. That being didn't create it, just utilized it.~

"This all makes much more sense now," Shay said. "But what do we get out of being councilors?"

Baneyarl shrugged his wings. ~What did you negotiate for? ~

We all stared at him, and I had the desire once again to beat my head against the stone. It was always what we didn't know that bit us in the ass.

"Wouldn't have the previous agreements with Earth carried over?" Citlali asked. "Cori, didn't you say we were represented when humans wore armor?"

I nodded, thinking back. "Yeah. I assumed it was during the time of Merlin, either before or after, but didn't the Egyptians and Greeks have armor, swords, other weapons? Merlin, for all I know, the Babylonians did too."

Citlali shrugged. "We know humans used to be here and they must have negotiated something. So that should still hold true."

We looked at each other and sighed. "Library of Magic."

~That is the most likely place to find any information of that sort.~ Baneyarl agreed.

My watch dinged. Two minutes.

"Show time, people." I redirected my attention to Brix in the center and I would have sworn he was smoking around the edges. But at least he wasn't glaring at me. Now he seemed to let his gaze bounce from being to being. It didn't matter. This had to end now.

My watch buzzed at the time indicated, and Brix raised brilliant wings. ~Council is now is session.~ The words beat into my mind and it felt extra cudgelly today. ~All non-councilors leave the floor.~

Beings headed up to the gallery, but I did spy that Zmaug and Onyx had shown up, though they looked like they were involved in their own discussion and ignoring the proceedings.

~Earth, why have your visitors not left?~ Brix snapped, the impact of those words making me cranky. Well, crankier.

"They are advisors, as defined in the council treaty." That was what Baneyarl had advised me to say. It also meant I really needed to get a hold of the treaty and read it.

Brix huffed, but didn't continue. Now his entire focus was on me. ~Lord Cori, why have you summoned a council meeting?~

I rose, kind of impressed he didn't attack me for daring to, but the session was still young. I stepped into the ring and looked at him.

"I, both as Earth Lord and Herald of Magic, have called a council meeting to require you to share what you know of the Undoing."

The room went silent and Brix changed from a rainbow of bright joyful hues to a cascade of colors that reminded me of sorrow.

CHAPTER
FORTY-FIVE

The tears of a phoenix are wonderous things, though not all are the same. But when they cry from grief, those same tears are a poison that can destroy even dragons. ~ Alchemist Text

---

B rix's feathers fluffed up and a sharp, harsh note slashed through me. ~You dare summon a council for this?~

"Yes. You have information I need and I will have it now. I don't care why you haven't freely shared. That is over. Tell me about the Undoing."

~Never.~ The word hissed through my mind like a skate over ice. ~You are the Herald. You can figure this out. It is not my responsibility to do your job.~

If the comment hadn't encompassed so much of my life, I might not have started laughing. I could feel the attention of everyone in the room on me. And I didn't care.

~Are you laughing at me?~ I didn't know if the tone of voice implied outrage or disbelief. Either way, I didn't care.

"Not really. More the comment," I managed, fighting back my chuckles. "You said this is what I was, not me. So, you could be seen as my employer and I'm telling you that I don't have the information I need to do this. So, you are going to tell me, or I'll say 'fuck off' and let the consequences fall where they may. I figure a few atomic bombs will solve the problem of too much magic."

My attitude was purely in the "no fucks given" stage, but the idea of that much death made my stomach threaten to empty on the floor. But if they gave me no chance...

~You dare threaten us?~ Brix had puffed up and flames danced around the perch.

"It isn't a threat, it is a statement of fact. If the rips continue, Earth will retaliate. If you don't help me, I can't stop them. If they get worse, more people will die and Earth will retaliate faster."

Brix raised his wings, color flooding back into them, bright, harsh, and it felt like malicious joy. ~You all need to die. It is your fault the Undoing happened. I will revel in your destruction. I have nothing to tell you. Council is dis——~

"Oh, no, you don't," I snapped out. "You will tell me the history and cause of the Undoing. This isn't a request, this is an order. My children were put in danger. That will never happen again." All humor had left my voice and rage beat at my mind.

There wasn't any calm logic left, just the deep primal desire to make sure those I loved were safe.

~Good.~ The word was a slap in my face. ~I hope they die. I ask Magic daily for all humans to watch their families die screaming for help and assistance, just like mine. This is all your fault. You can pay in blood the way I did.~ The words rang through the council chambers and the audible intakes of breath told me this wasn't something known or expected. The rage from the phoenix surprised me, but it didn't change a thing.

"I have no clue what happened. But either way, it was thousands of years ago. Are you going to blame me for what my ancestors did over three millennia ago?"

~I will blame humans until their ashes lay at my feet and create a sea of glass from their tears. Magic should have eaten them long ago. You'll never find the information and I couldn't be more delighted. Dismissed.~ Brix launched into the air, wings flapping as magic surged for a sidestep.

"No," I bit out, hard and angry. I slammed the tunnel back into the chamber. "You will tell me!"

A surprised squawk slipped out as Brix's wings beat rapidly to regain balance.

~You dare?~ Flames flew at my face and I batted them away with Air. My mind locked down into grabbing the truth from the blasted bird. I could do it, but while Brix was slinging magic at me and flying, I couldn't. I needed the phoenix down and exhausted to extract the information as easily as possible.

I struck out with a KO, but the beam was too narrow and Brix flew up to avoid it. The air around me dropped to freezing temperatures, and I narrowed my eyes. This was the reason I'd worn warm clothes. Because Brix used Fire, I assumed the phoenix was Chaos, but it could have been a natural ability. This solidified it. It kind of matched his personality. Fire could change the temperature, either pulling heat in or out. In a fight it could be deadly, but the right clothes helped.

I countered by pulling moisture from the air and soaking him with it, but the amount available steamed off as fast as I could add it.

~You disgust me. Why Magic ever graced you, I'll never understand. But if you die, then humans are dead. That would be excellent.~ Brix swooped up, and I got ready to block a side-step but instead I blinked, confused. I turned to watch the feathers train behind the bird as I tried to remember.

~Cori, stop him.~ Carelian's words cleared the confusion in my mind and I realized Disrupt Thoughts had been used on me.

Two could play at that game. I hit out with a Disrupt, then followed up with Illusion, creating a wall right in front of Brix's beak. A squawk and a flurry of wings as Brix flew out of the way.

Muttering started in the chamber and there were arguments on both sides, but I only caught words as I tried to beat the blasted bird down without a fatal injury. I couldn't pull information from something dead.

~Stop her.~

"This is a disgrace."

"Brix should have supplied the information."

I was at least slightly cheered that a few were on my side, but I couldn't focus on that. Instead, I threw Murphy at him and Lady Luck at me. Then I started casting lightning bolts. I tried to keep them at less than a Taser, but it was hard. The furor doubled as more than one missed the darting bird and hit the walls.

~Oh, nice hit. Fry the annoying feather duster.~ That voice I recognized, and I tried not to laugh. Instead, I darted to the other side of the ring as Brix dove directly at me, talons outstretched. I had zero doubt those razor-sharp feet would do massive damage to me.

"Stop her. She is challenging our chair."

"Jerk." I was getting annoyed, and I cheated. I had water in my tumbler. I made it evaporate, then I soaked the air around the flying form, hard and fast, forcing the bird down. Brix tumbled, and I turned the water to ice, freezing feathers and feet to the floor. Winded, I stalked over, crouching next to him. "You will talk, or I will rip every feather from you."

As proof I wasn't kidding, though mostly I wanted the information in the forefront of the phoenix's mind, I grabbed a primary wing feather and yanked. Brix shattered the air with a screech of outrage as it popped out.

"Tell me exactly how the Undoing happened." I paused and then a mix of guilt and curiosity forced me to continue. "And what happened to your family."

"This is unacceptable!" Shiarissa shouted. "This is an attack on a council member and we are supporting it?"

I sighed, but Brix had been beaten and I kept the cold up. Every time Brix's magic tried to melt the ice I pulled the heat away. It meant I was sweating as I pulled the heat away, but I'd deal with it.

~Cori Munroe has the right to demand answers.~ Baneyarl's voice rang through my head and I assumed everyone else's. ~When Brix tried to flee by dismissing the council and refusing her rightful request, Brix abandoned the duty of the office. That means it became a fight for chair, not an attack. And written in the bylaws, if the current chair attacks first—blocking a sidestep is not an attack—the defender has every right to fight back.~

Another wave of murmurs.

"I just want the information." I directed this comment to

the room at large, then Brix. "Tell us, or I'll pull it from your mind."

~If it was a challenge, this Cori Munroe is now eligible for the Chair,~ a voice said. I thought it might be the Aralez, but I wasn't sure.

~She would make a better one than Brix,~ Zmaug put in.

"Shush Dragon. You refused a seat, you have no input in this," Frej snapped out.

I wanted to turn to see expressions and body language, but I didn't dare move my focus from the bird.

"It seems to me there is an easier option, one we should have tried before," Tirsane said, her voice mild. The fact that most other voices silenced gave proof either to her power in the chamber or just her power. I had no idea which it was. Most likely both.

~And that would be?~ Esmere purred.

I wanted to roll my eyes. This whole set up seemed prearranged, but then what did I know? Everyone kept telling me this was where deals were made. I just didn't know what to deal for. Except this. I needed this.

"If the council as a whole demands Brix share this information," Tirsane said, her voice ice cold.

I grabbed two handfuls of feathers tight in my hand and swiveled to look at her. "What? That was an option? Why didn't we do that before?"

Tirsane smiled, not her I'm going to turn you to stone smile, but the one that implied you would taste good for dinner. "Because all councilors must agree and there were some that refused to vote that way."

"Huh." That didn't surprise me and to be honest, I didn't want to know who didn't want to tell me. Sometimes ignorance was bliss.

"I call for a vote of all councilors," Shay's voice rang out. I turned my attention back to the bird and froze the water again. Brix's colors were muted and exhaustion all but coated the phoenix.

"I call to vote that Brix, former chair of the Council, be required to share the information regarding the Undoing." There was an odd power to his voice, and I figured Baneyarl was coaching him. "Who is for this measure?"

"Aye," came from many throats and minds, but I had no way to tell who might not have been in there.

"And against?" I waited, ready to start yanking feathers and memories out of the bird's mind, but no one spoke.

"Then it is passed. Brix shall relay all that is known regarding the Undoing and the loss of family," Shay said clearly, and I felt Magic sweep around me and sink into Brix. Whereas not a minute before there had been defiance and resentment, muscles ready to launch up in the air the second there was an opening, now Brix sagged to the ground, defeated.

"Will you tell?" I asked, hands still wrapped around feathers.

~I have no choice,~ Brix responded, the anger mostly leeched from the words.

Nodding, I released the feathers and rose, stretching for a moment as I allowed the ice to melt. Brix shook out wet feathers and heat washed over them, drying the feathers back to their normal colors. Wings flapped, and I readied myself to stop an attempt to flee, but instead Brix settled on the perch in the center.

Had that been there all along? I couldn't remember, but for now, it didn't matter. What mattered was the information Brix had hidden from me, from everyone.

I waffled for a minute, then moved back to my chair, only taking my eyes off Brix for a moment. My trust level was still nonexistent.

Brix flapped on the perch a few times and preened. I almost said something, but I heard an upswing in voices above us.

~Patience, word is out, beings are coming,~ Baneyarl whispered in my mind. Instead, I pulled out a granola bar and unwrapped it, waiting for story time.

It felt like forever, but my watch assured me it was less than five minutes when Brix faced me, ignoring the others.

~I am seven thousand years old. I have returned to the egg four times. I never forgot the loss that led to my first Ashing.~

CHAPTER

FORTY-SIX

Stories of Atlantis have abounded as long as we have written stories, but no evidence has been found. At this point, Atlantis is assumed to be the literal interpretations of the dreams for a utopia. This is desire for a perfect civilization that exists at a primal level for humanity. But while there may have been a city or a country that had some aspects of this advanced civilization, we know it never actually existed except in dreams.
~ History of Magic

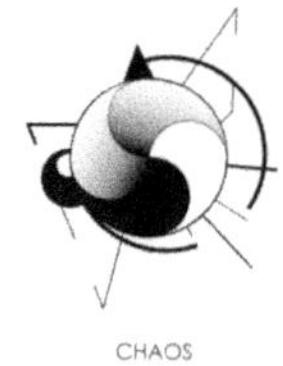

Brix's voice filled the room and once the venom faded from the voice in my mind, it caught you up in the sway of words.

~My world was vast. Plains and mountains, colors that have since faded, graced the trees and the flowers. The world smelled of joy and life. All around was magic. The unicorns ran with the hides, their white coats shimmered in the moonlight while dragons lived in high mountains, frolicking in the snow. There were these strange creatures on two legs that were weak and silly, but some found them good eating.~

I was lost in his words and I had to fight not lean forward enraptured.

~I cared little about any of that then. I had the world to explore. I soared in the clouds, across the oceans, to the heights of mountains, the bottoms of valleys. I slept in trees long gone extinct, flitted in and out of the realms as the doors were there open to any who knew them. Time had no meaning to me—then there was only life and the joy of every sunrise.~

Brix lifted wings, displaying the colorful feathers and sang a low, slow note that felt like a good stretch.

~The sun rose and fell and slowly those strange two-legs built silly things. I remember watching a big triangle being built in the land of milk and honey. Towers that scraped the sky. They rerouted rivers, created lakes, and killed each other. Some magical beings interacted with them, some were treated as gods, but most of us regarded them as either amusing, boring, or edible. I saw them as a passing fancy and followed the sun, watching the world change.~

The scope of time he spoke about was almost impossible for me to imagine, yet his words pulled us in. Part of me knew I should sit back and figure out which magic was being used, but I needed to hear this story.

~My kind is rare. And in the beginning, we were magic-created. I was the only one, but I knew not loneliness, for I had the world. But one day I heard a song. It twisted through my heart and soul and I knew there was another out there. Day and night I flew, following the song on the breadth of my wing, around clouds, through showers, and into the light of the moon. I found my Shera. You know of my colors, all of them, the image of rainbows shattered across the surface of a placid lake. Shera was the moon. Silver and white, with touches of rainbows when she moved. Her feathers were almost radiant with magic and her song could craft stone. Then there were her eyes. They were the sun itself, luminous with gold and flecks of green that made the trees turn orange in shame.~

The joy in his voice as he talked about Shera made me ache. I knew love, but what he put into his words made my love for Jo and Carelian seem almost shallow in comparison.

~She matched me wing for wing, song for song, joy for joy. I saw a million sunrises in her eyes. We created nests and were granted a viable egg. That one hatchling was full of magic and mischief and we set him loose on the humans as he grew, watching as they called him a trickster and a savior. He disappeared into their lives as something cherished and feared. We tried to call him back, but he had changed into a being that didn't want our life of flight. Saddened, we sought things to distract us and found that humans had become more interesting over the seasons. Curious as to what our child found so fascinating about them, we found a group on an island that had many wondrous things. Wheels that moved under the power of water, mirrors that sent sunlight to underground gardens, farms of fish, textiles and crafts that we longed to line our nests with. We swept in to interact.~

I swear I could hear the pounding music of something bad about to happen and I wanted to clutch the arms of my chair and tell him not to go, but all I could do was listen. He was letting loose a song of joy and loss, and I managed to glance around. Everyone else was as enraptured as I, even the dragons and Bob.

~They were surprised that we spoke, but soon we were hailed as messengers from the gods and our discarded feathers were prized for their beauty. The greatest gift we could bestow on someone was one of our molted pinions.~ He did pause to cast me a dirty look, which helped lessen the spell he wove just a touch. ~As a people they leaned into magic and used it in their life as naturally as Shera and I did. As their magic improved, their city became more marvelous and fantastic as they learned the laws of the world around them. Their magic users were some of the premier in the world and they interacted with nations all over the globe. They sat in on the council of Lords and were regarded as equal among the denizens.~

He drank a bit of water, shuffling his feathers closer to him and flat. It was as if he dimmed the bulb in the room.

~One of theirs was a Herald of Magic. Zenobia had succeeded Solomon when he left his physical existence.~

I jerked at the name. It sounded familiar. Someone Tirsane had mentioned as the last Herald.

Brix kept speaking. ~She walked with Magic and worked for her good, but Zenobia was arrogant and greedy. She wanted more than what she had. We had talked freely with her people and they knew we would resurrect if we were killed but not destroyed, though Shera and I thought nothing of sharing that knowledge. We had no reason to fear."

"Time passed, and we were ready to nest again, and we were granted a spot at the top of their government building. We built our nest with fabrics and yarns, it was full of comfort and warmth. To my delight we had three eggs. We would have children again." Those last few words had so much joy and agony in them, I felt tears spring to my eyes. If this was a movie, I might have closed my eyes for the next part.

His mental voice grew darker, and the joy faded from the room. ~We trusted freely, too much so. I didn't realize, we didn't realize, Zenobia craved more than she had, though she had everything. She was regarded as gorgeous by her people, had a devoted spouse, children to be proud of, and was not only a herald of Magic, but a high ranked person in their government. Their city knew no want. They had springs which provided fresh clear water, the trees were so laden with fruit they had to support the branches, the fish jumped into their nets, and the animals were healthy and fecund. It was like living in paradise. I never saw the rot.~

~The temple lay beneath our nest. We didn't mind people being able to see our eggs, though we were not easy to reach. We watched our eggs grow and felt the life in them. Three. Three more. Joy filled me and I flew toward the sun to proclaim my joy. They would be hatching soon. There was no way life could be better. Then I froze as I felt magic swell beneath me, a strange combination of Order, Spirit, and Chaos in a way I've never seen since.~ All of Brix's feathers were held tight against the bird's small frame as shivers racked it.

~There came an explosion of sound, magic, and force. I knew no more. I woke two hours' flight away on a piece of debris floating in the water that might have once been a door. I roused and flew back to Atlantis as fast as I could manage.~

The name hit me like a physical blow and I could hear the sharp inhales from behind me.

~It took me centuries to piece together what happened. But here is what I know and believe at this point. It has been at least three thousand of year since it occurred. I do not know the difference anymore.~

The statement rang of truth and I played back everything

Brix had said. None of it had been a lie, or at least not a conscious one.

~Zenobia linked all the realms through our nest. Each of our eggs, of my children, was attuned to a different realm. She sought to pull the power into her, to make her a god essentially. To help with it, she linked also to the dormant volcano under their small continent. Then she used her power to pull it into her. It didn't work. Instead, the power of the volcano, her, and my children snapped the cord she had wrapped around Magic and the backlash was so great that it sundered the connections of the realms with Earth and cut off the flow of magic to the world.~

Brix inhaled sharply, as if trying to calm nerves and focus on the story. I mimicked the action, knowing that if I had been Brix my rage might have broken the Earth. My mind whirled with what I might have done and part of me waited to hear the consequences.

~With one selfish act, a being that had everything—power, wealth, family, love—sundered it all for the desire for more. And in doing so, sacrificed not only the lives of every person on her continent, but my spouse and eggs. Their lives were ended before we had even named them. In my grief, I took my own life, going back to a chick, hoping it would remove the memories, the pain, the knowledge. It didn't.~ The flat hard words felt like a blow and I wanted to close my eyes in sympathy. After the zoo, I understood his rage all too well.

~It took me until Archimedes discovered the lever and in turn provided a clue as to how I could open a door back to the realms. I left the world of men then and vowed to never return. My spouse was dead, my children unmade, my only child vanished into the world of men.~

He stopped and focused on me, the rage, sorrow, and desire to burn down the world, my world, clear in his eyes. ~So yes, I blame Earth. I blame the human Heralds, who were so arrogant as to think what they had was not enough. But I place so much on you, Corisande Munroe. You remind me of her. Of the woman who stole everything. She was fair and dark like you. She had multiple lovers, as you do. Everyone loved her. But she destroyed all that I held dear and sundered the world from magic. You don't know how many died that day. How many unicorns, gryphons, dragons, creatures that no longer exist, because when the realms were sundered, the food they needed or the magic that let them live, was destroyed. There you have it. Everything I know about the Undoing. It was caused by Zenobia of Atlantis, and she doomed her world and ours, and I'll gladly see all of you burn to Ash before I assist.~

There was a stunned silence through the room and finally Esmere spoke. ~You would see us destroyed as well, the denizens?~

Until that moment I hadn't known that birds could sneer, but the look he sent her way was a sneer.

~Yes. All of Chaos, all of Order, all of Spirit. None of you cared that yours had died. You all shrugged, treating it as if we had suffered an earthquake. The realms being blocked from Earth was an annoyance, not something that mattered. The only ones that cared were the ones whose spouses, families, lovers were on the other side of the Undoing. Those found the lords and begged one-way doors to be opened. Most of the time, they were granted. Those that I talked to wished they had never looked. In almost every case, their loved one was dead, skinned, often eaten. Grief took families who had never realized they were mortal too. As far as I'm concerned, all of you deserve every action the humans perform.~

"How can I stop the rips?" I demanded. This was the one bit of information I needed.

~I have no idea. But a Herald caused it, her notes, her

research would also include hints as to how to repeat what she did. If you sunder the worlds fully, so there are no links left to Earth, we will be safe from the predations of humans.~

I just stared at him, stunned, and my hand reached for Carelian. The idea of losing him or, even worse, him losing access to his mother, to my friends was almost unthinkable. A cold, hard lump sat in my chest.

Brix flapped his feathers. ~I have done my duty, I am done. The council chair seat is vacant. I have achieved what I wanted and may you all burn in the darkness of the Void.~ Before I could do anything, there was a strange magical shift, and the feel of the room, the feel of Brix's presence changed. Then Brix flapped hard, wings flaring in colors, the ring around the bird's left foot glinted and then dissolved. A moment later Brix disappeared in a cloud of flames.

EPILOGUE

The end times are upon us. Once again the world will sunder apart and we shall fall into the grasp of nothingness. Say farewell to those you love, for soon it shall all be for naught. ~ Doomsayer on a street corner

---

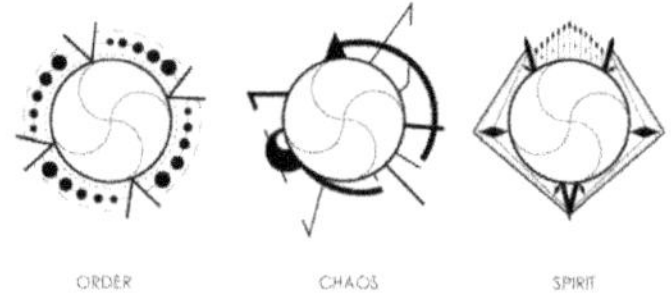

The council erupted into chaos as Brix vanished. At some point in his retelling, I'd returned to my chair and now I just stared at the center, at the perch. I understood his anger, his rage, but it didn't solve or change anything. And it didn't help me figure out how to stop it. Had he been lying?

"Tirsane?" I said her name, but not a shout, just saying it. She paused and turned to look at me, others noticing and quieting down.

"Was he lying about the Herald needing to figure it out?" I could tell when people were lying, but people didn't lie a lot and everyone was very good at avoiding active lying. Which meant most of the time I paid no attention to the little buzzes.

Tirsane tilted her head, obviously thinking. "No. Or at least he believed everything he said. But that doesn't mean it was the truth."

I nodded, grimly aware of that fact from a few people I'd dealt with. "And his comment that he doesn't know how to fix it, but that I am the one that can?" The idea of cutting off access to the realms permanently made me nauseous.

"I do not know," she admitted. "I knew of the Undoing, but not what he mentioned."

My eyes narrowed as a thought struck me. "Zmaug, you mentioned Atlantis should be a warning to us all. What did that mean?" Again, I didn't need to speak loudly. The dragons could have heard me if I was whispering.

Zmaug turned her head to look at me, eyes a bit redder than usual. ~That a city based on magic vanished from the world and knowing. It was never linked to the Undoing that I know of because we thought it happened after the Undoing. The Undoing was why they disappeared. But we all know how stories passed down over generations can change and twist things. I will say that the rips are starting to affect us though. I know of at least one dragon that has stepped through the rips. She wasn't that impressed with what she saw. Too many people and buildings.~

I sighed and sat back. The denizens were all talking, chattering, and I could tune into conversations, but right now it didn't change anything. I turned in my chair to look at Citlali, Scott, Shay, and Baneyarl. "Thoughts?"

"I need more coffee," Shay said, but his voice carried a level of exhaustion I recognized. "But now we have something to look for."

A flicker of memory. "I think there was at least one book about Atlantis in the Library and I wouldn't be surprised to find others, but even if it had all the notes Zenobia left, is it going to be enough?"

Citlali shrugged. "We won't know until we try, and any information is more than we have. None of my people are that old. It is possible from the time periods Brix spoke of that Babylonia might have some info. My suspicion is we may need to read a lot to find any hints as to what is possible. At least now we know we can read."

Shay nodded. "I've put out some feelers to see if there are any merlins that might be interested in this type of research. Even just having knowledge of the languages could help."

A surge of warmth hit me. At least these people weren't just saying it was my problem. That had been what I got with Brix. That it was my problem, not ours. Ours was decidedly better.

"I'll need to let Stephen know the rips are going to escalate. I think he is setting up teams, but I don't know how much is getting spread to other countries."

~We can help with that,~ Kesis said.

I turned to look at her. "Oh?"

Her tail flipped at me in an obvious laugh. ~After your

comments, Carelian and I talked. We have always had the ability to find and talk to other focuses, most of us just don't. Our mage provides what we need emotionally, or at least what we thought we did. It turns out having...friends, is good for you.~ She hesitated on the word friends and it made me want to hug her.

Carelian stood up and took over the thread. ~So, we have been spreading the word to other focuses and from them to their mages. It won't happen overnight but we are creating a network that allows information to be passed.~ He licked my hand. ~They will understand what is coming and hopefully by the time you have found the solution, we will have a method to get the information out.~

Shay stared at them. "You're creating a phone tree?" His voice was a bit incredulous.

The three familiars just stared at him. I did too. Scott laughed. "They've never used one, Shay. They aren't that old."

~I help!~ Dahli put in, her tail wagging like she was trying to fly.

Carelian cleaned his face. ~Yes, even the canine is helping.~

I chuckled softly. "This means we have a path forward. Lots of research, getting the word out. But there is one more thing." I stood and faced the council. "I, Lord Corisande Munroe, Herald of Magic, have a request I ask of the council and all those who live in the realms." My voice had an eerie weight to it. I really didn't understand the magic of this room.

A hush swept over the room. The spectators had come down from the gallery and it was full of beings mingling and talking, the previous floor show on the tip of everyone's tongue. They all turned to look at me, and I just stood there.

"I request that you talk to your friends, your relatives, and see if anyone knows of someone that was alive before the Undoing. We need to talk to them. I want to make sure you understand the danger. If Earth decides they are at risk, the realms have the most to lose, and not even dragons will be able to withstand the weapons that will come to bear." My eyes swept the room, trying to convey the seriousness of this. "Please let me know if there is someone that will talk to me."

A murmur that I interpreted as acceptance washed the room. I turned back to the humans. "I don't know what else to do, but for now, I'm going to go home. I have children to hug, a dryad to remind she is family, and my partners to discuss all this with. I might still be a danger and until the rips are stopped, I need to take precautions."

Citlali looked at me for a long time, to the point I began to shift uncomfortably. "Cori, I believe if there were more people like you in the world, this planet would be a different place." She heaved a sigh and stood. "Unfortunately, you seem to be unique. I will go home and search to see if anyone has any information about Atlantis, but that is doubtful. Most of our cultures didn't have written languages until two thousand years ago, well after Brix is saying Atlantis was destroyed. There is one thing I want to point out though: our timelines and his may not be the same. I have zero idea when Archimedes discovered the lever, other than a long time ago. What if his time sense isn't accurate? If it was only two thousand of our years not three, there might be much more information. Didn't Plato write about Atlantis? There are no seasons in the realms that I have seen, so their sense of the passage of time might not be correct. Or Brix may not realize how much time passed, just assumed."

It was more than I'd heard her speak in one go. But I turned that over, looking out at the grass where Zmaug lay. As always, the diffuse light was present.

"Maybe. If nothing else, I'll make sure to extend my research farther up." I spoke slowly as I thought. There were also some of the memento stones I'd never bothered with. Now might be the time.

"Cori?" Scott said, looking at me. I shifted my attention to him. "You got this, but you aren't alone."

I smiled and looked at Carelian. "Let's go home. I have kids to hug." Without a word, he created a rip to the house. I ached to hug Jo, Sable, Jaz, and Magne. Then I'd start on figuring out how to solve this.

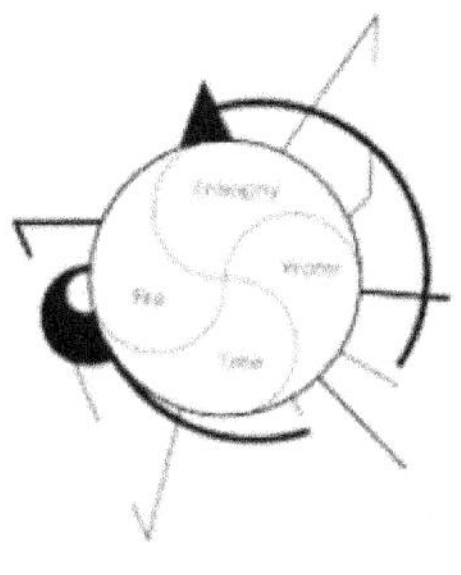

CHAOS

Chaos:
- Entropy
- Fire
- Water
- Time

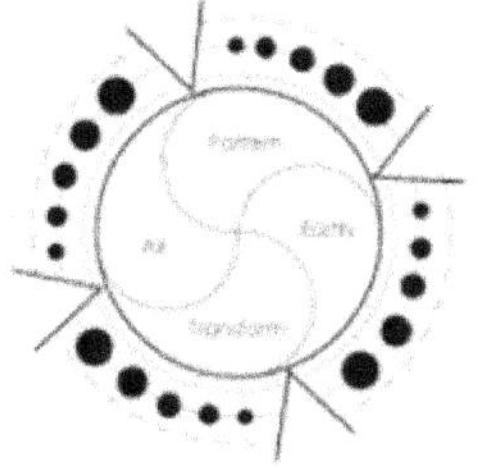

ORDER

Order:
- Pattern
- Air
- Earth
- Transform

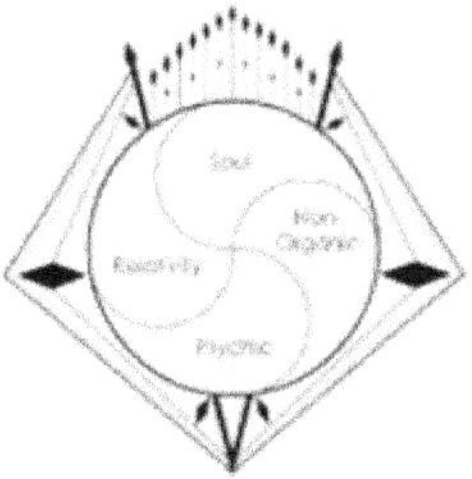

SPIRIT

Spirit:
- Soul
- Relativity
- Non-Organic
- Psychic

AUTHORS NOTES

This is book 7 in Twisted Luck, based in the Ternion universe. Balanced Luck, book 8, and the last book in the Twisted Luck series is available now! But it won't be the last book in the Ternion universe. I have at least one, if not more stand alone novels planned, including one for Scott Randolph and his start as a Rogue Mage Hunter. Plus a trilogy called Noble's Luck that is placed in the late 1800s. Don't forget there are the novellas out there for you to read as well.

If you loved this novel, please take the time to leave a review, you will be amazed at the difference it makes.

There is a lot more stories coming both in this universe and others. I'm writing as fast as I can.

If you'd like to stay in touch, you can follow me on social media at the following places:

Website: https://badashpublishing.com/
Facebook: https://www.facebook.com/badashbooks/

Twitter: https://twitter.com/badashbooks
Instagram: https://www.instagram.com/badashbooks/
Bookbub: https://www.bookbub.com/profile/mel-todd

There is a Twisted Luck Fan Group. I can't wait to see you there - https://www.facebook.com/groups/1500124503671599

If you're interested in free books, keeping up with what is going on in my life, as well as sales and launch announcements, you can sign up for my newsletter at my website. You never know what freebies might be in it

Take care!

Mel Todd

About the Author

Mel Todd has over 44 titles out, her urban science fiction Kaylid Chronicles, the Blood War series, and the Twisted Luck series. Owner of Bad Ash Publishing she is working to create a place for excellent stories and great authors. With over a million words published, she is aiming for another million in the next two years. Bad Ash Publishing specializes in stories that will grab you and make you hunger for more. With one co-author, and more books in the works, her stories can be found on Amazon and other retailers. You can follow her on Facebook at - https://www.facebook.com/badashbooks/ You can also sign up for her newsletter and follow her blog at https://www.badashpublishing.com

facebook.com/MelTodd.Author